Dreams
Unspoken

RJ LAYER

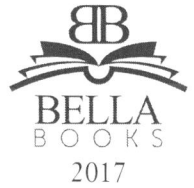

BELLA
B O O K S
2017

Bella Books, Inc.
P.O. Box 10543
Tallahassee, FL 32302

Printed in the United States of America on acid-free paper.

First Bella Books Edition 2017

Editor: Medora MacDougall
Cover Designer: Sandy Knowles

ISBN: 978-1-59493-584-8

Other Bella Books by RJ Layer

Judge Me Not
The Real Story

Acknowledgment

First and foremost I want to thank my publisher, Linda Hill, and the incomparable staff at Bella Books for making it possible for me to share my passion for writing. Bella's dedication to bring queer literature to readers is coveted, and I count myself fortunate to be a part of the Bella family.

As Nathaniel Hawthorne said, "Easy reading is damn hard writing." Thanks to my beta reader, Sue Hilliker, for her invaluable input. To my editor extraordinaire, Medora MacDougall, a million thank yous for your guidance and expertise. You inspire me to improve my work with every word.

Thanks to my family and friends for a lifetime of love and support. The biggest heart-felt thank you to my readers for motivating me to write the next book. And, Lori—my one—my all—my forever.

About the Author

Born and raised in the "heart" of the Midwest, RJ still resides there with her spouse of twenty-eight years and counting, and their two feline bosses. She loves her work writing lesbian stories that capture the heart of the romantic. In addition to traveling to new places, RJ can be found in the rolling hills along the water. Their hideaway is the perfect setting for dreaming up engaging characters and moving stories. Additionally she loves taking photos and reading every free moment she can find.

Dedication

For Lori—because my heart is perfect with you inside.

CHAPTER ONE

Jo sat on the fence enjoying her favorite time of day, wisps of steam rising from her coffee cup as she warmed her hands. She snugged the collar tighter on her jacket. Chilly or not, there was no place she'd rather be, waiting and watching as the first rays of sun broke the horizon while the rest of the world still slumbered away. The only thing that came close to this moment was a star-filled, crystal clear night sky.

She gave a whistle for her oldest mare and best friend, Daisy Mae, and looked around with wistfulness at her sixty-acre horse farm. Mid-April in Kentucky and the daffodils and irises were already in full bloom. New beginnings were in motion. Steam puffed from Daisy's nostrils as she ambled over, snorted and lifted her head. She repeated the ritual until Jo produced an apple from her pocket. She rubbed Daisy's head as the horse devoured the goody.

"Well, old girl." Jo's breath steamed the brisk air. "Are you ready to see if the grass really is greener on the other side?" Daisy Mae snorted again and rubbed her head against Jo's thigh as a thank you for the early morning treat. Jo hopped off the fence when Daisy Mae moseyed back out in the pasture.

After dropping her truck at the repair garage, she picked up a Toyota Prius at the rental place and by a quarter past eight was driving the 250 miles to the place her life had begun, contemplating if she were about to come full circle.

She found the property easily, and with thirty minutes to spare, was glad to have time to look around on her own without a pressuring real estate agent. After a stroll around the farm, she climbed up on the fence surrounding the pasture to the south of the rustic frame house. Chewing absently on a piece of wheat, she looked out over the land beyond the homestead.

Finally she saw dust rising from the road in the distance. The approaching car was traveling faster than was wise for the loose road surface, kicking gravel in every direction. She glanced at her watch. It was ten after one. The black Volvo station wagon came to an abrupt halt, sending up a dust cloud like a wind twister in the middle of a riding corral. The vehicle's paint quickly changed color as the dust settled, and a petite, dark-haired woman emerged from the car waving a folder before her to cut through the fog. Jo jumped down when the woman neared.

She shielded her sunglass-covered eyes. "Can I help you?"

Jo ran a hand through her hair. The woman who materialized from the dust cloud was a vision of beauty, curvy in all the right places. Jo found herself smiling as she stepped toward the woman.

"Ms. West, I presume."

The woman flipped over the folder in her hand and took a closer look, then cocked her head and looked back at Jo. "The horse breeder." When she smiled, Jo's heart raced like a thoroughbred.

Jo extended her hand, nodding nervously. "Yeah, that's me. Jo Marchal. Sounds like," she touched an index finger to her nose, "shawl. Marchal. Hi!"

"Jo Marchal," she repeated before giving Jo a firm, business-like handshake. Her hand was as velvety soft as a horse's nose. The sensation gave Jo's heart a little kick.

Jo swallowed. "Let me guess. You were expecting a man in a pickup truck wearing boots with spurs and a cowboy hat."

She shrugged. "My secretary's fault."

When she held out the folder she was carrying, Jo noticed her rings. So it was Mrs. West. She was married.

"She spelled your name like a man's, so yes, I guess I was expecting a cowboy."

Jo shoved her hands in her pockets. "And a little thing like you meeting a cowboy out in the country all alone."

She reached deep into the bag hanging from her shoulder and pulled out a very small caliber handgun. "I'm not alone. I have company."

"Okay." Jo whistled as she raised her hands. *The woman had moxie.* "But actually I am." The real estate agent eyed Jo over the top of her sunglasses, giving Jo her first glimpse of mesmerizing dark eyes. "A cowboy, ma'am." She hooked her thumbs in the top of her khaki pants and nodded her head toward the south. "I left the truck, my boots and hat back at the ranch with the horses."

Jo tipped her head at the real estate agent and she laughed. There was something about this woman. She looked forward to doing business with her. Ms. West fanned her face with the folder, and Jo noticed for the first time it was rather warm for April.

"With a sense of humor, no less." She stepped past Jo to the shade of a tree along the edge of the drive. "But aren't you considered a cowgirl?"

Jo shoved her hands back in her pockets and raised a shoulder. "Yes, ma'am. I s'ppose."

She turned back to face Jo. "That's what they'd call you down in Texas." Jo picked up a hint of an accent. She tucked the folder under her arm. "So what would you like to see first, the house or the out buildings and property?"

"Well, Ms. West—"

"Please, call me Maria."

"Okay then, Maria. I really hate that I dragged you all the way out here." Maria's smile vanished. "This place just won't work for me."

"You really should at least see the house before you decide. It has all new fixtures…" Maria scrambled into sales mode and Jo let her talk. She liked the sound of Maria's voice. Plus, she was real easy on the eyes.

When Maria finally took a breath, Jo interrupted. "I have no doubt the house is magnificent. But I've already walked around and the out buildings aren't quite what I need and the fence around both pastures nearest the horse barn are in bad repair. I was hoping for a place more move-in ready."

"But the house—"

Jo raised her hand to halt another sales pitch. "The house isn't the problem. Shoot, if it were in serious need of repair I could always bunk in the barn. But I need a place that's move-in ready for my horses."

Maria nodded. "So you want horse-ready, not necessarily house-ready."

Jo laughed. "Yeah, something like that."

"How quickly do you need this move-in ready farm?"

"Soon as I can find the right place, I s'ppose." Jo ran a hand through her hair before she could stop herself. She wasn't sure why Maria made her nervous. "My parents are getting on in years. I want to be closer than a four-hour drive."

Maria jotted down every detail Jo provided. "Where do your parents live?"

"'Bout fifty minutes or so from here, over in Campbell."

She continued writing. "I can check for other available listings close to Campbell if you have some time." She motioned to her car.

"This might sound kinda strange, but I don't want to actually be in, or right around, Campbell. I was thinking more like, close. Say…within an hour's drive."

Maria again looked at Jo over the top of her glasses. "Got it, close but not neighbors."

"Exactly." Jo gave a thumbs up.

She closed the folder. "So do you have some time today before you drive back to the ranch?"

"I wish I did, but I have an appointment at three." She hooked a thumb over her shoulder. "In Campbell."

"I can assure you, Jo Marchal, that I will work diligently to find just the right place you need for you and your horses if you'll give me the opportunity."

Jo knew she was sporting a dimpled, full-face grin. "I imagine you will, Ms. West, and I'm counting on it." She imagined other things about Maria too, then remembered the rings signifying that she was already spoken for. Not that Jo ever needed to be involved with another woman. Not even one as beautiful as Maria West, despite her allure.

"All right." Jo strode over to the compact rental, Maria following in her shadow. She rummaged in her backpack and came up with a dog-eared business card. "Call me when you've got something."

She couldn't stop herself from admiring Maria's shapely figure as she handed over the card.

Maria glanced at the card, shaded her eyes and looked up at Jo. "Lazy Daisy Farms."

Jo tilted her head. "There's a story there I'd be happy to tell you sometime, but for now," she peeked at her watch, "I need to get on the road."

"Of course." Maria extended her hand, offering Jo another soft touch of her velvety light brown skin. That and her warm smile gave Jo's heart another little kick. "I'll call you within a few days."

"Works for me." Jo bounced her head. You'd think she had made a date with the woman. She folded her five foot nine frame into the little car and watched while Maria walked back to her own car. Jo thought she looked every bit as good from behind, and she hadn't looked at a woman like this in a very long time. When Jo drove past, Maria gave a little wave and another dazzling smile. Jo tipped her head.

* * *

She had sufficient time to get to Campbell and drove at a leisurely pace. Arriving too early and having to make polite conversation with her parents was not at the top of her list of favorite things. She'd have preferred to stand around talking to Maria West. Exiting the elevator on the fifth floor of the downtown building minutes before three o'clock, she entered the door marked Hanson, Brewer and Fox. The names sounded like characters from a children's story. Jo knew that Mr. Brewer and her dad went way back, but the details eluded her at the moment. She stepped up to the receptionist's desk.

"Jo Marchal. I have an appointment with Mr. Brewer."

The receptionist nodded. "Yes, please have a seat. Mr. Brewer will be with you shortly." She looked past Jo to the waiting area.

Jo turned, only then seeing her parents seated in the corner, crowded with chairs and small tables. She joined them, although tentatively, as if someone were behind pushing her.

"Hi, Mom." Her eyes shifted. "Pops."

"Jo Lynn," her mom said, "you look thinner than you did at Christmas. Don't you eat?"

Her dad looked up, met his daughter's eyes briefly and returned to the magazine in his lap. Jo sat bedside her mom to avoid feeling scrutinized and prayed the lawyer would summon them quickly. She pulled repeatedly at a loose thread on the fabric arm of the chair and bounced her leg.

Not one to endure long silences her mom said, "They're calling for a hot dry summer. Will your horses be okay?"

Jo bounced her leg, her mom's attempt at conversation doing little to ease her tension. She could as easily be having this conversation with a stranger. "They'll do okay."

The receptionist opened the door out into the waiting room. "Mr. Brewer is ready to see you."

"Eileen, Walt." Brewer gave them a nod and extended his hand to Jo, which he shook with vigor. "Well, my, my. You realize the last time I saw you, Jo Lynn, was a Christmas gathering at your parents when you were barely a teenager." He released her hand and stepped back. "Look at you now, all grown up and such a pretty one." He moved behind his massive old wood desk. "You obviously take after your mother." He motioned them to the chairs in front of his desk. "No offense, Walt."

Her dad gazed momentarily at her mom and smiled. "None taken, Doug." He cleared his throat, signaling the lawyer to get down to business. Jo understood her dad's philosophy that time was money.

"Well, Jo Lynn, I couldn't tell you this on the phone, but your dad wants you to have power of attorney for any matters requiring his signature in the event he is incapacitated or…" He crossed himself. "God forbid, passes on."

Jo glanced from the lawyer to her dad, who looked completely indifferent and to her mom, whose eyes glistened with the beginning of tears.

Jo had gotten a call on Monday from Mr. Brewer letting her know she would be receiving some legal documents requiring her signature. He directed her to her parents for an explanation, citing attorney-client privilege. When she called, her mother informed Jo her dad had been feeling bad the last few months and the doctors were running every test under the sun. Jo had only ever known her dad to be healthy and strong, and the thought of him being ill, especially for months, came as a shock. Her mother began to cry when she tried to tell Jo they suspected some kind of a cancer.

Jo had offered the only words of comfort she could think of. "Dad's a tough ol' guy and never been sick a day that I know of. Whatever it is, he'll beat it."

"From your lips to God's ears," her mother had stated.

Once all was said and signed they waited in the lobby for the elevator. Her mom insisted she come by the house for dinner before she made her long drive home. Jo wanted to decline but couldn't come up with a good excuse. Plus she knew she had to face the changes their lives were about to take. It was time for some kind of reconciliation.

She watched as her parents left the building and got into their ten-year-old Buick. Gleaming in the late afternoon sun like a brand new showroom model, it reminded Jo that her mom had never learned to drive. Unlike mothers of Jo's friends, Jo's mom couldn't drive the car pool, but she made up for the shortcoming in other ways. Hanging at the Marchal house was considered the best, and Jo's mom treated all her friends like family. Turning the corner and walking the half a block to the rental car, she wondered how her mom would get around should anything happen to her dad. On the drive she considered how many things were about to change in her life besides her address.

It had been years since Jo visited home during the spring. Nothing much seemed different about the brick ranch they had moved into when Jo started high school except the size of the maples that flanked the driveway on either side and shaded the house. The shrubs and flower beds remained unchanged. She took a calming breath as she walked up to the door, knocked lightly and let herself in.

"It's me," she announced.

Her dad was sitting in his recliner with the paper in front of his face and her mom emerged from down the hallway a moment later.

"Jo Lynn, I don't know why you think you need to knock. You are family." Eileen had changed into a cotton blouse and slacks, and she had traded her heels for flat-soled shoes. Comfortable clothes, as she called them. Jo, dressed similarly, was less than comfortable. Jo found comfort in jeans, a T-shirt or a denim or flannel shirt and, of course, her favorite broken-in cowboy boots. But she had dressed "properly" to meet the lawyer and avoid embarrassing her parents.

Jo followed her mom into the kitchen. "I always knock before going in anyone's house. It's a polite habit." In actuality, Jo hadn't felt a part of her family for more than a decade. It's why she stayed away. She leaned in the doorway.

"Something I can help with, Mom?" Eileen poured three glasses of iced tea and handed one to her, nodding toward her father.

"Here's your tea, Pops." Jo placed the glass on the table beside his recliner. He neither looked up nor lowered the paper, only grumbling a "thanks." Back in the kitchen, preferring her mom's awkward attempt at conversation to her dad's stone cold silence, she set the table. Her dad said grace and her mom continued her attempt at conversation by asking Jo about her horses, her farm and the people she employed.

Jo became lost in worry about all the things in her life that would be impacted by the changes coming. There was no way to know if a new owner at the farm would take over the horses she boarded and trained and keep on the three guys that regularly worked for her. Over and over so many questions kept rolling around in her mind. The one bright spot, though, in this utter chaos, was her "new" real estate agent.

Her mom wouldn't let Jo help clean up after dinner, instead shooing her from the kitchen. With feet like lead blocks she dragged herself to the living room and found her dad leaned back in the recliner with his hands crossed on his waist. His eyelids appeared heavy as if ready for sleep.

She took a deep breath. "You look tired, Pops. How you feelin'?"

"I'm fine, and I wish everyone would quit worrying over me. Been up since six is why I'm tired, like anybody else would be."

It never changed. The tone of his voice reaffirmed for Jo that things would never again be what they had been. She choked back the hurt.

"I'd appreciate it if you and Mom would call me as soon as you know anything about the tests they've done."

"I'm sure it's nothing for you to be worrying about. It's probably a bug. You know the Lord takes care of those who take care of themselves."

His voice was edged with the familiar sharpness, and Jo knew enough to let it be. If she were going to be kept informed, she knew it would be by her mom. She returned to the kitchen where her mom finished the dishwashing.

Jo grabbed a towel and asked, "He won't tell me anything. Can we talk?"

Eileen nodded and took her sweater from the hook by the back door. "Let's sit on the patio."

She joined her mom on the swing. "This is nice. Is it new?"

Her mom rubbed her hand over the wooden arm. "Your father got me this for my last birthday." Her hand persisted in its motion as if she were summoning a genie from a magical lamp. "He said we should get out here more often and stargaze." Her eyes misted with tears.

"And do you?"

Eileen looked at the cloudless sky. "It's been too chilly for him. He gets cold easily these days."

Jo saw a tear slide down her cheek. Being a poor source of comfort, Jo hoped her mom wouldn't cry as she had on Monday. "I'm looking for a farm around the area. I'm going to move back up this way. I'll be closer if you need me for anything."

She patted Jo's leg. "You're a good girl, Jo Lynn."

Jo welcomed the touch, as small and insignificant as it was. She placed her hand over her mom's and gave a squeeze. "I'm sure everything's going to be fine, Mom. He's a tough old bird."

Eileen inhaled a sharp breath before a sob escaped. "Oh God, Jo, I don't know what I'll do if—" She placed her hand to her mouth.

"Mom, let's not think like that. There's no reason to yet." She took her mom's hand. "Let's be positive, like you raised me to be."

Unlike the way I've thought about generally everything in my life for the last few years.

Jo scooted over and slipped her arm around her mom's shoulders. When Eileen stood abruptly, Jo was fully aware that the fractured relationship still existed.

"I need to check on your father."

Jo followed back into the house and left almost immediately, saying her good-byes at the door. She was in for a long drive home. Heading up the highway on-ramp, she pushed thoughts of her family crisis out of her mind and called up an image of the lovely

Maria West. Jo was sure she would enjoy farm shopping with the attractive Hispanic woman—more than she probably should.

* * *

Maria replayed the meeting with the cowgirl on the drive to her sister-in-law's house. The sale of a farm the size Jo Marchal had in mind would earn her a nice commission. She was gradually building a nest egg for herself, unbeknownst to her husband. Nothing had changed in their marriage that she'd been able to discern, but his most recent promotion took him away on business more now than ever, and that gave Maria pause.

Kathleen had been kind enough to pick up her son from his school when she'd gotten held up with a client. She knocked before pushing through the door.

"We're in here," Kathleen called from the direction of the family room.

"Thanks for rescuing me again."

Kathleen smiled sweetly. "Sure thing, honey." She waved a hand. "He's fine, they're watching a movie." Kathleen had three boys of her own, ages six, eight and ten. They accepted their cousin without reservation, despite his slightly darker skin. Kathleen looped her arm through Maria's. "Come on, let's have a cup of tea and relax for a few minutes while they're still occupied."

She steered Maria to the counter that separated the kitchen and dining room. As Maria slid onto a stool she allowed her shoulders to slump and her purse to drop to the floor.

"I'm sorry to have to call on you so much. They couldn't tell me where Jack is, only that he couldn't be reached. I tried his cell and he's either out of coverage or has it turned off."

Kathleen sat the teakettle on the stove and readied two mugs before turning to Maria. "Don't worry about it. The boys love when they get to run out and pick their cousin up and bring him home with them."

Maria let out a tired breath. "I don't know what I'd do if I couldn't count on you."

"Jack still won't help with Matt?" Maria shook her head. Kathleen stepped beside her, placing a comforting hand on Maria's shoulder. "I'm always available to help out if you need me. Please don't ever hesitate to call. We're family and I love Matty like one of my own."

Maria touched her hand. "You're a godsend. I don't know how I'd manage without you."

Kathleen patted her shoulder. "Well, you're not going to have to find out, so don't worry about it, honey."

The kettle whistled, interrupting Maria's distressing thoughts. When Kathleen slid a mug in front of her, Maria decided to lighten the conversation.

"I met the most unusual woman earlier today." Blowing on the steaming cup, she took a sip.

"Unusual?"

Maria nodded. "She's a horse breeder." She chuckled. "She reminded me of a Texas cowgirl that someone had forced to get gussied up for the big city."

"What's unusual about that?"

Maria felt her cheeks warm. "I got this peculiar feeling that she might have been flirting with me."

Or maybe I just hoped she was. And why would I hope that a woman flirted with me?

Kathleen's brows arched sharply. "Really? So she's gay?"

"How would I know? I mean, I'm not sure I know any gay women."

Kathleen grinned. "Oh, you probably do, you just don't know it. Sometimes it's easy to tell, sometimes not. Does she look butch?"

"Butch?" Maria asked uncomfortably.

"Such the naïve one. You know, does she look masculine or act manly?"

Maria closed her eyes for the briefest moment and saw Jo Marchal in her mind. Her pretty pale eyes and that charming smile. "She looks strong and confident like a Texas cowgirl—or like a female horse breeder, I suppose." She shrugged.

"Well, did you get any vibes from her?" Maria simply looked at her. "Unusual feelings."

Maria hid a smile as she remembered the handshake accompanied by butterflies. "I don't know."

"Hmm…Maybe I should meet her."

"Why?" Maria sipped more tea.

"To see if she flirts with you."

Maria was certain her face registered the embarrassment she was feeling. "I'm sure I imagined it." And as if on cue to save her further uneasiness, Kathleen's boys came rushing in with Matt in tow. He hugged his mother's waist as she kissed the top of his head. "Hey, Matty boy. You ready to go home and have some dinner?" He responded by releasing her waist and taking her hand. With her free hand Maria rested it on Kathleen's arm. "Thanks for picking him up, Kat, I owe you some sitting time."

Kathleen gently tapped her hand. "At this rate, honey, you owe me enough for a nice long vacation on some tropical island." She laughed. "But who's counting?" Kathleen stood and placed her arm around Maria's shoulder. "Call anytime you need help with Matt." She tousled Matt's hair. "The boys love having him here and he's no trouble at all."

Maria smiled at the wonderful friend her sister-in-law had always been. "Thanks again. We'll do a girls' night out soon and make the guys watch the kids."

"Oh please, let's do. I could use a night without hearing the word 'Mom' repeatedly." Maria's smiled faded. "I'm sorry, hon. Listen, don't give up. They're making progress every day with kids like Matt."

In the car she watched Matt in the rearview mirror. Her beautiful boy, trapped inside himself by autism. "To hell with Jack," she muttered, starting the car. As long as she had her son, she didn't need Jack in her life any more than he appeared to need Matt in his life.

CHAPTER TWO

A little after four on Monday Jo headed from the office in the stable to the one in the house. She listened to several voice messages, the last, much to her delight, from Maria West. Maria emailed Jo links on some properties for Jo to take a look at. She played the message a second time to hear Maria's voice again. When she logged on her computer, she opened the email, which listed a few specifics about one of the properties, contained four links and ended with a note saying that Jo could reply at her convenience. Jo took a look at the properties, then typed a reply letting Maria know the best time to reach her.

Jo's cell rang around two o'clock Tuesday afternoon with an unknown caller.

"Hello."

"Ms. Marchal, it's…West. Sorry…your return…yesterday." Maria West's voice was broken and garbled. "I…you a number… properties to look—"

"We have a terrible connection. Can I call you back from my land line?"

Jo barely made out, "Sorry, darned…phones, take…look…call…evening."

She rushed outside in hopes of a better signal, but the call dropped. "Damn," she cursed under her breath. She hurried back into the stable and told the first hand she saw she'd be up in the house if anyone needed her. She checked her email and found multiple new listings from Maria. She replied to the email and returned to the stable. Jo was expecting a new rider for lessons on her newest boarder, an American quarter horse, which happened to be the twelfth birthday present for a young girl named Kaitlyn from her daddy.

"Darlin', you're killing me," Cecile admonished.

Jo was kicked back in her office with her feet on the desk when the land line rang. "Cil, I've got another call. I'll call you back." Her feet hit the floor as she grabbed for the other phone before voice mail could pick up. "Hello."

"Ms. Marchal," the familiar voice purred. "I apologize for that awful call earlier. I was trying to catch you between my appointments and wasn't in the best reception area."

"Jo, please, and it's quite all right. I imagine you keep very busy doing what you do."

"Ah, the nature of the real estate business." She paused. "I see from your emails there are five properties you're interested in seeing."

Jo caught herself in a daydream remembering how Maria West had looked so beautiful standing in the afternoon sun last Friday. "Um, yeah." She realized she sounded like an uneducated hick. "Yes, that's right." It was like being a schoolgirl again for Jo trying to make a first date. "What's your schedule look like?"

"My schedule is what I make it and I don't have to drive four hours to meet you."

The cadence of Maria's voice told Jo she must be wearing the killer smile that she had seen when they met and she couldn't stop her own smile. "How's Friday again?" She knew whenever she left the farm the hands would take the opportunity to ease off a bit, but at least at the end of the week, most of the work would be done.

"I can do Friday. What time?"

"What time do you need me there?"

After a momentary pause, Maria said, "Well, I wouldn't ask you to meet me as early as nine since that would require you having to get up before the chickens."

Jo heard the faint accent again and guessed again she might be a Texas gal. She laughed. "I'd only have to get up an hour earlier. I can do nine o'clock if you want."

"You get up that early every morning?"

"Yup."

"In any case, let's say ten on Friday, and you won't have to get up any earlier than usual."

"Works for me."

They discussed exactly where they'd meet. The second Jo hung up she was again reminded she'd soon be leaving her homestead and starting over. She walked to the chair on the front porch and sat down for a moment. She wanted to enjoy every minute she had left at the old place.

* * *

Thursday before turning in, Jo pressed creases in a fairly new pair of jeans and the wrinkles out of a denim shirt. She wasn't sure why she wanted to impress Maria West tomorrow. She just did.

The drive was no less boring than last week's, but definitely more comfortable in her Super Duty Ford truck. Today wasn't going to be a round trip. She planned to spend the night in southern Ohio, at a motel possibly, if her mom didn't invite her to stay with them. She picked out Maria's little black station wagon right away and pulled in a few spaces over from it. Maria didn't notice Jo until she walked up to her car door.

She scampered out of the car. "Good morning!"

"That it is." Jo grinned.

"I found a couple more properties you may want to look at." She extended a file folder to Jo. "I think we can fit in the time if you're interested."

"I don't s'ppose we'd have time for a cup of coffee, would we?" Jo raised the file. "I can take a look at these and take a little break from the windshield time I'm doing today."

"Sure, of course." Maria reached back in the car for her purse. "There's a coffee shop here in the shopping center." She led the way across the parking lot to a quaint little place situated between a hardware store and a drycleaner's.

"I suppose the last thing you want to do right now is sit in the car." At Jo's nod Maria continued, "We don't have any time constraints today, unless you do. You can take a look at those," she indicated the file in Jo's hand, "and I'll adjust the route if we need to. We're basically going to drive in a big circle."

Once seated, Jo flipped open the folder and assessed the two farms. When she looked up and met Maria's dark eyes, the intensity in them caused her breath to catch. Jo sat unable to formulate any words for several long moments.

She finally cleared her throat and tried her voice. "I was thinking I probably should have said something before. These properties are all relatively large, acreage wise, but I'd be most interested in the ones that have surrounding land that could be potentially acquired in the future. My long term goal is to establish a kind of dude ranch. You know, a place for horse enthusiasts to escape to where there are hundreds of acres to ride and camp out in the country." Jo took a quick drink of her coffee. "I'm sorry. I should have mentioned that."

Maria waved her hand. "Not a problem. These are all quite rural, but I'll have my office check on them before we waste time driving to them." She pushed out of the booth. "I'll be right back."

Jo focused on the information before her. When Maria returned, she pulled one of the listings. "We can cross this one off. It won't meet your future needs. So, that leaves us with six locations and even as spread out as they are, we should have plenty of time to get to all of them. Whenever you're ready to go."

Jo drained her cup. "Let me hit the bathroom."

"I'll meet you outside."

Maria was standing with a map spread over the hood of her car when Jo emerged. Sliding her sunglasses in place so it wouldn't be obvious she was scrutinizing the cowgirl, she noted Jo's confident stride. Today Jo was dressed somewhat boyishly, although Maria still wouldn't immediately label her as gay. She folded the map and opened her car door.

"I'll drive and bring you back when we're done."

Jo put on her own sunglasses and grabbed her backpack from behind her truck seat.

Maria grinned. "You really do drive a pickup truck." She started the car. "So, where are the boots and hat?" She pulled them into the morning traffic.

"Still back at the ranch with the horses. I didn't want to overwhelm you with too much at once." Jo gave her a wink.

Maria felt the warmth in her cheeks, thankful her skin tone made a blush hard to detect. "So you really are a cowgirl?"

Jo mimicked tipping a hat. "Yes, ma'am. Right down to the spurs on my boots."

When Maria laughed, Jo felt warm all over. And wow, not only was Maria West gorgeous, but her perfume was making Jo's head swim. The best part was that she could make Maria laugh and smile.

She slung her backpack into the back seat, noticing as she did the booster seat installed there. "Got yourself a little one, I see."

"I have a six-year-old named Matthew. We call him Matt." She said little more, redirecting the conversation with question after question about horses and horse farms.

Jo talked about boarding horses and teaching youngsters how to ride, whether for fun or competition, and how she was getting away from breeding. They grabbed lunch at a little family-owned diner in a small town after their third stop but were quickly on the road again, making it to the last property around three. It was by far the largest, in the best shape and of course the most costly of the places they had seen.

Jo pulled herself up to stand on the pasture fence and scan the open field. She closed her eyes, deeply inhaling the fresh air. It wasn't hard to envision her horses running in these pastures. The sudden ringing of Maria's cell phone shattered her daydream.

Maria walked back toward the car as she talked on her phone. Jo was only able to hear parts of her side of the conversation, but she gathered it had something to do with her son. Eventually she rejoined Jo at the fence.

"Everything okay with your son?" Maria's smile was forced when she nodded. She was noticeably distracted. Jo detected worry. "I think I've seen enough for one day." Climbing off the fence she followed Maria to the car. "I've got plenty to think about now. I appreciate you driving all over creation."

"You're welcome."

Yep. Definitely distracted since that call.

Seated in the car, Jo said, "Look, this is none of my business, so you're welcome to tell me to take a hike, but you seem terribly troubled since that darned call you got. Is there something going on you need to deal with? 'Cause I would certainly understand if there was."

Maria stared blankly for several minutes before she spoke. "It's my son. He's having a difficult time at school today." She gave a long sigh. "But my sister-in-law is going to pick him up." She started the car and headed out to the road.

Jo wasn't fooled by Maria's attempt at calm. Something was eating at her, so she persisted. "So, your boy—he's in some trouble at school?"

Maria shook her head. "Not really trouble. He attends a special school. My son is autistic."

Wow! That was as unexpected as a horses' kick. She knew nothing about kids with autism, but she gathered from Maria's current mood it must be tough to deal with.

"So where do you live?"

Maria gave a sideways glance. "In Midland."

"How far are we?"

"About twenty-five minutes away."

"And your sister-in-law," Jo asked, "she lives there too?"

"Yes."

Jo shifted in her seat. "We should swing by there then so you can check on him before you drive me back."

Maria glanced over again. "It's not really en route. It's out of the way."

"Ah, that's all right." Jo grinned. "I'm not in a big hurry. Just gotta stop by the folks for a bit."

"Really, it's not necessary. I'll be heading back to pick him up after I drop you off."

Jo cocked her head. "Yeah, but you could be seeing him sooner instead of later." She noticed that Maria checked the clock. "I say we stop now so you can surprise the little guy." Maria's expression brightened. "Like I said, I'm not in any hurry." *So not in any hurry.*

"Are you sure?"

"Heck yeah, absolutely. My folks aren't even expecting me. Thought I'd surprise them, you know."

"I'll run in real quick. Thank you for your understanding."

Jo waved her hand. "Oh sure. Hey, when we're troubled we all want our moms. *Too bad all moms aren't like you, Maria West.*

They pulled into the drive of a modest-looking home on the far north side of town. "Would you like to come in for the restroom or something to drink?"

"I'm good." But for some reason, Jo was strangely curious to meet Maria's son. "I wouldn't mind meeting your boy."

Maria turned to look at her. "I don't know how much you know about autism, but my Matt isn't very social."

"Okay, good to know." Jo shrugged. "That makes two of us."

Kathleen looked surprised when she opened the door. "I wasn't expecting you this early."

Maria stepped inside. "We were sort of passing by so I wanted to check on him." Kathleen's eyes settled on Jo behind her. Maria touched her arm. "I'm sorry, Kat, this is a client of mine, Jo Marchal." She looked at Jo. "My sister-in-law, Kathleen."

Jo had already sized up the petite blonde. She extended her hand. "Nice to meet you."

Kathleen accepted Jo's handshake. "Nice to meet you too." She eyed Maria. "They're in the family room."

"I'll be back to get him once I drop Ms. Marchal off."

They entered a large comfortable room where four boys of various sizes sat watching a children's movie on the big TV screen. Jo didn't miss the smile that warmed Maria's face. One of the boys nudged and pointed. Matt looked up, then got up and came toward them. He tightly circled his arms around Maria's waist.

"Hey, sweetie, are you okay?" Maria asked softly and kissed the top of his head.

The tender moment touched Jo somewhere deep inside. It'd been such a long time ago that Jo and her mom had shared any similar kind of closeness.

"I have to go back to work for a little bit, but I'll be back to take you home. Okay?" The boy didn't move or make a sound. Maria stroked his hair and looked over at Jo. "My son, Matthew." Jo nodded and smiled. "Can you say hello to our guest, Matt?" Again he remained motionless and silent and Jo saw a flicker of pain in Maria's eyes. Maria kissed his dark curls. "Okay, sweetie, I'll be back soon." She had to release his arms from her waist.

"Does he like riding in the car?" Jo asked.

Maria looked puzzled. "He doesn't dislike it. Why?"

"Why don't you bring him along? I mean, we're just driving back to my truck."

"I don't usually—"

"Ah heck with all that proper business stuff. I don't mind, and if he don't mind and wants to be with you, I say let's bring him along."

Maria ruffled Matt's hair. "Would you like to go for a ride in the car with me and this nice lady, Matt?"

He responded by taking hold of Maria's hand.

Jo grinned. "I take it that's a 'yes.'"

"Okay, big guy, let's get going."

Kathleen silently watched the exchange. "Thanks again." Maria directed to Kathleen.

"No problem, hon, whenever you need me call."

Jo looked at Kathleen. "Nice to meet you."

Kathleen smiled at Jo. "You too. Good luck with the house hunting."

"Actually it's a farm I'm looking for, but thanks."

Jo pulled open the door for Maria and her son. Kathleen didn't miss the gesture, and Jo didn't miss Kathleen mouthing the words "call me" to Maria. Maria strapped Matt in his seat and slid behind the wheel.

"He's usually very good in the car. Thank you for allowing me this comfort."

Jo looked at the boy in the back seat, staring out the window. "Hey, the way I see it, he's already got it tougher than most kids." She directed her eyes to Maria. "It's no hardship for me."

Maria smiled over at her. "You're the biggest hearted cowgirl I've ever met."

"Thanks." Jo laughed. "Believe it or not, that is the number one attribute all cowgirls strive for." When Maria laughed, the sound warmed Jo inside like nothing else ever had.

Jo sat in her truck watching as Maria drove away, waiting until her station wagon was out of sight before trying her parents' number. Her mom finally answered after six or seven rings, Jo lost count.

"Mom, is everything okay?"

"Yes, dear."

Jo sighed. "It's…well, it took you so long to answer."

"I was out tending to my flowers and didn't know your father was snoring in his recliner. Is everything all right with you?"

"Sure, Mom. I thought I'd stop by if it's okay."

She made a "tsk" sound. "Jo Lynn, now you know you can stop by anytime. Do you have plans for your dinner?"

"I was going to get something on the way."

"We're having vegetable soup. I'll set a place for you. You forget about that fast stuff that passes for food and come on by."

"I'll be there in a bit, Mom."

The evening mirrored last Friday. Her dad showed no interest in talking with her, so she again sat out back in the swing with her mom.

"Any word from the doctor?"

Her mom gave a push and set the swing in motion. "We have an appointment on Monday. They're waiting on the results of one more test. You know how they are, all secretive."

"I'm sure they want to be accurate with their findings. I wished you'd told me about the appointment. I could be here with you."

She tapped Jo's hand. "Oh, Jo, you don't need to be here." Eileen forced a smile. "They're probably going to tell us the only thing wrong with your father is he's hard-headed and stubborn."

"No news there," Jo muttered under her breath.

Her mom looked over. "Pardon?"

Jo hoped she hadn't heard. "Uh, you'll let me know what's up after you've been there."

"Of course, dear."

Jo gave the swing a push. "I looked at several farms today, all within about an hour from here."

"I think the Pierson place is up for sale. You know where that is, don't you? Right outside of town on Route 60."

"Yes, I know where it is, but it's too small for what I need."

"They always used to have horses. You remember your father used to take you out there sometimes on Saturday afternoons to ride? You were, what, about ten or so."

The memory brought a smile. "I think I was older. It was right before high school."

She remembered exactly when it was. It had been the summer after she'd attended summer camp. And as it turned out, summer camp became one of the best summers she'd ever had.

Jo had had a few crushes before, but for lack of a better understanding, she'd assumed it was something normal girls experienced but didn't speak of. Jo fell in love the first day with one of the camp counselors. At least she thought so at the age of thirteen. Judy King was pretty. She always wore her long brown hair pulled back in a ponytail and had a fit, athletic body. Jo's heart would do little flip flops whenever she was around. She was also the riding instructor, so Jo fell in love with not only women that summer but horses too. She participated in everything she could that pertained to horses to be around Judy King.

One of those things was grooming the horses. That's where Jo met Debbie. Debbie was a really quiet girl and kept to herself. But she knew a lot about horses. She lived about sixty miles away from Jo and had her own horse. She promised to teach Jo everything she knew. Little did she know that Debbie would teach her so much more. She was fourteen and they became good friends the first week. By the third week, Jo was spending more time with Debbie than anyone. Jo felt especially comfortable around her and they could talk about everything.

Three days before camp was to end, she and Debbie were brushing down the last horse in the old barn. Everyone else had run off to take a dip in the lake before dinner. Without warning Debbie reached over and took hold of Jo's free hand.

"I'm gonna miss you so much when we have to leave, Jo."

Jo stopped and turned to look at her. There was something in Debbie's eyes Jo had never seen before. She felt hypnotized. They stood in silence for the longest time. To break the trance-like stare, Debbie reached up and stroked her fingertips over Jo's cheek. Jo's legs became rubber bands. When she didn't flinch or move away, Debbie leaned in and lightly touched her lips to Jo's. A sensation rushed through Jo's body that took her breath away.

Debbie leaned back. "I'm sorry. I shouldn't have done that," she said softly.

Jo swallowed and looked down at her feet. "It's okay," she whispered.

Debbie raised her chin. "You're so cute. I couldn't not do that." She searched Jo's eyes, but Jo said nothing. "I want to kiss you again."

Jo's cheeks flushed with heat. She nodded. She couldn't say no. Their next kiss lasted longer, and when Debbie pulled away, Jo's heart was pounding fiercely. Jo only waited a second before she leaned in to press her lips to Debbie's. Warmth flooded her body from the contact and Jo realized that's what she wanted to feel every day—forever. Another long minute later they separated.

Debbie smiled. "Wow! Cute and a good kisser." Jo's cheeks burned hot. "Have you kissed girls before?" Jo shook her head. "Me either, but I really like it."

The tiniest smile curled Jo's lips. "Me too."

They heard the barn door creak and quickly moved apart.

Judy King approached. "Don't you girls want to take a swim before dinner?" She patted the horse's neck. "I think ol' Duke is ready to retire for the day."

As Judy led the horse to his stall, Jo and Debbie smiled knowingly at each other, then raced from the barn to get into their suits.

For the next two and a half days the girls were inseparable and would sneak off to steal every moment alone they could. The heartbreak of the whole experience, of course, came the day they had to part. Jo never forgot the feeling of their last hug.

Debbie wrapped her arms tightly around her. "I'm going to miss you so much," she whispered.

Jo didn't think she'd ever felt more completely loved than she did in Debbie's arms. Choked with emotion, she barely managed to say, "I'm gonna miss you too."

Jo had never forgotten the desire she'd felt that summer. To this day she was still searching for it.

"Jo Lynn. What's wrong?"

Jo hadn't heard a word she'd been saying. "What?"

"You got all glassy-eyed and didn't answer." She put the backs of her fingers to Jo's cheek. "You're not coming down with something are you?"

Jo shook her head. "I'm fine, Mom."

"Well, you didn't look fine just now. Why don't you stay the night instead of driving all the way back home? I'll worry if you do."

Jo searched her mom's eyes for something more than simple hospitality.

"The bed's made up in your old room like always. You're welcome to stay."

"Thanks, Mom, I think I will. Are you sure Dad won't mind?"

"Tsk…What can he say? I invited you and you're staying." She pushed up from the swing. "Speaking of, I should go check on him." She pulled her sweater across her chest. "Do you want anything?"

A cold beer or two would be good right now. "No thanks, Mom, I'm fine."

Eileen turned toward the door. "Don't stay out too long. It's been getting chilly in the evenings."

Jo nodded, but her mom was already through the door.

Maria had Matt settled in bed when she called Kathleen at nine thirty, hoping she already had her brood wrestled down for the night.

"Are you free now?"

Kathleen sighed. "Yes. I've put up my feet and I'm enjoying some wine. How's Matt?"

"He's been perfectly fine all evening. I don't know what could have happened to him at school. I can't even speculate about what might have agitated him."

"Is Jack home?"

It didn't matter if Jack was home or not. He refused to have anything to do with Matt, and of late, she felt more and more like his housekeeper than his wife. He'd become distant. She wasn't sure if it was his job or something worse, like an affair, because he never seemed to want to talk either. It was Maria's turn to sigh.

"No. He left yesterday for a business conference. He won't be back until late Sunday."

"Well, listen, sweetie, if you need me to watch Matt so you can grocery shop or anything this weekend, let me know."

"Thanks, Kat. You're my guardian angel, you know."

Kathleen giggled. "Angel, right, that's me. Do you suppose you could convince my boys of this and that they should treat me with great reverence?"

Maria loved that Kathleen could always lighten her mood and make her laugh.

"So—" Kathleen hesitated. "Did you sell a farm today and earn a big commission?"

"Not today, but I hope to soon." And be less reliant on her husband.

"Oh, I'm sure you will."

"I like your confidence in me."

"The gal that was with you today, she's the one from last week?"

"Yes. Do you think your speculation about her is correct?" Maria asked, unsure why it mattered.

Kathleen paused. "I'm no expert mind you, but from what I saw she seemed interested in you."

"That's absurd." Maria laughed.

"No, I don't think it is. I watched how she looked at you. And…well…when Matt hugged you, I thought she was going to hug you both."

"Oh Kat, that's ridiculous."

"Maria, I think this cowgirl just might be smitten with you."

Maria couldn't believe she couldn't see it. "She knows I have a child. Surely she would also know that I'm married."

"Oh, honey." Kathleen sipped her wine. "You're a very attractive woman."

"Oh and now you're flirting with me?" Maria's cheeks suddenly felt hot at the thought of a woman flirting with her.

Kathleen chuckled. "Gee, even if I was, I don't think I would have any time or the energy to follow through. Sorry."

"Is that the wine talking?"

"Probably, or me thinking about something more than being the mother of three."

"Would you ever do that—be with a woman?"

"Lord no! I was kidding. I'm strictly a man-loving woman. How else could I manage living with four of them? I know you and Jack have been together a long time, but be careful around this woman, Maria."

Maria cringed. She wasn't born in the Middle Ages. She knew how gay women were stereotyped, and Jo Marchal just didn't fit with that image.

"Maria?"

"I heard you, and don't worry, Kat. I don't intend to complicate my marriage with an affair and certainly not with a woman. Listen, I'll let you go. I'm beat. Too much driving today."

"Call me if you need help this weekend."

"Thanks, Kat, I will."

As she tidied her home office to wrap up her day, Maria looked at the card attached to the horse farm file. Jo Marchal might be a lesbian, as Kathleen suspected, but there was no way she had any romantic interest in Maria. She opened the file to the note with two more properties listed. She'd send the email in the morning. She turned off the light, quietly peeked in at her son and went to bed.

Jo didn't sleep well in her old bed. Despite her restless sleep, she woke precisely at five and was having coffee at the kitchen table when her dad came in at six thirty. He poured his own coffee and sat down.

"You're up early, Pops."

"Don't make good sense to sleep your life away," he said, his voice gravelly.

"I'd have to agree with you." She might as well be having coffee with a stranger. Why was it so hard to talk to him? They'd been like buddies when Jo was young.

He took a drink and cleared his throat. "You're still planning to move up this way?"

"I looked at several nice properties yesterday."

"Market's just starting to rebound right now. You ought to get a good price on something."

"True, but I'll probably end up paying for it when selling my place."

He nodded. "Suppose so." And with that, the conversation died. They sat in silence until Eileen joined them at seven.

Jo didn't stay for breakfast, making an excuse about an appointment. She entered the light highway traffic around seven thirty. All she wanted was to be on her farm.

Jo arrived home to an email from Maria—she had found two more properties. She sat looking at the info and pictures of the biggest, most expensive one she'd already seen. It wasn't much over an hour's drive to her folks, which was doable. And it was less than a half hour from where Maria West lived. She could deny it all she wanted, but Jo knew she'd developed a bit of a crush on the married mom. Well, Maria wouldn't be the first unattainable woman she'd felt this way about.

She spent the remainder of the day helping the guys muck out stalls and out in the pasture with her horses. When she finally made it back to her office, she was thrilled to have a voice mail from Maria asking if she'd received the email and was interested in seeing either one of the other properties.

Following a late dinner Jo settled out on the porch, debating whether to call Maria back so late. Long moments of back and forth passed before she decided to go for it.

After Maria's warm greeting, Jo said, "Hope I'm not calling too late."

"No, I was doing a little work on the computer."

"Well, I figured I should let you know I got the email. Both places sound like what I'm looking for, but I'm not sure how soon I'll be getting back up that way."

"I understand. You've got my number, call me."

"And what shall I call you?"

Maria chuckled. "You're quite amusing, Jo Marchal. Do you have any interest in the properties you looked at yesterday?"

"Possibly, but I've got to get a few things in order down here before I can get too serious about picking my new place." Plus she needed to know the outcome of her dad's tests before totally uprooting herself. She knew she was already leaning heavily toward one place, but she was enjoying the attention Maria was bestowing on her.

"Well, of course you do." Jo thought she could listen to the sound of Maria's voice forever. "If you have any questions at all or need any further information, please let me know."

"That's exactly what I plan to do."

Glad that she had found the courage to call, Jo leaned her head back and soaked in the country quiet. Eyes closed, she played through the clips of Maria West she had stored in her mind.

Maria considered Kathleen's appraisal of Jo Marchal and decided the cowgirl's sexuality didn't change her opinion of the woman she was getting a glimpse of. Jo made her laugh and forget the difficulties in her own life, and she wanted more people in her life besides Kathleen who could do that. Heaven knows Jack had barely given her a reason to even smile in longer than she could remember.

CHAPTER THREE

For a distraction on Monday, Jo worked with one of the boarded horses. She'd just returned the horse to its stall when her phone began vibrating. Racing out of the stable, she didn't connect the call until she was fifty feet beyond.

"Hello…Mom?"

There was a brief pause. "Yes, it's me, Jo Lynn." Her voice quivered.

Jo's stomach knotted. "Mom?" Jo heard her sniff.

"It's—" Her mom couldn't muffle the sob.

Jo ran toward the house. "Oh God, Mom, I'm driving up there. I'll be on the road as soon as I can grab a few things."

Her mom sucked in a deep breath and finally spoke. "No, there's nothing you can do."

The knot tightened in Jo's stomach. "I can be there, I don't know…be there."

"Really, Jo Lynn, there's nothing you can do at this point."

Tears streamed down her face. She cleared her throat. "So what exactly did they say?"

"It's in his pancreas." Her mom seemed to gain a tiny measure of control.

Jo didn't make it to the door. She dropped in one of the chairs on the porch. With elbows on her knees, she lowered her head. She didn't know much about cancer, but she knew this was one of the worst. She felt as though she might throw up. Her stomach churned and burned.

"We have an appointment with the oncologist Thursday. We'll know more about this whole thing then."

There were dozens of questions flying around in Jo's mind, but she only asked one. "What time?"

"What?"

"What time is the appointment on Thursday?"

"Ten o'clock." Eileen sounded distracted.

"I'm coming up and going with you. I'll be there Wednesday evening some time."

"That's really not necessary dear." Her voice was distant.

"Didn't you tell me I don't need an invitation?" Jo held her breath, but her mom said nothing. "I'm part of this family and I'm coming Wednesday night. Can I please talk to him?"

Eileen sighed. "Oh dear, I don't think that's a good idea now. He's in the den with the door closed. I think he needs this time to himself."

Jo couldn't begin to imagine what he must be going through. They'd fallen so out of touch over the last twenty years. "All right."

"I should go now, Jo Lynn. I need to think about doing something for our dinner tonight."

Jo thought she sounded undone or in a haze. "Sure—Mom?"

"Hum…"

Jo swallowed the lump in her throat. "Will you tell Pops I love him and I'll see him Wednesday?" She thought her tears started again, when in actuality they'd never stopped.

"Of course, dear. Drive carefully."

"I love you, Mom." Jo nearly whispered the words, unsure that her mom had even heard her and then all was silent.

She slumped back in the chair. She was only thirty-six, and, granted her dad was seventy-four, that wasn't old by today's standards. He was too young to leave her and her mom. He'd given the Postal Service forty years of dedication and had spent the five following years working part-time at a local hardware store for one of his fishing buddies. He only retired completely four years ago. How could life be this unfair? And what would become of her mom without him? The tears continued steadily as she went inside to the kitchen cupboard that held a few bottles of liquor. She pulled out an unopened bottle of Kentucky bourbon. She tried recalling who'd given it to her during a holiday visit last year as she poured three fingers in a glass.

In the living room she plopped into her comfy old chair. The first drink gagged her. She waited several minutes before taking another. It went down only slightly easier, the warm burn sliding down to her already churning stomach. Whiskey was probably a bad idea. She should have guzzled a couple of beers. She took one more drink, leaned her head back and closed her eyes.

Once the alcohol made it to her head she allowed her mind to drift away. She was riding in a pasture, drinking in the sense of freedom it gave her. She always felt safe and comforted there, astride a horse. And she stayed there, in her mind, until the glass slipped from her hand and hit the floor, startling her back to reality. She took the empty glass to the kitchen and got a beer. Back out on the porch, she called Cecile.

"Hey, darlin'! You callin' to give me a big ol' fat commission?"

Jo took a gulp of beer. "Yep. Put her on the market, 'cause I'm movin' to Ohio."

"What's goin' on hon? You don't sound like yourself."

Jo drew on every bit of self-control she could muster. "Family stuff. You know how that's always been."

"I do. So why you movin' closer? You gonna rub their faces in it 'til they give in an' embrace your lifestyle?"

"My dad…" Jo heaved a sigh and cleared her throat. "He's sick, Cil, real sick and I need to go back home and try to mend fences."

"Ah, darlin' I'm so sorry."

"Yeah, thanks. Will you at least come visit me?"

"You gonna have any good hot spots up thata way?"

"For you, Cil, I'll find one."

Cecile snorted. "Count me there, darlin'. Meanwhile I'll get you listed ASAP. And Jo, if there's anythin' you need…"

"Thanks, Cil. I'll be talking to you."

Jo finished the beer, leaving the empty can beside the chair, and wandered out to the stable.

"Any idea where Tom is?" she asked the first hand she came across.

"Sorry, ma'am." He shook his head.

The tack room was empty, but one of the two-way radios was missing, so she picked up another and keyed it.

"Tom, you on the radio?"

She waited and nothing. Finally there was a crackle of static. Tom's voice was faint. She strained to hear him.

"I'm riding the lower pastures, checkin' fences. What's up?"

"Would you stop in and see me when you get back in, please?"

"Sure thing, Jo. Anything wrong?"

"I need to give you an update."

"Okay, boss."

She returned the radio to its holder and returned to the house, poured more bourbon and went to her office. She spun her chair around to gaze out the window. She had an unobstructed view of the pasture north of the stable where several of her boarders grazed and a part of the gravel lot containing Tom's and two other pickup trucks. She sipped the bourbon, hoping to numb her mind so she wouldn't have to think about the worst thing she was going to face in her life. She had thought that losing Claire was the most devastating thing she'd have to endure. Hell, at least Claire was still living, breathing and enjoying life somewhere. Given the distance between her and her parents, she hadn't considered what losing either one of them might feel like. She took another drink. It sucked to feel.

Eventually she turned around, logged her computer on and found an email from Maria West. To make his farm more enticing for a buyer, an owner was willing to make a concession on one of the properties Jo had looked at. The woman's tenacity inspired a brief smile. She pulled up the color photos of the big farm, which was outside of Midland, where Maria lived. That's where she wanted to be when she went home again.

A knock on the doorframe brought her out of her daydreaming. Tom stood in the doorway holding the beer can she'd left on the porch.

"I knocked outside, didn't hear nothin' so I came on in." He raised the can. "You had a party and didn't invite me an' the boys." He grinned.

Tom was handsome in a rugged sort of way. He forever had a hat indentation in his thick wavy brown hair, and at least two days of beard growth. His brown eyes reminded Jo of a doe's eyes, soft and trusting. It was such a stark contrast to his well-muscled six-foot-plus frame. Jo noticed him eyeing the glass that still contained bourbon. She waved him in.

"Have a seat. I've got some kinda bad news." He tossed his hat on the coffee table and dropped on the couch. She took a seat a few feet away. She couldn't chance looking in his eyes when she broke the news. "I'm selling the farm." She braced herself when she saw his head jerk out of the corner of her eye.

"Damn! Sure wasn't 'spectin' that."

"Man, Tom, I'm sorry. I wish things could be different." She took a moment. "You and the boys do a heck of a job around here. I promise to make sure the new owner knows how valuable you are to running this place."

"Man, I'll sure be hatin' t' see you go."

Jo felt the lump growing in her throat. "Me too, Tom."

Tom had been like a surrogate big brother to Jo the last six years. He'd come on board from almost the beginning, and they'd worked hand in hand, reviving the old horse farm. From mending fences to filling the loft with hay bales, Tom had been right there with her. She wanted to take him with her now, but she knew the likelihood was slim that he could relocate his family. Tom was forty, married half his life and had two teenage girls. They'd hogtie their dad and drag him behind a horse until he relented if he tried to move them away from their childhood home. They were strong willed and as stubborn as their old man.

He picked up his hat. "I s'ppose that's why the trips up north the last few weeks."

Jo nodded. She wasn't sure if she could do this and not cry. She lowered her head. She didn't want Tom to see if she couldn't keep the tears at bay.

"My dad's real sick. I need to be closer to home to help out."

Wet spots formed on her jeans where the tears dropped. She had mentioned to Tom a few times about the less than amicable relationship she had with her folks.

He placed a gentle hand on her shoulder. "Anything I can help with, just ask." He stood and smacked his hat against his leg. "I mean it…anything."

Jo wiped her shirtsleeve across her eyes. "Would you mind breaking the news to the guys?"

"Sure thing, boss."

Sitting back in the silence, she asked herself how she'd ever find the strength to get through this.

* * *

She did her best to avoid everyone at the farm the next day or two and by mid-afternoon on Wednesday was packing an overnight bag in preparation for leaving. Checking her email one last time, she found another one from Maria West. Again the content was simple. It said only that she was touching base with Jo and if she had any questions or needed any info she should give her a call. Jo smiled. She'd do that.

She timed her departure so she'd arrive about bedtime. She didn't feel up to dealing with much tonight. The porch light came on as she made her way up the tree-lined street, signaling that it was time to turn in and her mom was leaving the light on for her. She stopped a few houses away, turned off the truck and waited for half an hour. Hoping they were asleep, she let herself in, tiptoed down the hall and quietly set her bag on the floor in the darkness of her room. A sudden sound startled her.

"I was beginning to worry about you," her mom's voice said softly.

Jo flipped on the bedside lamp. Her mom looked small in the doorway. Jo wanted to hug her and tell her everything would be okay.

"Sorry to be so late. I was trying not to wake you."

"It's all right, I wasn't asleep." She crossed her arms over the front of her nightgown and Jo realized just how fragile she appeared.

Jo sat on the edge of the bed. "Would you like to talk?"

Her mom lowered her head for a second before looking back at Jo. Pain filled her eyes. "I don't know what to say."

Jo stood. "Maybe we can make some tea and sit out in the swing for a little bit." Eileen nodded. Jo tried to take over in the kitchen, but her mom wouldn't allow it.

"I need to do the things I know how to do to keep my mind busy." Eileen pulled her sweater over her shoulders and they settled into the swing on the patio. The silence would have been deafening were it not for the sounds of the spring peepers.

Jo finally broke the quiet. "I found a place I want to buy about an hour from here. I'll be a lot closer if you need anything."

"You really don't need to uproot your life, Jo Lynn. Your father and I will manage this as we've managed every other trying time in our lives." She didn't need to say it. Jo knew that the "trying time" she was referring to was the first Easter weekend after she'd graduated from college.

She had come for the holiday. Since her parents always showed so much love and devotion, Jo was sure they would process and accept what she had to tell them about who she was. Nothing was further from the truth. Her mom flushed deep red and pressed her hand to her mouth, while her dad started reciting scripture. When he finally quit preaching, her mom said, "It isn't natural behavior, Jo Lynn." Her dad, furious, stood so abruptly his chair tipped over, and he stormed from the room. Shaking her head, her mom righted the fallen chair and followed him. Jo packed her bags and left. When she returned again at Christmas, she found the welcoming home she'd always known no longer existed. Nothing had been the same since.

She wished now she'd stayed in the closet the last twenty-plus years.

"I know you and Dad can manage fine without me, but I want to be here to help if I can." Jo saw the sheen of tears on her mom's cheek.

She patted Jo's hand. "Jo Lynn, I didn't mean to imply—"

"I know, Mom." Jo turned her hand to hold her mom's. "I know." She squeezed gently.

They simply were unable to communicate anything meaningful with one another. They swung in silence until it became too cool. Jo lay awake for hours trying to guess how their lives were about to change. And how, if at all, she could help her parents through the inevitable.

In the morning she was again at the kitchen table with her coffee when her dad came in.

"Morning, Pops."

He sat across from her. "You don't need to go with us today. Your mother and I can manage this."

"I know you can."

He reached for the paper Jo had placed on the table for him. "Well, I don't know what you think you can do by going." His words stung.

"Be there. I just want to be there for you, Pops." She took her empty cup to the sink. "I'm going to get my shower." She slipped from the kitchen before he could see the tears welling up in her eyes.

Her father sat stoically through the oncologist visit and her mom cried quietly while Jo fumed at her dad's insensitivity. She tried having a conversation with him when they returned home, only to have him close the den door in her face.

"Stupid old fool," she mumbled under her breath as she went in search of her mom. Eileen was on the patio, absently swinging and staring at nothing. Jo slipped out to her truck.

"Ms. West, Jo Marchal."

"Please, call me Maria. What can I do for you?"

"How busy is your schedule today?"

"I have some free time this afternoon. Do you want to look at more properties?"

Jo exhaled slowly. "Actually I was wondering if we could meet somewhere. I have some questions."

"Where are you now?"

"In Campbell."

"Let's see…there's a diner about twenty minutes outside of Campbell on Route 60. We can meet there if you'd like. What time are you thinking?"

"My schedule is completely open, so whatever time works best for you." The prospect of seeing Maria raised Jo's spirit a notch.

"How's two o'clock?"

"Two it is. I'll see you there."

She returned to the patio. Her mom looked so lost and lonely. Jo joined her on the swing and lacking words of comfort, she simply took her mom's hand.

"I don't know what I'm going to do, Jo Lynn." Eileen's tears started again.

"We'll manage somehow, Mom, we'll manage." Jo couldn't stop her own tears from spilling over.

When her mom sucked in a deep breath and expelled a torturous sob, Jo slid her arm around her shoulder and held her.

Eileen finally calmed enough to talk. "I don't know how I can live without him," she said in a hoarse whisper.

Jo's heart was breaking for them both. When Claire had left her two years ago, Jo felt as though her heart was broken forever. She couldn't imagine what it would be like to love and be devoted to someone for over fifty years and then lose them. She hoped somehow she could find the strength to get herself and her mom through this.

Jo was seated in a booth at the front of the diner with a view of the parking lot. It was now almost a quarter past two. Relishing the quiet, she felt the tension knotted in her neck slowly dissipating. She'd give the busy woman a little bit longer. A smile curled her lips as she pictured the attractive dark-haired, dark eyed woman. There was more there than met the eye, she suspected. An inner strength as well as an inner beauty. She'd bet that in a pinch Maria West could roll up her sleeves and change a flat tire on her car. She was petite, but Jo seriously doubted she was helpless in any way.

The jingling bell over the door brought Jo back to reality and to the sight of Maria rushing to the table.

"I'm sorry again." She dropped her purse and a folder onto the seat and plopped herself down across from Jo.

"Ah, don't sweat it. I appreciate you takin' the time to meet me." Jo realized she sounded like she was back down on the farm in Kentucky. Had she started to feel that comfortable around this woman? Maria smiled warmly as Jo waved at the waitress.

"Just coffee, please," Maria told the waitress and looked back at Jo. "I'm glad you got my message that I was running late." Jo patted her pocket. Her phone must be in the truck. She gave Maria a shrug. "Well, thank you for waiting."

The waitress brought her coffee and refilled Jo's cup. "You said you have some questions." She looked all business as she picked up the folder and laid it in front of her.

Jo recognized her dog-eared business card stapled to the top of the folder. She took a sip of coffee. "Only two. What would you consider the lowest offer they might take on the Buck Creek Road property, and how quickly could we close on it if we could agree on the price in the next week?"

Maria's all business expression became a wide smile as she pulled out the info on the property.

"May I?" Jo asked and Maria slid the sheets across to her. "Do you have a pen?" Jo scribbled on the top edge of the page and pushed it back to Maria. "Can you take this offer to them? I'd like to get my hands on this place as soon as possible." Jo raised an eyebrow and smiled as if her little flirt would get her what she wanted.

Maria's smile never left her face. "I assured you of my diligence, so I'll see what I can do." She slipped the papers back into the folder.

Jo didn't want Maria to leave and scrambled to make conversation. "How's Matt doing?"

Maria looked surprised by her question. "He's doing fine. Thank you for asking."

What else? She couldn't let her leave yet. She was the perfect distraction today. "Your sister-in-law, Kathleen, was it? She's sure got her hands full with three boys."

"She certainly does. I'm not sure how she manages." Maria's smile faded with her response.

Jo considered her lame statement in light of Maria's son's handicap. At a loss for words, she turned her coffee mug between her hands, noticing as she did that Maria was checking her watch.

Maria knew she needed to get back to work, but something made her want to stay and share more of Jo Marchal's company. She wasn't sure what was keeping her there. Maybe it was her smile and how easily Jo made her laugh. Jo's light-hearted persona seemed absent today, however, and her icy blue-gray eyes had a troubled look.

"Well, I've taken enough of your time." Jo said, catching the waitress' attention. "I appreciate you driving all the way out here to meet me." The waitress placed the check in front of Jo.

"I'll get you an answer on the property as soon as I can talk with the seller." Maria stood.

Jo dropped some bills on the table. "That'd be great, thanks."

Outside in the bright sunlight they both slipped on sunglasses.

"I'll be in touch," Maria said as she headed to her car.

Behind her dark glasses, Jo watched as Maria crossed the lot. Only after Maria pulled from the lot did she locate the phone she'd left in the truck and listen to the missed call message. She redialed the number.

"Hello."

Jo smiled to herself. "Jo Marchal."

"Yes?"

"You said inside you'd call, so I just wanted to let you know, I'll answer when you do." Jo kept her voice light and playful.

Maria laughed. "That's good to know, Jo Marchal, thank you."

"No problem, so, uh, you can call me…well, whenever."

"I will, and we'll do coffee again, my treat."

"Anytime." Jo sighed as she disconnected the call. Yep, she was smitten, and as absurd as it was to find herself attracted to an obviously unattainable woman, Jo admitted it felt kind of good.

CHAPTER FOUR

Jo stayed another night at her parents' house. Guilt, she surmised, was the only reason for her decision. As hard as she tried chipping away at the wall time had built between her and her parents, her dad seemed determined to reinforce it while her mom seemed…well, completely lost.

When she returned home, the "For Sale" sign by the road was a stinging reminder that the place she had grown to love as much as her horses soon would no longer be hers. She bypassed the house and drove straight down to the stable. Inside she found Jimmy mucking out a stall and asked if he would saddle up Cobalt for her. She poked her head in the tack room and found Tom sitting at the makeshift desk in the corner. He was on the phone.

He held up a finger to Jo and said, "Yeah, hang on a minute there."

"Sorry to interrupt, Tom. I'm gonna take a ride. Can you stop in the house on your way out today?"

"Sure thing."

She heard the clatter of horse's hooves behind her. When she turned, Jimmy placed the reins in her hand. "Thanks, Jimmy."

"Yes, ma'am." He tipped his head.

Jo felt a tremendous weight on her. She knew Jimmy was working full time for Tom while going to college. He was smarter than a whip and planned to be an engineer. She prayed the new owners would keep on Tom and his crew.

She trotted the stallion about a quarter mile until she was at the rise to the lower pasture. When they stopped, she leaned forward, stroked Cobalt's neck and gazed out over the forty acres coming alive with spring growth. She inhaled the fresh air and tipped her head to squint from under her Stetson toward a cloudless sky. When she looked back to the lush green pasture, her mind was devoid of everything except her and the wide open space. She nudged Cobalt into a trot again and after a moment she coaxed him to a gallop. She intended to let him run until one of them was worn out.

Tom knocked a little after four and Jo waved him in. He tossed his hat on the coffee table and dropped into the chair on the other side of her desk.

"How's the family?" he asked.

"Same as always. I got a father that's more stubborn than a mule."

Tom chuckled. "Don't we all?" Jo appreciated Tom's attempt at levity. "So what's up?"

Jo relaxed back in the chair. "Pretty sure I found the farm I'm gonna buy up in Ohio." He nodded. "It's bigger than this place with the potential for expanding."

"That's great," he replied without conviction.

She leaned forward and pushed a piece of paper across the desk to him. "It's this place." He looked at the spec sheet and pictures. "What do you think?"

"Looks like a nice place to have horses." He handed the sheet back.

"There's a lot of acreage with this place. I'd be willing to give you a piece to build a house on if you'd consider moving with me."

"Dang, Jo!" He shifted in his chair. "That's a mighty generous offer."

She shrugged. "Really? I thought it was kinda selfish on my part seein's how you helped me turn this place into what it is."

He shook his head. "An' nothin' would give me greater pleasure than to do it all over again with you. But I got three women in my life that'd hang me in that barn out back if I even suggested it."

"Well, hell, Tom, I figured I had to at least give it a try."

"Yeah, I sure wish I could."

"Me too," Jo said, feeling defeated.

He pushed out of his chair. "I need to git. I'm pretty sure those three women got some weekend planned for me."

"Have a good one, Tom."

He scooped up his hat and called over his shoulder on his way through the door, "Sure, you too, Jo."

* * *

For the first time in a long time, Jo spent a weekend at home filled with uncertainty. She'd not felt so alone since Claire left. She thought she was past all of it and content with the solemn life she lived, but something was terribly out of sync. It was eating her up inside. She wandered from the kitchen to the porch and eventually the stable. She did the same repeatedly throughout the day Saturday.

Every time she reentered the house after being with the horses she thought of Claire. Claire sitting at the dining table with legal briefs and documents spread everywhere. Claire, the woman she'd fallen madly in love with, who'd only loved her as long as Jo was willing to delight in the spotlight with Claire at her side. When Jo stepped further and further back from the limelight, Claire became more distant and the more time that went by it became apparent Claire wasn't happy in their relationship. Claire had become a lawyer because she wanted to make a name for herself. She wanted to run in the circles where the people with money ran—the kind of people that a successful horse breeder associated with in Kentucky—and she wanted to bask in Jo's light until she had her own. In the end it was clear that Claire used her as strategically as she used the law in court. When she moved out she'd gone directly from Jo's farm to a mansion with large stables and into the arms of the female owner.

Why now would she be thinking of Claire, the woman who never truly loved her? Frustrated, she called Cecile in late afternoon.

"Do you already have plans for tonight, Cil?"

"Nothin' set in stone. What's goin' on, darlin'?"

"I'm not sure, but I can't seem to sit still."

"Woo hoo! Let's kick up our heels and do some crusin."

"What time do you want me to pick you up?"

"There's a new bar I been wantin' to check out, but I'll pick you up. Around nine."

"All right. See you then."

Jo slid into the seat of Cecile's little red Fiat Spider. An extraordinarily successful realtor, Cecile didn't shy away from flaunting it.

"Sorry, the Caddy's in the shop, hon. I hope it doesn't cause a problem later." She flashed a devilish grin.

"You don't need to worry about it, Cil."

Cecile let her shifting hand come to rest on Jo's thigh after she ran through the gears and they were speeding down the road. "You need to get laid, darlin'. I'm tellin' you it cures everything." She gave Jo a wink. "Guaranteed." She squeezed Jo's thigh and returned her hand to the wheel.

Dressed to kill in a linen suit and silk blouse, in usual form Cecile had a pretty little thing hanging on her every word within ten minutes of positioning the two of them at the bar. Beer in hand, Jo leaned her elbows on the bar and faced the dance floor.

Before Cecile was dragged off to the dance floor, she leaned in close. "You look good enough to eat there, sweet pea. If someone don't take a taste of you tonight, somethin's not right in the world. Too bad we're such good pals." She gave Jo's rump a pinch. "Wish me luck."

Jo rolled her eyes. *As if Cecile needed luck.*

Not long after she disappeared a short, cute blonde slid onto the stool next to Jo, ordered a drink and turned to Jo.

"You're the hottest looking woman I've seen in this county in ages. Are you with someone?"

Jo looked into pale eyes, nodding her head toward the dance floor. "Uh, my friend."

The blonde's lips widened, revealing a perfect smile. She reached out her hand. "Callie, Callie James."

"Jo. Nice to meet you." She shook the woman's hand.

Callie picked up her drink from the bar, then turned back to Jo. "So Jo, do you dance?"

Jo took a long drink of her beer and shrugged. "Not so much." She caught Callie's eyes traveling from her worn boots to her slightly less worn jeans and up to her snug-fitted T-shirt.

When her eyes met Jo's, she sighed. "You are the best lookin' cowgirl I've ever laid eyes on."

Jo forced a smile, turned up her beer and drained it. Callie quickly caught the bartender's attention and ordered another. Jo tipped her head when Callie placed the cold bottle in her hand.

"Thank you."

Callie touched her glass to the beer. "You're very welcome." Jo resumed watching the dance floor. "A woman of few words. I like that." Callie sipped her drink. "Sometimes talk is overrated. Don't you think?"

"Sometimes." Jo took another long drink. The cute blonde wasn't picking up on her solemn mood, so Jo gave in. "So, what is it you do, Callie?"

She gave a smile that was bigger, if that were possible, and leaned close. "I'm a paralegal at a firm in Lexington." Jo stiffened. Callie ran a finger over Jo's bicep and down her forearm. "Are you really a cowgirl?"

"More or less." She met Callie's eyes while her finger traced circles on Jo's arm, then watched as her gaze wandered briefly down to Jo's jean-clad thighs. Why was it the pretty ones had to be legal somethings or others?

"So do you ride horses a lot?"

Jo waited until Callie met her eyes. "I do."

"Bareback?" A sexy inviting smile turned Callie's lips.

"Sometimes."

Either the heat had kicked on in the bar or the sexy little blonde was affecting Jo in ways she wouldn't have imagined possible. She was standing so close that when she turned to flag down the bartender again, her breast brushed Jo's arm. Jo had no sooner taken the last drink of her beer when Callie snatched the empty bottle and put another one in her hand. Jo felt as though she was beginning to relax for the first time in a week.

"I love to ride, but I hardly get the chance to. Maybe we could ride sometime."

Jo could only blame the beer for making her sneak a peek at the full breasts barely contained in Callie's designer top. When she got caught looking, Callie raised Jo's chin to meet her eyes and traced her finger along Jo's jaw.

The music had slowed. "Dance with me, cowgirl."

"Sure," Jo replied.

Callie led Jo to the dance floor where she moved effortlessly into Jo's arms, slid her hands up her back and pulled her close. Jo finally relaxed and swayed to the music in rhythm with Callie. Callie didn't want to stop, but Jo pulled her back to the bar. She emptied her beer and waved down the bartender for another. After a few sips, she excused herself to go to the restroom. As she weaved her way through the crowded bar, it became clear to her that she was well on her way to being drunk if she didn't slow down.

When she again maneuvered through the crowd, she spotted Cecile chatting it up with Callie, but she was gone by the time Jo reached the bar. Jo would really miss the ever-effervescent Cecile when she moved away. She reminded her of one of the wild and free-spirited horses she'd broken over the years, but she seriously doubted a woman would ever break Cecile.

Callie handed Jo her beer and met her eyes. "Your friend is very nice. She's so…" She shrugged.

"Full of abandon and only to be approached with extreme caution." Jo laughed.

She propped her foot on the rung of the barstool and leaned an elbow on the bar. Callie seized the opportunity to step against Jo's raised leg and rest her hand on Jo's thigh. Jo's blood moved toward a desire she hadn't felt in a very long time. She tipped her beer and took a couple swallows, hoping to extinguish what was beginning to smolder. When Callie again traced circles with her finger, this time on her thigh, Jo could barely stand it.

"Would you like another drink?"

"I'm fine, thanks."

Callie stood so close her hot breath caressed Jo's ear. She swallowed hard.

Cecile approached, Jo hoped, to rescue her. Pressing against Jo's side, Cecile dropped her arm across her shoulder. "Hey, darlin', how you doin'?"

"Great, Cil. Are we leaving now?"

Cecile looked from Jo to Callie and back. "Well…see…here's the thing. I met this gorgeous nurse." A smile spread on Cecile's face. "And well…she's offered to check my blood pressure." She wiggled an eyebrow. "If you know what I mean." She chortled. She looked again at Callie and touched her arm. "Don't s'ppose I could impose on you to give my friend here a ride home, could I?"

Callie cocked her head. "It would be no imposition to give your friend a ride—if she doesn't mind."

Jo opened her mouth to protest, but Cecile wrapped her in a bear hug and whispered, "Get you some tonight, hon. I promise it'll make you feel like a new woman." Cecile pulled back and eyed Jo until she gave a slight nod. "Wonderful! Thanks, darlin's."

As if on cue, a tall, slender brunette with unnaturally large breasts appeared and looped her arm through Cecile's. "Ready, sugar?" She batted long dark lashes.

Cecile grinned. "I'm gettin' there."

The brunette smiled and tugged Cecile away. She called over her shoulder, "You kids have fun."

"Sorry about that. She has a way of being very persuasive." Jo said. "Please don't feel obligated to drive me home."

"I was hoping to do more than drive you home." Callie offered her own seductive smile as she moved her hand dangerously high on Jo's thigh. "Darlin'."

Jo chugged the rest of her beer. "Ready to go?"

In answer, Callie grabbed Jo's hand and tugged her toward the door. Jo knew if she stayed she'd continue to drink. As for Callie… Well, if she decided not to take Cil's advice, she felt confident that she could limit their interaction to a goodnight kiss in the car. Probably.

Jo gave Callie directions to the farm, lowered the window part way to let in some cool night air, laid her head back and closed her eyes. The swirling air stirred Callie's perfume and Jo's mind wandered. Callie again placed her hand awfully close to the top of Jo's thigh.

"Are you okay there, cowgirl?"

Jo cracked open an eye and observed the hand close to her crotch. "Fine."

Callie murmured under her breath, "Indeed you are."

When the car stopped, Jo slowly opened her eyes, but Callie had already gotten out. A moment later Jo's door opened and Callie took her hand.

"Come on. Let me put you to bed."

Jo allowed herself to be led into the house, leaning on Callie for support more than she thought she'd have to.

Jo woke naked in bed, alone and relieved. Until, that is, she stood and saw Callie's top amidst the clothes strewn about the floor. She brushed the stale beer taste from her mouth, located her T-shirt and panties, then found Callie at the kitchen table drinking coffee. She smiled up at Jo before going to the counter.

"Good morning, cowgirl." Her eyes sparkled in the sunlight filtering through the nearby window. "I trust you slept okay."

Jo squinted at a developing headache. "I think I passed out."

"How do you take your coffee?"

"Black." She closed her eyes against the increasing pain in her head and dropped heavily into a chair. When the smell of coffee reached her senses, she became aware that Callie was standing very near. "Thanks."

Callie lightly stroked Jo's mess of hair. "You did pass out, but not before teaching me the finer points of riding a strong lean cowgirl."

Jo's stomach flopped over at the thought of having sex with someone and not remembering it.

Callie's hand slid down her back and she kissed the top of her aching head. "You should take something before you get a headache. Where's your aspirin?"

Jo tried nodding her head, but it felt like a bowling ball was rolling around in her skull. "Over the sink."

Callie placed the aspirin in Jo's hand. "Do you mind if I take a shower?"

Jo swallowed the tablets and leaned her head in her hand. "Not at all. Towels are in the hall closet."

As Callie walked from the room, Jo noticed for the first time she was wearing one of her denim shirts and nothing else. She caught the tiniest peek of a shapely backside. She stretched her arm across the table and laid her head down. She wasn't aware she'd nodded off until she felt the hand on her shoulder.

"Why don't you shower? It'll wake you up so you can nurse that hangover," Callie said in a tender tone.

Jo emerged from the bathroom to the smell of bacon and when she entered the kitchen Callie refilled her coffee mug.

"How about scrambled eggs since I'm not very good at frying them?"

Jo stood there, mouth agape.

Callie laughed. "Relax, cowgirl…I'm not trying to move in. I thought fixing you breakfast," she looked at the tiny watch on her wrist, "or brunch was a nice way of repaying your hospitality." Her smile was sincere. "Sit down." She placed a plate of toast on the table, and after she set the plate of bacon and eggs in front of Jo she took a seat across the table.

Jo took several bites. "You're a good cook. Maybe I should move you in." Now it was Callie who appeared like a deer caught in headlights. Jo ate a few more bites and laid her fork down. After a sip of coffee, she said, "I need to clear something up." Callie raised a brow. "I'm not in the habit of picking women up at bars." She avoided Callie's eyes. "Actually, I've never done it before."

"I knew we surely must have something in common…I felt it." They both laughed a little nervously. Callie raised her hand. "I admit, I'm a big flirt, but I've only ever left a bar with a phone number or a promise of a date." She winked. "You're my first, too, cowgirl." Callie's smile said so much, none of which was cheap or uncaring. She shrugged. "You looked like you needed a friend, and…when you went to the bathroom, your friend said you needed to get laid and she'd be eternally grateful if I could accommodate you. Of course there wasn't any question that I was attracted to you and I didn't get any bad vibes. That's some friend you got, but that's not why I slept with you. I wanted to." She took a sip of coffee, trying to hide her rosy cheeks behind the cup.

Jo shook her head. "Yeah, that's Cecile."

They finished breakfast in silence.

When Callie started to clear away the dishes, Jo asked, "Do you have somewhere you have to rush off to?"

Callie narrowed her eyes. "Depends…what'd you have in mind?"

Jo walked over to stand in front of her and reached out her hand. "I'm not sure we were properly introduced. "Jo, Jo Marchal."

Callie took her hand and gently squeezed. "I have a stable of horses. We could take a ride if you like." She kept hold of Callie's hand.

Callie made no attempt to pull her hand away. "That sounds nice, but…" She looked down at her Saturday night outfit. "I'm not exactly dressed for riding."

Jo released her hand and took a step back. "No, more like you're ready for dancing, but I might be able to find something that won't fall off of you. What do you say?"

"Sounds fun, as long as you keep in mind I'm an amateur."

Jo found a pair of Claire's jeans in a box in the back of the closet that had been left behind. They were half a foot too long, but the size was right. Callie came back into the kitchen in the rolled up jeans and Jo's denim shirt. When Jo frowned, Callie looked down at herself.

"What?"

"I'm not so sure you want to venture beyond the driveway in those shoes. They look kind of expensive." Jo looked at her own feet. "There's no way you could keep a pair of my boots on."

Callie snapped her fingers. "I keep a pair of sneakers in my trunk." She grabbed up her keys. "We sometimes go out and walk at lunch."

Callie was cute and sexy. Jo wished she remembered more of last night.

They were standing in the tack room. "When's the last time you rode?" Jo asked.

Callie ran a fingertip over the smooth soft leather of a saddle. "Oh, college, I think."

"So about a year ago," Jo said with a smile.

"Right, in my dreams."

Jo saddled Cobalt for herself and Calypso for Callie. These two could be trusted not to spook easily and no two horses of hers liked to run together more than they did. She placed water bottles in her saddlebag, boosted Callie up on Calypso and kept the horses at a walk toward the lower pasture while giving Callie a refresher. At the bottom of the pasture they took a break to let the horses drink from a small stream while they enjoyed a cool drink themselves. Jo asked Callie about her life and her job and nearly two hours later, after riding back at a full gallop, Jo turned the horses out to graze and sat up on the fence to look out over her land. Callie stood on the bottom rail, arms wrapped over the top.

"How come you're selling this place?"

Jo sighed, as she did every time she thought of letting go of the place. "I'm moving back to Ohio. I need to be closer to my family."

"Oh."

Jo glanced at Callie, staring out at the open field. "If I weren't moving away—I'd want to date, you know if you wanted to."

Callie looked at her and smiled. "So when are you moving away?"

"Soon as I can sell this place."

Callie's eyes held Jo's. "We could hang out 'til then. You know, go to dinner or dancing." She waved a hand in the air. "Or riding."

Jo nodded. "Yeah, sure."

She nudged Jo's thigh with her elbow. "Well, don't get too enthused about it, cowgirl."

Jo remembered Callie's earlier words, when she said she looked like she needed a friend.

"I'd like to apologize for any bad behavior I may have exhibited in my drunken state last night. I'm not in a habit of doing that."

Callie looked away shyly. "I wouldn't call what you did to me last night bad." Jo lowered her head in embarrassment and Callie rested her hand on Jo's thigh. "What I said this morning sounded kind of crude. You're very tender in your lovemaking."

"But…but I passed out," Jo stammered.

Callie took Jo's hand, turned it over and kissed her palm. "Not before taking me on the ride of my life." Jo felt the deep flush in her cheeks. "My only regret is that you're moving away and we can't date."

Jo knew better than to suggest anything beyond friends hanging out. She was certain that the long distance thing wouldn't work. Heck, the girlfriend-living-in-her-house thing hadn't worked out.

Turning her gaze back to the lush green pasture, she reminded herself it was time for things to grow anew—her life included.

CHAPTER FIVE

Jo and Callie made an early dinner date for Friday. While they were enjoying their meal, Jo's phone vibrated.

"Excuse me, I need to take this." She said a quiet "hello" and made her way outside the noisy restaurant.

"It sounds like I've interrupted something." When Jo didn't respond right away, Maria asked, "Have I?"

"I'm at dinner with a friend, but it's okay."

"There are a few things the seller wants me to run by you. I was wondering if you were going to be visiting your parents again soon or if I should email this to you."

Jo smiled. "I'm driving up in the morning. How's that for timing?"

"Perfect." Jo could hear the smile in Maria's voice, and it made her feel tingly inside. "I actually have some business I have to take care of in Campbell. I'll schedule it for tomorrow. What time can I meet you?"

"I'm flexible. You tell me."

"Can I call you tomorrow after I get my appointments set?"

"Works for me."

"Terrific. I'll talk to you tomorrow. Sorry for interrupting your dinner. Please pass my apology on to your companion."

"Sure."

Jo tucked her phone away. Interesting that Maria referred to her dinner guest as a "companion."

When Jo pulled up to Callie's place, Callie squeezed her hand and gave her a peck on the lips.

"Thanks, I had a great time and you're a wonderful dinner companion."

"You're a pretty great date yourself." Jo raised Callie's hand and kissed it. "Let's get together again soon. Okay?"

"Call me." Callie smiled.

"Count on it," Jo responded with a grin.

* * *

Jo knocked and let herself into her parents' house shortly after ten the following morning. "It's me, Mom…Pops…"

Her mom's voice echoed from the kitchen. "In here, Jo Lynn." Eileen was seated at the kitchen table, paging through a magazine.

Jo touched her shoulder as she passed in route to the counter. "Morning, Mom. Where's Dad?"

He mom expelled a heavy sigh. "Probably shut up in the den. He spends a lot of his time in there these days." Her voice cracked. "I don't know what to do for him, Jo Lynn. He won't talk to me." Jo poured a mug of coffee. "Oh dear, that coffee is hours old. Let me make some fresh."

Before Eileen could get up, Jo placed her hand on her mom's shoulder. "It's fine, Mom. Let me go see if I can talk to him."

Jo knocked on the door and he responded, but she couldn't quite make out what he said. It may have been "go away." She pushed through the door.

"Hi, Pops!" She closed the door behind her. As he grumbled a hello, Jo walked around his big old desk to kiss the top of his head. "How you feeling?"

"How do you think I feel?" he huffed. "Damn doctors say I'll be dead inside six months or less."

Jo bit back a retort while swallowing the lump in her throat which threatened to open the floodgates of her tears. She sat in the arm chair across the room. "Mom's sick about this. Why won't you talk to her?"

"You don't need to worry about me and your mother."

"You're my parents. Why wouldn't I worry?" Jo struggled for control.

"What do you know?" His voice rose. "You've spent more than twenty years avoiding us."

Jo raised her voice to match his. "You know very well why I stay away. You don't want me around. You don't want, God forbid, for anyone in this town to find out that Walt Marchal's daughter is not normal."

She stood and balled her hands at her sides. "Isn't that how you see me, Pops? Not normal. You can't stand the thought that you made me. Can you?" She took in a deep breath. This had been building for too many years, and she'd be damned if she didn't speak her mind before it was too late.

"I am who and what I am, Pops. Life's too short, as I'm sure you're coming to realize. I love you and Mom more than you care to know. The sooner you come to accept that—and me, because I'm the one you created out of love—the better you'll feel about the small piece of life you have left."

Tears streamed down her face, but she was beyond caring. She marched to the doorway. "You don't have to talk to me, but you damn well better talk to her. She's given you fifty-one years of her life. You at least owe her that much." Jo yanked open the door, then slammed it behind her. She grabbed her keys and without another word, left the house.

That had been coming for a long time, she admitted to herself as she drove a few miles north of town and pulled into a parking spot along the small lake there. She inhaled the fresh air and gazed at the rippling, sparkling surface of the water, hoping to calm the disquiet roiling inside her. When that didn't work, she crossed her arms over the steering wheel, lowered her head and cried. She cried because her parents hated who she was, because she'd lost twenty years of sharing with them and because she was about to lose her Pops forever.

When she'd cried out every tear, she got out and walked down to the lake. Strolling along the shoreline, she came upon a young boy of maybe seven or eight. He looked to be a year or two older than Maria's son Matt. The boy tossed a stick into the lake while a spry golden retriever fetched it.

When the boy saw Jo watching, he called out as if he knew her. "Hi!"

"Hi yourself!" She walked closer. "That's a fine-looking dog you've got there."

He beamed proudly when the dog laid the stick at his feet. He rubbed its head. "This is Lucky."

Jo knelt a few feet away. "Hey there, Lucky." The dog came right over and licked her face while his tail wagged vigorously. She scratched his neck. "I have a retriever. His name is Jake. He doesn't chase sticks, though." Jo rose to her feet.

"Really?" His expression showed confusion.

"Nope." Jo shook her head. "He likes to chase horses."

His eyes widened. "Cool." He handed Jo the stick. "Here, he'll fetch for you too."

Jo took the stick, smiling at the pure innocence of children. Why couldn't she be innocent in her parents' eyes? The moment she tossed the stick her phone vibrated in her pocket.

"How's your schedule?" Maria asked.

Seeing Lucky loping back to her, stick in his mouth, she asked, "Can I call you right back?"

"Sure."

She patted Lucky's head, took the stick from him and handed it to the boy, looking on as he threw the stick again and the dog dashed into the water after it. "Hey, I have to go take care of some grown-up stuff. It was nice to meet you fellas. Have fun!" He waved as Jo turned to go.

When Maria answered, she said, "I don't have a schedule. Just tell me when and where we're meeting."

"I don't know this town very well. I'm about ten minutes east of downtown. You'd be better at picking a spot."

Jo picked a little restaurant/bar north of town she was familiar with. She and the gal that ran the place had only been a year apart in high school and it was a place Jo had typically dropped in at whenever she stayed over at her parents in the past. It made for a nice escape from the uncomfortable stiffness, and she and Shirley had forged a casual friendship while sharing pieces of their lives. Nothing deep or revealing, though. Jo didn't even know if she was married.

At a quarter of one the place was nearly deserted, the lunch crowd long gone. Sliding into a booth sporting cracked and peeling vinyl seats, she gave a quick wave to Shirley. Minutes later Shirley made her way over and leaned a rounded hip against the opposite seat.

"It's not Christmas and it sure isn't summer yet. Can't imagine what brings you here."

"Family." Jo rolled her eyes.

Shirley looked away as the door opened and Maria entered. "Seat yourself."

"I'm actually looking for her." Maria placed a hand on Jo's shoulder and Shirley stepped aside.

The touch sent a tingle down Jo's spine. Maria slowly pulled her hand away and slid into the booth across from her.

"I'll be back in a minute," Shirley called over her shoulder.

Maria tilted her head and looked a long silent moment at Jo.

"What?"

Maria pursed her lips, worry creasing her forehead. "I'm not sure, but you don't quite seem like yourself."

Jo shrugged. "There's a lot going on right now." She finally smiled. "This is just the distraction I need, though. I'm glad you called."

Maria's concerned expression faded into a smile. "Well, then… I'm glad I called too." She leaned closer and crossed her arms on the table. "Anything you want to talk about?"

"Nah, nothing earth-shattering." Jo hoped for a convincing tone.

And in fact it was mostly true. She'd been dealing with the situation longer than she cared to remember. And now sitting across from the very attractive Maria West, gazing into her dark eyes, Jo wanted to put all of it out of her mind and simply enjoy the company.

"So…" Jo leaned back and stretched her arms across the seat back. "What's this homeowner wantin' me to give up on the deal?

Maria couldn't help but notice when Jo's long-sleeved jersey shirt pulled taut across her chest that she wasn't wearing a bra. She instantly pulled her gaze away and wondered when she had started noticing if women were wearing bras or not.

"Ms. West…" Maria looked at Jo's impish grin. "Something wrong?"

"Uh, no…" Maria shook her head. "I'm sorry, I got distracted by something…I was thinking about something…never mind, I'm sorry." She pulled a piece of paper from her purse as Shirley came back to the table.

"What can I get you gals?"

"Coffee, please," Maria replied.

Shirley looked at Jo. "Your usual?"

Jo's eyes moved from Maria to the waitress. "No, I'll have coffee too and a piece of whatever today's pie special is."

Shirley looked from Jo to Maria and back to Jo before she left.

"Should I ask what your usual is?"

"A beer. I sometimes stop in when I'm home visiting my folks." Jo shrugged. "They don't really socialize outside the church, so I usually come by here. Shirley and I went to high school together."

Maria turned a scrutinizing gaze at Shirley and back to Jo. "Your parents don't know, do they?"

"Know what?"

Maria leaned close and lowered her voice. "About…you know… your lifestyle."

"Excuse me!" Jo appeared stunned.

"I'm sorry. Maybe I've made the wrong assumption."

Jo said nothing.

"I assumed since you didn't want to live close to your parents, you're obviously not married and somewhat mobile that you, you know, bat for a different team than I do." Jo's lips twitched. "I apologize if I'm off base. No pun intended." Maria knew her cheeks were turning a rosy red.

"All pretty good reasons for making such an assumption, but you forgot the most glaring one." Maria furrowed her brows. "The way I look."

She gave Jo a long, lingering once-over. "Well you certainly appear much stronger than any woman I've met, I think, but I wouldn't presume on that alone."

"Okay."

"You know this really is none of my business. Forget I brought it up."

Jo ran a hand through her hair. "We don't talk about it. They act as though it doesn't exist. They're embarrassed by me, so I stay away most of the time."

"I'm so sorry." Maria knew all too well what it felt like to be ignored by someone you cared about.

Jo waved her hand. "Don't be. It's been this way so long I can't remember a time when it wasn't." She leaned close. "I hope this won't prevent our doing business together."

"Are you kidding? I'm a salesperson. We'd never let a tiny detail like this affect a business deal." She laughed and it felt good. She liked that this easygoing cowgirl could do that.

Jo liked when she could make Maria laugh. She got the cutest little dimples in her cheeks that she wanted to touch her lips to… *Whoa! Where on earth did that come from?* Maria was a straight mom and married in all likelihood, given the rings on her finger.

While they had their coffee and Jo shared bites of her pie, they hammered out the details on the property and Jo's offer. Jo noticed Shirley eyeing them curiously more than once before they parted an hour later.

* * *

The weeks flew by and Jo continued to see her parents once a week. The contract on the Ohio farm had been accepted thanks to Maria, and Cecile had worked overtime performing her magic to get a contract on the Kentucky farm. By the first week in June, with Jo's farm sold, she was driving her truck and horse trailer to their new home in Ohio. "They" being her faithful retriever Jake, Daisy Mae and Cobalt. She contracted the move of everything else, including her four remaining horses. Life was going to be very different, but Jo knew she'd adjust. She'd spent her life adjusting.

As Jo and Daisy Mae trotted through the pasture, Jo saw dust rising from the drive and caught a glimpse of a little black car headed down the drive from the house. She headed toward the road.

"Come on, girl, let's run." She clicked and gave Daisy a gentle nudge. Angling toward the corner of the pasture where the drive met the road, they were about to catch up when the car came to a stop. Jo reined in Daisy Mae and circled around it. Maria seemed oblivious to their presence. Jo was ready to dismount when Maria finally saw them.

As the window lowered, Maria tossed her phone over on the seat. "I was just about to call you." She put the car in park and climbed out, shielding her eyes from the bright morning sun.

"Oh yeah?" Jo smiled and leaned casually over the saddle horn. "And what was it you were planning to call me?"

With a chuckle Maria approached but stopped a number of feet shy of the fence. When Jo climbed down and walked with Daisy Mae closer, Maria stepped back.

"I left a little housewarming gift on your porch."

Jo thought the sight of Maria was the best kind of gift she could imagine. "I was on my way in. If you have time, I can offer you something to drink."

"Okay."

Jo's stomach fluttered. "I've got to unsaddle her." She quickly mounted Daisy Mae. "But it'll only take a few minutes." Anxious to move, Daisy started to prance. Jo pulled her back around and gave her a pat. "The house is unlocked. Let yourself in." Jo gave the horse a soft heel, and she instinctively trotted toward the barn.

When Jo entered the house, Maria was standing in the middle of her empty living room. Empty, that is, except for two folding lawn chairs, a sleeping bag on the floor in front of the big stone hearth and Maria, holding a basket in her arms.

"I love what you've done with the place." She offered the basket to Jo with a smile. "I hope you can find room for this."

"Shouldn't be a problem."

Maria followed her into the house's large kitchen, where she put the basket on the center island. She replaced her worn, tan Stetson with the equally worn ball cap sitting there and pulled the fridge door open. "I can offer you beer or water."

Maria stood at the island. "It's a little early for beer, I think." Jo handed a bottle of water across the three-foot counter that separated them and looked over the contents of the basket.

"I didn't know if you drink wine. If not, perhaps you have a lady friend that does." Maria tilted her head.

There wasn't anything subtle about Maria's inference. "This is mighty nice of you, but you didn't have to go to all the trouble."

"I always give a buyer some type of gift. Usually a gift card, but I didn't have a clue what kind of gift card to give a cowgirl." She gave Jo a wide smile. "It's obvious now that you are indeed a cowgirl. The hat," she motioned toward the Stetson on the counter, "the boots and the pickup truck out by your barn."

"Don't forget the horses."

Maria laughed. "Of course, the horses."

God, Jo loved the way Maria laughed. They stood silent and when it lasted too long, Jo said, "We can sit out on the porch if you'd like." Maria nodded.

"Would you mind?" Jo asked in the living room and handed Maria her bottle of water so she could pick up the chairs. Maria held the door for her.

Maria sipped her water. "I love this versatile furniture. Use it inside or out. What a novel decorating idea. Are you actually sleeping on the floor?"

"Yep. Until the movers bring the rest of my stuff and I get a chance to put the bed together—the floor will have to do."

"That can't be comfortable."

Jo waved a hand. "It's better than sleeping on the ground outside." Maria's brow arched. "I took a vacation about ten years ago at a dude ranch out in Colorado. We rode trails and did all those cowboy things you know, like a sleeping bag on the ground under the stars." She shuddered at the memory. "I can tell you that floor in there is a whole lot better. No snakes, no bugs and no critters. They can keep their stars."

Maria laughed yet again. "I can't imagine *you* being afraid of bugs. You can stand next to an animal that could kick you to the moon, and you're afraid of bugs."

"Not just bugs…spiders." Maria laughed harder. "Big, hairy spiders."

Maria pressed her hand to her side. "Okay, I got the picture." She calmed her laughter. "I'm pretty sure Kathleen has one of those inflatable mattresses if you'd like to borrow it."

Jo gave it a moment's thought and decided the only mattress she wanted from Maria would have to come with her on it. *Dang, Jo, get your mind out of the gutter.* "Nah, it's not necessary. They're supposed to have my stuff here by Tuesday."

For reasons she couldn't explain, Maria wanted to invite Jo to come stay at her house. What with her husband traveling so frequently, she was starved for company. Jo could make her laugh. There wasn't nearly enough laughter in her life.

"Well, if you change your mind, it's no trouble for me to check with Kathleen."

Jo asked where the best places were to post job opportunities, and Maria provided a number of possibilities. They sat in silence for a bit, simply listening to the sounds of the country.

Jo finally broke the tranquility. "You're not afraid of horses, are you?"

"I think I am, yes."

"They're such gentle animals."

"I'll have to take your word for it."

"Well, you'll have to come out sometime and I can take you riding. Get you over your fear."

"I think my fear is fine where it is, but thank you for the offer."

A short time later Maria stood. "As much as I'm enjoying the tranquility here, I need to go. I have a date with my son to visit the zoo today." She smiled.

"Sounds fun."

Maria extended her hand. "It's been a pleasure doing business with you, Jo Marchal."

Jo wrapped her fingers around Maria's soft skin. She wanted badly to come up with a reason to keep her there or at the very least a reason to return soon, but there wasn't one. Maria West had helped Jo find her new home, period. That's all there was to their relationship. There were likely a hundred other people clamoring for her time and attention, and she'd already gotten all she was getting. Sadness settled over her and made her next words hard to speak.

"I appreciate all your help. Take care, and if you ever decide to get over your horse fear, give me a call." Jo released her hand, pulled off her ball cap, ran a hand through her hair and forced a smile.

"I'll keep that in mind."

Maria's smile was warm and inviting, and Jo wished for the life of her she could see it every day. She watched Maria walk to her car. It reminded her of their first meeting. She was more than another attractive woman—she was a heartstopper. She gave Jo a little wave as she circled around the drive, and then all that was left in Jo's life of Maria was a cloud of dust. She stepped off the porch, kicking the ground as she returned to the barn.

She busied herself organizing in the tack room, but hours later when thoughts of the woman wouldn't leave her alone, she went to the house for a beer. Swallowing a gulp, she leaned over the island and peered into the basket Maria had brought, recalling her words about the wine. Jo smiled. Maria didn't appear to be bothered in the least by Jo's sexuality. Another of her many redeeming qualities. Jo had never been a wine drinker, but she hoped, as Maria had put it, that she someday would have a lady friend to share it with.

She finished the beer and forced herself back out to the barn. Working like a machine, as she had when setting up her Kentucky farm, she didn't break until dinner time. Parked on a hay bale inside the barn, she heard car tires on the gravel and watched as a sheriff's car rolled toward the house.

The person who emerged from the Dodge Charger was a woman. There was no mistaking the curve of the hips as she stepped up on the porch. As Jo walked from the barn, Jake shot past her, barking furiously. Jo whistled loudly and called him. The deputy spun around, hand resting on the gun holstered at her hip. Jake stopped on command and stood wagging his tail until Jo was beside him.

She gave his head a rub. "Is that anyway to greet company, boy?" Jo took a good look when the deputy stepped off the porch. Yes, definitely a woman—and almost certainly a lesbian. "Can I help you?"

With hesitation the officer met Jo's eyes, then smiled. "You bought the Miller farm?"

"That's right." Jo extended her hand. "Jo Marchal. And you are?" The nametag on her uniform read only K Tyler.

The deputy swallowed noticeably and wiped her hand down her thigh before meeting Jo's firm grasp. "Uh…Deputy Tyler… Kate Tyler."

Her hand was damp and Jo wondered if it was the heat of the day or nerves. "Nice to meet you, Deputy Tyler."

When the deputy took her hand back, she tucked it and its counterpart into her pockets. "Everybody around calls me Kate." Jo nodded. "I saw the For Sale sign, then it was gone and then I noticed your farm sign out there." She nodded toward the road. "Anyway, thought I'd stop in and meet our newest resident. I patrol this part of the county most of the time. Our office is in town and I live the next town over. So…if you have any trouble or anything… at all, call nine-one-one and we'll be out."

When Jo simply nodded again, Kate's head bobbed. She twisted the toe of her shoe in the dirt. Definitely nervous, but cute.

"Well, thanks for stopping by." Jo offered a smile.

"Okay…so uh, maybe I'll see you around."

"Right." Jo tipped her head.

Deputy Kate squared her shoulders, pushed out her chest and headed for the patrol car. Her gait reminded Jo of a rooster strutting around the hens. Yes, the sheriff's deputy was unquestionably gay.

Jake barked as the car drove off. Jo called to him. "Jake, what is the problem, buddy?" He came back, rubbing against her leg. She knelt and scratched behind his ears. "But thanks for looking out for me."

CHAPTER SIX

As promised, the movers arrived with her things on Tuesday. Setting up her house demanded more hours in her day, but at last she was ready for the rest of her horses. Well, except for the matter of hiring new hands to help take care of them. She was in the barn fiddling around with tack the following Saturday, waiting for a fellow to show up for an interview when she heard a car outside. When she went to greet him, however, she discovered it was the sheriff's car again. Jo stepped beside the car as Kate Tyler got out.

"Problem, Officer Tyler?"

Kate immediately shoved her hands in her pockets. "Uh, no…I was patrolling out this way and thought I'd stop and see if you're settling in okay." She smiled nervously.

Jo nodded. "Fine, thanks."

They both turned at the sound of another vehicle. It was the guy about the position as her farm manager.

The older Chevy pickup pulled alongside the cruiser and a young man who looked to be in his teens said through the open window, "I'm looking for Jo Marchal."

His voice was deep and didn't come close to matching his boyish face. "I'll be right with you." She turned back to the deputy. "You'll have to excuse me. I'm working on hiring someone to help me run this place."

"That's the other reason I stopped," Kate said. "I saw your sign on the board in Millie's diner up the road about the job. I may know someone that's interested."

"Sure, tell him to give me a call. Number's on the sign." She turned to walk away.

"It's a her."

Jo turned back around. "Okay, tell her to call."

"Yeah, I will. I'll see you." She tipped her head.

The young man climbed out of his truck and thrust his hand at Jo. "Tucker Lawson, ma'am." He gave Jo's hand a strong, firm shake. When she looked him over, he grabbed his hat off his head. "Sorry, ma'am."

Jo scrunched her face. "This will go much better if you don't call me ma'am."

"Sorry, ma'—sorry."

She smiled. "Let's talk in the barn."

"Nice spread you got here," he said as they walked.

"Thank you." Jo hardly considered her modest farm a spread. A spread was one of those places out west that consisted of thousands of acres. She did note he was dressed for the job, right down to his big silver belt buckle. "Exactly how old are you Tucker?"

He rotated his hat in his hands. "Twenty, ma'…uh, sorry again. I know I look like a kid, but I've spent years workin' for my dad on his farm. I'm a hard worker and I learn things real fast." Tucker's head bobbed. "I'm hopin' to get my own farm someday an' have my own horses."

Jo tilted her head. "You're a handsome young man. I bet you've got all kinds of girlfriends." She liked the boy, but she didn't want to have to deal with one in the throes of sowing his "wild oats," as most fellas did at his age.

He shook his head. "Nah, me an' Judy go out every once in a while, but it's not serious, and I don't go carousing around with a gang of guys neither. This kind of job is a lot of responsibility. I know I can do it if you just give me a chance. My pops says I can do anything I put my mind to."

Him calling his dad "pops" tugged at Jo's heart.

"The position is more than physical labor. I'd need you to be able to assist me hiring help when needed and supervising them."

He nodded. "I get along real good with people and I can learn anything you can teach."

She'd never worked with anyone so young, but considering all the major changes happening in her life, one more would hardly ripple the water.

"That's a fine belt buckle you've got there."

He smiled broadly as he rubbed his fingers over the silver. "Got this for a junior roping and riding competition at the fair a few years back."

"So you know horses pretty good then?"

"Oh, yes, ma'am." He slapped his hat on his leg. "Dang, I'm sorry. I can't quit saying that."

Jo laughed. "Do you have brothers or sisters, Tucker?"

"Two older brothers."

"And how old are they?"

"Twenty-seven and twenty-nine." His face flushed red. "Think I was an accident."

Normally she would ask for some references, but something about Tucker reminded her of Tom. When she'd hired Tom she trusted her instincts. Just like she trusted them now. "Maybe you can think of me like a big sister, and call me Jo."

He grinned. "You mean—"

"What do you say we try it and see how it goes?"

His head bobbed. "Sure thing! You wait, you'll see, I'm the best darn guy you could hire for the job." He reached his hand toward Jo and gave a vigorous handshake. "You won't be sorry. When do we start?"

"Bright and early Monday."

He looked at the bales of hay that had been delivered the day before. "You sure you don't need me today?"

Jo considered how much help he could be today getting the bales up in the loft. It would take her until past dinnertime working alone. If she could even finish.

"We haven't even discussed your pay."

He settled his hat on his head and waved a hand. "I trust you to pay me fair."

Jo smiled again. She really liked this kid. *Maybe, when I'm old and gray—and alone—he and his family will adopt and take care of me.* If… she could keep him around.

"I got gloves in my truck. Be right back."

By the middle of the afternoon they'd finished in the big barn and moved to one of the smaller out buildings to straighten and clean it out. At four thirty, Jo halted work.

"Time to quit. I don't want your mother holding dinner for you and mad at your new boss on the first day."

He shrugged. "I can call her."

Jo was beat. She'd thought a young man full of energy would be a big asset, but she was second-guessing that assumption and wondering whether she could keep up anymore. She placed a tired hand on his shoulder.

"Tucker, this stuff isn't going anywhere. I can say with certainty it'll be here come Monday morning."

He pulled off his gloves and tucked them into his back pocket. "So, no work tomorrow?"

She chuckled. "We won't work on Sundays."

Her parents had instilled in her the notion that Sunday was a day of rest. And after today's physical labor, she'd need to rest. They entered through the back of the house so Jo could get more bottles of cold water. Tucker took in the haphazardly placed furniture and boxes stacked everywhere.

Out on the porch he nodded toward the house. "I could get my mom to come over and help with that in there."

"I don't think there's any help for that mess." Jo laughed. "But thanks for the offer. I'm more concerned about where they live." She pointed to Daisy Mae standing at the fence by the big barn. "Them and as many boarders as we can fit in. They'll be our bread and butter." She turned her gaze to Tucker. "We may have to build another barn if we can get enough horses to board." His eyes brightened as if he lived for hard manual labor. He stepped off the porch.

"See you Monday, Tucker."

"Yep, bright and early, Jo."

As soon as his truck was out of sight, she dropped into one of the lawn chairs and leaned her head back. Maybe she was getting too old for this kind of work. She drained her water bottle, reminded that the truly exhausting physical labor would only last until things were in order. It dawned on her that she'd not given a thought to her family's ordeal while she and Tucker were working. A tiny smile curved the corners of her mouth as she remembered the time when she and Tom had done the same, down in Kentucky. Tucker was like a young version of Tom. She felt confident in her decision to hire him.

She pushed up from the chair, her smile quickly fading under the protest of her thoroughly aching body. She traded the water bottle for a beer, ran the tub full of hot water and slid her well-used body into it for a long soak.

* * *

Jo thought she was dreaming the pounding in her ears until she rolled over and felt the cool, hard floor. The bright sunlight through the barren window was blinding and the pounding was actually at her door. She struggled up with great effort and trudged to it, rubbing sleep from her eyes with aching hands. She opened the door to the largest woman she'd ever laid eyes on. *This* woman dwarfed Cecile. With a grin, she looked Jo up and down.

"Something I can help you with?"

The woman's grin widened. "I sure hope so."

Jo yawned and tried to shake the fog from her brain. "Excuse me?"

The woman shifted her weight to one foot and slipped her hands in the back pockets of her tighter than tight jeans.

"I came to see about the job you posted at Millie's up the road. I been tryin' to call since late yesterday, but only been getting voice mail. Kate…Officer Tyler that is, suggested I might stop in if I couldn't reach you this morning again, so here I am." Her eyes traveled the length of Jo's body and back to her eyes. "I sure would like the job."

Jo became conscious that she was wearing only a T-shirt and boxers. And it seemed the woman was interested in more than a job. She crossed her sore arms over her chest where the woman's penetrating eyes seemed focused.

"The job's been filled. I'm sorry."

"That's a shame."

"Yes, well, I planned to take down my postings today. I apologize you drove out here for nothing."

She waved a hand. "I'm not." She looked Jo up and down once again. "Maybe sometime we could go out and do something."

Oh lord! She's looking for a date.

"Running this place will take all the time I have, but thank you for the invitation."

The woman nodded. "Well, okay, maybe I'll see you around." She appeared puzzled.

"Something wrong?"

She shook her head. "You are the best damn lookin' woman I've seen around here in years. Such a shame." She turned to leave but stopped. "I really do hope to see you around sometime."

"You never know."

The woman had a swagger like Cecile's, and it didn't surprise Jo to see her mount a large motorcycle when she left. Her mind had simply been too exhausted to notice the sleeveless black T-shirt, black jeans and boots she'd been wearing.

As badly as she wanted to flop back on the couch, Jo waded through the boxes stacked everywhere to get to the kitchen to make coffee. With the brew cycle started, she located her cell phone on the counter—and discovered it had a dead battery.

"Damn! Where the heck is the household charger?"

While coffee dripped she pulled a pair of jeans over her boxers and walked barefoot to her truck to plug in the phone. Back inside she poured a cup, but instead of sitting on the back deck like she really wanted to, she went to shower.

She'd promised her mom she would start coming to Sunday dinner after church. Her mom was pleased. However, neither parent suggested that Jo might attend church with them. She figured her dad thought she would burst into flames if she crossed the threshold of a church. And her mom, she was sure, probably felt Jo had no business going to a place of worship unless she was there to repent. She let out a big sigh and reminded herself that she was doing this so she wouldn't live her life in regret for not having attempted to reconcile things between them earlier.

As she eased her truck down the road to her parents' home, she listened to no fewer than nine voice messages. Six were from the motorcycle woman, whom Jo now knew was named Bobbie. She deleted those and returned calls to three others that had called inquiring about the job.

Today's visit wasn't any different than the last. Her father was obstinate and curt and her mom struggled at conversation. After dinner and clean up, she and her mom sat out in the swing. When silence lingered too long, Jo launched into conversation about her newly hired farm manager. Her mom barely uttered a word. Frustrated, Jo finished her coffee and made the excuse she needed to get home to unpack boxes and move furniture since she couldn't find anything.

She walked in the door at home, gave a quick look around, then located a clean T-shirt, her jeans, boots and hat. She headed to the barn. The unpacking could wait. She placed a bridle on Cobalt and mounted him bareback.

Leaning down, she hugged his neck. "Let's take a little stroll, boy."

They ambled out to the gate that divided the east and west pastures. After closing the gate she let the horse graze a few minutes while she climbed on the fence to look over her property to the south. *This* was living—the great outdoors.

She was proud of what she'd accomplished so far. The farm was a hundred fifteen acres, nearly double the size of her Kentucky farm, and the eighty acres that stretched to the south was planted with hay. She'd have to contract someone to harvest it for her, but it would be enough for her needs and leave plenty to sell. She was anxious to ride through the fifteen wooded acres that backed up to the local reserve, which had a small lake. If she could acquire the surrounding farms, maybe one day before she was too old to ride, she could turn her place into a Midwest vacationing dude ranch.

* * *

Jo had been up for hours on Monday when Tucker arrived promptly at seven. He was hard-working and easygoing. A Tom, Jr., if there ever was one.

Things continued to fall into place at the farm. The landlines were installed and Jo received a few calls to board horses. She gave Tucker the responsibility of hiring a fellow part-time for an extra pair of hands. All was coming together nicely, with the exception of her personal space. She looked around at the mess and figured since her life was in such turmoil, the house might as well be too.

The following Saturday, when the now-familiar sheriff's car appeared again, Tucker found Jo in the tool shed to let her know. She rolled her eyes.

"You want me to deal with whatever it is?"

Jo gave his shoulder a pat. "Thanks, I've got it."

He walked with her only as far as the big barn and ducked inside. She found the deputy leaning against the cruiser door.

"I must be the best protected resident in the county."

Kate stepped away from the car and shoved her hands in her pockets. "I was patrolling close by, thought I'd stop and see how things are going."

Jo said only, "Great," creating an uncomfortable silence.

"I noticed on your sign you board and train horses."

"Uh huh. You have a horse?"

"Oh no! Don't even ride them."

Jo cocked her head. "Really? It's a great way to relax."

"I'll take your word for it."

Jo nodded. "Your motorcycle friend stopped by about the job—"

"She's not really my friend. She's someone I've run into a few times at a bar. She mentioned she was looking for a job so I said to call you. You say she stopped by, though?"

Jo smiled. "Yeah, woke me up Sunday morning." She thought she saw a flash of something in the deputy's eyes, but it happened so fast.

"Guess I must've mentioned where your farm was. Sorry."

Jo shrugged. "No harm, but I'd already hired someone." She stood waiting but Kate said nothing further. "Well, I need to get back to work." When she started to step away, Kate caught her arm. Jo's arm tensed as she quickly spun around.

Kate removed her hand. "Sorry, uh, I was…uh wondering… maybe we could catch some dinner in town sometime. I know all the best restaurants."

Jo slipped her hands in the pockets of her baggy cargo shorts, clenching her hands. "That's a real nice offer, but I'm so busy with this place here I don't really have time for socializing." Kate nodded and pulled open the door of her car, her expression showing what looked like disappointment and embarrassment. "Thanks for stopping by."

Kate slid behind the wheel and called through the open window while starting the car, "Yeah, well maybe I'll see you around."

Jo gave a nod as she drove off. When she headed for the barn, Tucker came out, wiping his brow with his bandana.

"Everything okay there, boss?"

"Yes." She smiled. Definitely a Tom, Jr.

He followed her back inside to the tack room where she pulled bottles of water from the mini fridge. She leaned against her saddle on its perch while he pulled the stool from under the old scarred wood desk and sat.

"You know how you told me to think of you as a big sister?" Jo tipped her head. "Well, I been thinking 'bout that and I think if I had a big sister, I wouldn't mind her being you."

"Thanks, Tucker. I appreciate you telling me that."

His cheeks burned red. "Yeah, and I try not to judge people." Jo raised a brow. He took a gulp of water and looked down at his feet. "That lady cop, she's interested in you, isn't she?"

Jo studied him for a minute. "Do you think she is?"

He met her eyes, but only briefly. "Oh yeah, but it's okay with me…I mean, I don't rightly care if you don't like guys. It's none of my business."

Such open-mindedness was the last thing Jo expected from a young man raised in the rural Midwest.

"Well, thanks for sharing with me, Tucker. I officially feel like a big sister."

He smiled awkwardly. "If she's bothering you, well…I…I'm here if you ever need any help with anything."

Jo walked to the waste bin to toss her empty bottle and placed her hand on his shoulder. "Thanks, Tucker. I like knowing you've got my back."

He stood. "I mean it. If you need anything, I'm your man."

It was immediately obvious from his expression that he realized the potential awkwardness of what he'd said. His cheeks were a bright rosy hue.

"I'm going to the tool shed. You can call it a day."

He tossed his bottle and joined her out in the barn. "I can help you out there."

"Nah, you've put in enough hours this week. Go on home and take your girlfriend out to a movie."

"You sure?"

"Absolutely. See you Monday, Tucker."

He practically ran to his truck. Jo headed back to the shed, but only to close the door. She then made a beeline up to the house. Inside she ran a hot bath, grabbed a beer and sat in the steaming water, hoping it would relieve some of the tightness in her muscles.

After the bath, she put on cut-off sweats and a comfortable old T-shirt. With a fresh beer in hand, she started to survey the mess. If her mother saw this place, she would probably suffer a heart attack. She had always been after Jo to clean and straighten her room. She gathered up the dirty clothes scattered around and took them to the laundry room off the kitchen.

In the kitchen she opened a box and pulled out pots and pans to put in a cabinet by the stove. She carried the empty box to the garage and saw her computer sitting on the workbench. Now that the cable lines were in, there wasn't any reason for her not to get reconnected. After finishing laundry and a frozen dinner, she sat down with a beer at the computer in the nearly empty room and logged into her email. She sipped as the page loaded, secretly hoping there might be something in her mail box from a particular pretty realtor. There were dozens and dozens of new ones. She scanned the list, junk, junk and more junk. There was also one from Cecile that was a week old.

"Hey, woman! Hope you're settlin' into your new digs up north there. I have to say, cruisin' the bar just ain't the same without my bitchin' blonde babe." Jo laughed. "I'm ready to visit soon as you say the word. Oh, and I ran into your little cutie last weekend. She said you all spent some quality time together before you left. I'm tryin' to imagine what 'quality' means. The gal sure seems to like you a lot, darlin', so maybe I'll bring her along when I come a visitin'. Hope you got a good hot spot to take me to, to make my comin' worthwhile—wink! Okay, maybe we'll talk soon. Love and miss ya darlin', Cecile."

Jo smiled as she closed the email and shut the computer down. Cecile could be so crass sometimes. She wondered how she always managed to get any woman she pursued to sleep with her. No, scratch that. She didn't want to find out how. She didn't need the complication of a woman in her life.

She navigated the obstacle course back to the kitchen for another beer and went out back on the deck to watch as the sun slowly slipped behind the landscape. The wash of color this evening was as intoxicating as the country air. Her mind wandered, her eyes drifting closed. She wondered whether she'd ever see Maria West again. She couldn't put her finger on what it was about the woman that attracted her, but there was no denying it, there was something.

She decided to crash early, settling down for another night on her makeshift bed in the living room—only to wake in the early morning dreaming of Maria. And aching with desire.

Wanting to clear her head, she showered before the coffee was even ready. The shower spray against her head helped to remind her that there wasn't a place in her life for any woman, and she certainly wasn't about to let one into her heart. Especially a very straight, married one.

CHAPTER SEVEN

Life at the farm slowly fell into a routine. She acquired a couple of boarders, including one whose owners were paying for jump training. The situation between her and her parents, on the other hand, remained status quo. Jo still gave it everything she had, visiting every Sunday.

Two weeks into July, Tucker waved her down before she made it around the circular drive on her way to the feed store.

"You probably don't want to hear this, but we need to invest a little money in some tools."

"What kind of tools? The tool shed is full of them."

He cocked his head. "Turn-of-the-twenty-first-century tools." She sighed. "A hammer and nails just isn't workin' on the fence boards. That horse we took in a few weeks back is a head scratcher, an' every time he gets to rubbin' his head on the fence he's knockin' boards loose. If I don't catch 'em quick enough, I'm afraid the jumper we're boardin' is gonna head for the hills."

"What do you need, Tucker?"

"A decent cordless drill and some very long construction screws." She pursed her lips. "Ah, I know, you're gonna tell me to make do with the hammer an' nails like my pops does, right?"

She dug a small notepad and pen out of the console. "Write down exactly what it is you want." She handed them out the window. "And tell me where in town's the best place to get them, please."

"It's called Burton's Hardware, and it's in the shopping center on Canal," he said as he wrote. "Can you read my scrawl?" He handed the pen and pad back to her.

"Sure. Now what if I can't find these at that hardware store? You going to be around in the barn so I can call you?"

"I can be for a few more hours, but just ask for Ernie, he'll fix you up."

She checked the dash clock. "Got it, I should be back by lunchtime."

He headed toward the barn, waving a hand over his head.

Jo drove to the hardware store, looked up Ernie and had her list complete in no time. On her way to the checkout she heard a familiar voice in the next aisle. She stopped and listened to be sure. When she made her way around the end of the aisle, her heart missed a beat, fluttering at the sight of Maria West.

She was talking on her cell and she sounded frustrated. "Look, tell him I'll get back to him this afternoon with the information." Her tone softened. "Thanks, Karen." Snapping the phone closed, she shook her head and mumbled, "Idiot."

Jo moved down the aisle. "Excuse me, ma'am."

Maria spun around, her stern expression dissolving in an instant. She smiled warmly. "Jo Marchal." She gazed intently at Jo. "What do cowgirls shop for in hardware stores?" Jo offered a look at the boxes tucked under her arm. "That looks like pretty serious work."

Jo shrugged. "Not for me." She looked at the window shades and blinds where Maria was standing. "And what do realtors shop for in hardware stores?"

The delight on Maria's face disappeared. "New window blinds for Matt's room."

Jo didn't understand why shopping for something for her son would be upsetting for her. From what she'd observed, Maria adored her son completely. The love in Maria's eyes when she looked at Matt was clear.

"Well, good luck with your window shopping."

Maria caught her pun and chuckled, and Jo remembered how good it felt to be able to make Maria laugh. When she started to turn, Maria touched her forearm. The simple contact froze her in place. As Jo's eyes studied the soft, brown fingers resting on her forearm, Maria pulled them away.

Maria's voice was soft as a spring breeze when she said, "I was going to have a bite of lunch next door at Cate's Diner when I finish here. Would you like to join me, or do you have to rush back with your hardware?"

Jo held back the broad grin she was dying to show. "Lunch sounds like a great idea."

"Maybe you could go ahead and get us a seat before it gets too crowded."

Jo's stomach flipped and flopped. "Right, I'll just…uh," she nodded, "get us a seat."

Maria smiled. "I shouldn't be too long."

Jo's head was somewhere in the clouds when she checked out, tossed her purchases in the truck, called Tucker to say she'd be delayed and rushed into the diner. She couldn't believe her luck in running into Maria. What were the chances? She'd had another dream about her just a few nights ago. She'd awakened feeling anxious—as if something were about to happen. Of course it wouldn't, but that didn't stop her from seeing herself with Maria "that way" in her dreams.

Maria couldn't tear her eyes away as she watched Jo walk out of sight. There was something about the strong and quiet woman. Maybe she was just a little bit envious of the way Jo walked so confidently. Then again maybe it was because she looked so hot in her snug, worn jeans. *Oh my heavens!* She took a deep breath and forced herself to finish her task, excited by the thought of joining the cowgirl for lunch.

Jo was seated in a back booth and stood when she entered.

"Mission accomplished?"

Maria nodded as the waitress appeared.

Once she'd left with their orders, Jo asked, "So…are you redecorating your son's room?"

Maria blinked, rapidly trying to stave off tears.

Jo leaned toward her over the table.

"Maria, I'm sorry if I said something to upset you."

She shook her head and wiped at the tears that escaped down her cheeks. She closed her eyes briefly, took a long deep breath, then fixed her gaze on Jo. She tried at what she hoped was a genuine smile.

"Running into you today has been the high point of my week."

"Wow! If I'm the high point of your week," Jo placed her hands over her heart, "things must be pretty bad. But on a positive note I'm glad to be on the top of someone's list as opposed to the bottom." She gave Maria a mischievous smile.

"I didn't mean—"

"I know what you mean. I'm flattered." Jo gave her hand a quick pat. "If you need to talk, I can listen. Mind you, I probably can't do much more than listen, but I can do that pretty darn good."

"You barely know me. Why would you want me to burden you with my troubles?"

The deep sadness in Maria's eyes was evident to Jo.

"First of all, it's not a burden to simply listen. Secondly, someone with a pretty smile like you have shouldn't be carrying around anything that keeps you from smiling."

"You surely don't want to hear about the dysfunction in my family."

"If you want or need to talk about it, then I do," Jo said in earnest.

And so Maria started talking. "Matt threw a tantrum two nights ago, which is why I'm buying new window blinds. It caught me off guard, and then Jack threw his own fit in response." Maria's eyes continued to mist. "My husband has had a difficult time accepting our son's disability."

It was heartbreaking for Jo to think that anyone couldn't love the innocent child she'd met.

"He insists that Matt be placed somewhere so *we* don't have to be burdened with his care. And it seems lately that our arguments are happening more frequently."

Jo was angry at this man she'd never met for not wanting to raise his own son—his own flesh and blood.

Maria dug in her purse for a tissue. "I don't know what's going on with Matt that's causing him to have these fits recently." She dabbed at her eyes and blew her nose. "The doctor doesn't have any ideas about it either."

Jo wanted to hold Maria and tell her things would be okay, but she had no way of knowing if they would. "If you ever need a peaceful, quiet place to relax, stop out at the farm. With or without your son, you're always welcome."

Maria gave a weak smile. "Thank you, but I wouldn't think of imposing."

Jo held her gaze. "You wouldn't be imposing. And I offered because sometimes the quiet out in the country can be very soothing—therapeutic even."

She followed Maria out to her car. "Thanks for the lunch invite. I enjoyed it."

"Thank you for listening to my woes."

"And I mean it. If you ever need an escape, stop out at the farm."

"Thanks, but I don't think—"

"Don't think you could take advantage of my hospitality." She hooked her thumbs in her pockets and continued in a drawl. "Shucks, ma'am, if you're worried 'bout that, well, we'll put you to work."

Maria narrowed her eyes. "Work?"

"Heck yeah! Like my least favorite job…mucking out the stalls." When she grinned, Maria laughed.

Maria touched her arm again. "You are such an entertaining woman, Jo Marchal."

That touch scrambled Jo's nerves. "I…I try." She shrugged. "The invite stands, minus the work, anytime you want."

Maria gave her arm a squeeze. She also gave Jo a smile so warm she felt it to her toes.

Back at the farm, Tucker rambled on about a call he had taken, but Jo's mind was so far away she couldn't wrap her head around what he was saying. Maria consumed her thoughts.

"Tucker," she interrupted, "could you please handle it for me?"

He bounced around. "Sure, yeah, sure I'll take care of it." He zipped off to the tack room.

When she went in to get her saddle, he was talking excitedly on the phone. She trotted Cobalt a short distance before nudging him to gallop. Riding had always been her escape and the best way to clear her head. And she desperately needed to clear her head of Maria West. She had no business thinking of her in a romantic way. She finally returned to the barn an hour later and found Tucker dancing with excitement. She sat so he could share his news.

"Somebody with big bucks bought a large parcel of land on the south side of the lake and got permission from the reserve people to establish some riding trails. The group that bought the land intends to offer horseback riding and requested that we, or I mean you, handle the training of the horses for trail riding since the reserve backs up to your farm." He was bubbling over with enthusiasm.

"I haven't doubted for a minute you could run this place, Tucker." She gave his shoulder a pat.

"If they agree to what I'm going to propose, we should make some good money on the deal. With your okay, that is."

"You run with this, I trust your vision. You make us some added income and we'll talk bonus for you."

* * *

Jo headed into the house Saturday evening as Tucker kicked up dust on his way out. The temperature was hovering near ninety and all Jo wanted was a cool shower and a cold beer. Before she got to the fridge, though, she heard tires on the gravel. She wondered what Tucker had forgotten. At the front door she saw the sheriff's car, sighed deeply and stepped out onto the porch. Kate approached carrying a brown paper bag, then stopped and propped her foot on the bottom step with the bag resting on her thigh.

"Hi!"

Jo leaned against the porch post. "You're very persistent, I'll give you that, Deputy Tyler."

"We're real hospitable around here."

"Obviously." Jo nodded. "What's in the bag?"

When Kate lifted the bag, Jo could see the oily spots forming on the brown paper. "Only the best barbecued ribs you'll ever taste."

Jo took the offering and caught a whiff of the contents. Her mouth watered.

"I figure you have to eat. Everybody does, and if I couldn't get you to join me out somewhere for dinner, I'd bring dinner to you."

"That's very thoughtful. Thanks."

"No problem." Kate's hand fidgeted on the railing.

Jo resigned herself to company. "Come on in, but I have to warn you the place isn't quite put together yet."

"Wow! That's an understatement," Kate said as they entered.

Jo laughed. Kate Tyler always looked as sharp as a razor's edge, so sharp that Jo figured she lived a neat and controlled life. The chaos in the house must be causing her to itch.

In the kitchen she set the bag on the island and went about opening boxes, looking for plates and utensils.

"What do you need? I think I remembered everything." Kate unloaded the bag.

"Oh, plates…" Jo flipped open another box and dug deep. "And maybe a fork or two." When she pulled her hands from the box, pieces of packing foam scattered everywhere. "Success." She lifted her hands, each of them with a plate which she took to the sink and rinsed thoroughly.

"They did give us plastic silverware."

Jo finished drying the plates. "Great." She placed them on the counter. "What can I get you to drink?" She opened the fridge. "I've got beer and water and more beer than water."

"What kind of beer?"

"Light, of course. I don't waste my time with the full-bodied stuff." She patted her flat stomach. "Have to watch my figure, you know."

Kate's eyes traveled up and down Jo's body and when she met Jo's eyes, she blushed. "A beer sounds good."

She uncapped two bottles. "I'll be right back."

She grabbed a clean T-shirt off the pile folded neatly on the boxes outside the bathroom. She could smell the day's work on herself as she pulled the sweaty shirt over her head. She wasn't interested in impressing Kate, but she didn't want to repulse her either. Back in the kitchen she noted that Kate's beer was half gone and she seemed more relaxed.

"You didn't have to dress for dinner on my account."

Jo took a gulp of beer. "Oh this old thing." She pulled at the hem of her blue shirt.

While they ate, Kate asked about her move to Ohio, which she answered without giving up too much information. Heck, Kate was a cop. If she wanted to know about her, Jo didn't doubt she had resources to find out. Jo didn't have any trouble switching the conversation back around, though. Kate seemed to enjoy talking about law enforcement and how she got where she was. There was something likeable about her. Perhaps the conviction with which she spoke about her career and the fact that she didn't refer to it as a job.

Jo decided that maybe she had herself a new friend. After dinner she put on coffee while Kate cleared the counter. They had their coffee on the back deck and watched as the sun set over the horizon.

"It's beautiful out here."

Jo inhaled deeply. "Yep, about as close as you can get to heaven, I imagine."

When the coffee was gone, Jo walked Kate to the cruiser.

"Thanks again for dinner. It was definitely some of the best barbeque I've ever had."

"Maybe we can do it again."

"Maybe," Jo smiled. "You never know. Maybe I'll be able to get out of here one of these days and actually go somewhere."

"I'd like that."

Jo stepped back. "Well, goodnight."

Kate pulled open the car door. "Night, Jo."

Sunday was like all the ones before it. Jo returned to the farm feeling sad about her dad's declining health and beaten down by another unsuccessful attempt to fix what seemed unfixable.

Monday evening after a grueling ten-hour day, she cooled off with a cold drink of water on the back deck. As she sat absorbing the peacefulness that surrounded her, her thoughts drifted, unbridled, to Maria. Following dinner, when she was at the computer checking her email, she searched the Internet for information on autism. For more than an hour, she read numerous articles with facts and misconceived notions about children with autism. She wondered if she hadn't been told Maria's son was autistic, if she would have guessed. At their first meeting, the only things obvious to Jo were that he appeared very shy and attached to his mother. Of course, he didn't speak, but a lot of terribly shy kids didn't, she reasoned.

She recalled having watched a news story about children with autism interacting with animals. Grabbing a beer, she researched the topic further, finding an article about therapies and read countless parents' stories that praised the positive effect animals have on these children who seemed otherwise locked in their own little worlds. Remembering Maria's mention of taking Matt to the zoo when she dropped off her house-warming present, she decided she was going to make it a priority to get Maria and Matt out for a visit with her horses. She'd call later in the week and maybe, just maybe, they'd come by over the weekend.

Before Jo had a chance to call Maria, though, Maria left Jo a message to please call when she had a few minutes. Jo's heart pounded in her chest like horses' hooves in a full-out gallop. She gulped down a beer to calm the nervousness unsettling her insides. Out on the front porch she returned the call, disappointed when it went to voice mail. She left a message, tucked the phone in her jeans pocket, tipped her head back and closed her eyes to let the effects of the beer completely relax her. Ten minutes later her phone vibrated in her pocket and her heart started hammering again.

"Hi!"

"Hi!" Maria replied. "I'm sorry I missed your call. I had Matt in for his bath."

Jo hadn't given any thought to how busy Maria would be with Matt when they were home. "Don't give it another thought. I'm sure you have responsibilities I can't even wrap my head around."

Maria sighed. "I wouldn't trade motherhood for anything."

Jo didn't doubt that for a minute. "So, were you calling to take me up on my offer to visit the farm for some relaxation?"

"Actually I am."

Jo's heart danced a rhythm faster than she thought possible.

"I thought we could stop out sometime on Saturday if that would be okay."

"We?"

"Matt and I. That won't be a problem will it?"

"Heck no! Bring whoever you want."

"Is there a time that would be better than another?"

"Nope. Come whenever. I'll be around all day."

"If anything changes and we're not coming, I'll call, but I'm pretty sure at this point you can expect to see us in the late afternoon after my appointments."

"Great! I'll see you Saturday." Jo was simply giddy.

"I'm looking forward to it. See you then."

* * *

Saturday couldn't arrive soon enough for Jo. She worked in the room that served as her office, trying to put it in some kind of order, but failed miserably at the task because she couldn't stop going to the window to watch for Maria's car. By three she was so fidgety she gave up on the office and went to the barn. She grabbed a two-way radio, told Tucker she was going for a ride out towards the reserve and to call if her expected guests showed up. She and Cobalt had just passed through the gate to the field between the pasture and reserve when the radio on her hip crackled with Tucker's voice.

"Hey, boss, if you're expectin' someone in a little black car they're here. If not you have an unexpected guest."

Jo keyed the radio. "Thanks. Hey, Tucker, would you ask them to wait for me at the fence beside the barn? I'm on my way in now."

Jo hurried back through the gate and ran Cobalt as fast as he wanted to go. She caught sight of the two figures standing hand in hand as she neared and eased back on the reins to slow Cobalt to a trot. She was breathing as hard as the horse, and he'd been doing all the work. When she stopped shy of the fence, Cobalt danced around and something like fear sparked in Maria's eyes. Tucker ambled over as she dismounted and wrapped the reins around the fence rail.

She hopped up on the fence. "Glad you made it." Maria smiled apprehensively, keeping her eye on the stallion. "Can you tell if Matt's afraid of the horse?"

Maria's eyes never left Cobalt. "I don't think so. He's been tugging on my hand since he saw you ride up."

Jo straddled the fence. "But you're afraid."

"Yes, I guess I am." Maria swallowed.

Jo made a click so Cobalt would raise his head. She patted and rubbed his neck. "They really are gentle giants." She noted that Matt's eyes were fixed on the horse. "Would you like to pet my horse, Matt?"

He didn't utter a sound but pulled free of his mother's grasp and approached the fence. Maria remained frozen in place, terror in her eyes.

"It's okay, he won't hurt him." She continued to stroke the horse's neck. "Tucker, could you help him up on the fence?"

Tucker scrambled over the fence and lifted Matt up to stand on the fence so he could reach over the top rail.

Jo talked softly. "Cobalt here loves to have his chin scratched." Jo held Cobalt by the bridle and demonstrated where to scratch him. "I promise he won't hurt you."

Matt reached out tentatively and mimicked Jo's motion. When Cobalt lifted his head slightly and whinnied his pleasure, Matt jerked his hand away, but only briefly, before returning it to the horse's soft coat. She looked at Maria watching her son intently. When Maria's gaze drifted to her, Jo smiled.

"I think my horse made a new friend. You wanna…" Jo tipped her head toward Matt and Cobalt.

Maria shook her head. "I'm perfectly content to watch from right here."

It was tough not staring at Maria. She looked nothing like the professional businesswoman today. Her dark hair hung loosely around shoulders exposed by a white sleeveless blouse. Her longer than usual full skirt billowed every so often in the warm breeze and on her feet were flat-soled sandals. She looked comfortable and like she belonged on the farm.

"Whoa, boy." Cobalt was backing away and Matt could no longer reach him, but continued to try. "I think he's had his fill of chin scratching. How would you like to meet another one of my friends, Matt?"

He turned and looked at his mother. Maria's face lit up as she looked back at him. When Tucker helped him down, he returned to Maria's side and tugged her hand.

"I'll unsaddle him and meet you on the porch."

Maria coaxed Matt toward the house.

When Jo trotted Cobalt into the barn, Tucker took hold of the bridle. "I got this. Go visit with your company." Jo slipped into the tack room, returned the radio and met Tucker in the doorway carrying her saddle. "The boy is handicapped in some way?" Jo nodded. "He sure seemed to like the horse."

Jo smiled. "It appears so."

Tucker dropped the saddle on the stand. "Well, it's a right nice thing you inviting him out here."

"Kids deserve happiness."

Tucker lifted his hat and wiped his forehead. "Can't argue that."

"Have you seen Jake recently?" They walked out into the barn.

"No, but he's been keepin' an eye on somethin' I'm pretty sure is livin' under the tool shed out back."

Heading out of the barn, she whistled loudly and by the time she got to the porch where Maria and Matt stood, Jake came running around the corner of the house. He stopped at her side and she grabbed his collar when he barked at the strangers on his turf.

"Jake," she scolded. "I told you that's no way to greet company." His tail wagged his whole body as he pulled her toward the steps. Matt escaped Maria's grasp, dropped to his knees at the bottom of the steps and let Jake proceed to lick his face.

"Jake, stop!"

Maria smiled. "He's fine. I'm sure dog saliva isn't hazardous to his health."

Jo stepped beside Jake and brushed her fingers over his back. "It's not that. I'm hurt that he doesn't kiss me like that anymore." She frowned and Maria laughed. She joined Maria on the steps. "What can I get you two to drink? I have water, juice and of course beer."

"I'd love a beer, but—"

"The horse thing has your nerves a little jangled."

"Yes, but Matt and I will share a juice."

Jo removed her Stetson once inside, ran her fingers through her damp hair in an attempt to make it look presentable in some fashion and returned to the porch with a juice and two beers.

"I shouldn't," Maria said right away.

Jo put the cold bottle in her hand. "A few sips couldn't hurt. Whatever you don't drink, I'll finish." She sat the juice on the steps. "Here's a cold drink for you, Matt, and don't worry, Jake doesn't like juice."

Jo motioned Maria to the lawn chairs while Matt and Jake continued to get acquainted. She took a long drink of her beer, noting the look of indulgence on Maria's face as she sipped her own.

"So, uh…uh…" Jo gulped a drink of beer and cleared her throat. "Where are you originally from 'cause I can't imagine it's Ohio?" Jo could not take her eyes off Maria.

Maria took only a small sip and placed her beer down on the porch. She shifted in the chair to face Jo. "I was born in Mexico.

We moved to Texas when I was four, so I grew up in the United States. My younger sister was born in Texas, and we have two older brothers."

"Ohio's a long way from Texas."

"I married right out of college." She hesitated a moment. "His work and family brought us here."

Jo hoped she wasn't being too nosy. "And Matt's father, what does he do?" The light in Maria's eyes faded.

"Sales in the beginning, but he's a regional vice president now, so he travels quite a bit." With sad eyes she looked down at her son. "It's just me and Matt a lot of the time."

She seemed happier talking about her biological family so Jo changed the topic back. "So, two older brothers, were they tough on you?"

Maria gave a little smile. "Actually, they weren't that bad. They were pretty protective when they weren't wrestling me in the dirt." Jo felt a pang of envy, which turned into regret when Maria continued. "They don't approve of my husband so we've lost touch since the wedding. My parents and I don't talk often either. They moved back to Mexico a few years ago to help take care of our grandparents. It might be different if they could talk to their grandson, but…"

"Do you ever wish you'd grown up in Mexico?" Jo asked, looking to move their conversation to a less painful topic.

Maria's gaze drifted to the tree-lined drive. "No. We lived so far south that we were almost at the border. When we were young, we used to spend a month every summer with our grandparents in Mexico, so I feel like I got plenty of exposure to my culture and heritage. I had opportunities in the states I wouldn't have had in Mexico. I do find as I grow older, I miss the quiet where we grew up."

Jo recalled her first taste of "peacefulness" that summer she spent at camp, far, far away from the sounds of the city. It was then she decided she wanted to live in the country when she grew up.

She inhaled the fresh air. "The country sure had its advantages."

Maria turned her attention to Matt seated on the bottom step, juice in one hand and the other repetitively stroking Jo's big gentle dog. "Yes, I suppose it does." She reached down for her beer, but stopped. "So how is your business doing here in Ohio?"

Jo talked with more confidence than she was feeling about things that had been going on since relocating. Maria listened intently. When a dusty brown car with the red and blue beacons on its roof rolled slowly up the drive a short time later, Jo sidestepped Matt and Jake and met Kate half a dozen feet from the porch. When Jake barked, Matt pressed his cheek to the dog's head and continued petting him. Jo frowned at the dog, looked at Maria with one brow raised and turned her attention back to Kate.

"Deputy."

Kate tipped her chin up. "Hey, Jo." She looked past her at Maria seated on the porch. "Sorry to interrupt." When Jo said nothing in response, Kate shoved her hands in her pockets. "Uh…some of us were going to go out, uh…you know, for a few drinks tonight. Anyway, I uh…thought I'd ask if you wanted to join us."

Jo slipped her hands in her back pockets. "Thanks, but I can't."

Kate looked past Jo again at Maria. "Oh, sure, maybe next time."

Maria stood. "Jo, don't let us keep you from anything. We should be going."

Jo spun on the heel of her boot and met Maria's eyes. "You're not keeping me from anything." Jo rolled her eyes, hoping that Maria would somehow read her mind. "I do have things to do later this evening." Maria gave a slight smile and sat back down, and Jo faced Kate again.

"Well, if you change your mind, Jo, we're going to a little place called Whispers up in Prescott. It's right on Highway 10 as you head into town. Hope to see you."

Jo stayed put until the patrol car was headed down the drive.

"Not to sound school-girlish, but I think the deputy likes you, Jo," Maria said teasingly. Jo closed her eyes and shook her head. "Did I read something wrong?"

Jo sighed. "God, I hope so. I've got enough on my plate already."

"Really?"

Jo waved her hand around the farm even though her property was only a tiny portion of what was presently causing her plate to overflow, and Maria nodded.

Jo dreamed of Maria again that night and then on Sunday shared another agonizing dinner with her parents. On the drive home, she found herself recalling the day before with so much clarity that it warded off her usual depressed feelings. The sight of Maria waiting by the fence yesterday had nearly stolen her breath. She was that beautiful. Jo couldn't help smiling every time she thought of Maria. She didn't want to.

CHAPTER EIGHT

A week passed without anything from Maria. Jo wanted to call her but resisted the temptation. It seemed Maria had found the farm relaxing and that Matt found a kinship with her animals, so… with an open invitation Jo could only hope they would return. Of course Kate didn't stay away. She stopped in Saturday afternoon with another dinner invite. Jo finally accepted, but only because she planned to use the occasion to let Kate know that she wasn't looking for any involvements.

They had a pleasant time, actually. Jo liked talking with her, and when she broached the subject Kate appeared okay with the fact that Jo wasn't interested in dating. Back at the farm, Kate walked her to the door. Jo placed a chaste kiss on her cheek and thanked her again before slipping into the house—alone.

Way to go, Jo. That is the stupidest thing you've ever done. First tell Kate you're not interested in anything beyond friendship and then send a mixed signal like that kiss.

She dropped her head back against the door.

When two weeks slipped past and she still hadn't seen or spoken to Maria, Jo began to wonder if maybe Maria had been put off by Kate's surprise visit and the reality of Jo's lifestyle. Maria's teasing comment could have simply been a way to cover her discomfort. Jo was sitting on the porch fretting about it and nursing a beer when Kate pulled in. She drained the last sip as Kate got out of the car, a familiar brown bag in her hand and a smile on her face.

"Dinner break." Kate raised the bag as she stepped on the porch. "Thought I'd see if you want to join me."

Kate didn't lack tenacity. She was also focused and driven, both qualities Jo respected. And it was kind of cute how nervous Kate got when she was around her, in complete contrast to her tough cop bravado. She waved her inside.

"Wow! Still can't decide what to put where?" Kate eyed her makeshift bed, now located on the couch.

"I've had other, more pressing things to deal with."

"Oh? Like the woman that was here a few weeks ago?" Kate asked pointedly.

Jo bristled. Kate's tone hinted at jealousy. Did she think that they were such good friends that she was entitled to an answer? Jo pushed a bottle of water across to Kate, but she motioned to Jo's beer.

"I think I'd rather have one of those." Jo opened the beer and handed it to her. Kate took a gulp. "Is that Hispanic woman one of your more pressing things?"

Jo stared at her for a long minute before answering. "Not that it's any of your business, but that woman's son is autistic. Do you know anything about autism?" Kate shrugged and shook her head. "He's essentially locked inside himself. I can't even begin to imagine what that must be like, but he seems to enjoy animals. So there's an open invitation for him and his mother to come out here. Is that enough of an explanation for you?"

Jo knew she sounded antagonistic, but she didn't much care, dammit. Kate had no right to pry into her personal life. Jo's crush on Maria had nothing to do with her inviting Maria and Matt to come to the farm whenever they wanted. That was purely time for them. Hell, maybe she should forget all about boarding and training horses and teaching riders. Maybe she should get herself a stable of horses and offer services to kids like Matt who needed something in their life that made them smile the way Matt smiled around the animals.

"Whoa, I was only asking." Kate took a quick gulp of beer, keeping her eyes pinned on Jo's. "That's pretty unselfish of you."

Jo decided to let it go. She couldn't handle even one more stress, and Kate seemed earnest. As they enjoyed their food, Kate talked about the bar in Prescott and suggested none too subtly that Jo check it out when she wasn't so busy.

"You seem different tonight, Jo. I don't know, kind of sad. Everything okay?"

"Yep." Jo stared off in silence, but Kate needled her until she finally shared, "My parents are getting on in age so I moved back here to be closer. Our relationship is pretty strained…" Kate lent a sympathetic ear.

Later, standing out front at the cruiser, and to Jo's utter shock, Kate threw her arms around her and clasped her tight. Jo stiffened.

"I'm sorry about the whole parent thing. If you need anything at all call me…anytime."

"Thanks," Jo replied.

Watching the taillights disappear down the drive, Jo hugged herself, deciding she'd made a mistake sharing something so personal with Kate. *Won't be doing that again.*

* * *

Sunday evening Jo sat in her partly assembled office checking her email. With a smile she opened one from Cecile.

"Hey, darlin', I know they say no news is good news and absence makes the heart grow fonder, but I'm beginnin' to think you left me for another. And the only reason I can think of for blowin' off your friend is some hot lover! Could ya call or respond to let me know what's up so I don't have to drive up there and whoop it out of ya! Hum…whoopin' a cowgirl sounds kind of hot! Please call or somethin'. Miss ya—Cecile."

Wandering out to sit on the fence where several of the horses were grazing, she dialed Cecile.

"You are still alive." Cecile huffed and puffed loudly.

"You okay, Cil?" Jo heard music fade away in the background.

"Oh yeah. Havin' me some Saturday night leftovers." She chuckled.

Jo closed her eyes as if that would erase the image of Cecile stopping in the middle of sex to answer the phone. "God, Cil, why did you answer the phone?"

Her voice was muffled. "Don't move there, darlin,' I'll be right back." To Jo, she said, "Cause I been worried 'bout you. You don't call, you don't write. How am I supposed to know what's goin' on with you?"

Her old friend's soothing voice was a comfort. "There's nothing going on you'd want to hear about. That's why you haven't heard from me."

"Well, I think I'd like to see that for myself, darlin'. Whatcha doin' next weekend?"

Jo sighed. "Cecile, I'm fine. You don't have to come and check on me."

"What the heck is wrong with spendin' some time with my friend? I'm visitin' next weekend so clear your calendar and send me your address. I'm not takin' no for an answer. I'll get your address and find you anyway, so you might as well give it up. Like I said, I don't want to have to whoop you." She chuckled again.

"Fine, I'll send it to you. Can you at least let me know when to expect you?"

"Sure thing, darlin'. Listen, I need to get back to my hot body before it cools down. See you soon."

"Yeah, have fun, Cil."

"It ain't no good if it ain't fun, darlin'. Remember that."

"Uh huh."

She clicked off and before going to bed emailed Cecile her address.

Monday Jo commandeered Tucker's help after they were done in the barn to set up the beds in her bedroom and the guest room.

"I can still ask my mom to stop in and put your house together for you if you want," Tucker joked while surveying the stacks of boxes that remained unmoved after two months. "Unless you're not plannin' on hangin' around here, boss." He cocked his head.

Jo frowned. "I've unpacked what I need. I'll get to it one of these days."

Tucker only smiled and shrugged.

* * *

Cecile was scheduled to arrive by dinner time. She told Jo she expected her to have a nice restaurant and a hot bar lined up for them. Jo had done her homework and was prepared. She wasn't prepared, however, for Kate to show up unexpectedly in the early afternoon. When Kate asked her out for dinner, though, she had recovered enough to politely decline. She was happy to have a reason to do so, though she didn't share with Kate what it was.

Jo was sitting relaxing on the porch when Cecile's little sports car raced up the drive hours later, kicking up dust and gravel in its wake.

When the car halted, Cecile climbed out, waving her arms in the settling dust. Jo was shocked out of her chair when Callie emerged from the passenger's side.

Cecile bellowed as she strolled toward the house, "Look here, I brought you a nice little surprise."

Callie looked like a deer caught in headlights, and Jo suspected Cecile might not have been completely forthcoming with Callie about the invitation. Cecile grabbed her and squeezed her in a hug that forced the air from her lungs.

"Well, darlin', ain't you a sight for sore eyes." When she released her, Jo took a much needed breath.

Standing beside Cecile, Callie shrugged her shoulders and shook her head. Smiling, Jo stepped around Cecile, slipped her arm around Callie's waist and kissed her on the cheek. For her, Callie was a sight for sore eyes. She leaned back with her arm still around Callie's waist.

"I'm glad you came."

"So you got our evenin' planned, hon?" Cecile asked, arching her brows so they formed two mountain peaks. "Dinner, a little dancin'?" She made the peaks dance.

Callie looked Jo over. "I feel a little overdressed."

Jo stepped back, looking her up and down. "You look perfect to me." Callie blushed. Cecile cleared her throat. "You look perfectly lovely too, Cil."

Cecile slapped Jo on the back. "I don't need compliments, darlin', I'm starvin'. I need food."

Callie rode with Jo in her truck and Cecile followed. She took them to the fanciest restaurant in town. Over dinner Jo confessed she hadn't actually been to the bar they were going to but had it on good authority from a deputy friend that it was the best place around. Cecile ribbed her about the "cop," but Jo adamantly declared they were strictly friends who shared an occasional dinner and nothing more.

"See, darlin', I keep tellin' ya, ya don't get enough." Cecile said a little too loudly for the quiet of the restaurant. She drew more than a few stares from a number of patrons. Callie flushed with embarrassment. Jo was accustomed to Cecile's boisterous "say what you think" manner. Clearly, Ohioans were not.

They pulled into the nearly full parking lot outside Whispers.

"You didn't say we had to cross state lines to get to this place," Cecile complained as they walked to the door.

Jo rolled her eyes. Cecile was used to cities like Lexington, not the small towns that dotted the countryside where she now lived.

"Cil, it was only a half an hour drive."

"Yeah, but it was over half an hour to the restaurant so that makes us more than an hour from your place."

"Not quite. We backtracked a little from the restaurant. Are you afraid you'll get lost driving home tonight?"

Cecile stopped dead in her tracks and placed a hand on her meaty hip. "Darlin', if I have to drive to your place tonight that would mean I struck out, and unless the women in this bar lack a pulse, I don't see that happenin'."

"Right." Jo nodded.

She pulled the door open and they stepped into a blast of cool air and loud music. They had been sitting with their drinks for no more than fifteen minutes when Jo spotted Kate making her way toward their table. Jo stood to greet her.

"When you wouldn't go out to dinner with me tonight I sure didn't think I'd be seeing you here," Kate said in a sharp tone before Jo could open her mouth. Her eyes looked dark as coal.

"These are my friends from Lexington. This is Cecile and Callie." Jo motioned to both gals. Kate grumbled a curt greeting.

"You could have told me. You don't have to sneak around," Kate said to Jo.

Jo didn't appreciate Kate's accusatory tone, but she also didn't want to make a scene in front of her friends.

Cecile took that precise moment to stand up between Jo and Kate and take Kate's hand. "I love women in uniforms. I understand you wear one."

"I wasn't talking to you, big mama," Kate snapped.

Cecile didn't flinch. "Ooh…a hot little fireplug." Cecile kept Kate's hand gripped in hers when she leaned a bit closer, "And I bet you scream real loud when you come. Jo wouldn't know that, though, would she? Seein's you haven't got in her pants yet?" Cecile leaned back and met Kate's fiery gaze. With her back still to Jo, she said, "She's my really *really* good friend, so don't you even think 'bout hurtin' her." She cocked her head, waiting for Kate's response.

Kate jerked her hand away and said to Jo, "I'll stop out sometime after I get off."

Cecile gave a snide smile as she murmured to Kate, "You keep on wishin' there, darlin'."

"That sure was an interesting exchange," Jo said after Kate stomped off.

"Sure was." Cecile chuckled. "She really didn't like me telling her I know she hasn't slept with you yet, darlin'." Jo rolled her eyes and looked at Callie. They laughed in unison.

Jo and Callie were ready to leave after another drink and several dances. Cecile wasn't, though. She was convinced she was going to get lucky with a butch construction worker. Wishing her luck, they headed home.

Back at the farm, Jo showed Callie to the master bedroom, complete with, well, just the queen-size bed. Callie realized then she'd left her bag in Cecile's trunk, so Jo rounded up a freshly laundered T-shirt for her to sleep in, bid her sweet dreams and went to sleep on her comfy couch. If Cecile unexpectedly ended up coming back during the night, Jo didn't want her crawling in with her in the guest room bed.

* * *

Sunday marked three weeks since Maria had been out to Jo's with Matt and three weeks that she'd been struggling daily with the emotion that had swept over her as she watched the easygoing cowgirl with her son. Matt's own father wouldn't give him so much as a minute of his time, and yet a virtual stranger had opened her home to him—to them. A few days following their trip to Jo's, Matt's teacher reported to Maria that his vocabulary had increased by another sound. Instead of only uttering "ma," which they knew to be Matt's sound for Mom, he was now saying "ja," which Maria was assured was for either Jo or Jake. Either way, she knew it meant that Jo had somehow managed to make a connection to Matt, even if it was through her dog.

She had made a connection with the cowgirl too, she had to admit. Emotions that she'd never felt before, frightening ones, had been swirling around inside her. Not knowing what to do with them, she had decided to avoid Jo altogether. Except even that wasn't working. She knew she had to quit hiding.

* * *

Jo had told her mom she wouldn't be coming for Sunday dinner because of her company, but Cecile returned at ten the following morning, earlier than expected, and sped off shortly thereafter with Callie. Now she didn't have an excuse to stay away.

Her dad was in a particularly foul mood, more so than usual, so as soon as she helped her mom to clean up after dinner Jo left. Back at the farm, overwhelmed with sadness, she was in the barn about to saddle up for a ride when she heard a car.

Steeling herself for a tense conversation with Kate, she was more than pleasantly surprised when she stepped outside to instead see a familiar black station wagon. Maria stopped the car at the edge of the drive, where Jo met her, bridle in hand.

"I'm sorry. I should have called first. I'm interrupting." Maria didn't meet Jo's eyes, looking instead at the bridle Jo held.

"No, you're not—interrupting, that is. I told you to stop by anytime." Jo raised her hand. "Let me put this away." She rushed into the barn, tossed the bridle on her saddle in the tack room and stopped only a moment to rub Cobalt's nose. "Sorry, buddy, maybe later." The horse snorted his dissatisfaction.

Maria was standing by the fence outside the barn when Jo returned. "Why do you suppose I'm afraid of horses? I've never been hurt by one."

Jo cocked her head and regarded Maria closely. She seemed sad today, kind of like Jo had been feeling herself. "Some people are afraid of heights, others, the dark. I don't know, but I think we all have fears."

Maria fixed her eyes on Jo's. "And what does Jo Marchal fear?"

The intensity in Maria's eyes seemed to reach into Jo's soul. She averted her eyes and looked out over the pasture. She shrugged, knowing the answer to Maria's question all too well, then masked the hollowness she felt by flashing a smile at Maria. "Would you like to get over your fear?"

"Exactly what are you suggesting?"

"Let me introduce you to Daisy Mae." Maria's eyes widened. "She is the gentlest horse I've ever been around in my life. And I've been around a lot of horses." Maria remained wide-eyed and motionless. Jo continued to smile and tipped her head toward the barn. "Come on. I promise you that you'll be safe."

Maria nodded slowly, but she didn't move. After Jo placed her hand lightly on her back, she finally took a tentative step toward the barn opening.

"Your farm is named for her?" Maria's voice was timid. "You said there was a story you'd tell me." Maria stopped dead in the barn doorway and no gentle urging got her to move.

Jo stepped in front of her and took her hand. "I promise I won't let you get hurt. Do you trust me?"

Eyes still wide, Maria nodded again, but she still didn't move. Jo pulled gently on her hand and started her story. "Daisy Mae is the reason I got my horse farm in Kentucky. One of her colts was a Triple Crown champion seven years ago." Jo stepped backwards, slowly pulling Maria along with her. "She's the most laid-back, easygoing horse I've ever known. That's where the 'lazy' part of the farm name comes from." Jo stopped in front of Daisy's stall. When the horse dropped her head over the gate, Maria sucked in a startled breath.

"It's okay…see." Jo rubbed under the horse's chin, but Maria refused to move. "I bet you liked to wear pretty dresses when you were a young girl, didn't you?" Maria's nod was almost imperceptible. "Did you ever have one of those fancy dresses made of velvet?" Maria answered with another tiny nod. Jo rubbed her thumb over Maria's hand. "Close your eyes." Maria's eyes grew huge again. "It's okay. I won't let anything happen to you." Jo placed her other hand over her heart. "I promised, remember?"

Maria swallowed and closed her eyes while Jo continued to stroke her hand. "Remember how soft that dress felt to your touch?" Jo touched Maria's fingers to Daisy Mae's nose. "So soft you couldn't keep from rubbing your fingers over it." Jo felt Maria's arm relax as she moved her fingers over the horse's nose. Jo smiled. "See, she's as harmless as that little dress you had years ago."

Maria opened her eyes, jerking her hand away when she realized what she was touching. When she tried to step back, Jo caught her arm. "Maria, she won't hurt you. Look…"

Jo grasped Maria's hand lightly and raised it, feeling it go rigid when Daisy pushed her nose beneath their joined hands. "She likes this soft part rubbed." Jo stroked the fingers of her other hand over Daisy's nose. Maria tentatively touched her fingers to Daisy Mae's nose. The horse pressed against Maria's fingers and snorted. Maria jumped back so abruptly she nearly fell. Jo caught her arm to balance her. "She really likes that. She was saying 'thanks'."

Daisy Mae rubbed her neck on the gate so Jo stepped back over to scratch her. "Good girl," she cooed. She looked at Maria. "She'd never hurt a soul. She doesn't even spook."

Maria stood back, watching. For as tough and strong as Jo Marchal appeared, she'd just witnessed how tender she truly was. That seemed only to further complicate what she was feeling when she was around her.

Jo faced her. "I'm sure this isn't what you drove out here for today."

Maria crossed her arms tightly over herself. "No, but it's all right."

"Are you okay?"

"I'm fine." Maria tried to make her smile convincing.

Jo stepped over to her and touched her elbow. "Let's get something cold to drink."

Maria didn't uncross her arms until she stepped from the barn into the afternoon sun. In the kitchen and seated at the island, beer in hand, Maria noticed the gift basket, which still contained the bottle of wine.

"Haven't found a lady friend to share the wine with yet?" The question was nosy, but she had an unstoppable desire to know if Jo was seeing someone. Why? She couldn't answer definitively. She only knew that she did.

Jo looked at the basket. "I've been a little busy." She shrugged. "Preoccupied with other things."

Maria took a sip of beer and glanced around. "Obviously not with your living quarters…no offense." She smiled.

Jo responded with a mock smile. "Obviously."

"I could help you unpack and organize your things." *And get a better sense of who you are, Jo Marchal.*

"That's very generous, but I'll manage it one of these days."

"Hum…one might wonder if you're planning on sticking around."

"Oh no, I can't leave. I have to…" Jo stopped.

Maria didn't miss the color shift in Jo's eyes. "Everything okay?"

"Couldn't be better." Jo's smile was forced.

She reached across the counter that separated them, touching her hand. "If you ever need to talk, Jo, I'd be happy to lend an ear." As the words left her mouth, Maria hoped that Jo wouldn't ever have a need to talk about any of her female relationships. She wasn't sure she could listen to her talk about the women in her life without feeling—*what*—jealous? She couldn't imagine for the life of her why she would feel jealous.

Jo nodded and picked up her beer. "Let's sit out back. The deck is still shaded now."

The day was warm, but a steady breeze blew out of the west. It was soothing looking out over the pastures and farm fields that gave way to the woods of the reserve. Jo sat silently, trying to focus on happier thoughts, like the way Maria's hand had felt in her own out in the barn. But her dad's mood and his harsh words earlier, to not only her but her mother, kept pushing everything else out of her mind. It dawned on her that she and Maria's son had more in common than their love of animals. Both of them had a father who was absent in too many important ways. She wanted to let it all out, have a good cry and be done with it. But even thinking about doing so made her feel so vulnerable.

Maria broke the silence. "I feel like there's something weighing on you, Jo. I wish you felt comfortable enough to talk to me."

Jo glanced over at her. Maria's face showed the tender caring she showed with her son. "It's nothing really." She attempted a smile.

"I'm not sure I believe you, but you hardly know me, so I understand your reluctance to talk."

Maria's dark eyes threatened to melt Jo's resolve. She hadn't told anyone about her dad. She'd only shared with Tom and Cecile that he was sick. But recalling now at how upset she'd been when driving home earlier brought tears to her eyes. She turned away. Maria was silent.

A single tear escaped and dropped in her lap. Jo swallowed the lump burning in her throat. "My dad is dying." She exhaled a deep breath. "And the stubborn old fool is determined to go to his grave hating his only child."

Maria looked over at Jo, her heart aching as she watched a steady trickle of tears run down her cheeks. This big strong woman had all the heart she had guessed from that first introduction to her son. She wanted to put her arms around her and hold her the way she did with Matt. To offer the comfort of a consoling embrace. Instead she simply reached over and grasped Jo's hand where it hung off the arm of her chair.

"I'm so sorry, Jo." She squeezed gently, holding on a moment longer. "I mean it, Jo, if you ever need to talk, I'm only a phone call away."

Jo glanced over at her. "Thanks."

Maria stood. "I should be going. Kathleen will be back with the boys anytime now."

Jo rubbed her arm across her cheeks and stood too. "I'll walk you out."

Maria knew if she were to stay, she would wrap Jo in her arms, and the thought scared her. Holding Jo's hand just now and earlier in the barn had stirred something inside her she hadn't experienced with any friends she'd ever known. It was terrifying and exciting at the same time. Although she didn't understand the attraction between same sexes, she wasn't bothered that Jo Marchal was a… lesbian. She was a kind soul, who had offered up her place as a sort of therapy for Maria and her son. The least she could do in return was to be a shoulder to lean on or cry on if Jo needed one.

Well, she'd made the offer. The rest was up to Jo. She would be quite surprised, though, if the cowgirl let down her guard enough to accept. Jo seemed very much the loner.

CHAPTER NINE

On the Saturday following Labor Day Maria and Matt visited the farm again. As they stood at the fence and Matt stroked Daisy Mae's head, Jo touched Matt's shoulder.

"Hey, cowboy, would you like to take a ride on the horse?" Jo looked at Maria. "I'll sit him in the saddle with me. He'll be perfectly safe." Maria looked apprehensive.

"Would you like to ride on the horse, Matt?" In response he scampered down from the fence and grabbed his mother's hand. "You have to ride with Jo. You can't go alone. Do you understand, sweetie?" He tugged her hand.

"He'll be fine, I promise."

Matt danced at Maria's side as Jo saddled Daisy Mae. Once she was seated on the horse, Tucker lifted Matt up to her. He automatically gripped the saddle horn.

"That's right, cowboy, you hold on tight while we ride." Jo gazed down at Maria's look of panic. "I'd invite you to join us, but this saddle is only big enough for two." Maria attempted a smile.

They started along the fence, Jo talking intermittently about horses, nervous with the young charge nestled in her saddle. She made sure not to lose sight of Maria as they walked the horse around the perimeter of the pasture. Reaching the crest of a small ridge, she turned Daisy Mae back toward the barn.

"Would you like to go faster, Matt?" He responded by rocking back and forth against her. "All right, buddy, hold on tight." Jo clicked and gave the horse a soft heel. Daisy trotted back to the barn where Maria waited with Tucker.

He appeared disappointed to end the ride so Jo called and whistled until Jake came running from behind the house. Matt stayed occupied with a juice and Jake while she and Maria sat on the porch. Maria declined the offer of a beer.

Jo took a swallow of hers. "You looked scared to death when Matt mounted the horse." Maria gazed down at Matt petting Jake's head. "You know I'd never let anything happen to him." Maria's eyes met hers. "You trust me, don't you?"

She gave a little smile and nodded. When Jo offered her beer to Maria, she took it and a small sip and handed it back.

Maria faced her. "How's your father doing, Jo?"

Jo took a gulp. "He's been having more trouble getting around and talking, but so far it's been infrequent." She knew his silence with her during the last visit wasn't because he was having trouble talking. He'd chosen not to talk to her. She looked down at the bottle in her hand. "Within the month I'd say we'll have to bring someone into the house to help care for him or put him in a facility."

"If there's anything I can do, please let me know." Maria placed her hand on Jo's arm.

Jo nodded and they sat in silence. It was obviously painful for Jo. Not only her father's illness, but the strained relationship between her and her parents. Maria knew something about strained relationships.

"He wants to remain at home," Jo finally said. "I don't see how she'll be able to live in that house if he dies there."

"I'm sure she's doing what's best for both of them."

Jo shook her head as she watched Matt and Jake.

"Jo…" Jo turned her gaze to Maria. "Have you ever thought of introducing them to your life?"

"My parents? You're kidding, right?"

"No. You should have them come out here and see what it is that you love to do so much and how you live."

"I don't think they would even consider the idea."

"Have you ever asked?" Jo shook her head. "Maybe you should then."

* * *

And so the following day during their regular Sunday dinner Jo did ask. Her mom seemed interested in seeing Jo's farm. Her dad, on the other hand, didn't have anything to say about it at all. Eileen walked out with Jo when she left.

"Would you talk to him, please? It would mean so much to me if you would both come see my place."

Eileen took her daughter's hand and squeezed. "I promise I will, honey. I think it would be good for the both of us."

A lump grew in Jo's throat. Finally after twenty-something years she had a glimmer of hope. Hope that maybe before it was too late, things could change between them. She choked back tears as she hugged her mom. "I love you both, you know."

Eileen leaned back and touched Jo's cheek. "I know, dear, and I'm sure he does too. I'll talk to him about coming for a visit."

Jo climbed in her truck. "Call me if you need anything at all," she called through the open window. Eileen waved.

For the first time Jo made the drive home feeling hopeful rather than depressed. And she had Maria to thank for this possible turn of events. But it really didn't come as a surprise that Maria would possess good instincts when it came to parent/child relationships.

* * *

Monday evening brought a surprise call from her mom. Eileen had spoken with her husband about visiting the farm and his only excuse for not making the trip was his inability to drive them there.

"How have you been grocery shopping?" Jo asked, wondering too if her mom would be open to learning to drive at some point.

"Someone from the church takes me. They've been very helpful through all of this."

Jo knew having someone from their church drive them to visit their lesbian daughter was not an option. "If I arrange for you to get here and back, will you come?"

"Well, what are you going to arrange? Your father was very clear that he didn't want you driving us back and forth."

"Don't worry, Mom. I'll take care of it. Will you make sure he'll agree to come?"

"I'll do my best, dear."

Jo contacted a medical transport company in Campbell that transported residents at area nursing facilities. She scheduled them for the last Saturday of the month. Unable to contain her excitement, she called her mom and then Maria. She owed Maria a thank you, and if she was honest with herself, she wanted to hear her voice.

Maria wasn't sure why she had bothered to carry her phone into the bathroom, but she was glad not to have missed Jo's call. Monday's were always the hardest day of the week. After two days away from his regimented school routine, Matt always seemed a little extra difficult, and by day's end Maria was worn out. With Jack holed up in his home office, she'd taken the opportunity to soak in the tub and relax with a cup of tea before bedtime. The sound of Jo's voice was relaxing too. She couldn't put her finger on what it was about her that made her anxious to see or talk to her in spite of the discomfort she sometimes felt in Jo's presence.

"Hi, it's Jo. Hope this isn't a bad time to be calling."

"Not at all. Matt's down for the night and I was unwinding."

"I don't want to cut into your down time. I just called to thank you," Jo said.

Maria took a sip of tea and settled back in the hot, scented bath, careful not to dunk her phone. "You're welcome. May I ask for what?"

"I took your advice. My parents will be coming to the farm at the end of the month. Providing my dad still can."

"That's so wonderful, Jo! With the weather change and the leaves starting to turn, it will be perfect. Your place will look pretty as a painting. I'm sure your parents will love it." She really wanted for Jo to feel the love that only a parent can have for their child.

Jo toed off her boots, leaned her head back and gazed up at the night sky. "Well, you were right about inviting them. I hope you're right about that too." A long silence ensued and she realized the courage she'd summoned to make the call was fading. "I was wondering what you're going to be doing the last Saturday of the month."

"That's nearly three weeks away. What do you need, Jo?"

"I'm, uh…lord, I'm a nervous wreck about this. I thought… well, maybe…if you and Matt might want to visit with me when they come. I don't know, provide a little buffer, you know."

"I'd love to meet your parents, Jo, but are you sure about having Matt there?"

"Absolutely, my folks love kids. Heck, they loved me 'til I grew up."

"Jo!" Maria admonished. "I'm sure your parents still love you."

Jo sighed. "I guess I'll be finding out. Will you come though and protect me, just in case?"

Maria laughed. "I'm sure we can probably help you out. Why don't we plan a picnic?"

"That's an excellent idea. I'll call around and find a caterer."

"Not if I'm joining your party," Maria said firmly. "I'll take care of the food."

"Absolutely not. You're helping me out by being here. That's enough."

"No, I insist, and besides Matt has a special diet. I'll take care of the food and you take care of getting your parents there. Agreed?"

"You sure?"

"Positively."

Jo stayed out on the deck another hour, enjoying the peaceful night and relishing the positive turn her life might finally be taking. After years of feeling isolated from her folks, she was getting the opportunity to mend fences with them. At least she hoped so. And the best part was that her two new favorite people would be there to help get her through it all.

Maria dropped her phone in the pocket of the robe hanging next to the tub and slid back in water, sighing as it rose up to her neck. She couldn't explain it, but Jo made her love life more than she had in years. She closed her eyes and pictured the cowgirl in her mind. A cowboy hat and boots, a T-shirt stretched taut over a hard, muscled torso and then tucked into faded blue jeans. And, of course, those blue-gray eyes that seemed to literally see into her soul every time she looked into them looking back at her. Jo Marchal made her feel things she'd never known before.

A loud rap on the door startled her.

Jack poked his head in. "Maria, Matt's banging something in his room and I'm trying to work."

She jumped from the tub and pulled on her robe. Her greatest fear always was that the thing Matt might be banging would be his head against something. She couldn't fathom why Jack wouldn't at least look in on his own son, but those were things, it became clear early on, he refused to deal with. He caught her arm as she tried to squeeze past him through the door. His eyes were on her partially exposed cleavage.

"Maybe after you settle him down we can have some time to ourselves."

Maria's skin crawled. His son could very well be harming himself and Jack's mind was on his own needs. *Heartless bastard!*

She rushed into Matt's room and found him rocking his bed, which banged the headboard against the wall. She touched him gently before slipping onto the bed to hold him and rock him in her arms. She hummed softly the lullaby that she had sung to him as a baby. In little more than ten minutes he was dozing, but she didn't intend to go to her bed tonight. Spending the night with Matt seemed a better idea. Once she was sure he was sleeping soundly, she pulled out her phone and called Kathleen.

"Hey, sweetie, what's wrong?"

"God, you know me too well."

"Well, it is almost eleven and—"

"I'm sorry, Kat, I didn't realize the time. I'll let you go."

"Maria, honey, you know you can call me anytime. So what did he do now?"

Maria sighed. "You know, Jack just being Jack."

"Is Matt okay?"

She gently smoothed his dark curls. "A perfect angel."

"Would you like me to come over and smack some sense into my little brother for you?"

Maria laughed. "Not that it would fix him, but knowing that you would makes me feel better." Maria knew that all the smacking in the world wouldn't bring Jack around to anything resembling parental behavior when it came to their son.

"Do we need a girls' day out or night…or both?"

Maria sighed again. "That sounds wonderful. I might have an idea for something we could do that might be relaxing, even if we take the kids along."

Kathleen chuckled. "That sounds interesting. I can't imagine my three boys and relaxation in the same sentence, let alone in the same place together."

Maria laughed again. "I'll check into it and get back to you this weekend."

"Sounds good. I'll be anxiously waiting. In the meantime, if you need anything or any help, call me."

"Thanks, Kat. I'll talk to you soon."

* * *

Jo got out of the shower Saturday evening to find she had missed a call from Maria. She listened with a smile to the voicemail she'd left.

"Jo, hi! I know we talked Monday and you're probably out having a good time with a lady friend, but could you give me a call tomorrow when you have a few minutes."

Jo couldn't imagine why Maria seemed to think she had lady friends. A light rain tapping on the roof sent her to the front porch to return the call.

She answered promptly. "You didn't have to call me back this evening. I'm sure you have better things to do on a Saturday night."

Little do you know. "Well, this Saturday night you're in luck. I have absolutely nothing going on. So, what's up? You coming out for a midnight ride?" She thrilled at the melodious sound of Maria's laughter.

"That's a good one. I'm terrified of horses in the daylight. It would be a cold day in you know where before I'd think about getting within a hundreds yards of one in the dark."

"Someday you might."

"My clone maybe, but not this warm-blooded woman you're talking to."

"So?" Jo asked.

"Oh, you got me off track with all the horse talk." Jo laughed. "I called to ask a favor."

"Okay, I will."

Maria giggled like a teenager. Jo loved the sound of it. "You might want some details before you agree."

"Okay."

"I was wondering…" Maria hesitated. "I wondered if you'd consider letting me bring Kathleen, my sister-in-law who you met, out to the farm sometime with her boys."

"Sure, fine, bring 'em on out whenever you want."

"Are you sure, because with Matt that's a lot of little boys?"

"Seriously, are any of them like the devil incarnate?"

Maria giggled again. "I don't believe so."

"Okay, no problem. I think I can handle it." Jo had spent most of her adult life around more males than females. She felt confident she could handle a bunch of small boys. "When can I expect this adventure?"

"You're being very optimistic calling this an adventure. Since Matty and I are coming out in two weeks, how about a few weeks after that?"

"Sounds great. Maybe we can do another picnic."

"We'll see."

Jo was more than excited about the family gatherings that were about to take place at her farm. This was all she'd ever wanted—family. She'd been sure that she and Claire would start a family. Of course Claire had shattered that dream and Jo's heart in a heartbeat…

"I have a better idea," Jo said.

"Should I be afraid?"

It was Jo's turn to laugh. "No. I was only going to suggest a cookout instead of a picnic. You know hot dogs, hamburgers and all that."

"That's a perfect plan." Jo could tell she was smiling on the other end. "We need to pick a date."

* * *

The following day at dinner Jo confirmed the plans for the picnic with her parents. Once she was assured the necessary arrangements were in place, her mom's spirits seemed marginally better than usual. And for a change her dad wasn't in a nasty mood, only a quiet one.

Kate showed up unannounced the following weekend, persistent to the point that Jo gave in and went out to dinner with her. Kate appeared to be satisfied with their friendship, although she managed to sneak a quick kiss on Jo's lips before bouncing down the steps and strutting to her car afterwards.

Jo couldn't wrap her brain around the unexpected kiss. She hadn't kissed either Callie or Cecile when they'd left. She and Kate might be becoming friends—they never had any trouble finding things to talk about. It was kind of nice being pursued too, even though she didn't feel the slightest spark between them. At the same time, she sometimes felt like Kate was pursuing her with all the ardor she'd devote to tracking down one of America's Ten Most Wanted.

None of it mattered, really, since she didn't have the time or inclination for a relationship. Especially considering how miserably the last one failed. And, as Cecile proved over and over and over, hopping into bed for lustful sex was not a foundation for anything lasting.

CHAPTER TEN

The big day arrived and brought Maria to the farm much earlier than Jo was expecting. Groggy, she answered the door still in her T-shirt and flannel boxers.

"I'm sorry. I should have called first to get you out of bed." Maria's eyes went wide. "Oh…goodness," she put her hand to her mouth. "Oh, no, I should have called first. You have company." Her cheeks flushed. "I'm so sorry."

Jo rubbed sleep from her eyes as she stepped back to let them in. "No, I don't have company. Late night."

Maria turned a complete circle in the spacious room, now void of all moving boxes. "Wow! You finally put it all away and organized your house."

On her way to the kitchen to put on some coffee Jo called over her shoulder, "Not exactly. Whatever you do, *don't* go into my office or the guest room."

Maria dropped her purse and a canvas shopping bag on the island. "I'm afraid to ask."

Jo started the coffee then leaned against the counter. "I put all the boxes out of sight." She shrugged.

When Maria finally took in what Jo was wearing, the first thing she noticed was Jo's nipples straining the fabric of her shirt. She was braless. Of course she was. Who sleeps in their bra? When she lifted her eyes to Jo's, Jo was smiling at her.

"Something wrong?" Jo asked.

Maria closed her eyes briefly and shook her head. "Are you ever going to settle in your home, or are you going to keep living like a tenant?" Jo crossed her arms over her chest, much to Maria's relief.

"What's the rush?"

Avoiding Jo's eyes, she pulled a few things from the bag. "I don't know how you find anything in all the chaos." Her nerves were tingling. She was sure Jo had noticed her noticing her chest and that now she was standing with her arms covering herself because she'd made her uncomfortable.

"I did put most of the kitchen stuff away. So if you need anything you can't find, let me know."

Maria raised a DVD case. "Do you have a player? I brought this for Matt to watch while I help you do whatever needs to be done to get your picnic ready."

Jo poured two mugs of coffee. "I don't have the one for the big TV in the living room hooked up yet, but the small TV in my room has one built in." Jo scooped up her cup. "Let me jump in the shower real quick and get dressed, then he can sit in my room."

Maria nodded.

Jo hurried into the bathroom and after the shower dressed in a V-neck sweater, a nearly new pair of jeans and her good boots. She applied some gel to her wet hair and ran her fingers through it a few times. She didn't want to try to look too much like someone she wasn't. She wanted her parents to accept her as she was, not for how she looked. Satisfied with the results, she found Maria in the kitchen with plastic containers of food spread out everywhere.

"I'd have carried all that in for you."

"We managed fine." Maria tousled Matt's hair as he stood pressed against her side. "Didn't we, big guy?"

Jo looked into Matt's expressionless eyes. "Well, I'm all done so he can watch his movie or whatever it is." She picked up the plastic case. "*Trains and Planes*. Gee, I want to watch too. Can I? Can I?"

Maria snatched the case from Jo's hand and gave a playful grin. "Only after all your work is done."

Jo feigned a pout. "Adulthood is so unfair." Her shoulders slumped as she led the way down the hall to her semi-organized bedroom and got Matt set up. "I'll be right back." Out front on the porch she whistled and Jake came running. He followed her in, tail wagging. She scratched his head. "Your buddy's here. Today's gonna be heavenly for you." Maria and Matt were seated on the end of the bed when she returned.

"I found you some company, Matt." Jake went to Matt and dropped his head in Matt's lap. He started rubbing Jake's fur while staring impassively at the picture playing on the TV. Jo patted the bed. "Come on, boy." Jake cocked his head and looked at her. She tried again. "Jake, come on, boy." The dog jumped up and sat against Matt's side, eyeing Jo curiously. "He won't get on the furniture without an invitation." She joined Maria in the doorway, where they stood watching the two for a moment.

"He won't move from that spot. They'll be fine."

Jo smiled at the picture. Jake had settled his head in Matt's lap. "I wasn't worried."

She let Maria take over the preparation of nearly everything for the "big day" as Maria called it.

* * *

The medical transport vehicle rolled up the drive right around twelve. Jo hadn't believed in the power of prayer for quite sometime, but she said a silent one as she watched the van approach. She wanted this day to be what she hoped for her family. She maneuvered her dad's wheelchair to the shade of the huge maple in front of the porch. Maria had brought several folding card tables with her. Together they had set them up with table clothes and pitchers of ice tea and lemonade. Maria had thought of everything. Jo knew she'd never begin to be able to repay her selflessness.

"You have a beautiful farm, Jo Lynn. And it's so big," Eileen said and nudged Jo's dad.

"It's a nice piece of property. You won't have any trouble getting your money back out of it."

Jo caught herself before stating that she intended to live there till she died. She set them up with cold drinks, then excused herself to go in the house. Maria was inside, allowing her some time with her parents.

"Aren't you coming out to meet my folks?" Jo shoved her hands in her back pockets.

Maria turned from the sink, wiping her hands. "I thought you were spending some time with them alone."

"Yeah, well, I'm a nervous wreck." She stepped in the direction of the fridge. "I need a beer."

Maria quickly blocked her way. "It's barely lunchtime. You *don't* need a beer." She placed her hands on her hips. "Go back out there with your parents. I'll be out in a few minutes. I want to finish things in here."

Jo dropped her head, her shoulders slumping as she headed back outside. True to her word, Maria emerged from the house with Matt about fifteen minutes later. The longest fifteen minutes of Jo's life.

"Mom, Pops, this is Maria West. She's uh…a friend. She's the realtor that helped me find this place." Jo swept a nervous hand around.

"It's very nice to meet you both. And this is my son, Matt." She paused. "He's autistic."

"Autistic?" Eileen asked.

Maria smoothed a hand over his curly hair. "He doesn't speak, but we're working on that at school. Right, big guy?"

"He's such a handsome boy," Eileen commented.

Maria's face glowed. "Yes, yes, he is." She drew him close, then looked over at Jo. "The food is ready whenever you'd like to eat."

They gathered at the tables, sitting in a most awkward silence. For Jo it was a lot like every other meal with her parents. She realized this was probably how it would end. She'd been foolish to hope for more. When Maria started clearing things from the table and disappeared into the house with Matt, her dad finally spoke.

"You still have that horse you bred the champion with?" Jo nodded. "I wouldn't mind seeing her."

Jo's heart leapt to her throat and she jumped to her feet. "Sure thing, Pops."

He exchanged a look with Jo's mom, who rose quickly. "I'm going to help Maria clean things up. Can you manage, Jo Lynn?"

Jo nodded again and pushed the chair down the bumpy stone walk to the barn. She joked as the chair bounced. "This could be a rough ride, you want me to get a rope and tie you in?" He only shook his head.

In the barn, she stopped the chair in front of Daisy Mae's stall. She'd brought her in earlier in the event Matt wanted to take a ride. She slid her hand under his arm and helped him when he struggled to push up from the chair. To Jo, her dad had always been a strapping big fellow at six-two and two hundred pounds. Now, though, he seemed so much smaller, his frame stooped and weighing forty plus pounds less. He clung to the gate while the horse ambled closer.

Daisy Mae snorted as he rubbed her neck. "She's a beauty." He glanced at Jo, then back at the horse. "Like you."

Jo choked back emotion. It felt like an eternity before she could respond, and when she did, her voice quivered. "I'm real sorry, Pops, that I never wore dresses and was girly like you and Mom wanted."

He laughed lightly. "My tomboy Jo."

Jo thought she was hallucinating. She couldn't remember the last time her dad had laughed around her.

"And I never gave you and Mom any grandkids."

He looked into Jo's watery eyes. "Are you happy with the life that you live?"

"Mostly."

He reached for her hand. "That's all I want for you." He squeezed gently. "Besides, there's still time to have kids if you want."

Tears slipped down her cheeks. It was too late to make her Pops a Grand-Pops.

He pulled Jo into a weak embrace. "Promise me you'll take care of your mother," he said softly.

Jo choked on the words. "I promise." She then cried against the hollow chest that had once been so strong.

The return ride for her parents came promptly at three. With Jake keeping Matt occupied on the porch, Maria accompanied them to the van.

"Oh…Jo Lynn, honey, I left my purse on the table. Would you be a dear and get it for me, please?"

Jo was gone in a flash, and when she started back she caught the handshake between her dad and Maria. Her dad was wearing a hint of a smile as he spoke, so Jo took her time returning. She hugged her mom and kissed her dad's cheek.

"I'll see you after church tomorrow."

"There's a dinner following the service tomorrow at the church. Would you like to go with us?" Eileen asked.

As monumental a step forward today had been, Jo wasn't ready to put herself under the scrutiny of the people at her parents' church.

"Actually I was planning to stop by later in the afternoon."

Eileen allowed the strong young fellow driving the van to help her inside. "All right, dear. We'll see you tomorrow."

Only after the van circled around and headed down the long drive did Jo exhale, the tension in her body beginning to abate.

"I think that went rather well, don't you?"

Jo faced Maria. "God, I need a beer. May I have one now?"

"You're a big girl." Maria grinned at her.

Jo frowned. "Funny, 'cause you weren't treating me like one a few hours ago when I wanted one."

"Your parents are church-going people. I didn't think they'd appreciate smelling alcohol." She caught Jo's arm and pulled her toward the house. "Come on, let's get you a beer."

Back out on the porch, bottle in hand, Jo relaxed back into a chair. "My dad shook your hand."

"Yes."

"I was shocked that he even spoke to you. Mind if I ask what he said?"

Maria looked out over the drive, avoiding Jo's eyes. "He said he liked the food and that I'm a good cook."

Jo watched her closely. If there was more, and Jo suspected there was, Maria wasn't giving it up. *Never play poker with this woman.*

"Thanks for being here today."

"You don't need to thank me. I was glad to be able to meet your parents. Besides, I had my own selfish reason for coming."

"Really," Jo sipped her beer. "And what might that be?"

"This." Maria raised her hands, palms up. "The peace and quiet of the country. And…" she smiled, "that my son gets to visit with one of his best friends."

It warmed Jo's heart to think she could be the source of some happiness for Maria and Matt.

"Maybe we should take Matt to visit his other friend. She's in the barn."

"Maybe you can take him to see her."

Jo cocked her head and held out her beer to Maria. "Here."

Maria took the bottle, but sat looking at Jo looking at her. "What?"

"Courage in a bottle." Maria remained seated, only gazing up at Jo with those dark eyes. "Come on, drink up. You'll never get past the fear if you don't keep trying."

Maria finally relented but didn't drink any beer. She seemed only slightly less apprehensive when they returned to the house later.

"See, that wasn't so bad."

"Says you."

"Surely you're not going to let a six-year-old show more bravery than you."

"He's a child…a male child. The only thing they're afraid of is soap."

Jo laughed. "You're kidding?"

Maria shook her head. "Oh no, I grew up with brothers and Kathleen has three. Believe me, hand washing and taking baths are pure torture for boys."

"Wow! I guess my folks were glad I'm a girl. I mean, I was a tomboy and all, but I didn't mind washing the dirt off."

Maria glanced at her watch. "We should be going."

Jo popped up. "Let me help load the stuff in your car."

Maria stooped to retie Matt's shoelace. "Why don't you keep the leftovers? I can collect my dishes next time we come to visit."

"You sure?" Jo relished the idea of missing a few frozen dinners in the upcoming week.

"Yes, but I will let you help me load the tables in the car."

Jo folded and carried the tables to the car while Maria fastened Matt into his car seat. As she placed the tables in the back of the wagon, Maria saw the car of Jo's deputy slowly approaching.

"Hey, Jo." She looked across the car's roof at Maria and nodded. "Ma'am."

Maria smiled at Kate, then at Jo. "Thanks, Jo. I'll talk to you soon."

Jo walked around and held the door for her. "Yeah, let me know about the cookout."

Maria gazed up at Jo affectionately, then started the car and headed out, keeping an eye on her in her rearview mirror—which also showed Kate watching Jo watching the car. Interesting that Jo hadn't mentioned the deputy. One thing was fairly certain. The officer didn't drink wine because the bottle she'd given Jo as a house warming gift still sat on the kitchen island.

Jo opened the fridge and pulled out beers.

"Wow, I've never seen so much in your refrigerator. You cook?"

Jo handed Kate a beer and leaned against the counter to face her. "Nah. It's left over stuff from what Maria brought."

Kate took a long drink of her beer, eyeing Jo intently. "You know, it may be none of my business, but is there something with this Maria?"

"You're right. It's none of your business. But no." Jo paused a long beat before taking a pull on her beer, annoyed by Kate's prying where Maria was concerned. "In case you couldn't tell, she's straight." Jo shook her head. "She's married with a kid…and oh, did I mention…she's straight!"

"Okay." Kate raised a hand. "I'm sorry I asked. It's just…well, I see her here all the time—"

"This is exactly the second time you've seen her here in four months. That hardly qualifies as 'all the time'." She stopped herself from saying more, knowing that it would likely sound defensive—or reveal that she did have a thing for Maria, hopeless as it was.

"Okay, okay, forget I brought it up."

"Forgotten." Jo sipped her beer.

"You look really nice." Kate flashed a smile. "How about you let me take you out some place for dinner?"

Guilt for not being completely honest about her feelings for Maria was the only thing Jo could fathom that made her accept the dinner invite. And dinner was pleasant enough that afterward Jo gave in and let Kate take her to a little rural bar that wasn't a gay bar, but had a number of obviously gay women there.

Standing in the drive around midnight and feeling the effects of her many beers, Jo pecked Kate quickly on the cheek and said her goodnight. *Why in the hell did I do that?* She asked herself as she strolled to the house. She opened the fridge and reached for a bottle of beer—then returned it to the shelf and closed the door. She'd been drinking more. Because of her dad's diagnosis, she reasoned, and in order to temper her anger at his stubbornness. But now that the visit with them at her farm had gone so well and they'd reconciled, she realized she needed to dial it back. Unless Maria unsettled her nerves. Then she might indulge a bit to calm herself.

CHAPTER ELEVEN

"I got something to show you in my truck when you have a minute, boss." Tucker was unusually jubilant for a Monday morning. Jo followed him out to his truck, where he threw a horse blanket off an old saddle that had a number of straps and add-ons attached to it.

"What is it?" Jo asked jokingly. "A saddle from another planet?"

Tucker laughed. "Nah, I know it looks…"

"Hideous," Jo supplied.

"Yeah, well, I guess it does, but I got the idea for it because of your friend's boy."

Jo cocked her head and looked at the apparatus. "Okay, show me."

He smiled and hoisted the awkward-looking saddle out of his truck and carried it to the barn where he set it on a hay bale. He straddled it to show her how it could secure someone undersized atop a horse. As he explained the purpose for each attachment, Jo realized it was one of her old saddles.

"I hope you don't mind my borrowing this from the tool shed."

"Not at all, Tucker." She continued to inspect the contraption. "As hideous as it looks, I'd say it's some imaginative engineering." She met his smiling eyes. "I suppose we're going to test this with Maria's son."

He shrugged. "If she wants. If not, I'll find someone to. Maybe I can sell this design to that big outfit that's going to open the stables with the riding trails through the reserve."

She considered again her dream of someday having a dude ranch. Maybe it could be more than that. Not just a dude ranch, but a place to serve kids like Matt. She'd have to learn a lot more about horse therapy, but the possibilities were endless, not only for the profitable operation she could run, but also for the charitable contribution she could make.

She smiled as she patted his back. "I'm proud of you, Tucker. Let me know whatever I need to do to help." She circled the hay bale, checking it from all angles. "I think I can persuade Maria to let us put Matt on it for a ride. If not, I know some other boys that would probably try it out in a heartbeat." Tucker grinned.

Jo was anxious for Maria to visit again, even if she would be accompanied by her sister-in-law and her brood of boys. She'd take time spent with Maria anyway she could get it.

Maria called Wednesday evening while Jo was eating dinner.

"I was just having the last of the leftovers and thinking about you."

"Do I want to know what you were thinking?"

Jo swallowed a mouthful. "I was trying to figure out how I could convince you to give up real estate and come work for me as my domestic engineer."

Maria chuckled. "An impressive title, but I'm not sure I could do that all day then come home and have to do the same here too."

"What if the job came with fringe benefits?"

"I'm afraid to ask," Maria said lightheartedly.

"How about free riding lessons and all the riding time you want?"

Maria laughed easily. "Such a funny one you are, Jo Marchal."

Jo loved when they could banter like the best of girlfriends. "Hey, I try. You know the more you laugh the longer you live. Heck, you might even live long enough to get over your fear of horses."

"Excuse me, oh great horse whisperer, but I think I've made great strides recently. At least I can stand near them without having an anxiety attack, and I can touch them without wetting myself."

"That's down right embarrassing," Jo howled. "And thank you for not piddling on my boots."

They both laughed wildly. "Stop it!" Maria exclaimed. "I can't catch my breath." Jo heard her gasp. "Promise me something, Jo."

Jo tamed her giggles. "Sure if I can. What?"

"Promise me you'll never stop making me laugh."

Jo smiled and wished with all her heart that she was looking in Maria's eyes at that moment. "I think I can keep that promise. We're like…good friends, right?"

"The very best kind."

* * *

It was several weeks before Maria and her posse pulled into the Lazy Daisy Farm for the Saturday cookout. Matt was content to sit in the yard with Jake, who seemed perfectly content to sit and have Matt pet him. The other boys ran off to explore, but only after receiving explicit instructions from Kathleen not to get into anything.

"I don't think there's anything they can hurt, except maybe themselves," Jo assured Kathleen.

"That's what boys do." Kathleen waved her hand. "I wouldn't know it was the weekend unless there was some blood and tears."

"I have a surprise for you," Jo said to Maria as she hoisted a heavy cooler from the back of Kathleen's van.

"O—kay."

Maria couldn't stop herself from staring at Jo's muscled arms as she carried the cooler. As she and Kathleen set everything up on Jo's newly acquired picnic table, Jo started grilling the hot dogs and hamburgers. Kathleen's boys were polite and well mannered, and after eating, when Jo offered horseback rides, there was hooting and hollering. Kathleen stood at Daisy Mae's stall with the four boys while Jo led Maria to the tack room to show her Tucker's invention.

"He did this for Matt?"

Jo ran her hand over the worn leather. "Basically, yeah, Matt was his inspiration. Tucker said he could see the joy in Matt's eyes when he rode with me. He thought he might really like riding on his own." Jo picked up one of the two-ways and keyed the mike. "Hey, Tucker, time to head in so we can try this new gadget of yours."

They waited a minute before the radio crackled with Tucker's voice. "I'm down in the reserve, but headed your way. Be there quick as Cobalt's bringing me, boss."

"Good, 'cause you got an anxious bunch of volunteers."

The saddle worked terrifically. Each of Kathleen's boys took a ride around the pasture first, then they put Matt on. The pleasure on Maria's face made Jo's heart swell as Tucker walked Daisy Mae slowly with Matt tightly secured in the saddle.

"Will you be around tomorrow?" Maria asked later as they were reloading the van.

Jo put the cooler in the back and closed the hatch. "Sure, after dinner at my folks."

"I might stop back out if that's all right."

"Yeah, sure, I'll probably be home by three." She did a mental fist pump.

Maria placed a hand on Jo's arm. "Thank you for today. I'll be forever indebted to you for giving Matt more joy than he's ever had. I could feel his happiness when he sat up on the horse."

Jo ran a hand through her hair. "You don't owe me a thing. I would have never thought to try and engineer something like Tucker did. He's a smart one, that boy."

Maria's smile was as warm as the spot where her hand rested on Jo's forearm. "In any case, it would have never happened if you hadn't invited us out here in the first place, so thank you. And don't change any plans you have for tomorrow on the chance that I can get away, but I do want to try and come back out."

"I'll be around."

Maria climbed into the passenger seat while Kathleen's boys pleaded for a return trip.

"Anytime you want to bring them out let me know," Jo said to Kathleen.

"Thank you. My boys will be reliving this day for weeks. You can probably count on seeing us again."

* * *

Jo hated that she had to turn down her dad's invite to watch the football game after dinner on Sunday, but something told her she needed to be home in case Maria showed up. She kissed his cheek and promised to catch next Sunday's game.

"She's a very nice woman." He took hold of her hand.

"Pops, Maria and I are just good friends. There isn't anything else." She was embarrassed having this conversation with him. His cheeks colored more than she had seen in a very long time.

He squeezed her hand. "I'm sorry for assuming."

Jo leaned down and gave him a quick hug. "It's okay, Pops. There isn't anyone right now in my life."

"But you're happy?" The wrinkles around his eyes deepened.

She smiled at the possibility of seeing Maria again. "Yeah, Pops, I'm happy."

He raised her hand and kissed it tenderly. "Then I'm happy."

"I'll see you for dinner and football next Sunday."

She said a goodbye to her mom and hit the road. As much as she wanted to keep her mind on her reason for rushing home, she thought about the exchange with her dad. There didn't seem to be any question that he now accepted who she was. And that single thought brought a torrent of tears as she pushed down the highway.

She was home forty-five minutes before she told Maria she would be. She wanted to ride—needed to—to lift the heavy feeling in her heart. Heading straight to the barn, she grabbed her saddle. Calypso was grazing the closest by, so she gave a whistle. She wouldn't get the wild ride on Calypso that she would on Cobalt, but he was nowhere in sight. She galloped the horse toward the lower field. If she could keep Calypso running, they'd have time to make it into the reserve to the creek and back before Maria arrived, if she was coming.

When they reached the water, she dismounted and Calypso dipped her head for a drink from the cool stream. This had become her new thinking spot. Here the peacefulness enveloped her like her favorite old flannel shirt. She sat on a fallen tree while Calypso nibbled on the lush grasses along the creek's bank.

She couldn't shake the heart sickening thought that after decades her dad finally accepted her and now he wouldn't be with her much longer. Why was life so damned unfair? Her parents were such religious people. Why was their god so unfair? The tears readily came again, but when Calypso snorted and something scampered under the tree where Jo sat, she snapped out of her negative thinking and took the reins.

"Come on, girl, we better get back in case we're getting company."

She laughed. *Yeah, so I'd rather talk to horses than people.* But then they never talked back or told her what she should do. They only offered companionship, loyalty, and Jo trusted them implicitly. As they rode back over the rise, she saw Maria standing on the fence beside the barn, looking out. Her mood swung as she trotted the horse closer, but when Maria looked like she was ready to bolt, she halted Calypso and quickly hopped down.

"I'm a little early. You're not late." Maria smiled at her.

Jo pulled the saddle off her horse and threw it over the fence rail. Once she removed the bridle, Calypso wandered away.

"That's a beautiful horse. What's its name?"

"Calypso."

"Calypso," Maria repeated. "How do you horse people come up with such unique and unusual names?"

Jo shrugged and looked back at the horse. "I'm not sure. Sometimes something just pops in your head."

When Jo faced her again and looked into her eyes, Maria saw a deep sadness. Her heart sank.

"Is everything okay?" she asked, knowing Jo had been to visit her parents.

"Yeah." Jo nodded. "My dad shared something today I never in a million years would have expected." She quickly looked away, but not before Maria caught the tears forming in her eyes.

Maria reached over the rail and touched Jo's shoulder. "Anything you want to talk about?"

"Nah." Jo picked up her saddle. "Let me put this up and we can sit on the porch or out back on the deck."

Maria returned to her car and grabbed the bag from behind the seat. She walked with more than a little apprehension into the barn, clutching the paper sack in both arms to her chest. She found Jo in the tack room. When Jo noticed her, she propped an elbow on the nearest saddle stand, looking rather surprised.

"Here." Maria crossed the room.

"What's this, more leftovers?" Jo took the offered bag.

Maria shook her head. "Courage."

"What?" Jo peered into the bag, a smile creeping across her face. "Courage for…"

Maria wrung her hands. "For me. I thought I could try this horse thing again."

"Okay…"

"Well, if my son is going to ride one of those big animals, I figure I'd better get over my fear of them."

Jo's smile didn't waver. "So, you want me to get you drunk so you're not afraid?"

"Oh no, not drunk!" Maria waved her hands. "Only one." She raised an index finger. "You know, to calm my nerves a little."

"Okay, but let's get some cold ones."

Jo motioned Maria ahead of her. She was dressed in jeans and a suede jacket, more casually than ever before. Her boots weren't exactly cowboy boots, with their two-inch heels, but overall she looked more like she could belong on a farm.

Maria drank an entire beer before she would let Jo take her out into the pasture in the four-wheel drive Gator to find Daisy Mae. Jo grabbed an apple in case Maria wanted to try feeding the horse.

She didn't. When they returned to the barn, though, she told Jo, "I think it's a little less intimidating out in the open than in the barn."

"Really? Why do you suppose?"

"I'm not sure. Maybe more room to run."

Jo laughed. "For you or the horse?"

"Both." She gave Jo's arm a light punch.

"How about we have another beer, or do you have to go?"

Maria checked her watch. "I've got time, but no beer for me."

Jo decided to follow suit and forgo another beer herself. They settled out on the deck with its spectacular view of the changing fall foliage. *God, why can't every minute of every day feel like this?*

Maria sighed. "God, I love it out here."

Jo wondered if God would hear them both and somehow make her wish come true. After sitting for long silent minutes, Jo finally asked, "So where's Matt this afternoon?"

"He went with Kathleen and her boys to the movies."

"He seems to get on real well with them."

"He's like a puppet for them. They can drag him along and into anything…literally."

It amazed Jo how Maria's eyes always twinkled when she spoke about her son.

"You don't ever talk about your husband."

The twinkle vanished as quickly as it had appeared and Maria gazed into the distance. "There isn't really anything to talk about."

"I'm sorry." Jo felt bad for bringing up an obviously unwelcome subject.

Maria faced Jo. "Don't be silly. I hardly think about it anymore." Jo kept her eyes on Maria's as she spoke automatically, it seemed, and without feeling. "He doesn't have anything to do with Matt. He won't even acknowledge him as his son. He's my son, my responsibility. Jack can't see past Matt's handicap and I can't see past that." She shook her head. "I can't believe he and Kathleen are brother and sister. They're as different as day and night."

"Sure seems pretty darn evident how much Matt loves you even if he can't express it like most kids."

Maria nodded. "I'd give my life for him."

As dusk cloaked them, Maria headed out.

"Be careful, it's that time of day the deer start to wander out."

"I will. And thanks, Jo. I'll talk to you soon."

Jo watched her disappear into the darkening evening. She hoped that Maria's determination to get past her fear would mean more visits. Whistling, she headed in.

* * *

Maria stopped out the next two weekends. Always on Saturday, though, so as not to interfere with the time Jo spent visiting her parents. On the first Saturday in November, with the temperatures predicted to hit sixty degrees, Maria felt as though she was ready to lead Daisy Mae on a walk in the pasture with her son aboard. She had, after all, braved standing next to Jo's biggest stallion, Cobalt, without suffering an anxiety attack. Daisy was like a grandma in comparison, but Maria seemed anxious as Jo placed the reins in her hand.

"You can't believe how nervous this makes me." Maria's hands trembled noticeably.

"It'll be fine. Think about how much enjoyment this is for Matt. Breathe deep and relax."

Maria led Daisy Mae slowly about a quarter mile around the pasture. She was smiling like a kid herself when they stopped at the hay bales inside the barn where Jo waited to help Matt off the horse.

"That was great. I'm so proud of you," Jo said, lowering Matt into Maria's arms.

Maria rolled her eyes. "If you could feel how fast my heart's beating, you'd understand how terrifying this is for me."

"Maybe we should have a cold one to calm your nerves."

Holding Matt at her side, she raised her eyes and looked at Jo. "I can't."

At that precise moment, Jake raced into the barn and to Matt's side. Matt let go of his mother's hand and knelt to let Jake lick his face.

"Jake!"

Maria watched with a grin. "He's fine." She looked again at Jo. "Still jealous?"

Jo laughed. "Yeah, maybe. Hey, I've got iced tea."

Maria looked at her son. "That sounds good."

Maria thought Jo's face might split with the wide grin she was wearing. On their way out, she admitted, "It was kind of thrilling. Thanks for nudging me to take such a big step. I will find some way to repay all your encouragement."

Kate showed up later unexpectedly, but Jo firmly declined her dinner offer, pleased that she was able to hustle her on her way in short order.

On Sunday, Jo was shocked to see what a downhill turn her dad had taken.

"Why didn't you call me?" Eileen was moving about the kitchen in a trance. "Mom?" She finally took her mom gently by the shoulders. "Mom, when did he get so bad and why didn't you call me?"

Tears welled in her mom's eyes. "Tuesday, he couldn't help me." Her voice quivered. "I couldn't get him out of bed, so I called the Hospice people. Oh God, Jo Lynn, what am I going to do?" When she broke down Jo did the only thing she could think to do. She wrapped her mom in her arms and held her.

"We'll get through it, Mom."

When Eileen quit crying, Jo made them tea, sat her mom at the table and excused herself. She stopped and looked in at her dad from the doorway.

"He's not in any pain." The voice startled her.

Jo spun around to see a fortyish woman sitting in the spare room across the hall with a book in her lap. She laid the book aside and stood.

"I'm Lena from Hospice," she said as she approached Jo extending her hand. "I'm here during the day shift to help your family through this. You must be their daughter, Jo Lynn."

Jo accepted the woman's comforting handshake. "Jo, please. They're the only ones who call me Jo Lynn." The woman smiled warmly. Jo sighed and looked back at her dad. "Just a week ago we watched football and I promised I'd come again and watch with him today." Guilt strangled her. How had she not known, not sensed that her pops turned this dreaded corner?

She placed her hand on Jo's shoulder. "Sometimes it happens quickly. He's not suffering, though. We're here to make sure of that."

Jo nodded as tears trickled down her cheeks. "He was such a big man, and now he looks so small lying there."

"Your mother says he has a heart of gold."

Jo let the tears go. She had come to know in the last month and a half that was true about her dad and that he'd spent the last two decades hiding behind his fear for her. Why hadn't she tried harder before to tear down the wall that separated them? All those years lost. Jo hated herself now for being as stubborn as he had been.

"Why don't you sit with him for a bit? I'm going to check on your mother."

She sat in the chair beside the bed and watched for a long time as his chest slowly rose and fell with each labored breath. She grasped his thin, frail fingers in her strong hand.

"Hi, Pops." She practically choked on the words. His hand finally twitched in hers and with effort he opened his eyes. When he parted his lips all that came out was a gurgled grunt. She placed her hand on his chest and patted lightly. "Why don't you let me do the talking for a change?" She was fighting with every fiber of strength she could muster not to cry. He squeezed her hand in response.

She sat for more than an hour telling him about everything that was going on at the farm, including the miraculous feat Maria accomplished getting past her fear to be able to share something her son enjoyed. He squeezed her hand and Jo knew he was letting her know he understood what that parent-child bond meant. It was more than she could stand. She needed to get out of there.

"I've got to go, Pops, but I'll be back to check on you tomorrow evening." She stood and leaned over to kiss his cheek. He squeezed her hand once again. In the kitchen, she placed a kiss on her mom's cheek. "I've got to go, Mom. I'll be back later tomorrow." Her mom stared blankly into her tea cup.

"Can I talk to you?" she said to Lena, who followed Jo to the living room. "I know she thinks I shouldn't be burdened with any of this," Jo said quietly, "but I need you to promise you will call me if there's anything you think I should know about. Anything at all."

Lena nodded. "We will have to speak with your mother about that. We were only following the instructions your mother gave us." She gave Jo a sympathetic expression.

"Can you please make sure anyone else that's here knows too?" Lena nodded once more. "Thank you. I'll be back tomorrow and every day he has left."

Lena put a comforting hand on Jo's shoulder as she had earlier. "Believe me they do appreciate your presence even if they can't say so."

Jo cried most of the way home. It was inevitable, and even though she thought she'd prepared herself for it, apparently this was one of those things you're never really prepared for. She had hoped—and yes, prayed—he would last until the New Year arrived. She had been hoping for one more Christmas to share with him, but now that seemed an impossibility.

At home and saddened beyond anything she could comprehend, she found the whiskey bottle packed away, along with most of her life, in one of the boxes. She dropped in a chair on the porch intending to watch the moon come up. As she took her first sip, Kate's car rolled up the drive.

Striding to the porch with purpose, she asked, "Where the hell you been all day?" Her tone was a little too harsh and hostile. Jo sat in silence. "You want to tell me where you've been?"

Jo heaved a heavy sigh. "Not that it's any of your business, but I've been helping my folks out with some stuff. I wasn't aware I needed to provide you with my schedule."

"Whoa." Kate raised her hands. "Looks like I hit on a nerve."

When Kate started up the porch steps, Jo raised her hand. "I don't much feel like company right now. I need some time to myself."

Kate started backing away. "Yeah, okay, I get it. I'll check back in with you later."

Jo took another sip of the whiskey when Kate's car turned onto the road and another until the fiery liquor began to make her head feel fuzzy. When the sun set she managed to stumble into the house and drop on the couch. The last image she had was of her parents as they said their good-byes on that day when she went off to summer camp with her friends. And now, it would be a good-bye forever.

* * *

The drumming in Jo's head was entirely too loud. But when she heard her name, she reasoned that the pounding wasn't only in her head. She finally cracked open one eye and saw Tucker standing a few feet away.

"Sorry to barge in here, but I was worried, and you didn't answer the phone, and I found this on the porch." He rambled on, raising the near empty whiskey bottle. "And the door was unlocked, so—"

"Tucker…" Jo raised her hand. "Please stop talking."

"Sorry, boss."

She waved a hand and tried to sit up, her eyes slamming shut as pain shot through her head.

"You okay?"

She dropped her feet on the floor and her head on the back of the couch while nausea turned her stomach. He stood silently watching her.

"What time is it?" she croaked.

"After eight thirty. You're usually out before I get here, so like I said, I was worried."

He placed the bottle on the coffee table and sat at the other end of the couch. "You don't got to tell me nothing. Your business is your business, but if there's something I can help with…"

Jo looked at Tucker through half-mast eyelids. "Would you happen to know how to make coffee?"

He popped up. "Oh sure, can't be a cowboy if you can't make coffee. How you like it, strong or weak?"

Jo cleared her throat. "Something between."

"You got it."

Jo closed her eyes until he returned with two steaming mugs. After several sips, she said, "My dad's dying, he doesn't have much time and I need your help." There, she said it so fast her brain didn't have time to register the words to make her cry.

Tucker sat his cup down and faced her. "Dang, that's awful. I'm real sorry, Jo."

"Thanks." She drank more coffee, hoping it would clear some of the fog from her head. "First of all, I don't want you to say a word to anyone."

"Okay."

She looked at him intently. "I mean not a soul. I don't care who comes around asking. You got it?" He nodded. "And I need you to handle whatever needs done here until this is over. I'll be in and out of here daily. But I need you to cover whatever comes up. I'll give you a key to the house and sign some checks so you can pay for anything that comes due."

He nodded energetically. "Sure thing, boss. Whatever you need me to do."

"Thanks, Tucker. I knew you were this dependable the day I met you."

He got up and carried their coffee mugs to the kitchen, then returned a few minutes later with only hers. "I left my cell number out on the kitchen counter. Call if you need me to do anything else…anytime." She forced half a smile.

She made herself stand in the shower, but it didn't help the sick feeling that consumed her. It was more than the hangover. It was the reality of what her life was.

She pulled on a T-shirt and crawled under the covers in her bed, confident that Tucker would step up and run the farm. She slept soundly until noon, at which time she showered again, dressed and went in search of him. After locating him with the two-way, she let him know she was leaving and wouldn't return until well after quitting time. He reiterated that she should call if she needed anything at all and not to worry about the farm.

Her visit was much like the day before, and when she returned home around eight she skipped the whiskey, opting instead for a beer. She turned in early and was feeding horses in the barn Tuesday morning when Tucker arrived. She headed out shortly after ten, wanting to be at her parents by lunchtime. Lena left at three and a woman named Donna, closer to her mom's age, came for the evening shift. Jo made sure before she left that Donna understood she was to be called if anything changed.

She didn't expect to hear the ringing phone at ten minutes after three in the morning and stared at it a long time, her stomach turning over. *Oh God.* She took a breath and picked up the receiver. "Yes?"

"Ms. Marchal, this is Helen with Hospice. I'm so sorry to have to tell you that your father has passed. The end came very quickly and he wasn't in any pain. Your mother wanted you to know, but didn't want us to wake you."

Jo rummaged for some clothes. "How's my mom?"

"As you might expect."

"Have you called for them to come for him yet?"

"No, I wanted to speak with you first. Your mother is still sitting with him."

Jo pulled on her jeans. "I'm only an hour away. Can you wait that long to make the call?"

"I'll wait."

"I'm on my way." Jo buttoned her shirt even as she grabbed her jacket and keys on the way out the door.

* * *

The following days blurred as Jo operated on autopilot. Having to be strong for her mom was the only thing that kept her moving forward. She didn't remember racing home Wednesday afternoon to pack a bag or sitting in her parents' bedroom while her mom picked out the suit her dad would wear for all eternity. Friday evening, thinking how horrible it was to stand for hours looking at the one you lost, she stood in a trance at her mom's side as hoards of people she'd never met paraded past his casket. She made up her mind then and there that she would be cremated and have someone, hopefully someone special that she loved, scatter her ashes throughout the hills and pastures where her horses grazed.

The graveside service tore at her heart. Saying good-bye forever—she couldn't imagine anything more difficult. Back at the house she could tolerate hearing only so many stories about her dad told by people she didn't know. She closed herself in his den, intending to call Tucker to check in. That was when she saw the missed call from Maria, made the evening before.

Part of her wanted to call Maria, but she didn't feel entirely in control. She was afraid that in addition to sharing how she was doing she would slip up and share with Maria some of what she felt for her. So she only called Tucker, leaving him a voice mail that apologized for leaving without warning and promised to get back as soon as she could.

She left the den for the kitchen and something to drink. A few minutes later, sitting in the swing out on the patio, arms wrapped tight around herself, she felt the phone vibrate in her pocket. It was Maria again. She almost answered—almost. Tucker called back an hour later, letting her know things were fine and to take all the time she needed. She told him what she needed most was a long ride on one of her horses.

"Yeah, I know exactly what you mean, boss."

* * *

A carload of church widows picked her mom up the following day for Sunday services, which Eileen tried to get Jo to attend with her. Jo couldn't take any more praying over her dad's death. She wanted the time alone in the house. She cried into his pillow. She missed him. For more than twenty years she rarely had given him a thought, but today she missed him like she had that first night at summer camp a lifetime ago. If only she could have broken down the barriers sooner, she knew they could have been best friends, but—too little, too late.

She and her mother had tea in the kitchen that evening.

"Jo Lynn, honey, you should go back to your home. I know you must have things you need to do there."

"I don't, Mom. I have someone taking care of everything for me."

Her mom stared into the teacup. "That nice dark-skinned woman we met?" she asked, avoiding Jo's eyes.

Jo saw how uncomfortable it was for her mom to ask the question. "Mom, Maria and I are friends. The young man that works for me is taking care of things at the farm in my absence."

She reached over and patted Jo's hand. "In any case, dear, I think you should go back to your own life." She looked away. "There must be someone waiting for you to come home."

To say Jo was surprised was an understatement. "There's no one waiting for me to come home, and I can't believe we're having this conversation, Mom."

Eileen's cheeks turned a rosy hue. "Your father, God rest his soul, made it impossible for me to have a relationship with my only child for over half of your life." She reached over and took hold of Jo's hand. "I don't know if I can make up for that, but I want to try." Eileen squeezed her hand. "You're all I've got." An errant tear escaped her lashes and slid down her cheek.

It was all Jo could do to speak. "There's nothing I want more, Mom." She placed her other hand atop her mom's. The tender moment touched Jo so deeply it threatened to unleash her own tears.

"Good, then as your mother I'm going to suggest you go home voluntarily so I don't have to throw you out."

Jo smiled for the first time in a week. "Let's compromise. I'll drive home tomorrow."

Eileen cupped Jo's cheek. "I'll be fine, dear, and I need some time…" Her eyes traveled around the room. "Some time alone. I have my church friends here." She patted Jo's hand again. "I will be fine."

CHAPTER TWELVE

Jo pulled into her drive mid-morning. A sense of peace washed over her when she stepped out of the truck and took a breath of the crisp fall air. This was the therapy that would assuage her grief. Locating Tucker in the barn, she got a quick update before heading inside to change clothes. She missed her boots and worn comfortable jeans almost as much as her horses. Tucker obviously read her mind since she found him standing outside the barn door with Cobalt already saddled.

He gave a tiny smile. "Thought you might need to take a ride and check things over for yourself."

She took the reins. "Thanks, Tucker."

She mounted the horse, grateful for that feeling she always got sitting high in the saddle. There was only one other thing that came close to it, and she hadn't experienced *it* or cared to in quite some time. As she settled into the aged leather saddle, her mind flashed on an image of Maria sitting astride a horse beside her. Having Maria around to share her life with would sure ease the grieving process, she thought, before quickly banishing the daydream.

As Cobalt danced, eager to run, she called over her shoulder, "Remind me to give you a nice fat Christmas bonus."

Tucker's smile went wide. She really liked him. If she could adopt a sibling, she'd want Tucker to be her little brother. Like Tom, he'd become like family.

She rode for more than an hour. When she returned she was shocked to see the black station wagon in the drive by the house. Maria got out the moment she saw Jo step out of the barn. Meeting on the front porch, Jo removed the Stetson and combed her fingers through her damp hair.

"Hi," she said timidly.

Maria glared at her for a moment. "You ignore my phone calls for days, I finally reached Tucker and all he would tell me was that you were away. I drove out yesterday, found the place deserted and all you have to say is 'hi'?"

Jo saw a fire simmering in her dark eyes. A bit fearful, she touched Maria's elbow ever so lightly. "Let's go inside. It's cold out here." *In more ways than one.* And apparently Maria was so fired up she didn't realize she was shivering.

Jo led her to the kitchen where she put the teakettle on to heat. Maria stood, arms crossed tightly over her chest in the doorway while Jo stood at the counter with her back to her placing tea bags into the cups.

"Well, are you going to tell me what's going on or not?" Her tone was only slightly less scalding than moments before.

Jo breathed deeply and exhaled slowly. "My dad died and I was taking care of all that stuff, you know, with my mom."

Maria was behind her in an instant. "Oh my God, Jo, I'm so sorry." When she put a hand on her shoulder, Jo's body went rigid, rejecting the solace she offered before she was even conscious of it. Maria immediately pulled away and gave her some space, moving to one of the stools at the island. "Is there anything I can do?"

The silence seemed to last forever. Jo poured the water, mesmerized by the rising steam. "Nah, it's over and dealt with." She set a mug in front of Maria and took the stool next to her.

"Do you have a close friend you can talk to?"

Jo stared off. This felt an awful lot like a wound that had only begun to heal, and now Maria was pulling at it, trying to open it up. "There's nothing I need to talk about," she said flatly.

Maria's voice, on the other hand, comforted like a favorite old blanket. "Jo, you must be feeling something about your father's passing. I can't imagine anyone that wouldn't. It might help if you talked to someone."

What Jo needed was to bury the pain deep inside. "What do you know? You don't really know me." She glared over at Maria and the hurt she saw in her eyes made Jo drop her head in shame. "I'm sorry."

Maria put her hand over Jo's. "I'm only trying to be your friend, Jo."

Jo sighed. "I know. I'm not real sure if I even know how to do that."

"I find that hard to believe." Maria studied her. "Is it because gay women don't befriend straight women?"

Jo shrugged. "I think that would be the other way around."

"Oh…"

"I mean, I don't know, but I'd think that generally straight women would be afraid of us hitting on them."

Maria squeezed Jo's hand and allowed hers to linger there. "Jo, I'm not afraid of you. Your choice of lovers doesn't change who you are. You're kind and caring, and I happen to like those traits in people, male or female, straight or gay. I want to be your friend." Jo batted feverishly at the tears forming in her eyes. "If you need to talk, about anything, I will always listen." Jo lost her battle and tears streaked down her cheeks. "Oh, sweetie, I didn't mean to make you cry. I'm sorry." She stood and hugged Jo against her. Jo nestled her head on Maria's shoulder and cried quietly. "And you can always… always cry on my shoulder," Maria said softly into Jo's hair.

The sensation of being in Maria's arms was unlike anything Jo had known before. Even with Claire, she hadn't felt this cared for. This was a new feeling. A feeling she liked—a lot.

After a good cry, she composed herself. "Sorry."

Maria pushed a lock of hair off Jo's forehead and their eyes met. "Sweetie, you don't ever have to be sorry for showing emotions."

Their eyes remained locked in a gaze so intense it made the old cliché about time standing still seem so real. They were frozen in this moment, and there was nothing else in the world but the two of them. Jo's heart pounded so hard she was sure Maria could see it, but she couldn't tear her eyes away from those deep dark eyes looking back at her.

Maria's breath had caught when Jo looked up into her eyes. She was still holding it. What was it about this strong woman exposing her emotions that made her want to hold Jo all the more?

Jo cleared her throat and broke the trance-like gaze that threatened to cause Maria to do something regrettable—like kiss her.

She finally took a breath and stepped back. "Are you going to be okay?"

"Sure. I'm a tough ol' cowgirl." Jo gave a half smile.

Maybe, Maria thought, tough on the outside, but on the inside...Jo Marchal was a big softie with a heart of gold. And, for some unfathomable reason, she wanted to pull Jo back into her arms, to hold her and feel that heart beat against her again. Maria sat back on her stool and sipped her tea.

The awkward silence grew long until Jo said, "You should bring Matt out this weekend. We're supposed to have an unseasonal warm up."

Maria needed to clear her head of thoughts about kissing Jo. "Horses don't like the cold?" she asked absently.

"It's not the horses that are bothered by the colder temperatures, it's us warm-blooded humans."

Warm blood, Maria thought, *that's what's flowing through Jo's heart. Which only moments before was against me and flooding my body in unexpected places.*

Jo's voice faded into the background and she drifted into a daydream. Jo's strong arms were around her, holding her while she looked into Jo's steely blue-gray eyes. She tilted Maria's chin up and leaned in for a kiss.

"Maria?"

Maria blinked. "Hmm…"

"I was asking if you wanted to take a ride this Saturday."

Maria snapped back quickly and laughed. "You're joking, right?"

"No."

"I appreciate the invitation, but I'm not ready for that. I might bring Matt out, though."

* * *

Jo woke in the middle of the night from the most vivid dream she'd ever had. Her heart was racing so fiercely she could feel it drumming in her ears. She had been holding Maria in her arms and looking in her eyes. She had professed her love and was sure that Maria was about to kiss her. It was so real that Jo could smell Maria's perfume.

"God, I must be losing my mind," she murmured as she stumbled to the bathroom for a drink of water. When she looked in the mirror she realized she still was wearing the T-shirt she'd had on when Maria hugged her. Stretching the fabric to her nose, she inhaled. Maria's scent all right. She closed her eyes and relived those few close moments they shared earlier. She looked again at her image in the mirror. "This is ridiculous you know? She's married with a kid. There's no way she'd give that away to take up with a lesbian cowgirl, so get over this crazy fantasy." Actually, of course, it was *she* who was crazy. She was talking to herself. Returning to bed, she worked at thinking of anything else until finally the sandman found her again.

When Maria hadn't called by Friday evening, Jo assumed she wasn't bringing Matt out Saturday, which was okay since Kate had been calling daily and bugging her to go to dinner. She needed to get the notions of Maria out of her head, and spending time with another lesbian might be the thing to do it.

Maria did call on Saturday morning. "We won't be able to make it out today."

"I kind of figured. Maybe next weekend."

"Maybe…listen, I don't know if you and your mother have plans for Thanksgiving, and I realize we're virtual strangers to her, but I wanted to invite you both to have dinner with us."

"Us?"

"We go to Kathleen's, so it's us, Kathleen's family and you and your mother if you decide to join us."

"We haven't even discussed it." Jo had spoken with her mom every day since she'd returned home, but her mom hadn't mentioned anything about the upcoming holiday. "I'm going for dinner tomorrow, I'll ask her. When do you need to know?"

"Whenever."

Jo and Kate had their dinner and rented a movie on the way back to the farm. Jo had no interest in the movie Kate picked and therefore spent the hour and forty-one minutes it was playing trying to imagine her and her mom with the West family for Thanksgiving. It was a picture she couldn't quite bring into focus. She practically threw Kate out after the movie, using the excuse she had to get up early to spend the day with her mom.

"You sure spend an awful lot of time visiting at your folks."

"Your point is…" Jo had never given Kate any reason to think there was anything but friendship between them. Or she had tried not to, anyway. She honestly would rather spend time with her mom or Maria. Having the two of them in her life mattered a lot presently.

Kate grumbled something under her breath and gave Jo a quick hug before leaving.

It was clear that Kate was feeling challenged by having to rein in her desires. Jo didn't want to think about that. She had more important things to worry about—like what to do about Thanksgiving.

* * *

Eileen surprised Jo. "Oh dear, I'm sorry but I've already made plans with Helen from church for Thanksgiving. I just assumed you'd have your own plans since we've not shared a Thanksgiving in—"

Eileen's eyes misted with tears as the words died on her lips. "I'm sorry, Jo Lynn, I need to change my thinking to include you."

Jo took her hand. "It's okay, Mom. I'm glad you have friends and you want to spend time with them and not stay cooped up in the house."

"Yes, well, Helen, Maxine and Emma are all widows so we decided to have a combined dinner and each of us is preparing part of the meal." She smiled and touched Jo's cheek. "You're welcome to join us, honey. One more at the table would be fine, I'm sure, and you're single like the rest of us."

Jo almost laughed out loud. Single, yes, but she had nothing else in common with these women, who Jo feared would kick her mom out of their little widows' club if she dared bring her lesbian daughter around for Thanksgiving.

"Yes, Mom, I'm single, and thanks for pointing that out." Jo gave her a grin. "I'm going to pass on the invite, but thank you."

"What are you going to do then?"

"Don't worry. I promise not to spend the day alone in my house."

"Next year, Jo Lynn, we'll plan ahead."

Jo nodded, but thought, *Not if the widows' club would be joining them*.

She didn't call Maria, hoping if she didn't Maria would forget the invitation. Such was not the case and Maria called Monday evening.

"So, what are your Thanksgiving plans, Jo?"

She considered lying, but couldn't do it. "My mom has officially joined the widows' club at her church. And as tempting as the invitation was to spend it with them, since I'm single too—thank you very much, Mom, for the reminder—I turned her down."

Maria laughed. "So you have no plans and nowhere to go?"

"I didn't say that."

"Well, do you?"

Like trying to avoid a bad case of poison ivy, Jo was trying to avoid answering. "Do I what?"

"Jo Marchal! Quit pussyfooting around and answer my question. Do you have plans for Thanksgiving or not?"

"No." Jo sighed.

"Okay. Why are you being so difficult about this?"

"It's my nature."

"I would very much like for you to join us at Kathleen's and I'm not taking no for an answer."

"I have one condition."

"Sorry…there will be no beer drinking on Thanksgiving."

Jo laughed. "That's not it."

"What?" Maria exhaled an audible breath.

Jo smiled to herself. "You have to come out here on Saturday and get up on a horse." The silence on the other end lingered, but she waited the long moment. "Maria, did you faint or what?"

"I must say you drive harder bargains than I do." Her voice was tight with fear or anxiety or both, Jo suspected.

"Well?"

Maria exhaled again. "Okay, but you have to promise me if this kills me, you'll raise my son."

Jo wanted to laugh. "Maria, you're not going to die, but yes, I would be honored to be Matt's guardian if you can get that past your family."

* * *

Nervously, Jo sat in her truck out on the street watching the house in suburbia. With the curtains wide open, she could see the big screen TV displaying a football game. She saw Maria pass in front of the window. A moment later Maria came through the door pulling a jacket over her shoulders as she headed down the driveway. *Busted…*

Maria walked to the driver's door, holding the jacket tight around her. Jo eased the window down.

"Hi!" Maria smiled at her.

"Hi yourself."

"I have to say I'm surprised you showed up."

Jo raised a brow. "Are you kidding? And let you out of your end of this bargain? I just bet you were hoping I wouldn't show."

Maria put her hand on the arm Jo had resting in the open window. "No, I wasn't. Come on, dinner will be ready soon."

Jo took a deep breath and grabbed the bottle of wine she brought for Kathleen. Maria introduced her to Jack and to Kathleen's husband, Tim, but both were too engrossed in the football game to give her much attention. Maria led her to the kitchen, where she handed the wine to Kathleen.

"Thank you for having me to dinner today. It's very thoughtful."

Kathleen gave Maria a quizzical look as she accepted the wine. "You're welcome, but this was not necessary." She raised the bottle and looked at the label. "It's a wonderful wine. Thank you so much."

Knowing nothing herself about wine, Jo had taken a chance that the type of wine Maria had put in the welcome basket was a kind that Kathleen might enjoy. Jo absentmindedly ran her hand through her hair. She noted that both Maria and Kathleen were dressed in skirts today. Looking down at her khaki pants, plaid shirt and loafers, she felt underdressed for the occasion.

"It smells great in here," she said, hoping her nervousness couldn't be detected in her voice.

Kathleen opened the oven. "We'll be ready to eat in fifteen to twenty minutes."

"Can I help with anything?"

Maria gave Jo an "I can't believe you asked" kind of look. Kathleen replied, "Nope, everything's about ready."

"Where are all the boys?"

"Jack brought them a football. They're out in the backyard."

Jo stepped over to the back door and looked out, then back at Maria. "Would it be all right," she tipped her head at the door, "if I hang out with these guys until dinner?"

After Jo had gone out, Maria went over to the door. Jo was sitting on the deck steps next to Matt and talking to an animated Ryan, Kathleen's youngest, who was parked on Jo's knee.

When they came inside for dinner, Jo asked if she could be seated at the kids' table. There wasn't one, but Maria seated Jo between herself and Ryan, who hadn't let go of Jo's hand since they had come in for dinner. Maria didn't miss how Jo helped Ryan fill his plate and tuck his napkin in securely over his shirt. Maria wondered if Jo had ever considered having kids. She'd add that to her list of things to find out about her.

After dinner, Jo helped clear the table, then asked for the bathroom. Entering it, Jo heard raised voices down the hall. She didn't want to eavesdrop, but she couldn't help it.

"I don't know what you could have been thinking." She recognized Jack's voice and he sounded angry.

"I don't know what's wrong with you. She's my friend and her father just passed away a few weeks ago," Maria replied.

"Maria, get a clue. She's a dyke, for crying out loud!"

"And that's a problem why? You're homophobic?"

"No. It's a problem because you're exposing her to our kids."

"And since when did you become concerned for your son's well-being?"

"Well, you're exposing Kathleen and Tim's kids."

"Well then, you should be having this conversation with your sister."

"I suppose you've brainwashed my sister about her too!"

Jo knew she shouldn't be listening to their exchange, but she couldn't make herself close the door all the way and kept her ear pressed to the small crack. If Maria was in trouble, she was ready to move mountains to help her.

"For your information, your son likes her."

"Well now, that's a shocker. He couldn't possibly even know *it's* a she."

"God, Jackson, you're an ass!"

"Where do you think you're going?"

"Away from you. Let go!"

Jo had her hand on the doorknob ready to storm the hall, but she heard heels clicking across the floor and gently eased the door shut. She waited until she heard the second set of footsteps before she dared leave the bathroom. When she did, she went straight to the kitchen where Maria and Kathleen were huddled close at the counter talking quietly.

"Well, ladies," Jo interrupted. "I hate to eat and run, but I need to head down the road."

Kathleen spun around. "But we haven't had Maria's wonderful dessert yet." Maria also turned around, visibly upset.

Jo patted her stomach. "I couldn't possibly eat another bite. I want to thank you both for inviting me today."

Kathleen took a step closer. "You're very welcome, and I want to say how sorry I am about your father." Jo nodded. "Stop over anytime. The boys still haven't stopped talking about the trip to your farm."

Jo tipped her head and smiled. What a wonderful woman Kathleen was. How could she be related to Maria's husband?

"We'll do it again when the weather's nice."

"I'll walk you out." Maria stepped beside her.

Maria got their jackets from down the hall and Jo mumbled a "nice to meet you" as she passed to the front door. Tim waved a hand over his head, thoroughly absorbed in the game, while Maria's husband, "the ass," didn't bother to acknowledge her at all.

Outside, Maria leaned against the inside of the open truck door. "I'm glad you came today, as uncomfortable as it probably was for you."

Jo cocked her head and studied Maria for a long minute. "I've been through worse family gatherings." She noted that Maria no longer wore the happy expression she'd had when she arrived. "You okay?"

Maria raised her eyes slowly to meet Jo's. "Please tell me you didn't hear us."

Jo bit the inside of her cheek. "I heard raised voices. Are you sure you're okay?"

Maria's smile was forced. "Of course, we argue like that all the time. You know how men are, they're always right and we're always wrong." She shrugged and wrapped her arms around herself.

If Jo couldn't read Maria's face as well as she did, she might be convinced it wasn't a big deal, but she wasn't fooling Jo. "It's cold, you should get back inside."

Maria remained planted against the truck door. Jo really didn't want to make her go.

"What time should we come out Saturday?" She must have looked puzzled. Maria reminded her. "For my first riding lesson or whatever you're calling it."

Jo couldn't stop a little smile from curling her lips. "I wasn't going to hold your feet to the fire on that. I just wanted to know that at some point I might convince you to give it a try."

"A deal's a deal. I'm not backing out."

"In that case, come whenever you want. I'm never more than a radio call away."

Maria placed her hand on Jo's. "We'll see you Saturday." She smiled a smile that chased the chill from the November air. "I'll bring you a piece of pie if they don't devour it all today."

"That'd be right nice, ma'am, thanks." She turned the key and started the truck. "See you Saturday."

Maria stepped back so she could close the door. As Jo drove away, she watched her walk slowly to the curb. God, she wanted to scoop Maria and Matt up and take them away from that bastard they lived with. No one, especially those two, should be subjected to the selfish, uncaring behavior of someone like him. They deserved to be treated with love and kindness and respect. Jo typically didn't hate people she didn't know, but at that moment she hated Jack West.

Maria passed through the living room without so much as a glance at her husband and found Kathleen in the kitchen pouring two cups of coffee.

She placed a cup in Maria's hand. "Come on."

Maria followed to the laundry room. "What's up?"

Kathleen eyed her suspiciously. "That's what I was going to ask you."

Maria sat the cup down and crossed her arms over her chest. "Jack is just being Jack."

Kathleen rubbed a hand across Maria's back. "I'm sorry, sweetie. And today is supposed to be a day of thanksgiving."

Maria gave a little smile. "I'll always be thankful for Matt." As quickly as she'd given way to the smile tears crowded her eyes. "And you."

"If there's anything I can do?"

She couldn't stand the thought of Jack being around for the next three days. "Can Matt hang with you guys tomorrow for a while? I want to try to catch some sales."

"Sure, hon, I was going to run out for a few things, but he can hang with Tim and the boys."

"Thanks. Do you think we could trade spouses?" She pursed her lips. "Oh, I guess not. How did you get so lucky?"

Kathleen laughed. "It's not luck, honey. You can't imagine how many guys I went through to find him."

Maria thought back to how hard and fast she'd fallen in love with the charming Jackson West. The wedding, pregnancy and Matt had all happened so quickly. Too quickly. Every day she regretted having let the wedding part happen so fast. She also knew if it hadn't happened, she wouldn't have her son. The son she would give everything for. She'd never seen the handicap, as Jack did. She only ever saw that precious little boy they had placed in her arms.

"As angered as I can get at Jack sometimes, I'm forever grateful he gave me Matt. No offense, Kat, I know he's your brother, but—" She shrugged.

"None taken. Believe me, sometimes I wonder if our parents didn't turn over a rock and find him." She laughed, which prompted a chuckle from Maria.

* * *

Maria dropped Matt off early, flying past every store on her way out of town. She knocked and waited. She tried the knob. It wasn't locked so she entered the house.

"Jo, are you here?" She checked the kitchen and called down the hall, "Jo?"

Jo had to be home. Her truck was in the drive backed up to the barn. The thought of entering the barn alone terrified her, but she walked out anyway. As she rounded the corner of the house, Jake came running and nearly knocked her over. She knelt and rubbed his head.

"Hey, buddy, where's your master?" The dog tipped his head to the side. "Where's Jo?" She stood. "Let's go find Jo." When he raced to the barn, she swallowed and muttered, "Great."

She saw Jake run through the barn and out to the pasture. But before she could reach the door he disappeared from sight. She stopped next to Jo's truck and called out again. "Jo, are you in there?" She waited, then finally inched her way inside the big barn opening. She heard the sound of heavy horse hooves and when she looked to the opposite barn doors they were suddenly filled with Jo atop her big black stallion.

Maria gasped and froze. The horse bellowed puffs of steam like a dragon breathing fire. But it was the sight of Jo that caused her breath to catch. She looked shocked at first. Then a smile spread across her face and made her eyes sparkle. Jo quickly climbed down and tied the horse's reins so he couldn't wander. She pulled off suede gloves and tucked them in her pocket as she approached.

"I wasn't expecting you until tomorrow." Her cheeks were rosy red and her words were accompanied by visible puffs of breath. Maria shivered. "Come on, there's heat in the tack room."

She realized the shiver hadn't been caused by the cold, but by the sight of Jo. Maria followed Jo like a pup after its mother. She was aware of the cold only after stepping into the warmth of the tack room.

"I'll be right back, I need to unsaddle Cobalt and brush him. Unless..." Jo grinned devilishly. "You want to take a ride on him." Maria adamantly shook her head. "Be right back."

Out in the barn Jo dropped the saddle on a bale of hay and walked the horse to his stall. It startled her to hear Maria's voice behind her.

"Can I help?" she asked timidly.

Jo looked around to see Maria standing in the opening to the stall with her arms wrapped around herself.

Jo cocked her head. "He's a far cry from Daisy Mae. You sure you want to get that close?" Maria gave a barely discernable nod and took a tentative step into the stall. "He's pretty docile when he's being brushed after a good run."

She slipped the brush off her hand and gave it to Maria. Once Maria moved next to her, Jo took Maria's hand with the brush and raised it against Cobalt's coat. She caught a whiff of Maria's perfume and had to rein in her desire to lean a bit closer.

"Brush from the top of his back down toward his belly."

Jo moved around to hold his bridle while Maria brushed. Maria looked over at the precise moment that Jo looked lustfully at her. Jo quickly avoided Maria's eyes, looking up at the horses.

Perhaps thinking she might scare the horse, Maria said softly, "My heart is pounding so hard right now."

Jo's heart was beating hard too, but for an entirely different reason. "I can imagine." After a few minutes Cobalt snorted and took a step. Maria jumped back and raised her hand to her chest. Jo patted his neck. "Whoa, boy, it's okay." Maria looked paralyzed with fear. "It's okay. He was letting you know how good it feels." Maria nodded but stood motionless. Jo gently removed the brush from her hand. "Why don't you wait in the tack room? I'll be right in to make some coffee."

Jo removed Cobalt's bridle and hung a feedbag of oats on the stall gate. She found Maria making the coffee when she returned to the tack room.

"Well, I'm impressed." Jo glanced over Maria's shoulder before leaning on the desk.

"With my coffee-making skills?"

Jo chuckled. "No, you just stood next to and brushed my biggest horse without fainting, and it looks like your pants are still dry."

Maria laughed. "That's very funny, Jo." The coffee began to drip.

"You never did say why you were here today instead of tomorrow. And where's Matt?"

"Matt's with his cousins and I wanted to get it over with."

Jo studied her face for a moment. "And…"

"And what?"

Jo stepped in front of Maria. "And I sense something else." Jo watched her eyes. "What's wrong?"

Maria looked at the floor between them. "Jack's home, and after his nasty mood yesterday I didn't feel like spending the day with him."

"So it would be more torturous to spend the day with your husband than face your fear of sitting on a horse?" Jo was pleased, and when Maria only shrugged, Jo again got a sense there was something more.

"I've mustered all the courage I have. Like I said, I want to do this and have it over."

The truth was that Maria wanted to spend the day in Jo's company. She didn't particularly care what they did. She was furious with Jack for saying the things he had about Jo yesterday, and after she'd gotten Matt to bed last night they'd fought about it. Jack had ended the argument by demanding Maria never allow that "freak of nature" to come around again. Maria called him a prick loud enough for him to hear, then sought shelter in Matt's room. No matter how mad he got, she knew he'd never come after her in there. He hadn't set foot in Matt's room since they received the diagnosis.

"Maria…" Jo stood holding a cup of coffee out to her. Maria wrapped both hands around the warmth. "I meant what I said yesterday. You don't really have to do this today. Or any day for that matter."

Maria lowered the cup from her lips. "No, I want to." She sipped again. "I want to be bigger than my fears."

"That's a good philosophy. So what other fears do you have?"

She stared off. "I'm not sure exactly, but I intend to figure them out and face them."

"Well, okay. If you need any help, you let me know."

"Let me finish this coffee and go to the bathroom so I don't accidently wet myself, and we're going to do this."

Jo laughed. "My saddle and horse thank you."

Ten minutes later, Maria placed her empty cup down.

"If you don't want to walk to the house, there's a bathroom back there." Jo pointed to a door in the corner. "But I have to warn you, it's only a slight step up from those portable things you see at the construction sites."

Maria opened the door and peered in. "I've seen worse in homes where people actually live." She slipped inside.

Jo left the tack room with a bridle for Daisy Mae. She was waiting with the horse out in the barn when Maria came out, but then stopped and leaned against the doorframe.

"Are you ready?"

Maria nodded a "yes" so Jo walked Daisy Mae next to the hay bales. "It'll be easier to mount her from here." Jo patted the top bale. Holding the bridle with one hand, she raised the other to help Maria up and onto the saddle. Maria's hand trembled and when Jo tried to release it, Maria squeezed tighter. Jo pulled harder, but she refused to let go.

"What's wrong?"

"Aren't you going to get up here with me like you did with Matt?"

Jo chuckled. "No offense, Maria, but you're a little bigger than Matt. You and I won't fit in that saddle together."

Maria's grip tightened around Jo's hand. "Well, don't you have a bigger saddle?" Jo shook her head. "I can't do this by myself. I thought you would be sitting here with me." She panicked. "Please…get me down."

"I have an idea." Jo tried again to pull her hand free.

"Please, Jo, get me down." She was on the verge of tears. Jo quickly helped her off the horse.

"I'm not sure you're ready for this."

Maria was standing beside Jo, holding her hand like a schoolgirl. She liked the feeling—more, she knew, than she should. Reluctantly, she let go, even though she was still trembling.

"No. You said you had an idea?"

"Yep." Jo hopped down and walked Daisy Mae a few feet away. Unbuckling the saddle, pulling it off and setting it aside, she walked the horse back to the stacked bales and climbed up. "Now I can sit with you."

Maria worried at her lip. "But…but, there's nothing to hold on to now."

Jo flashed a charming smile. "That's what I'm there for. Hop back on."

"Hop?"

Jo was starting to feel uneasy about the whole adventure. What if Maria fell off and got hurt? Who would take care of Matt?

"I think maybe we should put this off for another time."

Maria's expression softened. "I really want to do this. I want to face this fear and get past it."

Jo relented and helped Maria back on before throwing her leg over and sitting behind her. Maria instantly grabbed hold of Jo's arm when she leaned forward to pick up the reins from Daisy Mae's neck, and Jo inhaled the fresh scent of Maria's hair and her perfume. For the briefest moment, her breasts pressed into Maria's shoulders, making her feel a tiny bit lightheaded. Maria quickly grabbed her other arm when Jo reached around her. Maria had a death grip on both arms now.

"Relax, Maria."

"I...I can't...I feel like I'm going to fall off." Daisy Mae shifted under their weight, and while Jo didn't think it possible, Maria's grip got even tighter. "Sorry," she said, but she didn't loosen her grip.

Against her better judgment, Jo inched closer until her thighs touched Maria's backside. Maria leaned back and finally relaxed her grip on Jo's arms a bit. Jo's heart raced—pounded so hard she was sure Maria could feel it.

She leaned over Maria's shoulder. "You okay?" Maria's head bobbed. "All right, I want you to take the reins from my hands."

"I'm afraid...I'm going to fall." Maria's breaths came rapidly.

"Maria, stop breathing so hard. Relax. I've got you. You're not going anywhere."

Maria eased her hands down Jo's arms as Jo pulled them back, then gulped and took the leather straps. Her hands were cold and still trembling, so Jo placed her hands over Maria's and she pressed more firmly back against Jo.

It was Jo's turn to gulp. "You're doing fine. Steering a horse is like driving a car." Maria relaxed a little more against her.

"That's funny. I'm sure I never felt like I could fall out of my car."

Jo suppressed a laugh. "Okay, if you want her to go to the right, give the rein a gentle pull like this." She pulled lightly on Maria's right hand until Daisy Mae moved her head to the right. The horse shifted but didn't go anywhere. "If you want her to stop, pull back on both reins together and say 'whoa.' If you want her to back up—"

"Unless you're going to make me parallel park her, I don't see any need to go backwards."

Jo couldn't contain a chuckle. "Okay, you ready for a little stroll?" When Maria tried to turn and look at her, she slipped to one side. Jo tightened her arms under Maria's and righted her. "I've got you and I promise I won't let you fall."

"Oh, God…" Maria whispered.

"All right now, it's kind of like riding a bike. You've got to balance yourself side to side. If you were sitting in a saddle it would be easier, I can assure you. You ready?" Maria remained perfectly still, giving only a slight nod. Jo pushed her hands forward. "All right, just relax the reins, give her a soft heel and make a click sound. Come on, girl, let's go."

Daisy walked slowly toward the barn doors with Maria pressed as hard as she could be against Jo. The feel of Maria between her thighs was almost more than Jo could stand. She closed her eyes and tried to imagine Matt or one of Kathleen's boys sitting there, but Maria's scent made that impossible. She hoped she was only up for a short ride.

The movement of Maria between her legs with each step Daisy Mae took was pure agony. Jo could feel herself growing wet. She hoped Maria couldn't. She tried reminding herself that Maria was her friend, but dear lord, she couldn't deny the powerful attraction she felt for her. This was a slow kind of torture. When she could endure no more, Jo had Maria walk Daisy Mae back to the barn. Once the horse was back in her stall, they returned to the tack room for another cup of coffee to warm themselves. Not that Jo needed any additional warming. She was thankful when Maria left after her coffee. She was having a hard time looking Maria in the eyes after their little close encounter.

"Can I expect to see you back tomorrow with Matt?"

"I'm not sure. I'll let you know."

Maria hadn't wanted to leave. A part of her wanted to spend the entire day with Jo, but after feeling what she'd felt sitting so close to Jo on the horse, she was afraid. Her breathing had been rapid the entire ride and it wasn't from fear or anxiety. It was the feel of

Jo's strong thighs pressed against her and Jo's arms beneath hers alternately touching her sides each time the horse stepped. The more steps the horse took, the more comfortable she felt leaning back in Jo's arms. Her heart had pounded so fiercely that at one point she thought she might faint. But…the ache she felt between her own thighs as her backside rubbed against Jo's muscled legs scared the hell out of her. Remembering that sensation now as she headed down the road brought back the same ache.

"Get a grip," she chided herself. "Jo Marchal is your friend, and…and you're a married woman with a child. Getting involved with her would be insane, irresponsible, and not to mention ruin our friendship. And now I've resorted to talking to myself. I am insane."

CHAPTER THIRTEEN

Maria stayed away on Saturday. And for weeks afterward, as a matter of fact, not even calling to chat or check how "her friend" was coping with her father's death. She knew it was cowardly on her part, but before she saw her again she needed to be sure the unexpected physical attraction she had felt for Jo wouldn't lead her to do or say something to ruin their friendship. If Jo needed to talk to her, she surely would call.

Jo had not seen or talked to Maria in weeks, and the exchange she'd overheard between Maria and her husband on Thanksgiving Day kept niggling at her. Had Maria capitulated to his ultimatum? Surely not, but…

She could call her. After all they were friends, and friends checked in on each other from time to time, didn't they? Then again, taking a break was a better idea. She was having difficulty getting out of her head the overpowering physical attraction she'd felt when they'd taken their ride. She was feeling things she shouldn't for the very straight, married Maria West. Maria was her friend and there couldn't be anything more than friendship between them.

* * *

With Christmas arriving on a Wednesday, Jo arranged for Tucker to work through Christmas Eve and take off until after New Year's. She'd run the farm by herself. Doing so would be a welcome distraction after spending a couple of days with her mom remembering Christmases past. She waited until the Sunday before Christmas to call Maria.

"Jo, hi! I've been meaning to call you. Things have been a little hectic."

"Oh, uh, I figured you were really busy with family and the holidays and all." Jo felt strangely uncomfortable.

"So, is everything okay with you?" Maria sounded distracted.

"Sure, yeah, fine as frog's hair."

"What?"

Oh God, I sound adolescent. That was more like something Tucker would say. "Never mind. So how've you been?"

"You know, busy with the holidays coming, shopping and trying to get prepared."

It was as if they were practically two strangers again. Before Jo could stop herself, she said, "I miss you guys." She lowered her voice. "Miss seeing you." Well, she said it and there was no taking it back.

Maria seemed less distracted when she replied. "We miss you too, Jo." She sighed.

"Is everything all right?"

"Yes. I've been running around a lot and it's been so chilly I didn't think Matt should be riding."

"You could bring him out to visit with Jake in the house. I do have heat, you know."

Maria laughed. "Of course you do, but I don't want to invade your home."

"You wouldn't, and besides, Jake hasn't had a good kiss in a while."

Maria laughed again. "Yes, well, I suppose the same could be said for Matt."

Jo smiled. She liked it when Maria sounded happy. "What are you two doing on Saturday?"

"Nothing I'm aware of at the moment."

"Why don't you come out to the farm to see Jake? We can have cookies and milk or pop popcorn in the fireplace."

"Mmm, sounds inviting. Can I let you know later in the week?"

"Sure, sure. So…uh, I'll talk to you later in the week."

"I'll definitely give you a call."

Jo didn't want to end their conversation. She missed Maria more than she wanted to admit.

"Have a Merry Christmas, Maria."

"You too, Jo. I'll talk to you soon."

* * *

Jo arrived at her mom's in the afternoon on Christmas Eve.

"Where's the tree, Mom?"

"Your dad always took care of that."

Jo pushed up her shirt sleeves. "Guess that'll be my job now."

"You don't—"

"Mom, we can't have Christmas without a tree." She headed out to the garage to get the boxes of ornaments and the artificial tree.

They drank homemade eggnog and opened their presents that evening. Under pressure from her mom, she agreed to attend church with her on Christmas Day.

Her mom had a wealth of friends at the church and she seemed to be coping with her loss better than Jo would have guessed.

After the service, Eileen caught Jo's arm. "Let's wait right here. There's someone I want to talk to."

That someone was Maxine. She'd been singing in the choir during the service. She extended a soft hand to Jo.

"Of course dear, I remember you when you were a youngster."

Before I became an abomination, Jo thought, but said, "It's very nice to see you again."

"It's a shame you had to miss your parents' fiftieth anniversary celebration last year. Your father said you had to be away on business."

As her mother shifted uneasily beside her, Jo forced a smile. She'd not been invited and had wondered what they'd done to celebrate their milestone. They didn't talk about the exchange when they got home. Of course.

She couldn't escape fast enough back to the solitude of the farm. That she was alone at Christmas didn't matter. She busied herself wrapping the present she bought for Kate. She had been disappointed that Jo couldn't spend Christmas Eve or Christmas Day with her but had settled for her promise that they'd spend some time together on Friday evening.

Not knowing her well enough to come up with something that screamed Kate, she'd bought the deputy a jacket. The local leather store in Midland had marked every item in the store down sixty percent, so Jo got one heck of a bargain on the suede bomber jacket.

Maria and Matt's gifts were a different story. When she'd given a moment of thought, she knew immediately what she wanted to give each of them. She found herself hoping they would come by on Saturday. She really missed them—missed Maria.

* * *

Kate arrived after her shift on Friday, dropping her coat over the end of the couch. They toasted the holiday with a beer and Jo set up an informal dinner of baked ham and side dishes on the island. Kate seemed particularly antsy.

"I got you a Christmas present," Kate said as soon as they finished eating.

Jo wiped her mouth. "I happen to have something for you too." She stood. "Let me clean up here and we'll sit in the living room."

Kate excused herself to go to the bathroom. When Jo finished in the kitchen, she found her lighting a fire in the fireplace.

"I hope you don't mind." She stood, dusting off her hands.

Actually, she did mind—it felt presumptuous to have Kate acting as if she was a member of the household. But in the spirit of the holiday and her innate inclination to not make waves, Jo decided to let it slide. "You want something to drink?"

"Whatever you're having is fine."

She returned with two more beers. Handing her a bottle, she disappeared down the hall, returning a few minutes later with Kate's present. She took a seat on the couch, after placing the gift in Kate's lap.

"I hope you like it."

"You picked it, I'm sure I will." Kate tore into the package and pulled out the suede bomber jacket.

"I thought it matched your eyes."

Kate smiled. "It's great, thanks." She stood and slipped it on. "Wow! This feels so comfortable."

"I'm glad you like it. It looks nice on you."

Kate ran her hands over the subtle suede before taking it off. Laying it on the end of the couch, she reached into the pocket of her pea coat and pulled out a small gift box. Jo swallowed when Kate put it in her hand.

Apparently her apprehension didn't escape Kate's notice. She sat beside Jo and patted her leg. "Relax, it's not an engagement ring."

Jo removed the wrapping from the little square package. Tentatively she opened the velvet box and found inside a gold band with a pale blue stone flanked by tiny diamonds.

"It's a pinky ring. The color of stone kind of matches your eyes." She winked. "I thought you could wear it when we go out. I guessed at the size. If it doesn't fit, we can get it sized." Jo simply stared at the box. "Go ahead, try it on."

Jo slipped it on the little finger of her right hand. It fit perfectly. She couldn't decide if it was good the ring fit so she wouldn't have to venture into a jewelry store with Kate or if she should be scared that Kate had so accurately guessed the size. Stunned and speechless, she sat several long minutes until Kate squirmed on the couch.

"Uh, it's beautiful, thank you, but you really shouldn't have."

"I couldn't help it. It reminded me of you." Jo cocked her head and gazed at Kate. "Simple, but so beautiful." She reached over and stroked her fingers along Jo's jaw.

Jo stiffened. "Oh gosh, you're gonna make me blush." She drained her beer and popped up. She needed a break, time to get her bearings. "You want another beer?" she asked, even though it would be Kate's third of the evening, which might pose problems later.

"I don't know, do I?" Kate said, giving her a smile. "I think I can handle one more."

Taking refuge in the kitchen, Jo tried to shake the anxiety choking her. She couldn't breathe. Gulping deep breaths, she fought the unwelcome feeling sweeping over her.

What is wrong with me? It wasn't as if Kate were the first woman to come along since Claire had dumped her. There was Callie, of course. Who hadn't made her feel the way she was feeling now.

God, what if Kate drinks too much and says she can't drive? Well, then, she would handle it. She'd just put her in the guest room.

She took another deep breath and returned to the living room. She and Kate sat on the couch talking for a while longer. She finished her beer and was relieved when Kate took only a few drinks of hers before abandoning it. Jo didn't want to be rude and ask her to leave, but she was ready to go to bed—alone.

She pretended to stifle a yawn. "Sorry, I've been working double time with Tucker off."

"You shouldn't have given him so much time off."

"He works really hard. He earned it."

Kate leaned closer. "Seems to me that you work really hard too, but hardly take any time off for yourself." Jo didn't respond. "Well, you should." Without warning, Kate leaned in and kissed her. Not a peck, but a full-on-the-lips kiss.

It took Jo only seconds to gather her wits and pull away as Kate shifted to wrap Jo in her arms. She didn't look at Kate but jumped up from the couch.

Jo touched her mouth briefly. "I—I can't do this, Kate."

Kate stood too. "I can't help it. I want you so bad." She paused. "But I don't want to push you." She stepped to where her coat was. "I'll go before I do something I shouldn't."

"I'm sorry, Kate."

Kate gave a shrug and pulled her coat on. "Hey, nothing worthwhile comes easy." She picked up the new jacket. "Thanks for the gift."

Jo examined the ring on her finger. "I don't wear jewelry as a rule." She looked up. "But…thank you."

Kate nodded with a smile, said goodnight and headed out. Jo couldn't get the ring off fast enough. Claire had bought them matching gold bands for their ring fingers and called them commitment rings. As far as Jo was concerned, a little piece of gold didn't signify anything except that someone wasted their money buying it.

She stared at the ring sitting in the palm of her hand. She would wear it, as creepy as it had felt on her finger, but only once, the next time they went to dinner. Kate was, after all, a decent person.

After that it would find its way to the bottom of a drawer and she'd forget about it.

Jo tossed another log on the fire and stretched out on the couch to watch the flames dance. She woke chilled around three in the morning and stumbled to bed.

She was up the next day at her usual time of five o'clock, eager to get a jump on the day. Maria had left a message while she was working in the barn yesterday that she and Matt would be out later in the afternoon, and if that didn't work with Jo's schedule she should call Maria back. Otherwise, they'd see her tomorrow.

Armed with a caffeine boost, Jo worked feverishly to get done all the chores that she typically shared with Tucker or with him and Kirby. She made her way back to the house around one, cold and tired, but too excited to think about anything but seeing Maria. It had been over three weeks, during which time she had relived their riding adventure in her mind over and over, and over.

She had a fire going and was seated on the hearth attempting to warm her cold, tired bones when she heard the car drive up, then the sound of feet on the porch, followed by a knock on the door. She hollered for them to come on in. She jumped to her feet when the door opened and she saw Maria struggling with bags and a wrapped gift box.

"You should have yelled for me to open the door." She reached to take something. "Here."

Maria placed several things in Jo's hands. "I brought us some dinner, unless you already have plans."

Jo gave a wide smile. "The only plans I made were to spend some time with you two."

She whistled for Jake. He raced from the back of the house, wagging his whole body at the sight of Matt, who dropped to his knees on the doormat and allowed Jake to eagerly lick his face. Maria's face lit up with a smile.

"I told you. Jake's been pining for someone to kiss."

"Well, let's not camp at the door."

Maria helped Matt off with his coat while Jo carried things to the kitchen. When she returned, Maria had Matt settled on the large rug in front of the fireplace and stood watching him with Jake. *A perfect holiday picture.* Maria wore a long skirt that nearly reached her ankles and a very festive green and red sweater. Her hair was pulled back loosely, showing her neck and a hint of her shoulders. The firelight danced in her eyes. Jo leaned in the doorway, the sight too heartwarming not to watch.

Maria finally looked over. "What?"

Jo shoved her hands in her pockets, which seemed to be her new nervous habit. "I'm glad you're here." She motioned to the guys on the floor. "Probably not as much as those two, though. Can I get you something to drink?"

"Something hot would be nice."

"I have some spiced tea my mom made I can heat up."

"That sounds wonderful."

"How about for Matt?"

"He's fine until we eat."

Jo came back in to find Maria seated on the hearth near Matt. She sat on the end of the coffee table a few feet away. They talked about their Christmas days and Maria spoke quite animatedly about all of Kathleen's boys but was somewhat solemn when she looked at Matt. Jo's heart ached for Maria dealing with Matt's disability on her own. Jo tuned in a radio station that still played Christmas music and Maria moved to sit on the couch. As Jo tossed another log on the fire a knock sounded at the door. Jake jumped up and barked.

Jo patted his head. "Easy there, killer." She spied Kate through the tiny window in the door and hurriedly stepped out on the porch, pulling the door closed behind her.

"You got company."

"I do." Jo wrapped her arms around herself against the cold.

Kate shoved her hands in her coat pockets. "There's a New Year's party at Whispers, and, well, I thought I'd ask you to go with me."

"You could have called."

Kate shrugged a shoulder. "I was out this way so I just stopped."

"I'm not sure what my plans are yet. I'll call you tomorrow evening."

Kate bobbed her head. "Sure…okay." Jo reached for the doorknob. "Have a good evening, Jo. I'll talk to you tomorrow."

Jo didn't want to think about New Year's Eve or Kate Tyler. She rushed back into the house to her company who warmed her inside more deeply than any fire or hot tea ever could.

After an early dinner, they retreated to the cozy warmth of the living room where once again Jo added more wood to the fire and stoked the flames.

"I have a gift for Matt. I hope you don't mind."

"Of course not."

Jo made her way down the hall to the bedroom, pleased that the surprise hadn't been spoiled. She carefully carried the large cardboard box, flaps closed loosely, out to the living room. Maria watched as she placed the box close to Matt.

"You might want to help him with this."

Maria went to the box, eyeing Jo suspiciously. "Matt honey, do you want to help Mommy open your gift from Jo?" He stared blankly at her. She took his hand and pulled him up beside her before she knelt in front of the box. "Let's see what surprise Jo has for you." She gingerly lifted the box flaps and peered inside. "Oh, my…" She gazed up at Jo. "What a thoughtful gesture, but we can't possibly—"

Jo raised a hand. "I know you don't have time to care for a pet." She stepped back over to the box. "That's the beauty of this one." She reached in and pulled out the ball of fur. "He can keep her here at the farm." Jo squatted next to Matt while Jake sniffed the furry face and licked it. "Jake and I will help take care of her." Matt reached out and stroked the furry white Maltipoo puppy then pressed his face against it while Jo held her. Matt's reaction squeezed at Jo's heart. "I think he likes her." Tears formed in Maria's eyes. "I promise we'll take real good care of her for Matt."

"Here, sweetie, sit down so you can hold it…her?" Jo nodded. Maria steered Matt back down on the rug and with Jo's help placed the little fur ball into his arms. He hugged it to his chest, putting his cheek against her fur.

"I hope you're not mad. I saw a picture of her on the pound's website and I couldn't resist. I wanted to get Matt something extra special for Christmas. Since he likes Jake so much, I thought having his own pup would make him happy. She is just so loveable. She was recently surrendered when her owner passed away suddenly. She's only about three months old, so she'll only get a little bigger. She's a mix of Maltese and poodle."

Maria swiped tears from her cheeks. "How could I be mad?" She ran her hand over Matt's curly head of hair. "This is the most thoughtful gift he's ever received."

"Well, I happen to have a very special gift for you too."

Maria looked up at Jo as she stood. "Please, just tell me it's already in this house."

Jo tipped her head, then after a second or two laughed. "If I told you we had to go outside to get it, would you be mad at me?"

Maria bolted up. "Jo Marchal, no, I won't accept—"

"Relax, Maria. I'm not giving you a horse." Relief washed over Maria's face. "Be right back."

Jo disappeared again, this time returning with a wrapped gift box. While she was gone, Maria had produced the gift she'd stashed behind the couch when they'd arrived. Jo placed her box on the coffee table in front of Maria and sat beside her.

They each looked at the festive packages and said in unison, "You go…" They gazed at each other for another moment, smiling.

"Please, you go first." Jo said, and watched in amazement as Maria took her time removing the wrapping paper. "Why don't you rip it off?"

A coy smile played across Maria's lips. "The slower you go, the greater the anticipation."

Jo averted her eyes, certain her cheeks were coloring with a blush. Maria finally lifted the lid from the box and pulled back the tissue paper, but before she could say anything, Jo said, "For when you ride, because if I have anything to do with it, you will willingly ride one day." Maria pulled the riding boots and gloves from the box. "I guessed on the size. I hope they fit."

Maria kicked off her shoes and slid her feet in the boots. Standing, she walked to the middle of the room and hiked her skirt up to her knees.

"They're perfect." She met Jo's eyes. "Thank you."

"When's your birthday?" Jo smiled. "'Cause I think you'd look real cute in some riding pants."

Maria dropped her skirt and hurried back to the couch. "Your turn, open yours."

Wrapping paper flew as Jo ripped into the gift like an excited child. She opened the lid of the box, pleasantly pleased by the smell of new leather.

"Wow!" She pulled a black leather jacket from the box and stood, tossing the box aside.

"Something for you to wear when you dress up and go out. I hope you like it."

She pressed the jacket to her face and breathed. "I do. It's great."

"I tried it on and since the sleeves covered my hands I thought perhaps it would fit."

Slipping into the subtle leather, Jo pulled the lapels to her face for another sniff. It wasn't the smell of new leather that tickled her senses, but the scent of Maria's perfume. She ran her hand down the jacket front.

"It feels wonderful."

"Well, it certainly looks attractive on you." Jo raised her eyebrows. "I'm sorry. Is that not something one should say to a gay woman?"

Jo sat down. "Thank you for the jacket and the compliment." She settled back into the couch. "All dressed up and no place to go."

Maria pulled off the boots and put on her shoes. "Speaking of which, do you have big New Year's plans?"

"I'm not sure yet." It was too much, Jo knew, to hope that she could somehow ring in the New Year with this beautiful woman beside her. "You?"

Maria busied herself putting the boots back in the box. "Kat's keeping Matt so Jack and I can attend the big New Year's celebration at the Regal Hotel in the city. You know, dinner, dancing, the champagne toast and hotel room for the night. It's one of those package deals. One of the perks he gets through his job."

Jo felt all the air being sucked from the room. *God*, she told herself, *Maria's a married woman and she's going to spend New Year's with her husband. Has lust so skewed my view of reality I think Maria would chuck her family life to spend a night celebrating with me?*

"We should get going." Maria suddenly seemed uneasy.

"You don't have to," Jo responded, but her words lacked enthusiasm.

Jo held the puppy while Maria helped Matt on with his coat. "What are you going to name her?

Maria touched the ball of fur in Jo's arms. "I think…Rosie."

"Rosie, huh?"

"Yes, Rosie and Jake." She smiled. "It sounds cute together."

Jo gave the pup a rub on the head before placing her back in the box. "Rosie it is." She walked them out, holding the door for Maria after she buckled Matt in.

"Well, if I don't talk to you before, have a Happy New Year."

Maria brushed her fingers over Jo's hand on the top of the door. "You too, Jo, and thanks for today. We really enjoyed it."

Jo stood in the cold, watching until the taillights disappeared.

CHAPTER FOURTEEN

Jo only accepted Kate's New Year's Eve invitation in hopes it would provide a distraction. She was upset by the thought of Maria at a hotel with her husband. She didn't think she'd ever felt this way before, but she recognized what it was. "It" was jealousy, plain and simple. She talked Kate into meeting at Kate's place. She intended to drive her own truck to the bar so she wouldn't be stuck anywhere without a means of escape if she needed it.

She followed the directions to Kate's. It turned out she lived in a tiny cramped apartment in a complex of a dozen identical buildings. She felt suffocated just standing inside the door waiting for Kate to get her coat. She had swallowed her angst and slipped the ring from Kate on her pinky, knowing it would be the only time she'd ever do it. She was wearing her signature worn blue jeans, the simple blue V-neck sweater her mom gave her for Christmas and her favorite gift, the leather jacket from Maria. It still carried the faint smell of Maria's perfume. When she'd put it on earlier, she'd thought of Maria and wondered where she was. She shook the thought from her head. She was determined to forget about Maria any way she could, if just for the night. Only after they stepped out into the parking lot did she let Kate know her plan.

"What if you happen to drink too much?"

"I'll worry about that if it happens," Jo replied.

Kate didn't seem pleased, but she gave Jo another thorough once-over, jingled her keys and said, "Okay, follow me."

"I've never seen this place so packed," Kate commented when they claimed the only open stool at the bar.

Kate was buying and ordered a beer for herself, but Jo, wanting a quicker way to a buzz and forgetting about Maria, ordered Kentucky bourbon neat. It did the trick. By the time she finished the drink and Kate asked her to dance, it sounded like the best thing going. Something about Kate seemed more appealing than usual this evening, and Jo wasn't unhappy about being with her. She chased the bourbon with two beers rather quickly and felt the happiest she remembered in quite some time.

Shortly after the second beer she made her way to the crowded restroom. Unbeknownst to Jo, Kate followed. The second Jo opened the stall door to exit Kate flashed her badge and stepped in front of two other girls.

"Official business, ladies." She pushed into the stall, blocking Jo and closed the door behind her.

"Is there a problem, officer?"

Kate took hold of Jo's jacket lapels. "There should be a law against looking as hot as you do." When Jo only smiled, Kate whispered, "You can't believe how hot you make me."

Jo touched her lips to Kate's ear. "Really?"

Kate took Jo's hand and slid it slowly between her legs. "Really."

She could feel Kate's heat and she had had enough to drink that it stirred her own desire. Jo stroked her as her lips pressed firmly to Kate's. Kate grabbed onto Jo's hips, shoved her tongue in Jo's mouth and rode her hand. A moan escaped Jo's throat before she could stop it. She pulled back.

"Not here."

Kate rocked against Jo's hand. "My place isn't far."

Jo pulled her hand from between Kate's legs. "You got something to drink there?"

"We'll pick up something. Let's go."

It was obvious to Jo that she was in no shape to drive—or to do what she was probably going to do with Kate. But dammit, she was tired of always being sensible and responsible. What could it hurt? She'd deal with, well, whatever…tomorrow.

Kate assured her that her truck would be safe and she'd bring Jo back for it. On the way back to her place, she bought beer at a convenience store and Jo opened and drank one. They stumbled through the door a few minutes after eleven o'clock and Kate pinned Jo to the door the second it was closed.

"Whoa." Jo held up a hand and backed Kate up. She raised the beer in her other hand. "Buy a girl a drink before you try an' bed her."

Kate took a step back. "Sorry. I've just been waiting so long to touch you. Let's sit down." She motioned to the couch.

When midnight rolled around, something made evident by the noise and commotion outside, Jo raised her bottle. "Happy New Year."

Kate repeated the wish and after they both sipped some beer, Jo leaned over and kissed her. Jo was feeling like she could go through with it. Besides, she reminded herself, the woman she'd been lusting after for the last eight months was sharing a romantic night at a hotel in the city with her husband. Maybe sleeping with another woman was the best way to get over her infatuation. At least that's what the alcohol was telling her.

Kate's response to Jo's kiss was to take both their bottles and place them on the table, then straddle Jo's lap. And when the confines of the couch became impossible, she stood and took Jo's hand.

"Let's do this right."

Jo swayed a bit as she stood and quickly slipped her arm around Kate's shoulder to cover her state of inebriation, allowing Kate to lead her to the bedroom. Jo eagerly tugged at Kate's clothes until she was naked, dropping her own in a pile beside the bed. She lowered Kate to the bed and straddled her body. Their bodies rocked in a rhythm. Jo closed her eyes and let a fantasy she knew she shouldn't be having play through her mind.

* * *

"Hello."

Maria was completely thrown by the unfamiliar voice answering the phone and glanced at her screen to confirm Jo's name.

"Hello…" The voice said again.

"I'm calling for Jo." Maria responded.

The mystery voice said, "Sure, hold on." Then Maria clearly heard, "Baby, you've got a call."

Maria's stomach lurched.

"Jo baby, wake up."

Maria wanted to hang up, but it was too late. Jo would know she called. *Oh God, Jo's in bed with a woman, and I'm…I'm upset about it.* By the time she convinced herself to hang up and call later, when she felt more together, it was too late.

"Yeah, hello." Jo's voice came groggily through the phone.

Maria took a breath and closed her eyes. "Jo, hi!" She forced happiness into her voice that she didn't feel. "I'm sorry for waking you. You obviously had a great night celebrating." She winced, knowing she sounded like she was checking up on her.

"It was—"

"Listen, I called to wish you Happy New Year. I won't keep you. You're out and enjoying yourself…I'm glad to hear it. Go back to bed. I'll talk to you again soon." She hung up before Jo could utter another word and turned her phone off so Jo couldn't call her back.

So, Jo was in bed with a woman she spent the night with. *Why on earth would she care about talking to me?*

Maria felt like throwing up. Her hands shook noticeably as she haphazardly threw their things into the small suitcase. Jack had gone to settle the bill and get the car. She was to meet him downstairs in fifteen minutes. This had been the first moment she had alone to call Jo, and now she wished she hadn't. The saying, "What you don't know can't hurt you," Maria hated to admit, was so true. She ran to the bathroom and threw up.

Jo felt like she had a jackhammer hard at work in her head, but she was aware enough to know Maria wouldn't simply hang up like that. She rolled onto her back and tugged on the sheet to cover part of her naked body. On the recent calls list on her phone she found Maria's name and tapped it, closing her eyes against the blinding pain behind them as the phone began to ring. It went to voice mail so she left a brief message.

"It's Jo. I guess we got cut off or something. I'll call you later." She dropped the phone over the side of the bed onto her pile of clothes, then noticed Kate smiling at her from the bedroom door. "What?" Jo's throbbing head made her growl.

Kate crossed the room wearing a T-shirt and panties and sat beside her. "I was trying to decide what's hottest, clothes on or off." Jo rubbed at her temples and closed her eyes. "You've definitely got that whole 'something for the imagination' thing going for you." She traced her finger from Jo's breastbone down toward the top of the sheet before Jo caught her hand.

"No way, I can't."

"But I could go all day with you, cowgirl." Kate flashed a seductive smile.

"I feel like crap," Jo grumbled. "That's the last thing I'm in the mood for."

Kate stroked her fingers through Jo's hair. "I'm sorry, babe. What can I do for you?"

"Aspirin. And a beer to chase them."

"A woman after my own heart. Hair of the dog coming right up," Kate called over her shoulder on her way through the door.

Jo cringed—hoping…no, praying—that there wouldn't be anything "coming up." It was past ten. She needed to get home. She had responsibilities. Swallowing the aspirin with half the beer, she borrowed some toothpaste and finger brushed her teeth, then splashed her face with cold water. She looked exactly the way she felt—like crap. After running wet fingers through her hair she left the bathroom dressed.

"Can you get dressed and take me to my truck?" she asked as she went in search of her boots and jacket. "I need to get home."

"You really want to take off?" Kate frowned.

Jo grimaced as she sat and pulled on her boots. "Tucker's off and I told you before there's nobody to feed the horses but me. Do we really have to debate this? I need to get home."

Kate raised her hands. "Okay, okay, don't get your panties in a bunch."

Jo held her jacket to her face before pulling it on. Even after being in the bar last night it still carried a faint scent of Maria. God, she'd slept with Kate to forget Maria. But since hearing her voice on the phone, Maria was all she could think about. As she drove home, nursing a cup of stale drive-thru coffee for her hangover, her mind drifted to Maria. She hated to think of her husband touching her. *The way I touched Kate.* She was disgusted with herself for jumping in bed with Kate to try to forget about Maria and then fantasizing about Maria to get through sex with Kate.

She tried calling Maria when she got home, but again the call went to voice mail. She didn't leave another message. Instead, she spent hours in the barn and later dragged herself to the house for a hot bath and a beer. She tried Maria one last time. When she didn't answer, Jo left another message.

"Maria, hi…it's Jo. Sorry I was so out of it this morning when you called. Hope you're having a Happy New Year. Call whenever…if you want." She dropped the phone on the towel and slid all the way under the water.

Maria turned on her phone after she got Matt settled into bed and asleep. She listened to Jo's messages, Jo asking her to call. But she remembered the female voice that answered Jo's phone that morning. She needed to figure out where all the unexplained feelings for Jo were coming from. And then figure out a way to stash them somewhere hidden and safe. She was married, albeit not happily, but they had a child. It didn't matter that Jack was a father that didn't care about his son and a husband that she hadn't been in love with for years. Matt's father hadn't a fraction of the compassion that Jo Marchal showed for her son. Why wouldn't she have feelings for someone else? Even a woman. She was sick to her stomach that Jo had spent last night with a woman and done things she couldn't begin to imagine. When she was near Jo, she wanted to be closer. She wanted Jo to do to her those things she couldn't imagine. And that scared her to death. She mumbled to no one, "What's wrong with me? I'm straight. Straight women don't want other women."

But she did.

CHAPTER FIFTEEN

Weeks passed and Jo received only one returned call message from Maria that said she was sorry to have missed Jo. And so Jo started calling daily. Maria never answered, but Jo was tenacious, leaving a message every time to please call…if Maria wanted to. She couldn't fathom why Maria didn't want to talk to her.

Kate started coming by the farm more regularly, but Jo managed to keep things at arms' length. She knew they needed to have a talk about New Year's. Knew she needed to be honest with Kate about her feelings. She was starving for the company of a woman, but it was Maria's company she wanted, not Kate's.

When a month had passed, Jo couldn't stand it any longer. The minute Tucker arrived on Monday she let him know she had business in town. She parked within view of Maria's office, able to see anyone who entered or left. She saw a blonde go in around eight thirty, then nearly half an hour later Maria arrived. Jo's heart raced. Her mouth went dry. She had no idea what she was going to say. Maria was obviously avoiding her. Jo desperately needed to know why. *What if she won't even see me?* After fifteen minutes of debate, she finally mustered her courage and went in.

The blonde looked up from the reception desk. "Can I help you?"

Jo searched her memory and knew hers was the voice she'd heard on the phone last year when she called the realty office. "Karen, right?" Jo gave a smile. "I'm here to see Maria West."

She flipped open a book. "Do you have an appointment?"

"I was hoping she'd have a few minutes to see me."

Karen picked up the phone and punched in a few numbers. "There's a…" she hesitated, "a woman here to see you." She paused. "No, she doesn't." After another pause she looked at Jo. "Your name?"

"Jo Marchal."

Before she could repeat Jo's name, Karen hung up the phone. "Ms. West will be right out."

Maria appeared almost immediately in the long corridor to Jo's left. Jo leaned an elbow on the receptionist's counter and smiled as Maria walked toward her.

"We can talk in my office. I'm expecting a call from the Williamsons," Maria said to Karen. "Please put it through when it comes." Giving Jo a look she couldn't interpret, Maria turned and headed back to her office, Jo following close enough to catch a whiff of her familiar perfume. It seemed a small comfort to Jo. Maria closed the door behind them and remained against it like she might need a quick getaway. Jo gave a cursory scan of the room.

"What can I do for you, Jo?" She realized the second the words were out of her mouth how unfriendly her question sounded.

"Nice office." Jo dropped into one of the chairs that sat in front of the desk. "Gosh, Maria, I haven't seen you in more than a month. I kind of wanted to make sure you were still alive and kicking and that it wasn't some prerecorded voice that left me the one and only message I got back."

Although Jo's words dripped with sarcasm, it didn't have any effect on the way she looked to Maria this morning. Jo wore that damned leather jacket she'd given her for Christmas. Maria's fingers twitched. She wanted to run her hands over the smooth soft leather and her fingers through Jo's short hair. She wanted to stoke the fire burning in Jo's eyes. A fire burning for all the wrong reasons, ones that she was responsible for. She'd been hiding from her the last month. She'd been hiding from the attraction Jo caused her to feel. Maria sucked in a silent breath. She was getting good at keeping things quiet. At least outside her own head.

"I'm sorry." She moved to sit behind the desk. "As you can see I've been incredibly busy." She waved a hand over her desk which resembled the aftermath of a tornado.

Jo glanced at it, then up at Maria. "Are you sure this is your office? 'Cause I'm not picturing you being so…disorganized."

Maria slumped in her chair. "I'm not. My life demands structure and organization for Matt," she said with a sigh. "It's been a crazy January."

Jo leaned back in the chair and crossed her ankle over her knee. She looked cool and collected. Something Maria wasn't feeling herself.

"Well, I tracked you down because Jake and Rosie have been asking after Matt."

"They speak, do they?"

"Of course they speak. It just takes a trained ear to hear 'em." Jo touched a finger to her ear and watched as Maria's expression softened into a smile. The smile that Jo had been missing. "If you don't come see Rosie soon you won't recognize her."

"You're right."

Jo had difficulty reading her. "Maria, is there something else going on I've missed?"

Maria quickly averted her eyes and began flipping through calendar pages. "No…why would you think that?" When Maria looked up, Jo only shrugged. "We'll stop out for a little bit in the next few weeks." She met Jo's eyes again. "I promise."

"Great! The kids will be pleased."

Maria raised a brow. "Kids?"

"Jake and Rosie."

"Of course, your kids are the four-legged and furry kind."

* * *

Maria kept her promise and brought Matt to the farm. The day was blustery, so Jo built a fire to take the chill off. Maria seated Matt on the floor with his puppy Rosie and Jake.

"Can I get either of you something to drink?" Jo asked on her way into the kitchen. Surprisingly, Maria followed her.

"I don't think so. We can't stay long."

Jo pulled a beer from the fridge and leaned against the counter across from where Maria stood a few feet away.

She took a long drink, then said, "Those guys thank you for bringing their buddy out for a visit."

Maria became suddenly pale and bolted from the room. Jo stepped into the living room in time to see her disappear through the bathroom door. Matt remained contented on the floor with the dogs, unaware of his mother's race down the hall. Jo took a seat close by and distracted herself watching Matt with Rosie, but as the minutes ticked by she started to wonder about Maria's abrupt departure and whether she was all right. When Maria did finally return, as pale as before, Jo jumped to her feet.

"I must be coming down with something," Maria said before Jo could ask.

"Well, no offense, but you don't look so good." Maria wavered as Jo steered her to the couch. "Have a seat. I'll get you a cup of tea."

Maria closed her eyes, dreading the significance of what she had been sensing. This was the fourth time in as many days she'd thrown up for no apparent reason. She didn't think, though, that she needed to see a doctor to determine what was happening.

They only stayed an hour, Maria using the excuse of still feeling unwell. She stopped at the drug store on her way home and an hour later loaded Matt in the car and headed to Kathleen's. While Kathleen settled the boys in the family room at the TV, Maria made them tea.

When Kathleen returned and sat next to her at the counter, she patted Maria's hand. "You don't seem yourself, sweetie. What's going on?" Maria dropped her elbows on the counter and hid her face in her hands. Kathleen rubbed a hand across her back. "Come on, honey, talk to me. How bad can it be?"

Maria heaved a heavy sigh. "Oh God, Kat, I'm pretty sure I'm pregnant."

The deafening quiet unsettled Maria. She looked at Kathleen, sitting in stunned silence, staring back at her. Then Kathleen's expression transformed from shock to compassion.

She slid her arm across Maria's shoulder. "This is good, right?"

Maria tipped her head against Kathleen's shoulder. "I don't know Kat. I'm scared to death." She pulled away. Being this close to a woman made her think of Jo, and thoughts of Jo stirred so much inside her she felt lost.

"Well, talk to me, hon, we can figure this out."

"We?"

Kathleen rubbed her hand across Maria's shoulder. "That's right. I hope you know I've always got your back."

Maria shared all the emotions that had cascaded on her in the last hour. Kathleen reassured her she would support any decision Maria made, including not to tell Jack if she decided he didn't need to know what she decided. It was Maria's choice to make, difficult as it was.

Maria thought again that she should have married Kathleen instead of her brother. She worried over that thought the entire drive home. It was silly, of course. She wasn't attracted to Kathleen that way. Not like she was to Jo. And she was sure the only reason Jo Marchal was attractive to her was because of the kind of woman she was. She hated that she was married to Jack, but that was because he had turned out to be a selfish bastard, not because she was a lesbian. Damn Jo Marchal for instilling doubt that she was anything but a very straight woman.

Jo called Maria the following day after returning from her mom's to check on her condition, and to her surprise Maria called back later in the evening. After another few weeks of missed calls back and forth, Maria called and caught Jo soaking in the tub after a tiring twelve-hour day.

Jo loved hearing the honey-smooth sound of Maria's voice. Her pulse quickened and she couldn't help but wonder what Maria's touch would do to her. Jo's hand rested on her stomach, itching to move lower. Maria's voice turned her insides to liquid fire. After Maria agreed to stop out again the upcoming weekend, they ended the call. Jo melted into a daydream steamier than her bath water.

* * *

From inside the barn Jo heard the car pull in. Hoping today would be the day Maria finally took the reins for Matt's ride, she had already barebacked Daisy Mae around the pasture so the horse would be tired.

"Hi!" Jo greeted them with a broad smile.

Maria didn't return the greeting, instead saying anxiously to Matt, "Stay right here, sweetie," before bolting back through the doors and around the corner.

Jo rested a hand on Matt's shoulder. "Stay here, okay, big guy?"

As she neared the barn doors she could hear Maria retching and stopped. No woman wanted to be seen tossing her cookies. When she heard no further sound, she tossed a glance at Matt where he was gazing fixedly on his saddle on the hay bales, then stepped out of the barn. Maria was leaning against the barn with her hand to her mouth.

"Are you all right?" When Maria nodded, Jo walked over to her. She pulled a folded bandana from her back pocket. "Here, it's clean."

"Thanks." Maria pressed the soft cotton Jo knew smelled only of laundry soap to her face. "I'm sorry."

"Nothin' to be sorry about. Are you sure you're okay?"

"I'm fine. Let's take Matt for his ride." She raised the bandana and held it over her nose and mouth as they returned inside the barn. "I'll meet you guys out there." She motioned in the direction of the pasture and continued walking out of the barn.

Jo called Tucker out of the tack room to help her saddle Daisy Mae and get Matt strapped in.

"Hey, Tucker, would you mind walking Matt around the pasture for his ride? I need to talk to Maria and I don't think she's up for the walk."

The corner of his mouth rose in sync with his eyebrow. "Sure thing, boss."

Tucker took the reins and headed out. From the doorway Jo watched Maria at the fence beyond the barn. Her arms were crossed under her breasts and occasionally she lifted the bandana, still clutched in her hand, to her mouth and nose.

"He loves this, you know."

Maria focused her eyes on Jo. "Yes, he does, thank you."

Jo shrugged. "Heck, Maria, you don't have to thank me. He was destined to be a cowboy. I knew it the first time I met him."

Maria put her hand on Jo's forearm hanging off the fence rail. "Well, in that case, thank you for bringing me out of my comfort zone."

Jo felt a scorching heat from the spot where Maria's hand rested on her arm and it spread like an unimpeded wildfire to her belly. Desire rose uncontrolled. Standing there, in that moment, Maria had never looked more beautiful.

"I hope you don't live to regret it." Jo gave an easy grin. "Coming out of your comfort zone." *Damn…that was a blatant flirt.*

Maria's eyes seemed to smolder for a split second before she looked away.

Sunlight danced in Jo's eyes, making them sparkle. Her remark struck more than one chord in Maria, and she realized at the moment she wanted to push up on her toes and kiss Jo in the worst way. *Hormones…* It had to be her raging hormones. She raised the bandana to her face once again, hoping to hide any sign of desire that might be showing…

"You know you were sick several weeks ago. Seems an awfully long time to have a bug. You sure you're all right?"

They were friends, right? They exchanged gifts for Christmas. They had both sought out that special gift for one another, and Jo had gone above and beyond to give her son a perfect gift. They were definitely friends. And friends confided in one another, supported each other. Didn't they?

"I've become quite sensitive to some smells that never seemed to bother me before. Like manure," she swallowed, "and beer." She cringed at the thought. Jo's forehead creased with lines so Maria patted her arm. "Relax there, cowgirl. I'm only pregnant." Jo didn't utter a sound.

"You look shocked."

Jo shook her head. "Uh…not shocked. Surprised is all."

Maria searched Jo's eyes before Jo looked away. The sparkles created by the sun were gone. She couldn't help but wonder why.

"Your husband must be thrilled."

Jo's disheartened tone confused her. She thought Jo might be happy about her news. Although, she couldn't remember now why she'd thought so. Actually she had been hoping that Jo would be happy about her news. That would help dispel a lot of the anguish she felt about her choice to tempt fate and have another child.

"He might be if he knew," Maria finally said.

"Excuse me?"

"He might be thrilled if he knew, but he doesn't." Jo's eyes were full of questions when they met hers again. "I haven't told him yet."

Jo could have been knocked over by a feather in those few moments. It was the last thing she expected Maria to share with her. Wow! She needed to dislodge the imagery in her head that would lead to Maria becoming pregnant. Jealousy and envy battled inside her. And why was Maria keeping secret such big news from her husband? Fear? Fear that maybe she could give birth to another autistic child—give her husband another handicapped child? Jo wanted to take Maria in her arms and tell her she would always be there for her…no matter the circumstance.

"Well, my mom always said, 'there's no greater gift than a child'."

Maria's face relaxed into a tiny smile. "Thanks for saying that." She brushed her fingers over the back of Jo's hand. "You've become such a welcome friend for us." She motioned at Tucker, Matt and Daisy Mae making their way toward them.

Maria's eyes always took on a special brightness when she looked at her son. Jo loved that something as simple as a look could make a woman so beautiful. Her eyes drifted to Maria's middle. She'd heard women became more beautiful when they were pregnant.

Oh God, how am I going to maintain control around her if she becomes more tempting than she already is?

* * *

Maria found a certain peace in her own mind after sharing the pregnancy news with her friend. And she only need remind herself that Jo was too "hot" to ever be attracted to a "fat" pregnant woman…a fat, straight pregnant woman. Perhaps that would make it easier to be around her. And so she and Matt started making regular Saturday visits to the farm. During the moments when she did feel wistfully attracted to the rugged cowgirl, Maria simply chalked it up to the hormonal changes of pregnancy. Although she honestly didn't recall having ever felt the same around Jack when she was pregnant with Matt.

The last Saturday of the month she took Matt to the farm in the afternoon, but later than usual. She and Jo talked on the porch for a bit before making their way to the barn for Matt's ride. Jo walked Daisy Mae from her stall and barely had the saddle in place when she heard a car in the driveway. She and Maria were standing side by side on a hay bale hoisting Matt into the saddle when Jo spotted Kate.

"Hey!" Jo called to her.

"I thought we were going to dinner this evening."

Jo finished strapping Matt in, hopped down and helped Maria down. "Right." Jo gave her a smile. "Give me a couple of minutes."

Kate planted her hand on her hips, flashing angry eyes at Maria when Maria touched Jo's arm.

"I can do this, go on." Maria reached for the reins. "I'll ask Tucker to stay and help me when we're done if that's okay." Maria took the reins from Jo and rubbed her hand gently on Daisy Mae's neck.

Jo loved that Maria had finally gotten comfortable around horses, at least around Daisy Mae.

"You smell like those damned horses." Kate wrinkled her nose when Jo got close.

She took a step back. "Those damned horses are my life."

"And so what am I, a sideline?" Kate turned up her palms.

"All I have to do is change clothes and wash up."

"You just don't get it do you? You're never going to put me first, are you?"

"I'm not going to have this discussion. Let's go." When she reached for Kate's elbow, Kate jerked her arm violently. Jo was not in the mood for Kate's childish behavior and her demands of "why won't you, why can't you or when will you?" In an icy tone she said, "You know what? I'm tired, let's forget about tonight and maybe try again some other night."

Kate's mouth dropped open. "You're kidding?"

"No, I'm not."

Kate glared at her before stomping from the barn. A moment later Jo heard car tires spinning and kicking gravel. She spun around in time to see the threesome turn the corner out the opposite barn doors. She ran to catch up.

"I'm sorry we interfered with your plans. You should have said something when we showed up without calling."

"No big deal. She wasn't in such a great mood anyway. Must have been a bad day at work."

Jo shook it off to enjoy their quiet stroll. She tried getting them to stop in the house after Matt's ride, but Maria declined.

Standing beside the car before leaving, Maria said, "I'm glad you're getting out and dating. Sorry again about ruining your plans for this evening."

"You didn't ruin a thing. You and Matt are always welcome, anytime." Jo met Maria's eyes. She was more beautiful than the last time she'd seen her. "I'm glad you came."

CHAPTER SIXTEEN

Spring in southern Ohio, accompanied by spring showers, made perennial bulbs explode with color everywhere. But as beautiful as they were, they served to remind Jo that it had been a year since she'd learned she would lose her Pops forever. She understood love and that if you loved someone completely, it would eventually break your heart in a million pieces. She was sitting in the tack room running some numbers that Tucker had asked her to look over when Kate appeared in the doorway.

"Hey, cowgirl, how you doin'?"

Jo half turned in the chair. "I didn't even hear you pull in. And I'm really surprised to see you in here." Kate hated her horses. She said they smelled, but Jo suspected she was also afraid of them.

Kate walked behind her and placed both hands on Jo's shoulders. "Well, when you want something, you have to go for it."

She slowly slid her hands over Jo's shoulders toward her breasts. Jo closed her eyes for a second enjoying the sensations the simple touch aroused. Until she thought about whose hands were caressing her. She jumped up, knocking the chair back into Kate, and spun around.

"What the hell do you think you're doing?" She didn't wait for an answer. "Tucker and the guys are here and could be back any minute."

Kate raised her hands. "Sorry, Jo, I didn't mean to upset you." She reached to take Jo's hand, but she jerked it away. "I, um…"

Jo met her eyes. "I can't do this anymore Kate. I'm sorry," she said looking away.

"What…you can't do what?"

She made herself look Kate in the eyes again. "This," she motioned between them. "Hanging around all the time, going out…and it's not going anywhere." She looked at the floor. "It won't ever go anywhere."

Kate chortled. "You can't say I'm not trying."

Jo sighed. "I'm not. I don't feel it. I don't feel that way for you, Kate." Jo chanced a glance, noticing Kate's hands were tight fists at her sides.

"So what was New Year's about? You needed a good fuck or what?"

"I guess maybe I did." Jo couldn't stand Kate's icy cold stare. She dropped her gaze back to the floor.

"You guess?" Kate snapped. "You were riding me like a bronco and screaming the whole time. And you guess?"

God, she was going to recite all the details of a night that Jo could barely recall—and didn't want to.

Kate kicked the chair. "I was patient. I waited and waited for you to give me some clue where this was going. And I finally thought we connected on a whole new level, but it was just a fuck for you! Wasn't it?" Jo continued to stare at the floor. "So what the hell have you been doing with me all this time?" When Jo didn't respond, Kate grabbed her arm. "Answer me, dammit!"

Jo took hold of Kate's wrist and pulled the vise-gripping hand from her arm. What she saw in Kate's eyes when she stepped back shocked her.

"I…" She cleared her throat and tried again. "I thought maybe we could have a relationship and I tried. Like I said, I don't feel it. I'm sorry, Kate."

"Yeah, sorry." Kate looked strung tighter than a bowstring. Her cheeks burned red. "You keep me tongue wagging after you for months and you're sorry? Huh, you know, I'm sorry for you, Jo.

I would have given anything to take care of you. Good luck with your whole lonely hearts thing…" She turned and stomped out.

Jo's hands shook as she picked up the two-way radio. What she'd seen in Kate's eyes frightened her. She needed to be alone. She told Tucker she would finish going over the numbers tomorrow and asked him to close up when they were done. Inside the house she locked the doors and poured a short glass nearly full of bourbon. She finished it at the kitchen counter, filled it again and dropped on the couch in the living room.

The incessantly ringing phone was the next thing Jo was conscious of and only after the machine picked up and she heard Maria's voice did she drag herself to the kitchen. It was after eight. She brewed coffee, had a few swallows and called Maria back.

"Good morning!" Maria's voice sounded light and bubbly.

"Mornin'," Jo croaked.

"I didn't get you out of bed, did I?"

"No." That was the truth, she hadn't been in bed.

"Will you be around later today?"

Jo's head felt like someone had filled it with concrete while she'd slept. "Uh, yeah, sure."

"Kathleen has some plans with the kids so I can grocery shop and run some errands, so we won't be out until later this afternoon if that's okay."

After the call, Jo trudged to the shower. Since Maria had been witness to Kate's blowup several weeks ago, she made it a point to call before stopping out at the farm. Jo hated that she felt that way. She rather liked it when Maria showed up and surprised her.

They arrived around four thirty, Maria carrying containers of food for their dinner into the house before locating Jo in the barn. Jo sent Tucker on his way to enjoy what was left of the weekend.

Jo busied herself saddling Daisy Mae. "Would you like to ride too, or is that out of the question in your current condition?"

Maria shook her head. "I'm sure it would be fine, but I think I'd rather walk." She patted her growing tummy. "Exercise is good for us."

A quarter mile out, Maria broke the companionable silence they walked in. "There's something I've wanted to tell you."

Jo's heart leapt to her throat.

"But you have to promise me not to get angry or upset." Maria's tone grew serious.

"Okay…" Jo's mind flew in a flurry of "what ifs".

Maria's eyes stayed on the ground ahead of them. "You know I mentioned Jack wasn't ecstatic about this pregnancy." That had come as no surprise. "Well…that was a bit of an understatement."

Heat slowly crept up Jo's neck, but she bit her tongue.

"He was furious." Maria's voice shook in a way Jo had never before heard. "He said he would not be a part of another child with me."

"I'm so sorry, Maria."

Maria waved the hand that wasn't holding the reins. "I've had plenty of time to deal with it, and I'm pretty okay with it. It won't be any different for Matt and me than it is now."

Jo wanted to call him every nasty name she could think of, but she continued to honor her promise.

"He told me last night he's leaving."

Jo's mouth fell open. Someone could have slapped her and she wouldn't have felt it. "He's…he's abandoning you?"

"No, no. He's divorcing me and taking a transfer somewhere down south."

"What's the difference?" Jo asked, hearing the indignation in her own voice.

When tears slipped from Maria's eyes and raced down her cheeks, Jo grabbed the bridle and halted their movement. She stepped around Daisy Mae, reached out and gently touched Maria's hand.

"I'm sorry, that was pretty harsh." Maria lowered her eyes. "I'm not really good at this…you know…comforting, but please, if there's anything I can do, promise you'll tell me, Maria."

Maria's eyes rose to meet Jo's as she slipped her hand in Jo's hand. "Do what you do, Jo." Jo stared at her blankly. "Be someone I can talk to—and make me laugh."

When Maria squeezed her hand, Jo fought every urge she'd ever had to pull Maria into her arms. But she wasn't sure she knew the difference between the hug of a friend or the hold of a lover. She'd never really had any close friends except Cecile. And Cecile, well, she was cut from such a different fabric Jo didn't think she'd make the best comparison.

"Guess I need to work on the laughing part." She tipped her head with a smile. "But the talking, I've got covered—anytime."

Jo could tell Maria's smile was forced when she said, "Thanks."

Maria's gaze remained on her, and Jo wondered how it was that fate had chosen to bring the two of them together. Before either said another word, though, a deep rumble shattered the quiet evening. Jo looked around to see a sky filled with dark clouds rolling toward them.

"We better get back."

"I didn't know it was supposed to rain."

"Me either or we certainly wouldn't have walked this far out."

They walked at a brisk pace and were only fifty yards out when the clouds opened up, unleashing enormous raindrops. They half trotted, but they were soaked by the time they finally reached cover of the barn. In the tack room she grabbed a couple of horse blankets, draping them over Maria and Matt before returning to the barn to put Daisy Mae in her stall. When lightning cracked, Daisy Mae tried to pull from her hold.

"Whoa, girl." She rubbed the side of her head. "Come on now, you never spook." She talked the horse into the stall, closed the gate and hung a feed bag.

Maria and Matt were huddled together under the same blanket. Matt seemed fine, but Maria was shivering. Jo turned on the small electric heater in the corner.

"Sorry, I guess I should have turned this on right away."

"It's okay. Matt's pretty warm." Maria continued to shake.

"But you're not." Jo lifted the blanket enough to see Maria's sweater, soggy from their soaking, while Matt appeared dry under his jacket.

"You're soaked and you'll catch your death of cold, as my mom used to tell me, if you don't get out of your wet clothes." Jo peeled off her wet jacket and began to unbutton her dry chambray shirt.

"What are you doing?"

She finished with the buttons, pulled the shirt off and stood there in an undershirt. "Here, you need to put something dry on." Jo held out her shirt.

Maria's eyes traveled slowly from Jo's face to the waist of her jeans and back up as she reached to take the shirt. Her hand trembled noticeably.

Jo left the room again to grab a couple more hay bales to sit on. Maria was pulling the wet sweater off when she came back in, so she busied herself in the corner setting the bales, with a blanket over them, closer to the heater. When she turned around Maria was buttoning the top buttons of the shirt, which lay taut across her breasts and didn't quite close over her belly. The sight of Maria's bare abdomen caused a hot spark to radiate from Jo's belly. When she raised her eyes to meet Maria's, Maria was looking at her intently.

"It appears I'm a bit too big for your shirt."

Jo looked again at her bare belly. "At least it's dry." *Like my mouth.*

Maria wrapped her arms around herself. "Dry…yes, thanks."

Jo ushered them to the makeshift seat by the heater and, after they were situated, hung another blanket around them. Maria reached out and touched her fingers lightly to Jo's upper arm.

"What happened?"

"What?" Jo stepped back.

"That bruise on your arm."

Jo looked at her bare arm. She'd forgotten about the little souvenir Kate had given her. If Kate ever tried to manhandle her again, she would be finding out what cowgirls were made of.

"It's nothing. I got hung up in a horse lead the other day."

"You should be more careful." It appeared that Maria bought her story.

Jo hiked a thumb over her shoulder. "I've…uh…I'm gonna check on the horses." She grabbed a blanket and pulled it over her shoulders. "Be right back."

Jo felt naked under Maria's close scrutiny. She leaned against a post in the barn and knocked her head back into it. "Get a grip," she muttered. It was a good thing Matt was there, otherwise she was likely to do something totally inappropriate. Like put her arm around Maria on the pretense of warming her up, then casually lean in and kiss her. Jo's skin was cool, but her entire body was aflame.

Maria was certain her hormones spiked when Jo had given up her shirt. She'd never seen a woman's body that looked so lean and fit and so…so inviting. She was grateful when Jo finally covered her nearly naked upper body. She was barely able to breathe. It was entirely too easy to imagine what the cowgirl might look like minus those sexy jeans.

Oh God, and when she'd touched Jo, an electric hot charge had shot through her and settled between her legs. She couldn't remember ever feeling *that* sensation and couldn't believe she was having these lustful thoughts now…for another woman. She pulled Matt to her chest and, holding him tight, stroked his curls. She watched his eyes flutter, staring off at nothing.

She kissed his forehead. "You're going to have a little brother or sister before long, someone who will love you as much as I do." She slowly rocked, gathering him tighter against her.

Jo watched silently from the doorway for a few minutes before entering. She asked herself how stupid a person could be not to love such a devoted mother and son. She went to the mini fridge.

"All I can offer is coffee or water, and you're not supposed to do coffee."

"We're fine," Maria said softly.

She saw Matt's closed eyes and lowered her voice. "Is he asleep?"

"Hmm…all the excitement, I think."

Jo got a bottle of water and joined the twosome by the heat.

Maria pulled Matt into her lap. "Sit, I promise I won't let him kick you." Jo laughed lightly. "Since it seems you bruise easily."

Jo was ashamed for the lie, but she did it because…well, she wasn't sure why she lied. Oh, who was she kidding? That too was a lie. She didn't want Maria to think she could be weak or vulnerable in any way. She rubbed her hand over the arm hidden beneath the blanket.

"Apparently I do."

The uneasiness in Jo's eyes made Maria suspect there was something more to the story of the bruise. For now, though, she'd let her keep her secret, whatever her reasons. She tried to lean back against the wall, but her short legs wouldn't allow it.

"I don't suppose you have any pillows in here to go with all these blankets, do you?"

Jo chuckled. "No, sorry."

"Is it still raining hard?"

"Unfortunately, and there seems to be a moat developing around the barn."

Maria shifted. "I've got to get up. He's pressing on my bladder."

Allowing the blanket to slide off her shoulders, Jo stood and gently lifted Matt out of her lap and held him. Maria swiftly went to the closet-size bathroom. When she stepped back out, she stopped dead in her tracks. There Jo stood cradling Matt in her powerful arms, and she knew, unquestioningly, that she had never felt so much desire for another person in her life. Jo Marchal took her breath away.

They waited and waited for the rain to stop. Jo kept checking and they kept the conversation on non-personal topics. Both of them, she suspected, were feeling emotionally raw. Maria was more than a little fearful where things could go if desire reigned.

"It's still raining, but not nearly as bad," Jo came back and reported. "I can get the Gator and we can make a run for the house under the blankets if you want."

"I'm hungry so you must be starving."

"I'll be back."

Jo pulled on her wet jacket and disappeared. A few minutes later Maria heard the faint sound of an engine and Jo returned. Water dripped from her and her hair was plastered to her head. Even looking like a drowned rat, she was gorgeous. Jo threw an extra dry blanket over Maria with Matt in her lap and raced them to the house in the steady rain. She dropped her soaking jacket on the hearth and stooped to light a fire while Maria settled Matt on the couch. When the flames leapt toward the chimney she stood. Maria couldn't take her eyes off her. The rain had soaked completely through the denim jacket to her undershirt. She fixated on Jo's breasts. Given what it was revealing of her erect nipples, the material might as well have not been there. Jo turned back to the fireplace and rubbed her hands together briskly.

"I'll go find you something else to wear."

She tossed another log on the fire and headed down the hall. Maria was seated at the fireplace when she returned a few minutes later in a dry T-shirt and jeans. Jo handed over a well-worn sweater and as Maria started to unbutton the shirt, Jo abruptly headed for the kitchen.

Jo called into the living room. "I guess we better eat before it gets any later."

It was nearing seven thirty. Jo wanted a beer to calm her nerves, but opted for a water, knowing the smell of beer made Maria nauseous. After eating their dinner, Jo again started to feel more at ease in Maria's company. There'd been something in her eyes when they'd been out in the barn that made her more nervous than she remembered ever being around a woman. With Matt sleeping at the end of the couch, his head in Maria's lap and Rosie curled against him, Jo sat on the hearth poking at the dying fire.

"We should get going."

Jo peered out the front door. "It's still raining." She wanted to keep them safe there with her.

Maria startled Jo by stepping dangerously close behind her. "I have driven in the rain before." She smiled up at Jo when she looked around.

Jo swallowed. "Uh…I'm sure you have, but I bet with all this rain Buck Creek's running across the road." She took a step away. "I'll get online and check." Several minutes later she returned. "They got the bridge closed tonight. If you take the detour it could take you hours longer. I'm sure that's not the only bridge under water."

"I know the route." Maria walked over to where Matt slept.

"You should just stay here tonight," Jo blurted out.

"We couldn't possibly impose on you like that."

"Please," she waved a hand around. "I'm in this big house by myself."

Maria glanced back at Matt sleeping soundly. "Are you sure it's not an imposition?"

Jo tipped her head. "Heck no, I'll throw some fresh sheets on the bed and we'll be all set."

"Oh, don't go to all the trouble. Unless…" Maria hesitated. "Unless you…" Jo lifted a brow. "Unless you know…you…"

"Unless I recently had company in my bed," Jo said, her cheeks growing warm. She shook her head.

"I didn't mean to imply…" Maria shook her head. "I suppose I should drop it." She pulled her gaze from Jo.

She walked to the end of the couch. "I'll call Kathleen and tell her we're staying over just to be safe."

Jo waited until she finished her call, then asked, "Do you want to put him to bed now?" Maria nodded so she scooped him up and carried him to the bedroom. "You two take my room, it has the bigger bed."

When Jo stopped beside it, she felt Maria's touch on her arm. "We're not going to run you out of your own bed."

Jo looked at Maria's hand, then into her eyes. "Would you mind pulling down the covers?" Jo angled her head toward the door across the room. "Besides, there's a bathroom, it'll be more convenient."

Jo gently placed Matt down and Maria undressed him down to his T-shirt and underwear. Once done, she pulled the covers up and sat on the edge of the bed. Jo came out of the bathroom with her flannel robe and rummaged in the dresser drawers. She located an oversized novelty T that Cecile had given her as a birthday gift several years ago. Although she had never worn it, she'd kept it.

She handed Maria the robe and shirt. "These should work for you tonight."

Maria shook out the T-shirt and held it up. It read "Cowgirls do it in the dirt." She rolled her eyes up to meet Jo's. "Really?"

Jo grinned as if to say "but of course" as her cheeks burned with a blush. "Is there anything else you need?"

Maria scanned the room. "Would you happen to have a night light?"

"Sure." Jo got the one from the hall bathroom. "Anything else?"

"I think we'll be fine. Thanks for taking care of us."

"I'm glad to do it." Jo grabbed an undershirt and boxer shorts from the top dresser drawer, then shoved a hand in her pocket. "If you need anything, I'll be right across the hall."

"Goodnight, Jo."

She pulled the door closed. Settling herself in the guest room, she wondered how sleepless this night would be with Maria only twenty feet away.

Maria lay staring at the ceiling, distracted by the smell of Jo on the bed covers. In her mind she saw the defensiveness, then compassion in Jo's eyes when she'd told her that her husband was leaving and the image of Jo holding Matt in her arms as if he were her own. After an hour she gave in to the restlessness and quietly got up.

Jo had been watching the glowing digital numbers tick by on the bedside clock for at least an hour when her pulse suddenly quickened. Shifting her eyes toward the door, she saw Maria's silhouette there. She held her breath and lay motionless and watched Maria in the darkness watching her. After a very long moment Maria pulled the door almost shut and Jo finally breathed. When a faint light appeared through the crack in the door, she slipped from bed to take a look. The light came from the kitchen. She opened the door a bit more, hoping to catch a glimpse of Maria when she returned to bed. But after watching ten more minutes tick off the clock, she went to the kitchen. Stopping in the doorway, she observed Maria sitting at the island staring into a steaming mug.

"Couldn't sleep?" Jo asked softly, hoping not to startle her. She didn't seem surprised by Jo's appearance in the doorway.

"I'm sorry. I was trying not to wake you."

Jo crossed to the end of the counter. "You didn't. Do you mind if I join you?"

"No. Would you like something to drink?" Maria started to get up.

"Stay put, I'll get it." Jo moved behind her to the fridge and took out a beer, then, again recalling Maria's sensitivity to smells, traded it for a bottle of water. She sat across from her, wanting the counter as a barrier between them. Jo didn't trust all the feelings ping-ponging between her heart and libido. Maria stared again into the mug nestled in her hands. Jo took a drink, waiting another moment before breaking the silence.

"We should be more like kids and wear out quickly." When Maria looked up with sadness in her eyes and worry etched around them, Jo's heart broke. "Do you want to talk about it?"

Maria shrugged, but finally said, "I don't know what I was thinking." Jo's forehead wrinkled. "I don't know why I thought having another baby would bring Jack and me closer. All it did was to drive a permanent wedge between us."

"You couldn't have known that would happen."

She looked down into the cup. "New Year's Eve was the first time we'd been intimate in a year."

Jo's chest tightened. It hurt to know that this man who was undeserving of a woman like Maria could have her in that way.

"I don't know what we're going to do or how we'll manage."

Not for the first time, Jo wanted to take Maria in her arms. She wanted to hold her and tell her she'd take care of them, but instead she reached over and laid her hand on Maria's. "You have strengths you're not even aware of. You're all going to be fine, I know it." And she did, because she would take care of them if need be.

Maria looked weary when her eyes met Jo's. Her voice quivered. "I don't know. I'm not confident and self-assured like you. You manage a home, horses, a farm, so much at once." She sighed heavily.

"And I have people that help me with a lot of stuff." She held Maria's gaze. "You have people who care for you who will help you through this."

"I don't want to become more dependent on the people I care about."

"I know sometimes it's hard to ask for help, but I want you to know you can always call me…for anything, and if I can help in any way, I will."

A little sadness left her eyes. "How did I happen across a special friend like you, Jo Marchal?"

Jo winked. "Just lucky, I guess." Maria tried at a smile.

CHAPTER SEVENTEEN

In the weeks that followed Maria became a regular guest at the farm, showing up at least every Saturday with Matt in tow and sometimes unexpectedly. Jo was grateful for the time to share with them. They talked at least once during the week, and if Jo called Maria and had to leave a message, Maria always got back to her. The days of avoiding were behind them. Whatever had caused it, Jo still didn't know, and at this juncture she wasn't worrying about it. The relationship blossomed into a comfortable friendship. Jo relished any attention Maria bestowed on her, and in return Jo worked to build Maria's self-esteem and erase the self-doubt her husband—correction, almost ex-husband—had instilled. With the last weekend of May approaching, Jo asked Maria if she could stop out alone on Saturday for a while. Maria agreed to be there between three and four in the afternoon.

By four thirty, Jo was pacing the barn. Finally she heard the car pull in and stepped out into the bright sunlight in time to see Maria racing for the house. She leaned against the side of the barn waiting. When Maria emerged, she gave Jo a little wave, making her way over.

"Sorry." Maria placed a hand on her belly. "She's been pressed on my bladder for three days in a row now."

"She?" Jo pushed off the barn. "You found out the sex of the baby?"

Maria followed her into the barn. "Well, no, but Kathleen swears it's a girl because of the way I'm carrying."

Jo stopped. "You can really tell that way?"

"A lot of women believe so, yes."

She looked long and hard at Maria's extended abdomen. "Interesting."

"And what do you think?"

Jo gave a moment's thought. "That what they say about pregnant women becoming more beautiful is true." Her cheeks warmed.

Maria gave her arm a light jab. "That's cute, Jo, thanks."

Jo shrugged. "Are you still allowed to ride?"

Maria stepped over to the stall where Daisy Mae hung her head over the gate. She touched the top of her soft nose. "Yes, but no barrel racing."

Jo moved close and stroked the horse's neck. "Well, you know Daisy Mae, she barely trots. So, you up for a ride?"

Maria looked up into her eyes. "Sure."

They slowly made their way to a stand of trees in the northeast corner of the pasture.

As they neared, Maria asked, "What's that?" The large plastic box was hard to miss.

Jo glanced over at Maria, who now looked completely comfortable sitting atop a horse. She would have never guessed she could get Maria past her fear, and yet, here they were. Jo often reminded Maria that everyone has hidden strengths, you sometimes simply have to dig deep to find them.

Of course when Maria had asked Jo what fears she had to overcome, Jo assured her she didn't have any she was aware of. She wasn't sure if Maria believed her or not. And if Jo asked Maria if she thought there was anything she needed to work on, Maria told Jo she needed to work on being less charming. Jo would blush feverishly and Maria would chuckle.

Jo answered, "It's why I brought you out here."

Maria looked at her suspiciously when Jo hopped down and loosely wrapped Cobalt's reins around the fence.

When Jo offered a hand to help Maria down, she said, "You realize if I get off this horse there will probably be no getting me back up here. I don't see any hay bales sitting around."

"We'll get you up there. We have the cooler, but if necessary, I'll hoist you up on my shoulders."

Maria chuckled. "We? Have you got a strong man in your back pocket?"

Jo raised her arms and flexed them. "Don't need one. I got these." She pointed to a solid bicep.

"As much as I hate to admit this, I'm sure I outweigh you, and I don't think those," she pointed to Jo's arms, "will be enough to heft this." She patted her behind.

Jo reached up to Maria. "I bet you don't. Come down from there."

Maria didn't budge. "What are we betting?"

"Loser treats winner to a lavish dinner of winner's choice."

"Deal." Maria grinned. "So what you got there, cowgirl?"

Jo struck a bodybuilder's pose and flexed her arms again. "One fifty and still growing."

"Ha!" Maria laughed. "You lose."

"No way! Give it up."

Maria grinned again. "One fifty-five last week and definitely still growing. Like I said, you lose."

Jo smiled inwardly. It was one of the best bets she'd ever lost. She would gladly lose again for the chance to take Maria out somewhere to dinner.

Maria's back pressed into Jo, Jo's hands sliding from Maria's hips and up her sides as she helped her down. Maria's breasts were so close to Jo's hands she had to bite the inside of her cheek to keep from gasping. She smelled Maria's shampoo and her intoxicating perfume. Jo's thighs tingled and a slow throb started between them.

Dear lord, help me.

The feel of Jo's hands on her hips made Maria instantly horny. When she leaned into Jo as her feet touched the ground, she wanted to pull Jo's arms tightly around her. *Oh God, if my hormones don't settle soon, I'm going to combust.* And she would definitely have to start staying away from Jo.

Jo opened the large cooler, pulled out a blanket and spread it on the ground. She extended her hand to Maria.

"Will you join me for a picnic?"

Maria took her hand and allowed Jo to help her sit. She was awash with emotions as she blinked back tears.

"Are you all right?" Jo asked in alarm. "Did I seat you on a rock?"

Maria waved a hand. "No, no, it's just that no one's ever done anything so sweet like this for me, and my hormones are all over the place." She dabbed at her damp eyes. "I'm sorry."

Jo sat with her legs crossed a few feet away. "You don't ever have to be sorry about anything with me, Maria." She gave a wistful smile and pulled a bottle of sparkling cider from the cooler. "I thought we'd celebrate. I would have brought that bottle you gave me last year, but you went and got yourself pregnant." Maria raised her brows. "It's been a year since I bought this place." Jo looked around them. "This magnificent place." She began pulling food containers from the cooler. "So, I thought we should celebrate with a picnic in the middle of this majestic place *you* found for me."

Jo knew the first time she'd ridden to this spot that it was the most incredible place on her hundred and fifteen acres and she'd been waiting for just the right time to share it with Maria. She knew she couldn't ever share a life or love with Maria, but this special moment in time, along with so many others over the last year, would stay with her forever. She could be content to visit them in her dreams.

They snacked on cheese, crackers and fruit, enjoying the non-alcoholic bubbly, although Jo wouldn't have said no to a couple of beers to calm her jangled nerves. Being alone with Maria seemed to heighten sensations in every nerve of her body. There was no denying how much she loved every minute she shared with her. As they ate, Jo talked about her future plans to expand the horse farm into a ranch when she could acquire the surrounding properties, and Maria talked about baby names, diapers and doing three a.m. feedings again after so many years.

When Maria shifted, noticeably uncomfortable, and emitted a little moan, Jo asked, "You okay?"

Maria pressed a hand against her lower back. "Typical pregnancy pains." She winced. "It'll get worse as I gain more weight."

"Anything I can do?"

Maria leaned to one side and tried to stretch her back. "Not unless you packed a masseuse in that cooler."

"Well, I'm no masseuse, but I can rub your back if it'll help."

Maria exhaled a long breath. "Oh God, would you? I'll forfeit my winning bet for a back rub."

"You don't have to give away your free dinner."

Maria maneuvered herself half onto her belly next to Jo, who worked her hand in small circles beginning at her spine and out to each side above her hips.

Why couldn't she have found this wonderful woman before she met and married her husband? She might very well have been a lesbian too. No, she knew why. She wouldn't have Matt, and she lived and breathed for her son. *Everything happens for a reason*, she reminded herself. After so many years of loneliness, she was happy to have Jo a part of her life…if only to share some time with her.

"How's that?" Jo asked in a husky voice.

Maria groaned. "Mmm…I'll give you an hour to stop."

Jo chuckled. "Okay."

"You know, I've never known anyone I've been so comfortable with like I am with you. You're so easy to be around."

Jo wanted Maria to lay there against her thigh…well, forever. It felt so good that she had to force herself to not think about how comfortable she could get with Maria snuggled up against her. Maria aroused her in ways no woman ever had.

"I'm pretty laidback." Jo's hand paused briefly before continuing its circular motion. "I guess I'm a comfortable kind of gal."

Maria reached back suddenly and stilled Jo's hand. "She likes your back rub." She pulled Jo's hand around to her abdomen. When Jo felt the movement, her hand jerked. Maria giggled, but held on. "She won't bite. She's just getting comfortable too."

The repeated subtle movement in Maria's belly made Jo smile. It was extraordinarily special to have Maria sharing this with her.

"Wow! Doesn't that hurt?"

Maria kept hold of her hand and moved it, causing the baby to kick again. "Occasionally yes, but mostly you get used to it." Maria shifted over onto her back, pressing very firmly against Jo's thigh, and gazed up into her eyes while still holding Jo's hand against her. "I think she likes you."

Jo smiled down at the dark eyes holding her gaze. This could be one of those moments that could change a person's life. But her better senses prevailed, and she refrained from leaning down and kissing Maria, as much as her entire body ached for the touch and taste of her lips.

Maria felt as if she'd slipped into a fairy tale. Jo's touch made her heart pound so fiercely she was sure she would notice. She half expected her strong arms to sweep her into an embrace at any moment. As if sensing the moment might somehow turn dangerous, one of the horses whinnied, bringing them both back to reality.

"Does your back feel any better?" Jo's voice was hoarse.

Realizing she still held Jo's hand, Maria let go. "It does, thank you."

Jo's eyes wandered over the vast field that stretched out of sight beyond the corner of the pasture. "Thank you for finding me such a wonderful place to live." Jo reached with her strong arms to help Maria sit when she struggled to push herself up.

"I'm glad you're happy here." She wanted to touch Jo's face, slip her fingers into her hair and pull her closer than the space that separated them, but instead she said, "I hate to end such a wonderful picnic, but we should probably head back soon." She frowned. "I'm going to need the bathroom." She tipped her head. "Sorry."

Gauging from the sun, it was probably going on six o'clock and neither of them were dressed for the cool air that would descend with the setting sun. Jo started to get up, but Maria stopped her.

"This was more than thoughtful, Jo, thank you."

Jo gave a nod. "You're more than welcome."

They packed everything back into the cooler, and with only a minor struggle and Jo's assistance, Maria was back in the saddle on Daisy Mae. She made a beeline for the bathroom in the house while Jo carried the remainder of the sparkling cider to the kitchen. When Maria took her usual seat at the island, Jo slid a flute of the cider across to her.

Jo raised her glass. "To friends."

Maria sat staring at the counter. When she finally looked up, batting back tears, she tried to smile. "Yes."

Maria looked brokenhearted. Jo felt a sudden wave of guilt that she'd somehow caused it. She moved around the island to sit beside her. "I didn't mean to upset you, Maria."

Maria brushed her fingers under her eyes. "No, I'm sorry, it's not you."

Jo's heart ached. She turned Maria's stool to face her, but Maria wouldn't look at her. She lifted Maria's chin and when she raised her eyes to meet Jo's, mere inches separated them.

Desire sparked, and without a word or warning, Maria leaned forward and touched her lips to Jo's.

Her lips tasted sweet like the cider, Jo thought. But then again she guessed they always tasted wonderful. A moan escaped her throat, and Maria pulled back, emitting a tiny gasp.

"Oh God, Jo, I'm sorry. I—I'm—" Maria stuttered.

"Curious?" Jo said, offering Maria an out. Maria lowered her head. They were still so close that Jo could smell her fragrant hair. "'Cause I'm pretty sure you wouldn't be the first straight woman to kiss someone like me."

"Oh God, please don't let this ruin our friendship." Maria stumbled away. "I…I have to go." She rushed from the kitchen.

"Maria," Jo called. She caught her arm just before she got out the front door. She turned around but wouldn't look Jo in the eyes.

"Our friendship is fine," Jo said softly. "I promise." Maria still refused to look at her. "Please, Maria, don't leave upset." She held onto Maria's arm.

Maria shook her head. "No, I'm…it's okay, really."

Jo lifted her chin again, this time ensuring plenty of space between them. "I trust that's the truth."

Maria's eyes finally met hers. "It is."

Jo tipped her head to one side, eyeing her with suspicion. "Okay, I'll see you soon."

"Uh huh." Maria nodded.

Jo let her go, in spite of the overpowering desire to grab her and kiss her until their lips hurt. Maria had started a fire Jo knew she'd be a long time putting out. She stood in the dark watching through the front window at Maria sitting in her car for more than a minute or two. She wanted to go out, pull her from the car and into her arms. She wanted to tell Maria how much she cared for her. She wanted to take her to bed. But she knew once that happened the friendship would die and eventually the physical relationship would as well. It always did. She went to the door and grabbed the knob, but the brake lights finally lit and Maria's car rolled down the long driveway into the night.

Maria sat in her car staring out into the darkness, trying to even out her breathing and slow her pounding heart. She'd been with other guys before meeting Jack, but never, not even with Jack when their relationship was new, had she experienced a kiss like the one she shared with Jo. A woman! She kissed a woman and felt more passion in those brief seconds than she'd ever felt at anytime in her life. She touched trembling fingers to her lips. She didn't want to leave. She wanted to go back inside and find out what it all meant.

Hormones, it must be her hormones. She tried recalling how it had been when she was pregnant with Matt. "My hormones are running wild," she muttered. She looked in the rear view mirror and saw only darkness in the house. Jo hadn't seemed shocked by what she'd done. And why would she? Jo kissed women all the time. Jo had probably kissed her share of straight women too.

She's incredibly attractive. She probably has gay and straight women throwing themselves at her all the time. "I'm just another one," she mumbled and dropped her head on the steering wheel. "Oh God, I'm such an idiot." She tried focusing her thoughts on driving to Kathleen's and picking up her son, but her mind kept wandering back to Jo and the feel of her lips.

Kathleen directed Maria right to the kitchen when she arrived. She dropped her purse on the floor and herself into one of the chairs.

Kathleen placed the tea kettle on the stove. "How are you getting along, sweetie?"

Maria sighed. "Oh you know, some days better than others."

Kathleen perched on a chair across from her. "And today is one of the others?"

Maria closed her eyes momentarily. Jo's face flashed in her mind. Her eyes flew open and she nodded. "Do you believe it's possible to love more than one man?"

Kathleen frowned. "It wouldn't be for me, but you know, some people believe that saying that 'anything's possible'." Kathleen's eyes were laser focused on her. The seconds seemed to drag into long minutes. "Are you having an affair? Because if you are, honey, I certainly won't judge you." Maria shook her head. "So…you're attracted to a man other than Jack?" Again she only shook her head.

Maria was embarrassed to even think about this unexplainable attraction to another woman, let alone, talk about it with Kathleen. She looked away.

"Oh!" Kathleen reached for her hand. "Maria, honey, look at me." When she did, Kathleen stared intently. "Is it Jo, honey?" Maria dropped her head. "Maria, I won't judge you." Kathleen reassured her. "I see how this is upsetting you…weighing on you. Talk to me."

Maria sighed loudly. "I don't know what's going on with me. I really like being around her. She makes me laugh. I feel like I'm enjoying life when I'm with her." Something, she thought, she hadn't felt with Jack in a very long time. "And she's so good with Matt. It's obvious she cares about him." Her voice quivered. "Something Jack has never done."

Kathleen patted her hand. "Don't you think maybe that's the attraction?" Maria shrugged. "Jackson refuses to accept Matt and she does."

Maria shook her head. She couldn't begin to explain to her sister-in-law the powerful sexual desire Jo Marchal made her feel when they touched even innocently. "I don't know. Sometimes when I'm around her I feel like I want to be closer."

Kathleen took hold of her hand. "Sweetie, I'm sure you're not the first straight woman to develop an attraction to an attractive lesbian like Jo. And yes, I admit, she's a looker in a rugged sort of way. If I swung that way, I'd probably give her a second and third look." Kathleen released her hand and patted it again. "Don't beat yourself up over this. You've got enough on your plate without worrying about it."

Maria knew she wasn't likely to take Kathleen's advice. "You're right. It's probably just my hormones."

"I know from three pregnancies they can be all over the place."

Every time Jo closed her eyes she saw Maria, and when she did manage to fall asleep, she'd awakened to a vivid dream of Maria. A dream in which she wasn't kissing Maria, but Maria was kissing her and holding her tightly.

Unable to go back to sleep, her mind whirling with thoughts of Maria, she made coffee and sat on the back deck waiting for the sun to rise. She fretted and wasn't completely convinced that Maria hadn't been upset when she left yesterday. She feared the loss of their friendship, a friendship far more vital to her than any physical relationship. She'd never before felt that anyone cared about her the way Maria did. It made her feel special. She liked feeling special to someone.

Maria called later in the week to confirm they would be out Saturday afternoon to take a ride, weather permitting. They continued to visit every weekend, but Maria seemed to get tense if Jo got too close to her, and so she made it a point not to. Jo was prepared to do anything to preserve their friendship. Neither made mention of their brief kiss.

CHAPTER EIGHTEEN

It took weeks of pleading until Jo convinced Maria to let her pay off their bet of a lavish dinner. Jo had the perfect place picked out, except Maria didn't want to go out anywhere. She wanted to stay in and asked that Jo cook.

"You're kidding, right?" Jo laughed into the phone.

"Actually, no. I don't feel like being out in public. I feel like… oh, I don't know." She sighed. "I feel fat and I don't have any nice fat clothes to wear."

"Maria, you're not fat. You're pregnant. And I'm pretty sure you'd be beautiful in a burlap sack."

"And you think flattery or flirting or whatever it is you're doing is supposed to change my mind?"

"I'm sorry."

There was a long pause. "No, I'm sorry, Jo. I didn't mean to snap." She sighed again. "It's no excuse, but my hormones have my emotions all over the place."

"Apology accepted, but the fact remains, I don't cook. Never have."

"Oh, come on Jo, be resourceful. I have every confidence in you being able to prepare one simple meal."

"But that doesn't change the facts."

"If you want to have dinner with me, you're going to have to cook it and there's no negotiating on this. Does your mother cook?"

"Yes. Doesn't every mother cook?"

"Maybe you should talk to her."

"You mean have her come here and cook you dinner?"

"No, silly. I mean ask her for a recipe, something you can manage."

"Okay, sure, I'll do that. But you have to promise if I cook, whatever it is, you'll eat it."

Maria laughed. "If you'll eat it, I promise I'll eat it."

"All right, so dinner at seven."

"Can we make it six?"

"Sure."

"Great and I'll be sure to bring my appetite."

In a panic she called her mom. Eileen gladly provided Jo her favorite pot roast recipe, explaining, "It's very simple, Jo Lynn. Follow the directions and it'll be fine. What's the special occasion?"

Jo hadn't prepared to have to answer that question. "Uh… nothing special, just uh…Maria's coming out for dinner's all."

"Oh, that lovely Hispanic friend of yours. That's nice."

Jo caught the innuendo. "Mom, Maria and I are *just* friends and it's *only* dinner."

"Well, yes, of course it is, dear."

* * *

Jo was nervous Saturday as evening approached. She knew she shouldn't make such a big deal of a simple dinner, but it was Maria, and she had this need to please her and have a perfect evening. The pot roast turned out fine, and Maria was not only impressed with Jo's untapped culinary skills, but the flawlessly set dining table complete with candlelight.

Shortly after seven, they were surprised by the sound of a car skidding in the gravel out front. Jo's first fearful thought was that it was Kate. Confused, but relieved, she watched as Cecile strode toward the porch. She gave Jo a wide grin as she pulled open the screen door.

"Hey, darlin', how you doin'?" She softened her voice. "You haven't called or answered any emails since you gave up the cop,

so I thought I'd better make sure you were still alive and kickin'."
She grabbed Jo and squeezed the air from her lungs in a bear hug.
Then she saw Maria at the table in the candlelight and released
Jo. "Oops, you got company. Guess I shoulda called first." Cecile
lumbered into the dining room. "Sorry to interrupt, darlin'." As she
neared the table, she gave a low whistle. "Well now, aren't you just
a pretty little thing."

Behind Cecile's back, Jo turned up her palms, shrugged and
mouthed "Sorry" to Maria.

Maria wiped her mouth and, smiling, stood to extend her hand.
"Maria West. It's a pleasure to meet you."

"I'm Jo's friend, Cecile." She took Maria's hand, leaned over and
placed a kiss on it. "Believe me, the pleasure is all mine." She took a
step back and motioned to Maria's pronounced middle. "Is that for
real?" Maria touched her belly and nodded. Cecile spun around to
Jo, slapping her on the back. "You ol' dog you. I see why you been
too busy to bother with your old friend."

Jo shook her head insistently, and Maria only smiled at Cecile's
assumption and Jo's obvious embarrassment. "No, Cil, Maria and
I aren't…" Jo sputtered. "Maria's married and has another child
already, and we're not…you know, we're…we're friends."

Cecile arched a suspicious brow, turning back around when
Maria spoke.

"Actually soon to be divorced, but still straight." She gave Cecile
an engaging smile. "All my life."

Cecile shook her head. "Well, I'm sure I speak for all lesbians
when I say it's a damn shame." She looked back at Jo again. "Right,
darlin'?"

Jo's mouth hung partially open, but she didn't utter a sound.

Cecile pulled out a chair, dropped her huge frame into it and
waved a hand across the table. "Please, finish your dinner."

Before sitting, Maria asked, "Would you like something to eat?
There's certainly plenty. Jo cooked for an army."

Cecile turned a sly grin to Jo. "My Jo here cooked? I didn't
know she knew what a kitchen was for except a place to keep a
fridge to put her beer in."

"That's real funny, Cil. So you drove all the way up here to
insult me in front of my company?"

"Just kiddin', darlin'." She eyed Maria. "I'm only kiddin'. Jo's a wonderful gal and I love her to death." She blew a kiss at Jo. "Not literally, mind you." She winked at Maria.

Maria only smiled. She liked watching Jo and this friend of hers. It was fun and playful and she guessed they had some special kind of bond. Jo made Cecile a drink and Cecile told endless stories and gossiped about people, mostly women, that they knew down in Kentucky.

Jo finally stopped her. "Cil, I think Maria's probably heard enough lesbian gossip now to give her nightmares for months."

"Sorry." She addressed Maria. "Jo'll tell you I can get carried away talkin' sometimes."

Maria pushed her chair back from the table a bit. "It's okay." She gave Jo a look. "I don't think I'll have nightmares." On the contrary, hearing all the stories of women with women had only served to stir a longing to be closer to Jo. If she were to dream about any woman, it would be Jo. She got up with her plate and headed to the kitchen. Stopping beside Jo, she rested a hand on her shoulder. "Would you like me to put some coffee on for you gals?"

Jo hopped up from her chair, taking the plate from Maria. "Oh no you don't. Sit, please. This is supposed to be your reward, not mine."

The corner of Cecile's mouth lifted as she watched the more than friendly exchange between Jo and Maria.

"But I'm sure you two have a lot of catching up to do."

Jo put a gentle hand on Maria's low back to steer her to her seat. "Nice try, but Cecile and I will get caught up before she goes back. Please sit. I have dessert."

"You made dessert too?" Maria asked in surprise.

Jo headed to the kitchen. "No. You said I had to cook dinner. You didn't say anything about fixing dessert too."

While Jo was in the kitchen, Cecile called out, "Oh yeah, darlin,' I almost forgot, Callie wanted to come, but she couldn't get away. I'll give you what she sends later when we're not in mixed company." She again winked at Maria. Jo made it a point to be sure that Maria saw her roll her eyes behind Cecile's back as she placed the plates around the table.

Cecile washed the last bit of pie down with the last of her drink. "So, you s'pose I could convince you gorgeous gals to let me take you out dancin' for a spell?"

"As fun as that sounds, I have to decline." When Cecile gave a pout, Maria touched her hand to Cecile's. "Don't take it personally. You're simply charming and I'd love to join you, but I have to pick up my son and get him home." She stood and looked over at Jo. "I really should get going. I hope you two have a good time."

Jo stood too. "Don't feel like you have to rush off. We can go out later. The place is open till two in the morning."

Maria squeezed Jo's hand. "I really need to get Matt home."

Jo followed her to the front door. The last thing Maria wanted was for this evening to end. She wanted to be able to go out with Jo and her friend and see Jo having fun with other lesbians. She especially wanted to watch Jo dance or dance with her. The thought of being in Jo's arms stirred that familiar desire and that gave her the best reason to go home before she did something like she had before.

"Thanks for dinner, it was wonderful," she told Jo at the door. "You're a fine cook, Jo Marchal."

"Sorry for the interruption. I had no idea she was going to show up."

"Oh well, we'll have to do it again then."

"You got it." Jo smiled. "Drive carefully."

Maria called across the room. "It was very nice to meet you, Cecile."

"Pleasure's all mine, darlin'," Cecile called back.

"I'll talk to you later," she said to Jo and was gone.

Cecile was in the kitchen making another drink when Jo returned from the living room. She leaned a meaty hip against the counter while Jo cleared the dishes and loaded the dishwasher.

"That's a real pretty friend you've made there, darlin'. How'd you two meet?"

"She's the realtor that found me this place," Jo replied without looking up.

"Really, that's interesting. How come you kept that little tidbit of info from me?"

Jo spun around, drying her hands. "Because the two of you would have bored me to sleep with shop talk."

They spent an hour catching up, and Jo filled Cecile in on why she and Kate were no longer dating.

"Good! I didn't like that little Napoleon at all."

They left the house around nine for Whispers and, snagging a table not far from the dance floor, they settled in. They both had already spotted Kate lurking at the corner of the bar and when she came toward them, Cecile jumped up to cut her off before she reached Jo.

"Well, well, if it ain't the fierce little cop."

Kate tried to sidestep her, but Cecile blocked her way.

"Get out of my way!"

Cecile matched her steps each time she moved. "Gee, darlin', is that any way to talk to a lady?"

Kate snorted. "Give me a break."

Cecile cocked her head. "I sure hope it don't come down to that. Now where you headin' there?"

"I'm going to say hi to Jo," Kate said impatiently.

"Well now, I don't think that's a good idea." When Kate tried to sidestep Cecile again, she pushed the manicured nail of her index finger into Kate's chest. "You see here, she's with me." Cecile drew closer. "And I don't like to share."

Kate smacked her hand away. "I'm not afraid of you, you overgrown hillbilly."

Cecile's face flushed beet red. This time she hooked her finger inside the top of Kate's shirt and gathered the fabric in her fist. Leaning closer still, she said, "Listen here, you inconsiderate little worm. Jo's finished with you, so leave her alone. Don't make me have to come hunt you down." She pulled within a breath of Kate. "'Cause I will find you." She leaned back, released Kate's shirt and gave it a smoothing pat. "See ya, darlin'."

Kate's eyes glowered with hatred. She turned and stomped off to her dark corner.

When Cecile returned to her chair, Jo said, "I could have handled her."

Cecile scooted her chair close, draping her arm across the back of Jo's chair. "I have no doubt of that fact, darlin', but I think she'll leave you be now, so don't worry your little self, you hear? Besides, I was havin' me some fun."

Chuckling, Jo glanced to where Kate sat staring back at them. The expression she saw there made her uneasy.

Within an hour Cecile had found herself a tableful of women who were unsuspectingly about to have their pants charmed off. As Jo sat at their table alone, a tall, slender, ponytailed brunette walked up carrying two beers.

"I do hope that's not your girlfriend." She angled her head in the direction Jo had been looking—the lively corner where Cecile was sitting. Jo shook her head.

The brunette leaned down. "Good, because I have this extra beer and you look like someone I'd like to share it with."

Jo looked up to meet soft brown eyes and a warm smile.

"Do you mind if I join you?"

"Not at all." Jo flashed a smile of her own.

She set the beer in front of Jo and took the chair next to her. Wiping her hand first on her tight designer jeans, she extended it to Jo. "Hi, I'm Loren Mathews."

Jo enclosed the thin hand in hers. "Jo, Jo Marchal. Nice to meet you, Loren."

She kept a firm hold of Jo's hand. "And you." After a long lingering moment she released Jo's hand. "You don't look familiar and I'm sure I wouldn't have forgotten a face like yours. Do you live around here?"

Jo took a slow drink of the beer. "On Buck Creek Road outside Midland near the reserve. And you?"

"I'm a local, but I work at the hospital in Midland. I'm surprised I haven't seen you before now."

"I don't come out much."

Loren took a drink of her beer and leaned back. "Well, I'm glad you did tonight."

They talked easily until midnight when Lorne announced, "I have to get going. I'm on at six thirty." She stood taking Jo's hand. "It was certainly a pleasure meeting you, Jo Marchal." She leaned down and brushed her lips over Jo's cheek. "I hope to see you again sometime."

Jo nodded with a smile. She liked Loren. Her easy-going, laidback personality was refreshing compared to someone like Cecile. She glanced at the table where her friend sat. Or compared to someone like Kate, who seemed wound too tight and ready to uncoil at any minute. Yes, perhaps she would see Loren again. At one thirty Jo interrupted Cecile and her harem of women.

"Sorry, Cil, but I'd like to head home."

Cecile wrapped an arm loosely around Jo's waist. "Ah darlin', sit down and have a drink with us. These ladies are all nurses at the local hospital. They assure me they can cure whatever ails you."

Jo relented after a moment and pulled up a chair. "If I have a drink, can we go?"

"Sure, darlin'."

Jo leaned close to Cecile's ear. "You can take anyone of them back to the house if you want. I don't mind."

Cecile waved the waitress over. "Thanks, we'll see."

They finally left at two thirty, well after last call. Cecile had her arm across Jo's shoulder as they made their way out. More for support, Jo suspected, than camaraderie. Cecile seemed a tad bit on the drunken side.

"I can't believe you're going home with little ol' me," Jo joked as they crossed the parking lot.

Cecile let loose a belly laugh. "Don't get your panties all wet, darlin', I ain't gonna sleep with you." She stopped and squeezed Jo's cheeks in her large red-tipped fingers. "As cute as you are, it'd be sooo weird."

Jo shuddered. She loved Cecile dearly, but the thought of being naked in bed with her seemed…unimaginable.

She put Cecile in the passenger seat of the Cadillac. "So how come you're not bringing one of those nurses back to the house with you?"

"'Cause it was all or nothing and a couple of 'em was holding out."

Jo cringed at the thought of an orgy in her guest room and thanked the stars there wouldn't be one as she walked to the driver's door.

* * *

They had pie and coffee for breakfast, but Cecile left by lunchtime since all Jo had to offer in the way of other food was leftover pot roast. As soon as she could take care of the horses, she hit the country roads with the truck's windows down, heading for her mom's house and thinking of Loren Mathews. She hoped they would meet again. Loren was charming, good looking and someone Jo thought she'd like to date. Although, charming was something Claire been, and that relationship had turned out to be worse than bad.

At her mom's she repaired a leaky bathroom faucet and hung a shelf in the kitchen. Eileen insisted she stay for dinner. When Jo arrived home at eight she was exhausted, but not too tired to return a missed call from Maria.

"Hi!" Maria's voice gave Jo the warmest tingles.

"Hi yourself. What's up?"

"I called to see if you girls had a good time last night. I have to admit, I was a little concerned you might have gotten yourselves into trouble when you weren't home earlier this evening. Your friend struck me as someone that gets a wild hair on occasion."

Jo pulled a beer from the fridge, chuckling. "That's an understatement. Cecile *is* a wild hair. I was at Mom's the better part of the day doing some handy work for her." She took a drink of beer. "I think she thinks because I'm gay…well…I think she thinks all of us are handymen." Maria laughed. "Anyway, thanks for worrying about me."

"It gives me something to do."

"Yeah well, you'll know if I get thrown in the slammer. You'll be my first phone call. Lord knows I couldn't call Mom. Cecile lives too far away, but if she were here, she'd be sittin' right beside me. So…that leaves you, my friend."

Maria laughed again. "It's nice to be needed."

Jo sighed at the thought of how much she did need her, then squeezed her thighs to stop the pulsing between them.

"I'm glad you had a good girls' night out. Did you meet up with your deputy friend Kate too?"

That question she hadn't expected. "Uh…no. You know, I meant to tell you a few weeks ago that we weren't dating any more. Guess I forgot."

Maria exhaled in relief, glad that Jo was no longer having anything to do with that woman. She'd never gotten a good feeling around her and was pretty darn sure that the bruise Jo had gotten had been compliments of the deputy. It wasn't jealousy that made her distrust the woman. It was that she cared so much for Jo. She felt for Jo the way she did for her son and his soon-to-be sibling. She wanted them safe. She wanted to ensure no one hurt them.

"I'm sorry to hear that." Maria justified the lie in her mind. "Have you found anyone new to date?"

"No, not really."

"No, not really" didn't sound definite. Maybe this Callie person who Cecile mentioned last night was getting Jo's attention these days. Not wanting Jo to think she was keeping tabs on her or checking up on her, Maria let the questions she was dying to ask go—for now.

"When it's right, I'm sure you'll find that special someone."

"Yeah, maybe, but relationships are overrated if you ask me."

Maria wondered if someone had hurt Jo so badly in the past that she'd given up on love. "Well, I think if it's meant to be, it will be. Don't give up."

"If you say so, I just don't think it's meant for me. But hey, I've got a good life and no complaints. And with friends like you, who needs lovers?"

Lovers, the word sent hot desire straight to Maria's core. *Stop it, stop it, stop it*, she told herself. "I might be adopting that philosophy right along with you," she finally managed to get out.

"That's great! We'll start a club." Jo laughed.

Maria joined her. They confirmed plans for the following Saturday. "Thanks again for dinner last night. I'd say you did your mother's recipe proud."

"Thanks and don't forget we have to do it again since Cecile interrupted our evening."

"I'd like that. Goodnight, Jo."

"Night, Maria."

CHAPTER NINETEEN

Several Saturdays later, restless after Maria and Matt left, Jo showered, dressed and drove to the bar, promising herself to have only one beer. If she didn't see Loren, she'd leave. Jo was leaning on the bar nursing her drink when she saw her arriving with several other women. They had no sooner sat down when Loren zeroed in on her. Locking her sparkling gaze on Jo, she leaned to say something to the woman beside her, then walked to the bar.

She grasped Jo's hand. "I'm so glad to see you again."

"Can I buy you a drink?"

Loren leaned close. "Sure, but I need to get some for my friends." She squeezed Jo's hand, got the drinks and delivered them. When she returned, Jo had a beer waiting for her. "What brings you out tonight? I don't see your friend anywhere."

Jo got lost in Loren's eyes. "I was hoping I might see you."

Loren leaned on the bar, dangerously close to her. "I looked for you here last weekend."

"I don't really frequent bars much." Jo's shoulder lifted.

"And yet here you are." Loren flashed a pearly grin.

Jo put her arm on the bar and leaned close. "And here I am."

Loren moved to stand in front of Jo, placing a hand on either side of her on the bar. She had her pinned and Jo was rather enjoying it. "You suppose I might talk you into dancing with me tonight?"

Jo opened her mouth to answer when she saw Kate bearing down on them, a fiery glare in her eyes. Kate stepped behind Loren and placed a hand on her shoulder before Jo had a chance to warn her. When she pulled Loren around and cocked her arm, Jo jumped quickly between them—just in time for Kate's fist to land squarely on her cheek. It felt like she'd smacked her with a two by four. The blow snapped her head back and forced her into Loren.

"Damn it!" Jo placed a hand to her throbbing cheek. She shoved Kate back with her other hand. "Get the hell away from me!"

With her hand still cupping her cheek, Jo rushed to the door and outside.

As she reached her truck, she heard Loren calling, "Jo, wait… please."

Loren caught her as she reached the truck.

"I can't do this," Jo said, her hand on the door handle.

A few seconds later Kate burst through the bar's door and bulldozed her way toward them yelling, "God, Jo, I'm sorry." She moved lightning fast.

"Are you okay?" Loren asked.

Not waiting to answer, Jo pulled open the door and attempted to slide inside. Loren turned and stood protectively between Kate and the truck.

Kate yelled at Loren, "Get away from her!" and shoved Loren forcefully into the truck door. The door slammed, trapping Jo's hand in it.

Jo's breath whooshed from her lungs with the excruciating pain. Kate might as well have shot her with her service revolver.

God, what did I do to deserve this?

She pushed on the door enough to get her hand out of the frame, hit the door locks and shoved the key in the ignition and started the truck. Fighting the anger that was boiling up inside her, she didn't bother looking to see what the two women were doing. She eased the truck out of its parking space, intending to head home, but nausea swept over her and she had to stop before pulling out onto the road. When it passed, she headed out again. It felt as though fire was shooting up her arm. Several miles down the road she spotted the family market and whipped into the lot. She handed a five to the cashier in payment for a bag of frozen peas.

"Keep the change."

Back in her truck, she laid her damaged hand on her thigh and gently placed the frozen bag on top of it. The cold stung, biting into her flesh. She tugged her shirttail from her jeans, laid it over her hand and resettled the bag in place. Her cheek was throbbing too, and she could feel the skin tightening under her eye. It was swelling shut. Laying her head back, she waited until her hand was numb before starting the truck again and heading for home. Somehow, half blinded and broken, she managed to get herself there.

Shortly after she put Matt to bed Maria got an uneasy feeling. At nine thirty, she settled into her own bed and dialed Jo. Disappointment nagged at her when Jo's machine picked up. She left a message. Unable to shake the feeling that was unsettling her, it was midnight before she managed to drift off. She called Jo around nine on Sunday morning and again got no answer. When another half hour passed and she couldn't reach Jo on either of her phones, a feeling of disquiet assailed her. In a rush, she dropped Matt off at Kathleen's so he could attend church with them and she drove out to the farm.

She found Jo's truck parked haphazardly in the driveway, which only added to her mounting anxiety. She pounded on the door and after several long minutes tried looking through the front window. All she could see was a whiskey bottle on the coffee table. Jo wasn't answering the phone or the door. She might very well be in bed. Maria's mind came to an abrupt halt—Jo might very well be in bed with a woman. That thought unsettled her more than any other explanation for not being able to reach Jo.

She made her way around the house and found the back door unlocked. She fought a nervous feeling in her stomach as she entered. The answering machine light blinked like a beacon on the kitchen counter. From the doorway she caught sight of Jo on the couch. The whiskey bottle she had seen was empty, and as she neared Jo's sleeping form she stopped abruptly and placed her hand over her mouth.

"Oh, Jo," Maria whispered.

She moved her hand over her nose, picked up the empty bottle and set it aside, then perched on the edge of the table. She took in the dark bruise covering Jo's cheek, and the thawed bag of peas sandwiched between her hands. When she lifted the bag, she gasped.

"Oh, Jo honey. What have you done?"

She gave Jo's shoulder a gentle shake. "Jo." Jo didn't move. She watched Jo's chest rise and fall for a moment and tried again. "Jo, honey, wake up." Jo only moaned. She stroked her hair. "Jo, please wake up."

Jo's face contorted in pain and she exhaled a deep breath, then slowly cracked open her eyes.

"My God, Jo! What happened?"

Jo turned her head away and closed her eyes against the agonizing pain in her head and hand.

"Why do you subject yourself to the brutality of that woman?" Maria cautiously lifted her hand.

Hurt by the implication, Jo jerked her hand from Maria's and snapped. "I've still got a mother in case you forgot. I don't need another one."

She regretted the words the second they left her mouth and more when Maria's expression reflected how much they had stung her. Her head pounded harder, a reminder of the whiskey she drank last night to kill the searing pain in her cheek and hand. She knew Maria only wanted to help. Maria cared. They'd become such good friends, holding each other up through each other's challenges.

She turned back to Maria. "I'm sorry." She whispered shamefully. "I didn't mean that."

Maria lightly touched her fingers to her bruised cheek and pushed the hair back from Jo's face. Her voice was soft. "I know, sweetie." She stood. "I think that hand looks broken. You need to get it X-rayed." She took hold of Jo's good hand and gave a little tug. "Come on, I'll drive you."

She resisted. "There's nothing broken." Through excruciating pain, she wiggled her fingers slightly. "See, it'll be fine."

Maria gave a look of disapproval and tugged again on her hand. "Either you come with me, or I will call your mother." She looked at

Maria in disbelief, but at the same time reveled in Maria's sure soft grasp. "Surely you don't want me to upset your mother needlessly."

She gave in and allowed Maria to pull her to her feet. "God, you're a stubborn woman," she muttered.

Maria chuckled. "And look who's calling the kettle black."

Jo let herself be steered out of the house, and per Maria's instructions, tried to hold her damaged hand above her chest as they made their way across the yard to Maria's car. But the increasing pain made that impossible, and when her hand drifted toward her waist, the pain shot up her arm and straight to her head. Suddenly, dizzy and weak, she dropped to her knees, catching herself with her good hand barely in time to keep from falling head first. Within a second Maria was kneeling beside her.

"I think I feel—" Unable to prevent it, Jo felt her body heave. The taste of whiskey burned at the back of her throat. She prayed silently as Maria's hand came to rest on her back.

"Try to keep your head lower than your heart so you don't faint. Don't move I'll be right back." She rushed to the house.

Jo laid her forearm on the cool grass and rested her head on it. She choked back the whiskey that was trying to burn its way out of her stomach. Thank heavens she hadn't thrown up. Maria returned and placed a cold wet cloth against the back of her neck. The sickening feeling that had brought her to her knees only moments before abated.

Maria stroked her hand over Jo's back. "Better?" Jo mumbled her reply at the ground. "Can you get up?"

Jo slowly raised her head in response and offered no resistance when Maria slipped a hand under her arm to help her to her feet. Carefully taking hold of her wrist, Maria raised the crippled hand above Jo's shoulder and walked her to the car. After Maria belted her in, she reclined the seat back, wrapped the cool towel around her hand and rested it on her chest.

Maria thought Jo looked like a hurt child lying there. Despite becoming good friends with her since their meeting over a year ago, Maria hadn't been able to get to the bottom of what caused the deep sadness that darkened Jo's otherwise gorgeous eyes at times. Jo's eyes were closed when Maria brushed locks of hair from her damp forehead.

"You relax, sweetie." She gently pushed her fingers through Jo's hair again. "I'm going to take care of you. I'll always take care of you."

She'd spoken those same words to her son more times than she could count. But the ache in her chest today didn't feel maternal. It was something entirely different. No matter how hard Jo tried to keep her at a distance, Maria knew she'd always want to be around to take care of her.

When they'd taken Jo into an exam room, Maria stepped outside to call Kathleen and let her know what was going on. Back inside she discovered they had given Jo something for pain. It had taken affect, evidenced by the crooked smile Jo gave her.

Maria placed her hand on Jo's shoulder. "You look like you're in less pain." Jo's eyes were cloudy and unfocused. She looked like a broken soul that needed someone to take care of her.

"They gave me some good stuff and said my face isn't broken, but…" She raised her hand, wrist limp. "But my hand is. Gonna be late for dinner at Mom's."

"Would you like me to call her for you?" Maria asked.

Jo gave a slight nod. "Waitin' on the bone doctor."

"I'll step out and call her in a few minutes." Maria pulled a stool over to sit and wait on the doctor. She felt a need to stay as close to Jo as she could and reached out to grasp Jo's good hand.

"At least you're not left handed."

Jo knew the pain medication was pretty potent, but she was clear-headed enough to know that her increased heart rate and the warmth spreading from her chest wasn't the result of drugs. She gave Maria's hand a light squeeze.

"Good thing or I wouldn't be able to fill out all the insurance paperwork they're gonna want from me." She sighed, closed her eyes and relished the feel of Maria's hand in hers. When she opened them again, Maria sat gazing at her intently.

"I know. I look like someone that's been dragged out of the gutter after a bar fight."

Maria reached out and brushed her fingers over her forehead. "Not at all. We do need to find you a girlfriend to take care of you."

Jo chuckled. "You got Cupid in your back pocket there?" Maria only arched a brow. "What qualifications you got to play matchmaker?"

"I admit my past record doesn't speak well for itself, but I think I'm a much better judge of character these days." She gave a playful smile. "I'll get my resume together for you."

The full effect of the pain medication hit Jo like a brick between the eyes. "Okay," she said before closing her eyes.

When she opened them again, Maria was shaking her gently and she had a cast on her left hand and forearm. "Jo sweetie, wake up. Let's go home."

Maria helped steady Jo into the house. "Let's get you into bed first and I'll fix you something to eat."

Jo shook her head. "No food. My stomach feels awful. I need a shower and I can put myself to bed."

Maria stopped in the living room still holding onto the arm Jo had draped across her shoulders. "You can't shower. You can hardly stand by yourself. Besides, you'll get your cast wet. Your stomach feels so bad because there's probably nothing in it but whiskey and a pain pill." She steered Jo down the hall. "How about a bath first, then something to eat?"

Jo was too tired to argue. Maria helped her sit on the side of the tub, started the water running and reached for a button on Jo's shirt.

Jo pushed her hand away. "What are you doing?"

"Trying to help." Maria stepped back.

Jo shook her head. "I didn't become an invalid. I can do this." She realized her words were as hurtful as the ones she'd unleashed earlier.

"I'm sorry."

Jo caught her arm before she was out of reach and let her hand slide into Maria's. "No, I'm sorry, Maria. You should just slap me."

She cupped Jo's chin. "Someone beat me to it." The compassion in Maria's eyes was a salve not only for her physical wounds, but the emotional ones. "You've got ten minutes to undress yourself and get in the bath." Jo released her hand. "I'll be back." Maria closed the door behind her.

Maria returned as promised, knocking before opening the door and poking her head through. Jo was submerged to her neck, eyes closed with her casted arm hanging over the side of the tub.

"You are awake, aren't' you?"

Jo rolled her head to the side and opened her eyes. "Yes, Mom."

"Very funny." Maria smiled down at her. "How long before you're done? I want to fix you something to eat."

"May I have half an hour?"

"You certainly may. Can you manage getting out by yourself?"

Maria prayed the answer was yes. She knew it would be dangerous for her to see Jo naked. Jo was far too vulnerable now, and she herself was too emotionally raw. In her soul, she knew that the brief kiss over a month ago was a prelude to what could happen between them, but logic told her she couldn't allow it to. A physical relationship, as satisfying as it might be, would surely destroy their friendship. No, she wasn't about to lose the precious bond they'd forged.

"Maria!" Wincing, Jo waved her broken hand, snapping her from her daydreaming. "There's a draft."

Maria blinked. "Thirty minutes." She pulled the door closed and leaned against the frame, a flood of heat sweeping through her body. Back in the kitchen she prayed under her breath, "Please make it stop."

When thirty minutes came and went, Maria returned to the bathroom. "Jo?" She rapped on the door.

Jo's reply was so faint she barely heard it, so she poked her head in again. Jo sat on the floor, her head resting on her arm stretched across the toilet seat, her robe loosely covering her body.

"I felt too sick to stand."

Maria knelt beside her. "Of course you did." She felt Jo's neck for any signs of a fever. Satisfied that at least Jo's body temperature was normal, she pulled the robe tighter around Jo and tied the sash. "Come on." She stood, hooking her hand under Jo's arm. "I promise you'll feel better with something in your stomach."

Jo insisted on sitting at the dining table, and slowly but surely she devoured every bite of the soup and sandwich Maria had fixed for her.

"Thanks, I feel almost human again."

Maria's hand rested on Jo's shoulder as she reached for the empty plate. Jo loved the way it felt when Maria touched her. She had ever since that very first handshake over a year ago. The yearning sparked by gazing into her dark eyes hadn't subsided since then either. It had only grown stronger.

"Don't you need to get home to Matt?"

Maria returned from the kitchen, drying her hands. "When you're all tucked securely into your bed, I'll go."

Jo pushed up from the table, picked up the pill bottle and dropped it in her pocket on her way to the fridge for a bottle of water. "Then let's get me tucked in so you'll go home to your family."

With Jo settled in her bed, Maria shook out a pill for her and handed her the water. She placed the bottle back on the nightstand and slipped her hand into Jo's. "You're my family too, you know?"

"Thanks for taking care of me today." She squeezed Maria's hand then pushed it away. "Now go."

"Where's your phone?"

Jo shrugged. "I honestly don't know."

Maria searched Jo's clothes on the bathroom floor before tossing them into the hamper. She finally located the phone on the seat of her truck. When she returned to the bedroom, Jo appeared to be asleep.

"That's right, you sleep. I hope you'll call me if you need anything." She leaned over and kissed Jo's forehead, laid the phone on the nightstand and quietly left.

It took every bit of concentration Jo could muster to pretend to be sleeping so Maria would leave. While the pain pills made her drowsy and almost masked the pain in her hand, they also seemed to heighten her sensitivity to Maria's presence. She ached to touch Maria in ways she'd only ever be able to dream about.

CHAPTER TWENTY

Maria called daily to check on her and by Wednesday Jo had gotten the hang of working with a broken hand while under the influence of pain pills. What irked her most was having to hire someone temporarily to work with the horses that she'd contracted to train. Given her damaged hand, she didn't feel that she had the right touch for the job, a job she loved above all others. She parked herself on the sidelines, occasionally calling out suggestions to the guy Tucker had found to fill her boots.

As she climbed the porch steps Saturday evening at five, she heard a vehicle in the drive. She didn't recognize the Jeep that slowly crept toward the house, but when it stopped she was surprised to see it was Loren. Eyes hidden behind dark sunglasses, Loren wore a bright smile along with a tank top, jean shorts and sandals as she strode confidently to the porch. Stopping short of the steps she removed her sunglasses.

"Hi! I thought I should stop out and check on you." She squinted up at Jo. "I feel kind of responsible." Her shoulders pulled into a shrug.

Jo shook her head. "Well, you're not. I'm real sorry you got caught up in all that."

Loren propped a foot on the bottom step, drawing Jo's eyes to her long elegant legs. She pushed off the post and motioned with her good hand to the chairs on the porch.

"I was about to have a cold one. Would you like to join me?"

Loren ascended the steps two at a time and stood in front of her in an instant, pulling Jo's hand from where she'd hid it under her shirt.

"How's it feeling?"

Jo tilted her head. "How'd you know?" She didn't await an answer. "More importantly, how'd you find me?"

Standing face to face, Loren continued to hold the cast in her hands.

"I was on duty when your girlfriend brought you to the hospital."

Jo chuckled. "She's not my girlfriend."

Loren's brow rose. "You don't say."

"She's just a friend."

Loren gave a knowing smile. "And the one at the bar?"

Jo shook her head. "She wishes. Is that how you found me?"

Loren settled into one of the chairs, leaned back and draped one long leg over the other. Loren's sex appeal wasn't lost on Jo as she leaned back against the porch rail.

"You're joking, right? I threatened to call the cops. She begged me not to. She's not stupid in spite of acting like she doesn't have a lick of sense. If I ever see that one again, I'm pretty sure I'll be running in the opposite direction and dialing nine-one-one."

"Like I said, I'm sorry you got caught up in that drama."

She fixed Jo with her gaze. "It was valiant of you to step in front of that punch. I understand she's a cop."

"Yeah, a deputy sheriff. I'm pretty sure she suffers from a Napoleon complex." Jo gave a tiny smile. "You know 'cause everyone else is taller than her."

"Yes, I've known a few of her kind."

"So, can I get you a beer?"

"Sure, but only one, and I advise against more than one for you if you're still taking pain meds."

Jo returned with the beers and took the chair next to her. Loren tapped a slender finger on the cast.

"I'd say at the rate you're going this cast won't last but another week tops. I'd be happy to fix you up." She placed the bottle to her lips and took a slow drink. "You really should keep it dry."

Jo looked at the cast. "You still haven't said how you found me."

"Well, I was going to ask one of the officers I know to help me find you, but then the next morning you came to me."

Jo searched her memory for a sighting of Loren at the hospital. Nothing. Heck, she barely remembered even being there.

"You know—that pesky insurance paperwork you have to fill out to get treated."

"I thought that information was supposed to be protected under some privacy laws or something."

Loren smiled coyly. "I can assure you I have not shared a single thing I've learned about you with a soul." Loren tipped her head. "Your sign says this is a horse farm." She looked Jo down to her cowboy boots and back up to her eyes. "So are you some kind of horse wrangler?"

Jo lifted the cast. "Not at the moment, but usually, yeah." She bobbed her head. "You like horses?"

"I guess." Loren thought for a moment. "I've only been around a couple and it was back in high school. But what's not to like, right?"

Jo nodded. "You want to meet mine?"

"Sure."

Jo gave the fifty-cent tour, introducing her to three of her half a dozen horses. Loren seemed perfectly at ease around the horses and asked good questions. A short time later they were back on the porch sipping ice water with lemon slices.

"This is some place you have here."

Jo knew how true that was. "Maybe once I get this off," she lifted the plaster, "you can stop back out and we can ride…if you like."

"That sounds like fun, and I bet you can be a lot of fun." She scooted to the edge of her chair. "I should get going."

Jo stood also. "I appreciate you coming out to check on me."

Loren took Jo's cast in her hands as she had earlier. "My pleasure. I like you, Jo." She brushed the tips of Jo's fingers sticking out of the cast. "You really should come by the hospital and let me replace this for you."

"Yeah, sure. Maybe I can get by there this weekend."

"I'll be looking for you." She leaned in and brushed her lips over Jo's cheek. Releasing her hand, she stepped from the porch and slid her sunglasses down to cover her eyes. "Enjoy your evening."

* * *

Maria hurried into the house with Matt late Saturday afternoon after his ride. She quickly settled him with Rosie inside the door and rushed to the bathroom. She heard a car door as she came back down the hall and when she spotted who was driving the little blue car that had stopped out front she nearly tripped over Matt trying to get out of the house. She stood on the porch and felt in her skirt pocket for her phone.

Jo must have heard the car too. She was standing in the barn doors with her arms crossed over her chest.

Kate was talking even before she stopped a few feet away. "I am so sorry, Jo." Kate took another step closer. "I didn't mean to—"

"You've got a lot of nerve coming here."

She reached out for Jo's broken hand. "Jo, please, I just want you to understand how sorry I am and make sure that you're okay."

When Kate's hand got dangerously close to Jo's cast, she jerked it up and away and stepped back.

Maria bolted from the porch then, phone in hand, and headed toward the barn like a provoked bull, enraged and ready for attack.

"You need to stay away," Jo was saying.

Kate started to step toward Jo again, but Maria caught her arm. "Get away from her. Haven't you done enough?"

Kate wrenched her arm from Maria's grasp. Fear shot through Maria when her eyes met Kate's hate-filled stare. Maria pulled out her phone.

"I'm calling the police."

Praying it wouldn't turn into another bad judgment call, Jo quickly stepped between the two. With a hand on Maria's shoulder, she steered her a few feet away.

"I've got this. Really, Maria, it's okay." Jo kept a hand on her shoulder, Maria's anger was palpable, her eyes black as coal. "I promise if she tries anything, I'll smack her with this." She raised her cast with a smile, immediately diffusing Maria's anger.

Maria removed Jo's hand from her shoulder and shoved the cell phone in it. "Here." She looked past Jo at the glaring Kate. "Don't make me have to come back out here."

Jo took a breath as she watched Maria return to the porch. *One down, one to go.* She focused her attention back on Kate without a hint of the smile she'd given Maria.

Kate jerked her head toward the house. "So, does your little straight girlfriend know about the lesbian one?"

Jo fixed her eyes on Kate. "Maria and I are only the best of friends. She happens to care that whoever I date treats me right." She paused, hoping her words would sink into Kate's thick head. "Here's a piece of friendly advice. Stay away, Kate, because if you don't I will find a way to make your life as miserable"—she raised the cast—"as you've made mine." Jo sidestepped her and walked to the house without looking back. She joined Maria on the porch, dropping an arm gently across her shoulders. They faced the house.

"She thinks you're my girlfriend."

Maria slid her arm around Jo's waist and pulled her close. "Well, far be it for me to ruin anyone's fantasy."

Jo gazed down at Maria. "You're bad." She chuckled.

Maria met her gaze smiling. "Okay…"

Jo felt the all-too-familiar ache. *If only.* They walked with their arms around each other into the house as the sound of crunching gravel signaled Kate's retreat.

* * *

Jo stopped at the hospital around ten on Sunday morning and asked if Loren Mathews was working. The gal at information sent her to the ER. The place seemed vaguely familiar. At the glass-enclosed desk she asked again for Loren. She was shocked when the receptionist paged for Dr. Mathews.

"If she's with a patient, she could be a while."

"No problem. I can wait."

She picked up a year-old magazine and found an article on the benefits of fitness for women's health. Fifteen or twenty minutes later—Jo wasn't clock watching—she was greeted by a pair of sneakers attached to very long legs and a charming smile.

"Hi." Jo smiled in return.

Loren shoved her hands in the pockets of her white coat. "You came."

Jo nodded. "You told me to."

Loren sat in the chair beside her, took Jo's cast gently and turned it over. She lowered her voice. "I did, and apparently the assumption I've been under that all strong, gay women are bullheaded is ill conceived."

"I try real hard not fit the stereotypes."

Loren met her eyes. "I didn't mean to insinuate—"

"Relax. I haven't taken offense to anything you've said to me since we met." She couldn't stop a silly grin from claiming her face. Loren was one attractive woman. "So, watcha think, Doc?"

"I think this may need further examination."

As they passed by the desk, Loren called to the woman behind it. "Can you please pull the file for Jo Marchal?" She spelled the last name. "From last Sunday. Thank you." She led Jo to a large room with multiple beds and curtains hanging beside each and patted the first one. "Hop up."

"You really need me up there to look at my hand?"

"How else can you judge my bedside manner?" Loren said playfully. Jo laughed and followed orders. "The last time you were here you were so out of it you didn't even know I was the one who set and cast your hand."

"Really, so who gave you permission to do it?"

"Your pretty friend, Ms. West." Loren met Jo's gaze. "She asked me if I would also put big cumbersome casts on both of your legs so you couldn't leave the house." Loren laughed. "She was very worried about you, you know? That's why I thought you two were together."

"And so you thought what, I was cheating on my woman? Was that another of your assumptions about strong, gay women?" Jo's voice was kind of loud, although her tone was playful.

"Shh…you want to out yourself in the hospital?"

Jo shrugged. "Does it matter?"

"Not to me. The people I work with already know about me."

"You don't think when people get a look at me they don't automatically place me into one of those stereotypes? You know, 'one of them'?"

Loran spoke softly. "You know not every strong, attractive woman is one of us."

Loren cut the week-old cast off and after an X-ray to confirm everything still looked good, went about replacing it. Jo watched in amazement as her delicate fingers expertly performed the job. She guessed she was getting a firsthand look at who Loren Mathews was. And that was a woman strong in confidence, her convictions and her sexuality. All in all, Loren was an appealing package.

As she finished and was soothingly wiping away plaster residue from Jo's fingertips, she said, "I'm off in a few hours. Would you like to get something to eat somewhere?"

Jo's shoulders slumped. "I can't. I'm going to my mom's over in Campbell to have dinner."

Loren tipped her head. "You're serious, aren't you?"

"Yeah, why?"

"That's so sweet. You continue to amaze me." Loren leaned closer. "You're not at all what I expected."

Jo kept the space close and intimate between them. "And what was that?"

"A rough, tough, I don't know, maybe a possessive kind of cowgirl."

"And?" Jo leaned forward until there was only a breath between them.

Loren's smelled of mint as her breath whispered against Jo's lips. "You're soft." She touched Jo's good hand resting on her thigh. "And sensitive." She slid her fingers off Jo's hand onto her thigh. "And compassionate."

Jo's eyelids felt like lead. She wanted to kiss Loren more than she wanted her next breath. A loud crash somewhere close by startled both women and reminded them where they were. Loren took a step back, but neither broke the intense gaze they shared.

"I almost kissed you." A smile crept across Jo's face.

"And I was going to let you." Without breaking eye contact, Loren reached beside Jo and picked up the chart. "Too bad about lunch." She held the chart to her chest.

"Yeah," Jo nodded.

Loren stepped toward the curtain. "Well, maybe I'll see you at the bar again."

Jo nodded again. "Sure. Or…" She raised her new cast. "Maybe you'll come riding when I get this off?"

"Careful what you wish for." She backed around the curtain with a smile and disappeared.

Jo hated lying about what happened to her hand, although it wasn't a complete fib. She did tell her mother that her hand had got closed in the door of her truck, she just sort of alluded to the accident happening at her farm. There didn't seem to be any need to share with her mother the fact that she was hanging out at a bar.

Jo arrived home from her mom's around seven to a message from Maria. "Hi, Jo, I tried to call you around eleven this morning, but you weren't in. Or at four this afternoon, and now it's after six and I'm beginning to worry after yesterday. Your cell keeps going straight to voice mail, so please call me the minute you get this message."

She pulled her cell from her pocket and recalled turning it off before she went into the hospital. When she turned it on, it beeped letting her know she had new voice mails. She'd listen later. She grabbed a beer and headed out back.

"Hi!" she said before taking a swig of beer.

Maria sighed audibly. "Thank God you're alive."

"Of course I'm alive. It's Sunday, and you know I usually go to my mom's."

"I know." She sounded calmer. "But not usually for the entire day."

Jo leaned back, stretched her legs and took another drink. "I stopped by the hospital this morning to get my cast replaced."

"Why would you get your cast replaced?"

"Because she said I should."

"She who?"

"She the doctor that put the first one on."

"Oh…" Maria paused a long moment. "How do you know who put the first cast on? You were practically unconscious."

"It's an interesting story. I'll tell you after you answer a question for me." There was only silence on the line. "Maria?"

"What? Ask your question."

"Were you going to tell me what you asked that nice doctor to do to me when I was practically unconscious?"

Again, there was a lengthy pause. "I was only kidding. I thought she knew that."

"Well, you know she thought you were my girlfriend."

"Why would she think something like that?"

"I thought maybe you could tell me." More silence on the line. Jo waited a few seconds longer. "Let's see…masculine butch with a pregnant, overprotective femme. We're obviously not related, sounds like a perfect lesbian couple to me." She couldn't keep the laughter out of her voice any longer.

"Jo Marchal, you are so full of yourself!" When Jo continued to laugh, Maria finally joined her. "And I suppose she probably thinks you got me pregnant with the turkey baster after Thanksgiving?"

Jo laughed so hard her sides were hurting, but finally managed to say, "I told her the whole sordid truth."

She wiped tears from her cheeks. Once they controlled their laughter, Jo told Maria she already knew Dr. Loren Mathews and that Loren had actually witnessed Kate's barbarity.

There was a fondness in Jo's voice as she spoke about this Dr. Mathews. It sounded as though Jo really liked her, which started Maria's own emotions bouncing all over the place. The doctor was a very nice woman, and the Lord knew Jo needed someone to love and take care of her. But the thought of someone loving and taking care of Jo made jealousy rear its ugly head. She knew it was selfish to think that way. It wasn't as if she could be the one to do that.

"I'm glad you're dating someone like Dr. Mathews."

"We're not really dating…" Jo thought for a split second. "Not yet."

"Well, I think you should. She seems very nice."

"Nice, yes, she is nice."

Maria closed her eyes against the renewed stab of jealousy that Jo's words brought. They ended the call a few minutes later after she stated she'd check in on Jo tomorrow.

Jo finished her beer, closed her eyes and tipped her head back. It sounded like Maria was happy that she might be dating Loren Mathews. She would definitely be pleased to know that Loren seemed interested in dating her. But she didn't really care one way or the other. Jo knew full well she would never fall in love with another woman. She was already in love with the one in her dreams.

CHAPTER TWENTY-ONE

Jo loved the warmer weather and high humidity that made a person sweat standing still, but the damned cast on her hand was driving her crazy. She couldn't train horses and that was the equivalent of cutting off a painter's hand. Loren had told her six to eight weeks, which meant, at a minimum, she had another week to go. She wanted to find the necessary implement in the tool shed and remove the thing herself. There wasn't any pain in her hand and even with the restricted movement of her fingers it felt fine when she wiggled them.

She was standing in the tack room eyeing the plaster on her hand when Tucker came in.

"Would you mind driving to town to pick up a few things we need to finish the fence repairs? I'm pretty sure one of our new tenants likes kicking at fences."

"Sure, give me the list. It's not like I can do anything productive around here anyway." Tucker handed her the piece of paper and quickly ducked from the room.

She headed down the highway with the windows open and wondered what the chances were that she might run into Maria at the hardware store like she had last year. One in a million, she guessed. She'd swing by Maria's office after her shopping to take her to lunch. Tucker and Kirby could wait a little longer to start their work. She had spent the last five weeks miserable. They could have a turn at boring idle inactivity. Heck, who was she kidding? They were probably already in the tack room embroiled in a poker game.

She looked up Ernie to help her with her list, then drove over to Maria's office. Her car wasn't there, but she popped in anyway to see if maybe she was around town somewhere.

Karen gave a welcoming smile. "If you're looking for Maria, Ms. Marchal, she's not in."

"I figured." Jo returned Karen's smile and crossed her arms on the counter. "You suppose you could call me Jo?"

"Certainly." Karen pointed her pen at Jo's cast. "What happened to your hand, Jo?"

Jo glanced at the dirty worn plaster. "Horse bit me."

Karen's eyes grew big as saucers. "Oh my!"

Jo winked at her. "I'm kidding. If a horse bit my hand I probably wouldn't have one left." Karen scrunched up her face. "It got smashed, broke a couple of bones." Jo patted her good hand on the counter. "So do you know if Maria's due back anytime soon or if she's working around town?"

Karen raised a finger as she answered the ringing phone, pressed a combination of buttons then hung up. "She left about half an hour ago and said she was taking the rest of the day off." She stood and leaned closer as if she were about to share a national secret. "If you ask me, they're having a big sale at the outlet stores. I bet she went shopping for baby things."

"You're probably right. Well, if she does happen back in, tell her I was in town and stopped to say hello."

Karen grabbed a notepad. "I certainly will, Ms.—uh, Jo."

Jo spun on her heel and called over her shoulder, "Have a good one."

She sat out in her truck and contemplated either driving past Maria's house or the outlet mall. Ah, she'd be out to the farm tomorrow. Reluctantly, she pointed the truck toward home where she could have the pleasure of sitting on her rump and watching other people do what she couldn't. Lunch with Maria would have beaten that in spades. They hadn't been alone since the day Maria had taken her to the hospital. She was so out of it at the time, though, that she couldn't appreciate the time spent with her. It was a ridiculous fantasy, she knew. It wasn't as though anything could happen between them, but still…the unexpected kiss months ago flashed in her mind. "You keep dreamin', cowgirl."

She was pleasantly surprised to see the black station wagon in the driveway when she made her way home. She hustled to the tack room with Tucker's supplies and found them standing around looking guilty. Cards, she was sure, but she didn't care because Maria was there.

"Is Maria in the house?" She handed the bags over to Tucker.

He passed them on to Kirby, who stood beside him. "No, she took Matt out on Daisy Mae. Said something about needing a walk."

Jo stepped through the rear barn doors, shielding her eyes from the sun, and spotted Daisy Mae ambling towards her. There was a rider astride, but the reins dragged the ground. He was alone.

"Tucker!" she screamed as she raced out to Matt on Daisy Mae. Her heart thundered and a deafening sound roared in her ears. She gathered the reins and patted Daisy Mae's neck.

"Good girl." Daisy Mae rubbed her head against Jo's shoulder. Jo squinted up at Matt, took a deep breath and said, "Hey there, cowboy, you enjoying your ride today?"

Her mind raced. Where the hell was Maria? Where the hell was Tucker? Scenarios flew through her mind like movie credits on a screen. Finally Tucker was beside her.

"Where's Maria?"

She barely managed to whisper, "I don't know." She quickly scanned the empty pasture, then she turned to Tucker and handed him the reins. "Take Matt in, leave him on the horse or find Jake and Rosie and sit him down with them. He trusts you, Tucker, just don't let him out of your sight." She snatched the two-way radio from his belt. "Which way did they head out?"

Tucker's usual confident, kick-ass bravado was gone. "Uh… uh…along the northwest fence. She said—"

Jo took off at a full run, Tucker's words lost behind her. A quarter mile out over the rise, lungs burning, she spotted the form against the fence. When Jo reached her, she dropped to her knees, gasping long and hard before getting enough air in her lungs to speak.

"Maria?"

She lay to one side, perspiration glistening on her face in the bright sun. Jo reached a shaky hand to touch the side of her neck. She felt the beat, but wasn't sure if it was hers or Maria's. She scooted closer and pulled out her shirttail to dab Maria's face.

"Maria."

Maria finally moaned faintly and ever so slowly opened her eyes.

"Thank God," Jo whispered.

Eyes squinting into the sun, Maria murmured, "Jo…"

Jo moved sideways to shade Maria's face and leaned over. "It's me." She hurriedly unbuttoned her shirt and shrugged out of it. "Maria, what happened?" Her eyes closed again. Jo used her shirt to wipe the sweat from Maria's face and neck.

"I felt…light-headed, I…sat down for a minute." Jo wadded up the shirt and placed it under Maria's head. She grabbed Jo's hand. "Jo, I think…I think my water broke…unless…" She sighed. "I…I feel wet—embarrassed."

Jo pushed back the long locks of hair from her face. "It's okay. We won't ever mention it again." She smiled down at her. "Can you sit up?"

She clutched Jo's hand. "Think so."

Jo helped guide her to a sitting position against the fence, pulled the radio from her back pocket and called Tucker's name into it.

"Did you find her?" he came back.

"Yeah, have one of your boys bring the Gator out towards the northwest corner over the rise."

"You got it—"

She could hear Tucker shouting instructions to someone before he un-keyed the radio. Rising up on her knees, Jo propped her cast on the fence rail so she could shade Maria as much as possible. It felt like the desert as the sun dried the sweat on her exposed skin. Maria jerked her hand to her belly and suddenly leaned forward.

"Oh God…" she gasped.

Jo's blood ran cold. "Maria, what's wrong?"

She grabbed for Jo's hand, nearly crushing her fingers. On a deeply inhaled breath, she said, "Something's wrong…oh…God… it hurts."

The color quickly drained from Maria's face. She still gripped Jo's hand so tight her fingers were losing feeling.

Jo patted her pockets. "Damn," she muttered. She had left her phone in the truck. "Maria, do you have your phone with you?"

She nodded. "Pocket."

"Just…" Jo tried pulling her hand from Maria's iron grip. "Let me get your phone, Maria. Okay?"

She released Jo's hand, continuing to gasp for breath. Jo reached into one and then the other of the deep pockets in her long, loose skirt. She felt the wetness, but was ill-prepared to see her fingers and the phone covered in crimson when she pulled them out. Her breath caught. She grabbed her shirt to wipe the blood off before Maria could see it, but she'd closed her eyes again.

"Maria, you still with me?" She only moaned. Jo keyed the two-way again. "Tucker!" It seemed an eternity before the radio crackled with his voice.

"Kirby's headed your way in a minute."

"Make it faster."

She threw the radio down, brought the screen up on Maria's phone and dialed 9-1-1. One ring, two rings, three rings…

"Come on, damn it."

Four long rings later a calm female voice answered. "Nine-one-one. What is your emergency?"

"I'm with a pregnant woman. She's having pain and bleeding." The words rushed from Jo.

"What's the address?" Jo gave her address. "And how far along is she?"

Jo's brain wouldn't process the question. "Damn, I don't know. I need help, not questions."

The soothing voice replied, "Ma'am, I'll get you all the help you need, but I do need for you to just take a deep breath."

"Sorry," Jo mumbled.

"It's okay, honey, I understand," the calm voice of reason came back.

Jo forced her brain to think…to remember. "She got pregnant on New Year's Eve."

"Okay," the voice paused a long moment. "Do you know when the bleeding started?"

Jo cradled the phone against her shoulder and touched her hand to the side of Maria's face. "Maria." When her eyes opened slightly, she asked, "Do you know when your water broke?"

"Right before—" She cried out in pain and nearly doubled over, holding her abdomen with both hands. Her breathing came rapidly. "Before I…I got dizzy." She began panting. "I think…" she reached out for Jo and caught her cast. "I think…I'm in labor." She cried out again. "No, no, no…too soon."

The voice in her other ear sounded more urgent. "How much blood has she lost? Can you see if the baby's crowning?"

"A lot."

Maria exhaled a cry and slumped back.

The voice again asked, "Can you see if the baby's crowning?"

"No!"

"No, you can't see?" the voice asked anxiously. "Or no, it's not crowning?"

Jo closed her eyes. "No, I can't see, so I don't know."

In a soothing tone the woman said, "Listen, honey, I know this is difficult, but you need to look and see if the baby's head is trying to come out." Jo squeezed her already closed eyes tightly and held her breath. "Did you hear me?" the woman asked softly.

In a weak voice, Maria asked, "Jo, what's wrong?"

Jo shook her head and mumbled, "This ain't nothin' like birthin' a horse." Her voice took on the lazy hillbilly twang she had been so comfortable speaking when she was around the boys back on her old Kentucky farm.

"Jo?" Maria tugged at the casted hand resting on Jo's thigh.

Jo swallowed hard, slowly opening her eyes. She barely heard her own words. "I need to see if the baby's coming, but I don't—"

"Jo…" Jo raised her eyes to meet Maria's. "Please…"

Jo nodded. "I need to lay the phone down for a minute," she said to the dispatcher.

"That's fine. You're doing great."

Great, right. Jo took hold of Maria's skirt hem, but only looked at it. She couldn't do it. She shook her head and looked at Maria.

"I can't…I can't…" She was so afraid if she did this their relationship would never be the same, and she wasn't ready to have that happen. Tears formed in her eyes.

"It's not…like you haven't seen…it before…and if you…haven't you're not…a very good lesbian…Jo Marchal."

Jo wasn't sure if Maria had actually spoken those words or she imagined them. She didn't respond.

"Please, Jo…help me. Help us."

Maria's plea reached the deepest part of Jo's soul. She mentally slapped herself. Swiping the sweat from her face with her arm, she pushed the skirt to the top of Maria's thighs, grumbling to hide her embarrassment. "I sure as hell didn't sign on for nothin' like this." *Okay, you've got this. Put the emotions somewhere else.*

The sight of so much blood made her queasy, but she thought about the last foal she helped deliver and pulled the blood-soaked panties aside as Maria shifted her hips. All she could see was *a lot* of blood. She wiped her hand on her jeans and picked up the phone.

"There's so much blood it's hard to see," she said quietly into the phone. Maria's eyes, filled with fear, never left hers.

"Gently, using your fingers, see if you can feel the head at the vaginal opening."

Jo tossed the phone down without a word to the woman and mumbled "Shit!" under her breath. Maria's eyelids drooped over her eyes. "I have to see if I can feel the baby's head. Okay?" Maria's head tipped forward. Jo quickly slid her hand past the bloody panties to her opening. Relief washed over her when what she felt seemed very familiar. She pulled her hand out and the skirt back over Maria's legs. "I'm sorry for that," she whispered before hurriedly wiping her hand again. The sound of the approaching Gator was a second wave of relief as she picked up the phone. "I don't feel the baby's head."

"That's good. The ambulance is en route. Tell her not to push, even if she feels like she has to."

"Maria, don't push." Her head was hanging over her chest. "Maria!" Jo tipped her head up. The pulse was still there, but her breathing was shallow. Panic crept in again. "She's not conscious now and barely breathing and our ride to meet the ambulance is here."

"Where exactly are you at this address?"

Jo's patience slipped away. "Way the hell out in a horse pasture, but headed for the barn." When Kirby got out of the Gator, Jo tossed him the phone. "Your turn to talk to the nice lady." She reached both arms under Maria.

"Let me help." Kirby stuck the phone in his shirt pocket and stooped across from her.

In one fluid movement she stood with Maria in her arms. "Open the tail gate," she barked. He moved quickly. She set Maria's limp body on the blankets and scrambled in to cradle Maria between her legs. Kirby hopped in the seat. He was talking on the phone when Jo yelled, "Go, damn it!"

He dropped the phone on the seat and hollered over his shoulder as he bounced them across the pasture, "Ambulance will meet us at the barn."

"Is Tucker still on a two-way?"

"Yep."

She grabbed the radio and keyed the button. "Tucker?" She didn't wait for an answer. "Stand by the barn gate so we can get straight out to the driveway." Tucker's reply came back as she dropped the radio beside her. Holding Maria tight in her arms, Jo rested her cheek against her hair. "It's gonna be all right," she whispered, doubting her own words as she said them. "I promise." Tears clouded her eyes.

She stared at nothing. In a single heartbeat she saw Maria's face smiling at her the first time they met when Maria had tried to conceal her surprise that Jo was a woman. In the next beat, Maria's hand was in Jo's touching the velvety softness of Daisy Mae's nose. And the next, Maria was hiking up her skirt to show off her new cowboy boots at Christmas, and then…then she saw the look of desire Maria's eyes had held the moment she kissed Jo. Every time she thought of that moment, she could feel the warm softness of Maria's lips and the desire that consumed her soul.

The loud voices brought her back. "Ma'am?" They were at the edge of the drive next to the ambulance. Two EMTs were standing at the tail gate of the Gator with a stretcher. "We need to move her."

Jo nodded numbly, turning to locate Kirby. "Where's Tucker?"

He hooked his thumb. "In the barn with the boy."

"Go sit with him and send Tucker out…please?"

He bolted to the barn. Jo climbed out, picked up Maria's phone from the seat and slapped it into Tucker's hand.

"Find a number in this thing for Kathleen, her sister-in-law. Tell her what's going on and to please come get Matt and meet me at the hospital." Tucker nodded. "I'm riding with them."

She started to step away, but Tucker caught her arm, and in a much too mature voice, said, "Don't worry, she's gonna be fine, and you know I ain't never gonna let anything happen to that boy of hers."

Jo blinked hard against more threatening tears and choked past her tight throat, "Thanks, Tucker. I owe you."

He looked at the bloody phone. "Don't give it another thought." He waved his hand toward the ambulance where they were loading the stretcher. "Go be where you need to. I got everything handled here." He looked at the phone's screen as he turned to go to the barn.

She raced to the ambulance as the driver started to shut the door. "Whoa, hey, I'm going with you."

As they headed out the EMT sitting beside Maria asked, "Is all that blood on you hers?"

Jo looked down at herself. She didn't remember putting her bloody shirt back on, but there it was, covering her bloody undershirt. She gave a nod and swallowed to keep from retching at the sight. She shifted her gaze to Maria. She looked so peaceful. Jo concentrated on the slow rise and fall of her chest for a moment and the wires snaking out from under her blouse, then she focused on Maria's face.

"How's she doing?"

He gave Jo a reassuring look. "She's stable. IV's in and we're pushing lots of fluid. She's lost a lot of blood, so stable is good. Heart rate's still in a safe range."

Jo's eyes moved to Maria's abdomen and the blood-soaked skirt. "How's the baby?"

He placed the stethoscope on her belly. "I hear a steady beat. Here…" He handed the scope to Jo and when she had the earpieces in place he returned the bell to where he had it a moment before.

Jo heard the faint, steady drum of a heartbeat. *A tiny heartbeat.* Her mind now did the math it had refused to do earlier in her panic. *Seven months and a week. Or was it two?* It didn't matter. She remembered Maria said it was too soon. She lowered her head, closed her eyes and silently prayed. *Please, God, if there is a God, don't take this baby away from her, and don't take her away from me.* The tears dropped steadily onto her blood-stained jeans.

It seemed like an eternity and a fraction of a minute at the same time before the doors were bursting open and Maria was being rushed from the ambulance. She followed as they wheeled the stretcher inside, shouting medical jargon back and forth she didn't understand. When they pushed through doors into a sterile-looking room, a woman in brightly printed scrubs stepped in front of Jo.

"I need you to wait out here until I come back." She held Jo's arm. "Okay?" Jo only looked past her at the army of doctors and nurses closing in around Maria until she could no longer see her. The woman gave Jo a little shake. "You okay, honey? Do you need me to call someone for you?"

"No, it's done," Jo heard herself say, but she didn't recognize her own voice.

The woman patted her arm. "Okay, be patient and I'll be back, I promise."

She pushed through the doors. Jo stood in the noisy hall, feeling more lost and alone than she'd ever felt in her life. She watched for a few minutes through the windows in the door and then paced for a few. She repeated the action. Over and over until she felt like her body would simply collapse beneath her. She leaned against the wall beside the door and closed her eyes to say another prayer.

"Jo! Oh my God! Are you okay?" The voice grew louder. Jo opened her eyes and saw Loren standing, mouth agape, a few feet away. Her eyes traveled up and down Jo several times before she asked again, "Jo, are you all right?" Jo stared blankly at her and Loren stepped closer, taking hold of Jo's blood-encrusted hand.

Jo blinked repeatedly, trying to wake from the bad dream. "I'm okay," she finally said. "It's not me…it's…" Loren became a blur as tears formed in her eyes.

"It's okay, Jo." Loren squeezed her hand.

"No." Jo lowered her head and shook it. "It's not, it's Maria."

Loren stepped sideways and looked through the door. "She's in there?" When Jo nodded, Loren stepped back in front of her. "What happened?"

Jo rambled, "She's bleeding…she got dizzy, or she got dizzy and thought her water broke…she was way out in one of the pastures." She took a ragged breath. "The baby's coming too early, and I don't think I got there in time." She sucked in a deep breath and fought the sob trying to escape.

When her body began to shake uncontrollably, Loren pulled her hand. "Come with me." Jo resisted. "Look," Loren pointed to a chair fifteen feet from the door. "You need to sit before you fall down." Loren dragged her to the chair and sat her down. She watched helplessly as Loren returned to the door and disappeared inside. She watched…and waited, and finally Loren came back. Jo stood too quickly when Loren approached and nearly fell on her face. Loren steadied her, sat her back in the chair and stooped in front of her.

"They've got her stabilized enough to take her to surgery. They need to take the baby and find the source of her bleeding. Is there someone we can call? A family member? They don't want to wait too long to take her up."

"Her sister-in-law will be here eventually, that's it. The husband's gone." Jo's eyes pleaded. "They have to save her, whatever they have to do."

Loren placed her hand on Jo's shoulder. "They will, Jo. They will. Do you want to go in and see her before they take her up to surgery?"

Jo answered by pushing up from the chair. She followed Loren to the side of the bed that wasn't crowded with machines.

A voice behind her said, "They're prepping an OR now. It won't be long until they take her up."

"Thanks," Loren replied. "This is Jo Marchal. She'll be staying with Ms. West until they come for her."

Maria looked so pale. Her hand was cool to the touch as Jo held it between her own. "Please don't leave me, Maria. Me and Matt. We need you an awful lot." She closed her eyes, gently stroking her thumb over Maria's soft skin. "Pops, if you're listening, I sure could use your help right now." She opened her eyes and looked toward the ceiling.

A short time later they rolled Maria down the hall. Jo stood there, emotions raw, and watched as the elevator doors closed.

Loren again placed her hand on Jo's shoulder. "There's a waiting room upstairs for the surgery suites. I can take you up."

"I've got to find a phone and make a call."

Loren produced her cell phone. "Here," she placed it in Jo's hand. "Let's step outside and get some air."

Jo followed in a trance. She called Tucker to confirm he'd gotten hold of Kathleen. Kathleen had Matt so Jo called the number she had left with Tucker.

"God, Jo, what happened?"

Jo rubbed at her head and the intensifying headache. She closed her eyes and relayed everything she could force her brain to recall. "Are you coming now?"

"I'm trying, Jo. Tim's out on a job site and I'm waiting on a call back from him. I can leave our boys with a dozen different people, but not Matt, and I'm afraid to bring him to the hospital. The second I can put him with Tim, I'll be there."

"I'll try and call you back if she's out of surgery before you get here, but I don't have a phone. Otherwise I'll be in the surgery waiting room."

"I'll be there as soon as I can."

CHAPTER TWENTY-TWO

Loren sat her down in the waiting room with a cup of coffee.

"I've got to get back downstairs. I'll check back as soon as I can. If you need anything, have me paged." Loren took her hand. "She's in good hands. They'll take care of her and her baby." Jo looked at Loren, trying to imagine how she could know.

Thirty minutes later a doctor appeared asking for the West family. When Jo stood, he spoke quickly. "The baby's delivered, caesarean, and presently stable. She's been moved to the neonatal unit. Thus far we're unable to get the bleeding under control. We may have to do a hysterectomy. You're the family member?"

Jo shook her head.

"I was told there would be a family member to talk to."

"She's not here yet." Jo wrung her hands. "She has Maria's handicapped son. Please don't let her die. Do whatever you have to." Her voice quivered. "Please…"

"In the absence of a family member, another doctor and I will make the call. She'll not be able to have any more children." He said it as if Jo might not understand the implication.

Through fresh tears, Jo begged softly, "Please save her."

She had no clue how much time passed before the same doctor returned to inform her that the surgery had gone well, but Maria's condition remained guarded. He rambled on with additional information that seemed to float in the air around her. Jo heard what she wanted to. Maria was still alive. She was in the same spot when Loren came back and sat down in front of her again. Loren placed her hands on Jo's knees and squeezed.

"Hey, Jo." She blinked and registered Loren's comforting expression. "She's been moved from recovery. You don't have to wait here."

Jo thought a moment. There was a reason she was still sitting there. "I saw the doctor. But…uh…I told her sister-in-law I'd be here."

"Tell you what, I'm going to find you something to put on besides this," she touched the short sleeve of Jo's shirt, "so you don't scare anyone. I'll clean up your cast and we'll call whomever you need to, then get you something to eat. After, I'll take you to her room. Agreed?"

"I have to see her now."

When Jo tried to stand, Loren held on to her thighs and kept her in the chair. "Listen, Jo, if she saw you now, the way you look, she'd be shocked."

Jo looked down at herself and for the first time really registered how much crusted blood there was on her hands and clothes.

Loren pushed hair away from her eyes. "And you need to eat something. You're pale as a ghost, which I'm sorry to say only adds to your frightening appearance." She took Jo's hand. "Come on with me."

Loren grabbed one of her scrub tops and directed Jo into a restroom. She stood by as Jo scrubbed her hand and arms, stripped off her bloody shirt and stuffed it in a plastic bag, then cleaned up the cast as best she could. She had to keep hold of Jo's hand to get her to follow to the cafeteria, where she directed her to a seat. Loren filled a plate with food and placed it in front of her, but she only stared at it.

"Jo, you've got to eat something. How much good will you be for Maria if you run yourself down?"

Jo forced down several bites, drank the orange juice and picked up the coffee. "Can we go now?"

"Sure." She sighed deeply and stood. "At least take the cookie for later. The sugar will give you some energy. I know you're strong and unshakeable, but right now you look fragile enough to break."

Loren led Jo to the ICU, where she stopped at the desk. After conferring with a nurse, she told Jo, "She hasn't regained consciousness yet. Are you sure you're up for this?" Jo nodded, feeling the familiar sting of tears in her eyes. Loren said something else to the nurse, then placed a hand on her shoulder. "Come on."

Jo felt a building pressure in her chest with each step down the long hallway. Was she having a heart attack? Sounds and even Loren's voice right beside her sounded muffled and far away. When they stepped into the room, Jo's breath left her and she swayed. Loren steadied her with an arm around her waist. There were a number of machines on either side of the bed and tubes and wires running everywhere. Maria's naturally dark skin looked pasty, almost white.

"Why isn't she awake?" Jo barely managed to ask.

Loren pulled a chair to the bedside for her. "Her body's suffered a major trauma and she lost a lot of blood. They're not saying when or if she'll wake up."

Jo felt strangled by a fear she'd never known. "'If'?"

Loren rubbed a hand across her back. "I'm sorry, I wish I could tell you something more, but for now it's a waiting game."

Jo turned her eyes back to Maria's motionless body, tears flowing freely down her cheeks. "And the baby?"

Loren continued the soothing motion over her back. "She's in the NICU, and so far doing as well as anyone can expect. They can accomplish miracles for preemies these days." What Jo wanted was a miracle for Maria. "I'm going to call her sister-in-law for you. What's her name?"

"Kathleen," Jo whispered.

She sat vigilant at Maria's bedside, the flow of tears down her face a constant reminder of how precious love and life can be. She couldn't love Maria more if she tried. She had thought losing Claire was the most unbearable thing she would have to endure. Then she'd lost her dad. But losing Maria—well, Jo knew it'd be the one thing she would never recover from. She lowered her head and said another prayer.

If you're listening, God, please bring her back. She has kids that need her. I need her, and I promise I'll never love another woman again in my life if you do this for me.

The hand on her shoulder held comfort. "How is she?" Kathleen asked quietly.

Struggling to answer, Jo took a deep breath. "No change. Were you able to contact her parents in Mexico?"

"I know she talks to them about once a month. I'll find a way to contact them." Kathleen's hand stayed on her shoulder. "She'll be okay." Jo only nodded. "She's very lucky to have someone care about her as you do." Jo sniffed and wiped fresh tears on her sleeve. "I can see how much she means to you." She gave Jo's shoulder a squeeze.

Jo took another breath. As hard as she'd tried not to fall in love with Maria, she had. She swallowed the lump in her throat. "I tried not to care so much."

Kathleen rubbed her hand across Jo's shoulder, then touched Maria's still hand. "Oh, honey, I don't believe that's even possible. My brother is a selfish bastard, but if it weren't for him, she wouldn't be my best friend. I love her like she's my own sister." Kathleen's voice wavered. "She'll be okay. We'll make sure of it…you and me."

"You should sit with her." Jo started to get up, but Kathleen pressed gently on her shoulder.

"Stay put."

Jo took Kathleen's hand when she stood up. "I've got to go walk for a minute or two."

Kathleen squeezed her hand. "She really will be okay. We have to believe that." Jo saw the sorrow that Kathleen had been trying to mask wash over her face. Tears formed in her eyes and finally spilled over. Kathleen whispered, "She has to."

Jo put her arms around her and hugged her. She dropped her head against Jo's shoulder as a sob escaped. Her body shook in Jo's arms.

"She will. I have an 'in' with an angel and he'll be watching over her." She held Kathleen until her shaking subsided then leaned back. "Will you be okay for a little bit?"

Kathleen dabbed her eyes with a tissue. "Sure, honey, go do whatever you need to."

Jo stopped in the doorway. "Where's Matt?"

A tiny smile tugged at Kathleen's lips. "He and my boys should all be together by now. They finally located Tim at his job site. Matt will be fine." She waved her hand toward Jo. "Go on now, so you can come back and keep me company until I have to go back home."

Jo made her way to the neonatal intensive care unit and, after donning a sterile gown, mask and booties, stood looking into the see-through plastic box at Maria's tiny baby girl. Her heart swelled with the same kind of love she felt for Maria. An unquestionably protective love. After a moment a nurse broke the silence.

"She must come from good genes. She's a real fighter, that little one."

Jo couldn't agree more. When the nurse stepped back out of earshot, Jo said, "You fight with everything you got, beautiful one, 'cause you got an amazing mom you got to meet."

Back in Maria's room, Jo asked quietly, "Any change?"

Kathleen looked like she'd been horsewhipped. When she started to get up, Jo gently held her in place and she slumped back. "The nurse was in to check her blood pressure. She said every hour she hangs on is a step in the right direction."

"Did she say when she's going to wake up?"

Kathleen turned swollen, red eyes to meet Jo's. "They don't know. I'm sorry, honey. They're going to do some test for brain function in the morning if she still hasn't gained consciousness."

Jo turned to stare out the window at the evening sky as fresh tears wet her cheeks. After a several minutes, she composed herself and looked at Kathleen. "How long are you staying?"

She shifted in the chair. "I hadn't really thought about it."

"I'd like to run back to the farm. I don't even have my cell phone."

"You came in the ambulance with her?" Jo nodded. "Take my van." She reached for her purse.

""No, I'm gonna take a cab so I can get my truck."

Kathleen dangled the keys. "You sure?"

Jo nodded again, patting at her pockets. "Shoot." She frowned. "I guess I will. I don't have my wallet or any money."

Kathleen held out the keys. "Don't mind the toys and the crumbs."

"I won't be long. I'll take a quick shower and change my clothes." She looked at her stained jeans. "I'll get back as soon as I can."

Kathleen dropped the keys into her hand. "Take your time, honey, and do what you need to do. I'm not going anywhere before morning."

She gave Kathleen her cell number. "I'll have it in hand in half an hour. Call me if anything changes…please." Kathleen gave a nod.

Jo located the mini van in the lot and drove to the farm in a daze, reminding herself over and over about what the nurse had told Kathleen about things getting better every hour that Maria held on. Finally she reached the farm and grabbed her cell from the truck. Jo didn't take a breath till she confirmed there had been no calls. She put on coffee and quickly showered. Dressed for comfort in a T-shirt and jeans, she pulled on a decent pair of boots and checked on the dogs before filling a travel mug with strong black coffee. This was going to be the longest night of her life.

Entering the room in near darkness, she found Kathleen reclined in the chair, apparently sleeping. She quietly moved the only other chair around the bed where she could see Maria's face in the dim glow of light filtering in from the hall. She sat back, silently sipping the coffee until the wee hours of the morning.

"Jo." Kathleen patted her leg and stirred her.

Jo cringed from the pain in her neck as she lifted her head.

"Get in that recliner and sleep. I'm going to run home so I can get the boys up and fed for Tim and then I'll be back."

"Wait." Jo stiffly crawled out of the chair and followed into the hall where she got Kathleen's number to put in her phone.

"I'll call if anything changes."

Kathleen touched her hand to Jo's cheek. "I know you will, honey. Get some rest, I'll be back."

Jo couldn't lie back in the chair and sleep so she held Maria's still hand, eventually lying her head down on her arm where it rested on the bed. Some time later she felt sure Maria's hand twitched in hers and it startled her awake like a clap of thunder. She jerked her head up and studied Maria's hand in hers. When it twitched again, she gave it a light squeeze. "Maria," she sad softly. She was positive Maria's hand squeezed ever so lightly in response. Her heart flip-flopped. She raised their joined hands and rested them on her thigh as she sat on the bed.

"I'm right here, Maria, and I'm not going anywhere."

Jo waited impatiently, but there wasn't any further movement. After several more minutes she pressed the call button. The nurse appeared quickly and checked all the monitors.

"What's wrong, dear?" She moved around Jo to check the IV drip.

"She moved her hand. I was holding her hand and it moved, twice. And when I spoke to her I felt her squeeze my hand." Jo tried to remain calm, but her voice sounded rushed with excitement.

"Did she open her eyes or speak?"

"No." Jo felt like a balloon losing air.

The nurse slipped on the blood pressure cuff. "That's not unusual. Even in the deepest comas it's possible for the body to have involuntary movements." Her explanation further deflated Jo's optimism. She ripped off the cuff. "Her pressure is remaining steady now at a good level, but her body has suffered a major trauma." She patted Jo's shoulder. "Don't count her out. I understand she gave birth to a fierce fighter. Those genes had to come from somewhere."

She left Jo again amidst the whirls and beeps of the machines. It was four thirty and try as she might to stay awake, her head eventually found its way to a restful position on the side of the bed. Her mind floated in a dream. She and Maria were at the farm at their picture-perfect picnic spot out in the pasture and Maria was stroking Jo's hair as her head rested in Maria's lap. It was by far the most vivid dream she'd ever had about Maria. Then realization dawned on her that it wasn't a dream. Her head popped up and she opened her eyes to see tiny slivers of Maria's dark eyes. She sat for a moment stunned until Maria's struggle to swallow and open her mouth were apparent.

When Maria stretched her hand toward Jo, the floodgates holding her tears opened.

"Oh God," she exhaled in a whimper. "I was terrified I was never gonna get a chance to make you laugh again." Maria tried to speak. "Shh…Maria, relax. Let me get a nurse." She fumbled for the call button.

A moment or two later the same nurse reappeared. "Well, well," she gave Jo a grin. "What did I tell you? A real fighter like the little one." She whipped out the blood pressure cuff again.

"My—" Maria strained to speak.

"Easy, dear." She lifted Maria's arm. "Let me get your pressure real quick." She picked up the plastic pitcher from the small bedside table and pushed it toward Jo. "Could you ask for some ice chips at the nurse's station, please?" Jo started to protest. "I need a few minutes to check her dressing and sutures, and she needs something to wet her mouth, so you'll be doing us both a favor."

Jo started to leave, but stopped when Maria hoarsely said her name. Jo smiled for what felt like the first time in ages. "I won't be long. I promise I'll be right back."

Maria's glassy eyes held hers a little too long and the nurse waved her off. "Go on now so I can do my job."

She dropped the pitcher at the nurse's station and practically ran out to the parking lot. Dropping onto the bench inside the covered bus stop, she dialed Kathleen's number.

"I'll be back as soon as I can get everyone up and fed."

"Take whatever time you need to take care of the family. I'm not going anywhere. How's Matt?"

"He's doing just fine with his cousins."

She closed the phone. It was barely six o'clock. Tucker's update could wait a little bit longer. She closed her eyes. "I miss you so much, Pops. Thank you." She steeled herself against more tears and rushed back inside.

She picked up the pitcher, returned to the room, but waited in the doorway until summoned by the nurse.

"Give her the chips to moisten her dry mouth and throat. She can talk, but she really needs to rest."

"Thank you."

"Buzz if she needs anything." And so quietly Jo almost didn't hear her, she said, "I'm going to see what I can find out about her baby."

Jo stood beside the bed. "Can I sit?" Maria gave her a nod and Jo perched on the bed.

After several bites of the ice, she said in a raspy voice, "My baby's...gone." Tears formed instantly in her eyes.

Jo blinked back her own tears. "She's upstairs in the neonatal intensive care unit. They're taking excellent care of her."

"But she's—"

"She's the tiniest thing I think I've ever seen, but just like her mother, a real fighter." More tears spilled down Maria's cheeks. "Hey, hey, no crying. It's a joyous day. You're here and you've got a beautiful baby girl."

"But—"

Jo slipped her hand in Maria's. "No buts about it. I saw for myself. She's as beautiful as her mother, I swear." Jo smiled when Maria squeezed her hand.

"Matt?"

"He's fine at Kathleen's. You know, that's one smart boy you've got. He rode Daisy Mae all the way back to the barn for help."

"Daisy's the smart one."

Jo couldn't keep from smiling at the glorious eyes looking back at her. "Let's agree they make a good team."

Maria gave a slight nod before her eyes drifted closed. Jo stood and tried to withdraw her hand, but Maria held on. She pulled the chair back over, got comfortable and closed her own eyes.

A deep male voice woke her sometime later. "Can I ask you to step out of the room while I examine Mrs. West?" Jo recognized the doctor from last night. It was after nine o'clock.

She was leaning against the wall out in the hall when a woman dressed in a business suit approached with a folder in her hand.

"Are you the West family?" The woman looked at the closed door.

Feeling protective, Jo moved between the woman and the door. "No," she answered. "Something I can help you with, though?"

She looked Jo up and down. "No. I have a question about insurance coverage that I need to discuss with Mrs. West."

Jo crossed her arms over her chest, remaining steadfast in front of the door. "I don't want Ms. West bothered right now," she emphasized the *Ms*. "So how about you discuss it with me."

The woman narrowed her eyes. "And exactly who are you?"

Jo cocked her head. "The person that's going to keep you from bothering Ms. West with insurance nonsense. Let's call me her bodyguard. So, you want to discuss this with me now or later? 'Cause you aren't going to bother Ms. West with it as long as I'm around, and I'm not going anywhere."

"Fine," she huffed.

As the woman explained the dilemma, Jo got angrier by the second. Like a rodeo bull wanted to trample its rider, Jo wanted to step on Maria's soon-to-be ex. Instead, she poured on the charm. The woman left with a smile, satisfied the hospital would receive payment for services one way or another. A moment later the doctor came out, but he stopped Jo before she could enter.

"You might want to give them a few minutes. The nurse is helping Mrs. West to the bathroom."

Jo was still waiting and deep in thought about how to best help care for Maria after the hospital when Kathleen surprised her.

"Jo, is there something wrong?"

"No, they need a few minutes of privacy."

Kathleen leaned against the wall beside her and Jo couldn't hold her tongue. "You know that brother of yours is a real piece of work."

Kathleen met Jo's gaze. "I'm afraid to ask. What's he done now?'

"He dropped Maria from his insurance coverage and only has it for his children, even though the divorce isn't final yet." Kathleen sighed heavily. "Don't worry, though, Maria and her kids will never want for a thing as long as I'm alive."

CHAPTER TWENTY-THREE

By evening they had moved Maria from the ICU. After she had settled into the new room, Jo put her in a wheelchair and took her to the NICU. They donned masks, gowns and booties, then Jo helped Maria stand so she could get her first look at her baby girl. The tears began silently, but quickly evolved into hushed sobs. Jo put an arm around her in comfort.

"Shh…don't upset yourself, you'll be sick. She's gonna be fine. I feel it in my gut." She held Maria close to her side. "Matter of fact, I predict she's gonna grow up strong enough to be a cowgirl if she wants."

Maria placed her hand against the plastic enclosure and dropped her head against Jo's chest. "Promise me, Jo."

Jo's voice trembled. "I promise I'll do everything I can to make sure this little girl gets to go home with you."

Maria wanted to see Matt, but she was afraid bringing him into the hospital would be too traumatic. Instead, she had Kathleen help him with the phone so she could render words of endearment to him. After having sat with her newborn for a while the following day, Maria announced to Jo she'd picked her name.

"Camilla Jo," she said. "Camilla is my grandmother's name. And if she grows into a strong woman as you've predicted and thinks it's too girly and wants a tomboy name, she can go by 'Jo.' Right, Jo Lynn?" Jo smiled proudly.

Maria only had to stay four more days until they were certain there was no threat of infections but was torn between finally seeing Matt and leaving her littlest one behind. The NICU nurses assured her they would care for little Camilla as if she were their own, and Maria could come and go as she pleased. Jo didn't allow Maria any say about the bag she'd packed so she could sleep on Maria's couch. Things were running smoothly at the farm under Tucker's command and Jo had been informed she still had at least a few more weeks to go in the cast. Maria finally managed to Skype with her parents so that they could see for themselves that she was all right, and they got their first look at their new granddaughter.

They quickly found a routine. Jo would drive them to Matt's school, drop Maria at the hospital and return for her truck to drive out to the farm. In the afternoon, the routine reversed, and Jo found herself sitting down with them to a home-cooked meal—like a real family. On the weekends, they got creative, but typically at some point during Saturday, Kathleen or Tim would deliver Matt to the farm. He and Daisy Mae would take a ride around the pasture and then he'd spend hours with Rosie and Jake. For Matt's benefit, they tried to keep life as normal as possible. Jo promised her mother they would return to their Sunday dinners as soon as Maria had her newborn settled at home.

Jo got to be a master at living out of a duffle bag, chauffeuring Maria and Matt and consulting with Tucker regarding farm operations. For the first time since college she again felt part of a family. A close-knit, loving family. She didn't ever want the feeling to end.

At the four-week mark, the doctors declared Camilla the strongest and fastest growing preemie they'd ever seen. Barring any unexpected results from a battery of tests they were performing, she could be released in another week or two. That evening at dinner, Jo asked the question she'd been sitting on for weeks.

"How are you planning to handle Cami and working?" She had nicknamed the baby Cami from "camouflage," for her ability to hide her strength. She watched frustration cloud Maria's eyes.

"I don't know." She sat her fork down and pushed her plate away. "I had originally been planning to take some time off. Jack's income was always more than enough to run the household, but now…" She stared off.

Nervous, Jo stood and began clearing the table. "I was thinking maybe you and the kids should come and stay at the farm with me." Jo cut off Maria's protest with a raised hand. "Wait, please hear me out before you let pride and stubbornness sway you."

"You know what they say about living in glass houses." Maria narrowed her eyes at Jo.

"At least I'll admit to being stubborn. So anyway, there's more than enough room in that big house for all of us. It doesn't have to be forever, only until you're ready, but you can rent this house I'm sure for more than enough to pay the mortgage. I'd feel more comfortable if you weren't living alone and trying to manage everything, and I think Kathleen would too, even if she's only fifteen minutes away."

Jo threw the dishtowel over her shoulder and shoved her hands in her pockets. "Please think about it. You can put the real estate thing on hold or work part-time if you want and, well, I'd be there to help take care of the kids." She shrugged. "I know, I'm not parent-of-the-year material, but I can raise a colt from birth to be a champion. How much difference could there be?"

She gave Maria a big grin, which made a smile grace her beautiful face. *God, I've missed that "almost ready to laugh" kind of smile.* She quickly added, "They eat, they sleep, they poop and you clean it up. Sounds the same to me." Finally, she managed to get a little laugh from Maria. "Just think about it."

Maria stood. "I will." She placed a hand on Jo's arm and leaned in to kiss her cheek. "Thank you." She moved around the table to get Matt up. "For everything."

Jo felt the warmth from her heart creeping into her cheeks and ducked hurriedly into the kitchen.

She was having a beer out on the back patio when Maria joined her. Pulling the bottle from her lips, she offered, "Drink?"

Maria sighed. "I'd like nothing more, believe me, but I've been nursing Camilla every day when I visit her and pumping as much breast milk as I can for them to feed her so when we bring her home we'll hopefully spend more time up close, if you know what I mean."

She prayed Maria wasn't going to go into details about breastfeeding and all its benefits. Maria pulled her feet under her and faced Jo.

"I talked your proposal over with Matt."

Jo smiled. "And what did the two of you decide?"

"I love the idea of being out there in the peace and quiet, but I don't want to be a burden on you. You've already gone above and beyond any friend I've ever had."

Jo slid her hand over Maria's. "You and your children would never be a burden on me. Please believe that." Maria turned her hand over, intertwining their fingers, her eyes shining darkly.

Maria looked at the strong hand holding hers. "You have to promise me you won't change how you live your life to accommodate us if we move in with you. Temporarily, of course."

"Okay. But I'm not sure what you're talking about changing."

Maria continued to gaze at their interlocked hands and realized she wanted to hold onto Jo's hand and never let go. But she released her fingers and slipped her hand away.

"You have to continue to date and go out and spend time with your friends."

Jo chuckled. "Ah yes, my active personal life. We can't possibly have a lull in it. It might actually cease to exist."

She smacked Jo's arm. "I'm very serious about this."

"Okay, but I'm not sure what exciting nightlife, or whatever, you think I might be missing out on."

Despite the niggling fear of having Jo's answer, she asked, "What about Dr. Mathews?"

Jo stretched her fingers and made a fist with her left hand, remembering the last time they'd talked. "I haven't seen her since I got my cast off." Maria didn't need to know that they'd not even spoken since that day. "Our schedules are so different."

In truth, Loren made it clear that she couldn't see Jo as long as Jo was in love with Maria. Jo tried arguing that Loren's perceptions about her feelings were wrong, but could only do so half-heartedly. In the end, she knew Loren was right. Hell, even Kathleen was able to see that Jo had serious feelings for Maria.

"Maybe if you're not devoting so much time to me and my kids, you two can find some mutual time." Jo only shrugged. "Unless you promise me, Jo Marchal, to quit hovering like a mother and go back to the life you're accustomed to, I won't even entertain the idea of living at the farm, for any amount of time."

Silence loomed between them before Jo finally responded. "Okay, okay, but what, you gonna hold me to some kind of quota on dates or something?"

Maria pursed her lips. "Only if I think you're neglecting your own life." Jo turned her head and rolled her eyes. "Are we agreed?"

She returned her gaze to Maria and said, smiling, "I can live with those terms. Should we be drawing up a contract and sign in blood or something?" She immediately regretted her choice of words, but Maria only narrowed her eyes at her.

"I'll give you the benefit of the doubt."

* * *

They made their plans and by the end of September, Jo had worked out everything so they could be a settled, happy family out at the farm. Within the week, the necessary things were moved and stored and a renter for Maria's house had been found. They established a good working routine in the first few weeks. Maria would have the kids ready to go in the morning, dropping Matt first by his school and the baby at Kathleen's for a few hours while she did some work at her office. She returned to the farm by lunchtime to feed Jo, Tucker and whoever else was working at the time. She scheduled her appointments for late afternoon whenever possible and Jo gladly sat with the baby. Maria would return with Matt and they'd have a family dinner. The evening routine included Jo cleaning up the kitchen, starting laundry when necessary, while Maria readied the kids for bed and tucked them in. They could generally manage to meet at the kitchen island by nine or so to unwind from their busy days.

One such night in the middle of October, while sipping her herbal tea, Maria said, "You look worn out, Jo. You don't look at all like the laid-back cowgirl you used to be."

Jo took a swallow of her beer. "Well, that's why little Jo likes me so much. She thinks I'm her ol' nana."

"Nice try at steering the conversation away from where I was going with it."

Jo furrowed her brows. "Which was?"

"You need to go out and relax and have some fun. Like you used to before we invaded your life."

"Yeah, well, running around and hanging out in bars is overrated, believe me."

Maria shook her head. "In any case, I want you to go out to a movie or dinner with a friend, someone…something, but I want you out of this house Saturday night."

Jo's eyes widened. "Ah, and the truth shall be revealed. You want me outta here because you're gonna have some guy over for a little hanky panky." She gave what she hoped was a devilish smile. "Why didn't you just say so?"

Maria wadded up her napkin and tossed it at her. "Hardly. That is the furthest thing from my mind. I want you to go out and forget about dishes and diapers, laundry and grocery runs. I want you to kick back, have a few beers and, as you so aptly put it, have some hanky panky." Maria tilted her head with a smile as Jo tossed the napkin back at her and laughed.

"What, you think I can walk into a bar and pick out a woman to go home with?"

Maria blushed. "I can't imagine there's any shortage of women that would want that with you."

Heat warmed Jo's face. "Be that as it may, or not, it's not me. And I'm not interested in a relationship."

Sighing audibly, Maria reached across the counter and touched Jo's hand. "Oh sweetie, I'm not trying to push you into a relationship. But who hurt you so deeply that you won't even try and let someone love you?" Jo lifted a shoulder. "I can't stand watching you sit around the house night after night. That's what I do. I'm a mother, that's what we do. Look…we had an agreement, did we not?"

Jo averted her eyes and pretended to search her memory. "Did we?" When her gaze moved back to Maria, she narrowed her eyes at Jo.

"Don't play naïve. You know very well we did, and if you don't go out Saturday night, I will move us out of here so fast your head will spin. Then maybe you'll get on with your life." Maria's attitude shocked Jo.

"Wow! That kinda sounds like a threat." Jo smiled.

Maria's expression was as stern as Jo had ever seen. "If that's what it takes to get you to honor the word you gave me, yes, I'm threatening to pack me and the kids and move back to town."

Jo rubbed her hands over her face and through her hair. "Okay, I'll go out to the bar in Prescott Saturday night."

"Maybe you can call your friend Cecile to come for a visit and go out with you."

Jo laughed. "There's definitely not enough room in this house for Cecile to visit. I'd be seriously afraid she'd scare the devil out of Matt."

Maria's tight lips curled into a smile. "Thank you." Jo nodded. "And can we not make this such a hard-fought battle in the future?"

Jo nodded again. "So if I go out and get drunk are you going to load the kids in the car at midnight to come and get me if I call?"

Maria got up and set her cup in the sink. "If you need me to, I will. Isn't that what friends do for each other?" She placed a hand on Jo's shoulder. "Thank you again." She pressed her lips to the top of Jo's head. "Goodnight, Jo."

"Night."

Jo's breath caught and she held it until Maria was out of the kitchen. She shook off the shiver that had raced through her from Maria's nearness and the innocent kiss.

As she sat finishing her beer she stewed over how much she didn't want to go out to the bar Saturday night. But since she had given her word, she'd have to suck it up.

CHAPTER TWENTY-FOUR

Jo was so apprehensive about having to go out she couldn't enjoy dinner Saturday. Maria insisted on cleaning up, pushing Jo from the kitchen to go get ready. She carried a beer to the bathroom and took a leisurely hot shower, even shaving because she had the ridiculous thought that Maria might check, or, even more ridiculous, that she might get lucky.

Wiping the fog from the mirror, she told her reflection, "The luckiest thing ever happened to you, cowgirl, is that woman in your kitchen." Using some gel, she combed her hair into place and spent more than twenty minutes deciding what to wear. She mumbled in front of the bedroom mirror since the baby was sleeping. "Just be comfortable. It's not like you have to dress to impress." She finally rejoined Maria in the kitchen and tossed her empty bottle in the trash.

When Jo emerged from her bedroom wearing a T-shirt that matched the blue of her eyes, faded jeans torn at the knees, a well-worn pair of boots and the leather jacket she had given her at Christmas, Maria immediately regretted insisting that she go out in search of some fun. She wanted to keep her home, to herself, and see what kind of fun they could come up with. Jo looked perfectly delectable and Maria's thighs clenched involuntarily at the sight of her. She struggled for nonchalance when she finally spoke.

"Is that the look the women go for?"

Jo looked down at herself. "I don't dress to be looked at. I like to dress for my own comfort."

Maria smiled. "Well, you certainly look comfortable." She dropped her eyes to the tea bag she dunked in her cup. If she looked at Jo any longer, she would feel a need to bodily block Jo's exit, arms outstretched in the doorway.

"Okay, I'm off. I've got my cell." She patted her jeans pocket. "If you need anything at all, call me."

Maria glanced at her briefly. "We'll be fine. Go have fun." And if Jo's sex appeal wasn't torture enough, Jo placed a quick kiss on the top of her head.

"Don't wait up, Mom." And with that Jo was gone.

Maria sighed deeply. She had planned to soak in a hot bath, but it now seemed more like she would need a cold shower.

Reluctantly, Jo entered Whispers and found a spot at the bar. She stood with her back to the crowd in her own little world, ignoring a brush against her as rudeness since the place was busy, but a familiar voice interrupted her thoughts.

"Didn't think I'd see you out here." Jo turned around to see Loren waving her empty beer bottle at the barmaid. "So where's the little woman? Maria, right?"

"Home with her children, I imagine," Jo answered.

"How's the baby?"

"Healthy and growing," Jo responded flatly.

"Can I buy you a beer?"

"Sure, thanks." When the fresh beer came, Jo tipped her bottle. "Thanks again." She took a drink.

Loren scrutinized her closely. "You seem down in the dumps, Jo. Anything you want to talk about?"

Jo shook her head and took a long pull on the beer.

"Would you rather I leave you alone?"

"Only if you want to." Jo forced a smile.

She didn't leave. And Jo eventually relaxed into an easy exchange of conversation with Loren, even buying the next round. The more they talked, the closer they stood to one another. Jo couldn't deny what an attractive woman Loren was, and she smelled heavenly.

The music slowed and Jo asked, "Would you like to dance?"

Loren emptied her beer and studied her for a second before grabbing Jo's hand. "Sure."

Jo's body warmed holding Loren in her arms. Or maybe it was Loren's hot breath on her neck. Loren's eyes sparkled with desire when Jo leaned back to look at her, so she closed the distance between them and pressed her lips to Loren's.

Loren's tongue darted into Jo's mouth, begging to be challenged. The kiss so heated that Loren stopped, grabbed Jo's hand and tugged her off the dance floor. Part way down the semi-dark hall to the bathrooms, Loren stopped and pinned her against the wall. Jo's lips were eager and hot, much like the spot between her legs where Loren had slid her thigh. She could feel her own wetness soaking her underwear. She wanted nothing more than soft fingers touching her there. It was as if someone had stuck a match to dry kindling. She was burning hot inside.

When Loren pushed her hand between them, Jo cried out, "Oh, God—" barely managing to stop herself from uttering Maria's name. She wanted Maria in her arms, she wanted to kiss her. She stilled Loren's roving hands and moved her back an arms-length with her hands on her shoulders.

"I can't, Loren," she croaked hoarsely. "I'm sorry. My mind's somewhere else and I can't do this to you."

Loren took a step back shaking her head. "I got it…you're still hung up on the straight lady." She used her fingertip to trace a line from Jo's breastbone to her navel and with a "sorry you're missing out" look, said, "I might still be around if you ever get over that."

Jo dropped her head and Loren walked off. She went to the bathroom and splashed cold water on her face before slithering out. She knew better than to drive after downing three beers in a relatively short period of time so she spent an hour sitting in her truck with the windows down. Eventually she made the trip home, driving slowly and deliberately. Turning the truck into the drive, she breathed a sigh of relief and swore to herself never to do that again.

* * *

The moment Jo walked out of the door, Maria regretted having been so insistent that she go out and have fun with other gay women. She couldn't wrap her brain around the jealousy that flared at the thought of a woman's lips on Jo's. The very lips she'd kissed once. She'd relived that moment in her mind every day since.

She struggled daily with the undeniable attraction she felt for Jo. She'd never had more than a passing curiosity about women "in that way." She'd always dated boys, not a lot, but certainly enough in high school and college to be considered normal. Married for seven years, with a child, that was normal. Wasn't it?

She couldn't be a lesbian. Jo had some masculine characteristics, no question, but there was no mistaking her womanhood. She never tried to appear male. She was simply comfortable with who she was, a strong and very attractive woman.

No, it wasn't "women" she was attracted to, Maria decided—it was Jo Marchal. She couldn't sit down and relax while she was out. She paced between the kitchen and the front window. When the headlights flashed across the darkened living room, however, she made her way down the even darker hall and slipped into bed.

Jo crept quietly into the house, trying with desperation not to run into anything in the dark. She bumped the entry table, rattling a horse statue, which she skillfully caught. Disaster averted. Had it fallen, it would have sounded like a bomb going off in the silent house. Maria would panic and the baby would cry. She tiptoed down the hall and peeked in both bedrooms. Matt was sleeping soundly. Across the hall Maria and the baby were as well. Jo leaned in the doorway a long moment, watching Maria's still body. She'd give anything in the world to snuggle up to the woman in her bed, to hold her and be near.

Staring at her reflection in the hall bath, she mumbled, "In your dreams, cowgirl." Pulling the covers back on the sofa bed in her office, she flopped down on it. She tossed and turned for hours before sleep ever found her, thinking about Loren's kiss and seeing Maria in her bed. The images went back and forth, over and over, until she could imagine it was Maria's lips that had been so warm and inviting on hers hours earlier.

When the baby cried around four o'clock, Jo couldn't pry her eyes open, but she heard Maria shushing as she started nursing her. After the first few nights, Jo was able to sleep through the baby's cries most of the time. She'd offered to help Maria with the late night, early morning feeding, but Maria informed her that for some reason Camilla wouldn't accept anything but her breast during the night since she came home from the hospital. A bottle, even though it contained breast milk, would not be so welcome, and unless Jo could produce milk, she couldn't help. The conversation came back to her now as she listened to Maria's quiet humming.

Maria pulled the office door closed even though Jo appeared to be sleeping soundly. She hoped since Jo had made it home before midnight she hadn't met up with a woman. If she had, wouldn't she have stayed out the night or have another body on the sofa sleeper? She clearly did not. She'd ask about Jo's night at breakfast.

Camilla was still sleeping and Maria had only just sat Matt down for his breakfast when Jo trudged into the kitchen looking rather bleary-eyed. Jo reached for the coffee maker. "It's ready to go," Maria told her.

Jo flipped the switch and scrubbed her hands over her face as she leaned against the counter waiting on the coffee.

Maria masked a smile. "Late night?" Jo merely grunted her reply. Maria leaned against the island. "You look like…well…like you had a rough night." Jo didn't respond and simply rubbed her hand over her forehead. "Rough night?" Maria persisted.

Jo squinted as she looked in her eyes. "Can we put this on hold 'til I've at least had a cup of coffee?" Her voice was raspy.

Maria turned around for her tea, hiding her smile. "Sure."

When Jo sat across the counter, her red eyes glowed like beacons. Maria wondered if it was too much alcohol or something else. She let Jo have half a cup of her coffee before she resumed her questioning.

"I didn't expect you home last night. Did you get in late?" She eyed Jo over the top of her cup while sipping her tea.

Jo cleared her throat. "I got in around midnight. I didn't really sleep until early this morning for some reason."

Maria no longer cared if Jo had met, talked to or done something more with another woman last night because she'd come home. "You're not coming down with something are you?" She moved around to feel Jo's neck and forehead. "Hum…no fever."

After everything that had gone through Jo's head last night, Maria was definitely standing too close now. She pushed up off the stool. "I'll feel better after a shower." She refilled her cup, in a hurry to vacate the kitchen while Maria was sitting with Matt as he finished his breakfast.

An hour or so later Maria asked Jo if she could sit with the kids for an hour or two.

"I have a couple who are serious about finding a home. I think I can get a quick sale. We could use the money."

"You do not need to worry about money."

"I will not be a kept woman. I can pay my own way." Jo conceded.

A knock sounded on the door as she sat in the rocker by the fireplace. "Darn," she mumbled. She forgot Tucker was supposed to stop in. "It's open," she called.

Tucker entered, a grin spreading ear to ear.

"What?" she asked.

"I don't think anybody'd believe it."

"What?" she asked again.

"You," he motioned at her, "this." He chuckled. "I never would have imagined it and I sure bet nobody'd believe me if I told them."

Jo looked down at the bundle in her arms happily suckling on the bottle. She raised her narrowed eyes to Tucker. "If you tell a soul, I'll have your head."

He raised his hands. "Heck, boss, like I said, nobody'd believe it anyway."

She eyed him critically. "As long as we're understood."

He tapped his hat on his thigh. "Yeah, I kinda like my job…and my head." When he laughed, she smiled. "So…what's up?"

Jo tipped her head toward the coffee table. "It's right there in that envelope." He picked up the large manila envelope and carefully removed the contents. "You know I bought the old Wagner farm next door." He nodded. "I'm gonna keep about twenty acres and lease out the rest for farming for now."

He looked up from the papers, his eyes big as saucers. "This is…" Stunned, he looked back at the papers in his hand. "This is a deed," he finally said looking back at her. "With my name on it."

"That's right. I'm giving you five acres. It's my way of saying thanks for everything you've done for me in the last year." He stood there, mouth agape. "It's a small gesture compared to the invaluable help you've been to me."

"But, I…" he stammered, "I don't know what to say."

"Tucker, shut up and take it," she said playfully. His head bobbed as he shoved the papers back in the envelope. "You can do what you want with it. Build on it or sell it. Of course, if you sell it it has to be to me, but if you build on it, you'll never have an excuse for being late to work." She grinned.

He laughed. "Yeah, I can always walk to work if I have to."

"That wasn't my intention, but it would be nice someday to think of you as my neighbor."

"You'd make a fine neighbor, Jo."

"There's cold beer in the fridge if you want one to celebrate your new status as a landowner."

He tucked the envelope under his arm. "Ah heck, I can't, but thanks. If my momma smelled alcohol on my breath on a Sunday, she'd tan my hide and I'd never hear the end of it." Jo smiled, not completely surprised that Tucker's mother was such a righteous woman. "But maybe tomorrow after work."

"I'll keep 'em cold."

Jo thought of her own mother. She'd never think of drinking in front of her either. She had been so sweet, offering to come for a visit and help out with the new baby when Jo told her she might not make it as often for Sunday dinner. Of course there weren't enough sleeping accommodations unless Jo turned the living room couch back into her bed. Her mom had assured her she could share Sunday dinners with her church widows when Jo couldn't make it.

Both Jo and Camilla were sleeping when Maria arrived home half an hour later. Her heart melted at the sight of Jo cradling the baby in her arms. She slipped quietly down the hall and found Matt curled up in his bed between Jake and Rosie, all napping away. Deciding to take advantage of the quiet time, short as it might end up being, she ran a hot bath and slid in. No more than fifteen minutes had passed when a light rap sounded on the door.

"Maria?"

She didn't open her eyes. "Hmm…yes."

Jo's voice came softly through the door. "I didn't realize you'd gotten home."

Water splashed as Maria sat up. "I'll be right out."

"No, enjoy your time. I just wanted you to know I put Camilla in her bassinette so you don't wake her when you come out."

Maria didn't want to get out. What she wanted was for Jo to come in and slide her strong hands in the soapy water and—" Thanks…I won't be long."

"No worries."

Jo was right there. So close, but so far away. Maria's blood ran hotter than the bath water and pooled between her thighs.

CHAPTER TWENTY-FIVE

It puzzled Jo that in the following weeks Maria made no further mention of her going out and trying to meet someone. And she had no intention of bringing it up or going in search of lesbian companionship. She also had no desire to have any liaisons only for sex. It wasn't her. She would just continue to dream about that special someone that she wanted to spend the rest of her life with.

November rolled around, bringing with it a sadness and loneliness that settled into Jo's heart. As the anniversary of her dad's death neared, it seemed mostly to serve as a reminder that her parents had spent more than fifty years happily married while she would likely spend her old age as a lonely lesbian cowgirl.

On the Friday night before the dreaded anniversary, which Jo had promised to spend with her mom, she was seated in her usual spot at the kitchen island nursing her second beer. Maria entered later than usual, well after ten o'clock. "Your namesake is being quite the stubborn handful tonight. She refused to go to sleep." She put the teakettle on and leaned against the counter, waiting.

Jo thought how much like an old married couple they had become in their nightly routine—sitting in the kitchen to relax a bit before bed and discussing the day's events or whatever subject happened to come up.

Before moving around to her side of the island with her tea, Maria put her hand on Jo's shoulder. "Thanks for running out to the store for me this evening."

"You're welcome."

Maria took her seat across from Jo. "You don't have to give up so much of your time or yourself taking care of us."

Jo cocked her head, sensing she was about to receive a lecture about going out and finding some fun again. "I don't mind taking care of you all. It gives my life purpose."

Maria frowned. "I can think of other things that can give your life purpose."

Here we go. "Like?"

Maria's eyes were focused on the spoon stirring her tea. "Like someone to take care of you."

Jo smiled. "I seem to recall you were supposed to be taking care of that, weren't you?"

"Yes." Maria returned her smile. "Cupid and I. And I think I may have found someone for you."

Jo's brows rose high in surprise and anxiety. As if knowing she needed rescuing, Cami let out a wail and Maria dashed down the hall to get her before she woke Matt. Jo waited and waited for Maria's return, but when the clock on the stove read 11:47 she knew their conversation would have to continue another time. She needed to get to bed since she was heading out in the morning to spend the weekend with her mom.

When she entered the kitchen the following morning Maria was seated at the counter, cooing and making faces at Cami in her lap, and Matt was eating his cereal.

"Good morning," Maria said in a chipper tone.

"Morning," Jo replied feeling like a wrung-out dish rag after lying awake for hours before falling asleep. She hadn't been able to keep their interrupted conversation from looping in her brain.

"Are you feeling okay?" Maria asked. "You look a little worn out this morning.

"I'm fine," Jo mumbled. She poured a cup of coffee and sat opposite the Wests at the counter.

"Are you going to be okay spending the weekend with your mother? Or would you like our company?" Maria smiled warmly.

"I need to be a big girl and do this, but thanks for the offer."

Jo couldn't imagine the shock on her mom's face if she showed up with Maria, Matt and the baby in tow. Then again, maybe her mom would rather have a very straight woman and her kids as weekend house guests. Jo finished her coffee and moved to the sink to rinse her cup.

"I should get going in case Mom has lunch plans."

"I made enchiladas for you to take. Your mother seemed to really like them at last year's picnic. They're in the casserole dish with the blue lid on the bottom shelf. The carrier is on the dining table."

Jo slid the dish out of the fridge, lifted a corner of the top and sniffed. Even early in the morning it made her mouth water. There wasn't any better Mexican food than Maria's grandmother's enchilada recipe.

"Thanks. That's very thoughtful and I'm sure Mom will be really appreciative." She put the dish in the carrier, then leaned down to place a kiss on the top of Cami's head. "Be a good girl for your mommy." She stepped around Maria and lightly ruffled Matt's curls. "You're the man in charge, Matt." She scooped up the casserole and met Maria's gaze. "And no wild parties, young lady."

Maria giggled. "As if…" She motioned to each of her children. "Drive safely and tell your mother we send hellos."

Strolling to the front door, Jo called over her shoulder, "I'll see you guys tomorrow evening."

During the entire drive to her mom's, Jo puzzled about what Maria was alluding to when she said she thought she'd found someone for her. The second she pulled into the driveway, though, an image of her dad in the barn flashed in her mind. She'd been to her childhood home dozens of times over the last year. She'd never felt as solemn as she did today. Grabbing her duffel bag and the food carrier, she pasted on a smile, knocked on the door and let herself in.

"Hey, Mom, I'm here."

"In here, sweetheart," her mom called from the kitchen.

Would she ever get used to hearing the endearment? She couldn't remember even as a child her mom calling her sweetheart. Jo set the casserole on the counter and kissed her mom's cheek.

"Well, what have we here?" Her mom slid the zipper around the carrier.

"Maria made enchiladas."

"And here I thought you cooked something."

Jo chuckled. "You know better than that, Mom."

Her mom gave her a pinch on the cheek. "You have many other talents, Jo Lynn. Cooking isn't for everyone. So how are Maria and her children getting along at your farm?"

"Just great! And Camilla is growing like a weed." She whipped her phone out of her pocket and scrolled through her photo gallery. She held it out to her mom showing a picture of Cami in her swing, taken during a fit of giggles. She scrolled through several more.

"She's as cute as her mother is pretty. And here you are, showing pictures like a proud parent."

Jo stepped over to the coffee maker to hide the blush she felt rising in her cheeks. After taking her time pouring a cup, she turned and leaned against the counter. "What would you like to do today, Mom?"

"After lunch can we drive out to the cemetery? I want to put fresh flowers on your dad's grave."

"Sure." Jo sipped her coffee. "How about if we go out for dinner so you don't have to cook."

"That sounds lovely."

They sat around the kitchen table with their coffees, her mother talking about what she and the church widows had been up to and peppering Jo with questions about how her life had changed with the West family living there.

"It actually works out well. My schedule is flexible enough to help with babysitting, and as you know Maria's a great cook so she keeps me fed."

She was glad to be able to spend this weekend with her mother, Jo thought, taking another sip of coffee. She realized, however, that she'd only been away from the farm for a few hours and already wished she was back home.

Jo loved the weekends. In spite of Maria having to run out for appointments, they had more time to spend together. She reflected again on how much their living arrangement mirrored that of a family. A real family. She liked the feeling. And dreaded the day it might come to an end.

Not that real families didn't have their downsides, she reminded herself. People make mistakes. She undoubtedly would too, if she was lucky enough to be able to spend a significant portion of her life with the Wests. Never, ever, though, would she judge Cami when she grew up and made her life choices. Not the way her parents had judged her. They had lost so much precious time together because of that. Thank God, she had had enough time to reconnect with her father before his death—and had the opportunity now to strengthen her ties with her mother.

Life, she decided, was too short not to do what it took to make the most of every chance for wholeness and happiness. Maybe it was time to tell Maria about her feelings for her and the kids. Even if that was scary as hell.

Then again, she thought, *look what happened when I came out to Dad and Mom*. Would Maria welcome her into the family or would she run?

She thought she knew Maria well enough to think she wouldn't run away even if she didn't think she could ever return Jo's kind of love. Would she withdraw, though, the way she had before?

She went back and forth on what she should do. Only one thing was clear—she loved Maria and the kids with every piece of her heart.

When Jo walked out of the house Maria felt what seemed an awful lot like heartache. This would be the first night she and the kids had spent at the house alone. She was already missing Jo and their daily routines. Jo had become not only a big part of her life, but Matt and Camilla's too.

She couldn't decide if the baby's crying last night, just as she was about to share with Jo what she was thinking about relationships, was an intervention to keep her from making a big mistake and ruining a perfect friendship or simply a matter of bad timing.

After putting the kids down for a nap, she sat at the kitchen island with a cup of tea, making a mental pro and con list in her mind.

The biggest pro was how Jo made her feel—simply by being around her. Jo made her heart beat faster, she made her feel desire she'd never felt before in her life.

The biggest con? She wasn't a lesbian and if she got involved with Jo and couldn't be who Jo needed it could ruin everything they had.

In the end, Maria decided, she and Jo needed to have a conversation. She needed to unburden herself of the internal battle she'd been experiencing. Who knows? Maybe it was just a crush and if they talked through it, she'd feel differently about Jo.

"Who are you kidding?" she mumbled as she made her way down the hall to check on the kids.

Following lunch and the trip to the cemetery, Jo's mom started reminiscing about the past—the times before Jo's announcement had blown apart her family.

Having a family was important to Jo—the most important thing in her mind, in fact. She wanted to be a caregiver, to nurture young minds. That was one of the reasons she'd decided to leave the high-stress world of horse breeding and work toward opening a dude ranch.

She had thought all that would happen with Claire. But when Jo proposed to Claire following the Supreme Court's ruling on marriage equality, Claire had made it clear that she wasn't interested in marriage to some run-of-the-mill horse farmer. She had no intention of having rug rats under foot either.

The woman now sharing her living space would make a perfect partner for her, Jo realized. She sighed heavily. The only way she and Maria could ever have a chance at anything, though, was if they talked. Wasn't it?

Jo sat patiently with her mom, watching television and making small talk, filling up some of the space, she imagined, that her dad had. She hoped it gave her mother a measure of comfort, but she itched to be home and outside in wide open spaces. She turned in earlier than usual. She was going to try and head back to the farm after breakfast—if her mom didn't object.

* * *

"Sweetheart, I didn't plan on you spending the entire weekend with me. I know you have work to do on your farm, and honestly, the gals from church keep me quite busy. I promise you I'm doing fine." Her mom reached across the table and squeezed her hand.

Jo had no idea that her mom could be so independent, but she was happy that her mom wasn't sitting alone in the house. "I do have some things to tend to at home," she said. *For one thing, I have to get home and find out what Maria was about to share with me on Friday night.*

She kissed her mom's cheek and left her on the porch waiting for her ride to church. She was anxious the entire drive home.

"I'm home," Jo called out entering the house.

"We're back here," came Maria's response from down the hall.

Jo peeked in the master bedroom. Matt sat on the end of the bed with Rosie watching a children's program on the TV and Maria and Cami were stretched out on the bed, Cami sleeping soundly.

"How was your visit with your mom?" Maria whispered to Jo when she sat next to Rosie on the bed.

"It was great. Mom is getting along A-okay," Jo said quietly.

"Let me put her in her bed and I'll meet you in the kitchen for lunch."

Jo was seated at the island turning a water bottle in her hands when Maria entered.

"What sounds good for lunch?"

"Maria, you know me, I'll eat anything that's called food."

She fried turkey bacon and made Jo the tastiest BLT she'd ever had. Once they'd eaten, Maria brought Matt in to feed him his lunch. An hour later she was putting him down for a nap. Returning to the kitchen, Maria sat across the island from Jo.

"So…" Jo began. "Shall we pick up our abandoned conversation from Friday about your collusion with Cupid?"

Maria exhaled a long sigh. "How about if we talk after the kids are in bed for the night? Like we do every night?"

Jo gave a nod.

CHAPTER TWENTY-SIX

Seated at the island that night, Jo said, "Okay, so as I recall you were about to share something."

Maria stared at her hands fidgeting on the island top. After another deep breath, she finally said, "I think Cupid and I have found someone for you."

"Really?" Jo nodded. "Who?"

Maria's eyes turned black as a moonless night, her smile fading. "Me," she said timidly.

Jo laughed nervously. "I think you have our roles reversed. I'm the one that's supposed to make you laugh. Remember?" Jo took a long drink of her water. She regarded Maria's serious expression.

"I'm not joking. I've never been more serious in my life."

Jo's mouth went dry as cotton. She drained the bottle before attempting to speak.

"Maria, Maria, I admit to having been with a few straight women in my life, but it's never worked out. It's not meant to be. Besides, I could never risk the friendship I have with you." Maria's gaze pierced her. "Listen, I'm beyond flattered, believe me, but this is not a life for you." *Are you crazy, Jo Lynn Marchal? This is what you've been dreaming of.*

"But it's an okay life for you?"

Jo set the bottle down and spread her hands. "This is who I am. I was born this way. Look at me. I'm as queer as the day is long. My being such a private person is the thing that helps me live my life without too much trouble. I don't really put myself out there. There are so many more people in this world that don't accept what I am than those who do." Jo dropped her head as the thought of her dad became a painful reminder.

"Some people love unconditionally." It was as though Maria knew what she was thinking.

She looked up again. "Oh, don't think I don't know that, but all it's ever got me was gut-wrenching heartache." She lowered her head again. "And I can't do that anymore."

When Maria touched her hand, Jo met her gaze. "He loved you Jo. In the end, he loved you unconditionally, even if he didn't say it." Jo wanted to believe it was true. "He asked me to take care of you." Jo picked at the label on the water bottle. "The day they visited and you asked me what your father said to me. He did tell me he liked the food and that I was a very good cook. And then much to my surprise, he asked me to take care of you." Jo blinked back threatening tears. "I think he thought you and I were…you know…together maybe."

Maria got up and walked around the counter. Placing her arm across Jo's shoulder, she pulled her close and pressed her cheek to Jo's head. "He loved you more than he could tell you," she said softly. When Jo exhaled a deep sigh, Maria briefly pressed her lips to Jo's hair. "The way I love you." Jo shook her head and Maria relaxed her hold, then tipped Jo's chin up to look into her eyes.

"You're afraid. I can see that in your eyes. But please, Jo, don't be afraid of me. Let it go. This is meant to be, I can feel it in my soul." She touched her fingers lightly to Jo's cheek and Jo closed her eyes. "I'll admit I'm afraid. This is all so foreign to me, but I'm not going to run away from how I feel—not anymore." Her last words drew Jo's eyes back to hers. "I want to trust my feelings for you. I want to make your life everything you want it to be. I trust you enough to give you my heart. Can you trust me and take a chance on us?"

Jo wanted to believe—believe this was right. She didn't doubt that Maria cared for her, but she had trusted feelings like this before only to be betrayed in the end. She knew she was in love with Maria—had known for a very long time now. But she wasn't as sure that Maria was "in love" with her. Doubt, fear and anxiety swamped her all at once. Maria's touch caused an ache in her heart, born not of pain, but intense yearning and desire. She remembered the feeling well. The feeling she got when she gave all of herself to a woman. She tried to resist. It was a losing battle. She dropped her eyes.

"Jo, please look at me."

When Jo again looked in Maria's eyes, she saw a longing there that pulled as strong as a riptide. She couldn't stop her hands from reaching up and cupping Maria's face. They shared a lingering gaze before a force Jo had no power to fight brought Maria's lips to hers. The first soft brush of Maria's lips ignited Jo's passion like kindling. Maria moaned softly and the fire in Jo's belly erupted. She pulled back, gasping for a breath.

She searched Maria's eyes long and hard. "There's no going back from here," she said breathlessly.

"I don't ever want to go back." Desire flashed in Maria's eyes and her lips parted slightly. "I want you."

Jo took a deep calming breath, pulled Maria firmly into her arms and kissed her like she'd been waiting her whole life for her. She had.

Maria placed her hands on Jo's shoulders to steady herself. She felt lightheaded from the kiss. Never, ever in her life had she desired so desperately to be touched by someone. Jo's hands were like fire on her skin, burning everywhere, and when Jo's tongue parted her lips warmth flooded her body. She couldn't stop the groan that escaped, and Jo responded by pushing her tongue deeper as Maria slid her hands around Jo's shoulders to draw her closer. When her breasts pressed into Jo's chest, the heat between their bodies opened floodgates that neither could shove back any longer.

Jo's lips traveled to her jaw and down her neck while nimble fingers methodically unbuttoned the top of her blouse and slipped it off her shoulders. Jo trailed kisses over one shoulder and the other, returning her lips again to her neck. She'd never been so wet…so wanting.

She lowered her head and placed her lips to Jo's ear. "Please… Jo, make love to me." Jo pulled back to look in her eyes. In a throaty whisper, Maria said again, "Please…"

Jo led her to the bedroom, pausing inside the doorway. "Is it okay if I put Cami in the office?" she asked in a hushed voice.

Maria nodded a "yes" and followed Jo as she carried the sturdy bassinette like it was nothing more than a sack of light groceries. She was anxious to feel Jo's solid body pressed into hers, her strong hands touching her skin. She placed the monitor close by Cami and took Jo's hand. Jo gave her hand a squeeze as they stood there a moment looking at the baby. The emotion nearly brought Maria to tears. This was why she loved this woman, because Jo had the capacity to love unconditionally. She finally led her back to the bedroom, where they stood beside the bed.

She ran her fingers through Jo's hair and looked deep into her eyes. When she leaned in to kiss her, Jo freed the remaining buttons on her blouse and slid it from her shoulders. Jo's hands moved slowly up her arms, over her shoulders and to her breasts. She flinched.

"I'm sorry." Jo pulled back.

She took Jo's hand and kissed her palm. "Please don't apologize for touching me. You feel wonderful." She kissed Jo's wrist. "They're very sensitive." She placed Jo's palm over her breast again. "No one's touch has ever felt so…so," she inhaled sharply, "so arousing." She could feel her temperature rising.

Jo stroked a finger up and down between her breasts. "I'll be gentle. Maria…" Her eyes met Jo's. "Are you sure this is what you want?"

"I've never been surer of anything in my life."

Jo wouldn't fight the desire any longer. The sound of Maria's voice, her touch, had made Jo want her from the time they'd met. She wanted to show Maria how exquisitely a woman should be loved. Their lips came together, tongues dancing with urgency. With an arm around her waist, Jo slid her knee between Maria's and guided her down onto the bed. She sat beside Maria and worked open the button and zipper on her slacks. "You are so beautiful." When her fingers brushed the satin of her panties, Maria moaned and caught Jo's hand.

"I feel very self conscious about my body."

Jo stroked her fingers down her arm. "You shouldn't." She stood, pulled her T-shirt over her head and tossed it over the bedside lamp to soften the light. She knelt before Maria. "Please let me take away any doubt you have."

She touched her lips to the scar above her panty line and traced her tongue to the top of it. Maria's legs clenched Jo's sides in response. Jo raised her head, meeting Maria's eyes. "I don't want to hurt you or do anything you're not comfortable with." Maria was silent, eyes dark with desire. "Please say you'll tell me if I do."

When Maria nodded, Jo laid her back on the bed. She removed Maria's slacks, making sure to touch her legs all the way down to her ankles, and placed feather-light kisses from her knee to her thigh as she moved onto the bed beside her. Maria pulled her into a hungry kiss that told her she wanted this. She went slowly, touching and tasting Maria in the places she knew to be sensitive to a woman, and Maria didn't fail to respond. When Jo finally slipped her fingers in Maria's wetness, she trembled in orgasm almost immediately.

"Oh God!" Maria gasped, clutching Jo's shoulders until her body stilled under her hand.

Jo nuzzled her neck. "Are you okay?"

"Better than," Maria whispered breathlessly. Her thighs clenched around Jo's hand and fingers where they remained in her wet folds. "I'm not sure what to do," she said with steadier breath after a long moment. "Please tell me how to satisfy you, Jo."

Jo kissed her neck and next to her ear. "There's plenty of time to learn."

"Will you take off your jeans so I can feel you against me?"

She stood and after removing the remainder of her clothes, slipped off Maria's bra and panties. Maria's hands roamed over her shoulders, down her back and settled on her ass. Jo moaned, stroking her fingers again through Maria's wetness and coaxing a moan from her.

"I want to be inside you," Jo murmured. She wanted to touch every part of Maria.

Maria guided Jo's fingers inside her, her hips rising in sync with Jo's slow gentle thrusts.

She took Maria to her edge, then pulled back over and over as Maria whimpered and her own release neared. When Maria pleaded, "Please, Jo…" Jo pushed her back to the edge and tumbled over with her.

"Maria!" Jo called out as the orgasm rocked her. "Ah, Maria," she gasped, shuddering through the aftershocks. Maria held her face in her hands, kissing Jo hungrily until they were both breathless.

"I've never experienced anything like this."

"What…multiple orgasms?" Jo asked, suddenly feeling shy.

"Feeling like I've been drugged. I'm so high I never want to come down." When Jo rolled onto her back, Maria snuggled up against her side. "I had no idea lovemaking could feel so…so rousing and exhausting, and so…freeing. I don't ever want to move from this spot."

Jo wrapped her arm around Maria as she settled her head against Jo's chest. "I don't think I *can* move from this spot." She exhaled a contented sigh. She was a goner. She'd fallen helplessly in love with Maria, and the knowledge that she was the first one to take this amazing woman to ecstasies she'd never before known filled her with untold pleasure.

They lay, limbs entwined, fingers stroking—exploring. Maria's warm breath whispered across Jo's chest while her heart pounded in perfect rhythm with Maria's heartbeat against her side.

After a while, Maria stirred. "I want to please you, Jo, but you have to tell me how."

Jo squeezed Maria's thigh between hers. "You can't believe how much you already have."

Maria reached between Jo's thighs, but Jo caught her hand. She kissed her palm and sucked a finger into her mouth. "I'm not done with you." She barely recognized the deep, low tone of her own voice.

"Oh, Jo, I can't—"

She guided Maria over onto her back. "Let's see." She kissed her way down Maria's silky warm skin, feeling her own arousal reigniting against Maria's thigh. Jo's lips lingered on the scar before moving to her hip, then the tender spot at the top of her thigh. Maria's legs opened to her. Jo painted the inside of her thigh with her tongue. When she heard the familiar whimper, she pressed her tongue to Maria's sensitized flesh and was rewarded with a deep, low moan. Maria clutched at the bed covers and arched against her mouth. Her tongue slipped through her wetness, inside, out, over and over until Maria shuddered in orgasm.

"Oh my God!" Maria's body fell limp. Jo rested her head on her thigh and watched Maria as she threaded her fingers into her hair. "Mmm…you've rendered me helpless." Jo kissed her thigh, making her flinch. "Come up here." Jo moved up to settle against Maria's side. "As soon as I can breathe I want to make you feel like this."

Jo pulled herself tight against her side. "Ah, but you already do."

She had climaxed as she enticed the second orgasm from Maria. She couldn't be more sated. She pressed her lips to Maria's temple, rolled onto her back and pulled Maria half on top of her. She stroked her fingers up and down Maria's back. It wasn't long after Jo could tell she had drifted off by the soft, steady sound of her breathing.

This is what it's supposed to feel like. Loving and being loved. Jo knew it in her heart. She prayed for no regrets in the morning. The clock glowed one fifty-three a.m. It already was morning. She lay awake for another hour, feeling Maria's breath across her skin. She could do this every day for the rest of her life. She *wanted* this every day for the rest of her life.

Maria had been sleeping soundly with Jo pressed against her back when she heard Camilla's tiny cry through the monitor. She turned it off, hoping Jo wouldn't wake, and slipped from the bed, pulling on her robe. Her body felt as though she'd run a marathon, then her mind focused on the reason her body felt so spent. She smiled. Warmth spread again from her belly to her center as she settled down on the sofa with the baby. She hummed and rocked Camilla side to side as she nursed, reliving how completely Jo had pleasured her, not once, but multiple times in the hours they'd spent making love. She had never known it was possible to have more than a single orgasm. She wanted Jo to feel the same. When she finished nursing and got the baby down, she was far too keyed up to go back to sleep.

* * *

Jo slept like a baby. But, when she rolled over in the bed she realized she was alone…in her bed…and wondered if it had all been a dream. She sat up and ran her hands through her hair and over her face and then she knew it hadn't been. Maria's scent lingered on her fingers. The memory was vivid. The feel of Maria's body under her touch and the way she had responded.

It was nearing eight o'clock. She couldn't believe Maria was already up, knowing she hadn't drifted off to sleep until almost two in the morning. Padding naked into her bathroom, she brushed her teeth, then pulled on a T-shirt and boxers before venturing out into the hall, no longer able to walk around the house naked with children under her roof.

She couldn't find any children, though. The diaper bag and Matt's backpack were gone from their spot by the kitchen door. She rushed back down the hall to check the office and guest room. Panic strangled her as she ran to the front door. Her heart dropped to her stomach when she stepped out on the porch and saw that Maria's car was gone. She could barely breathe as she ran barefoot to the barn, yelling for Tucker when she raced through the doors.

He bolted from the tack room, halting immediately and turning his head when he spotted her.

"Tucker...have you...seen Maria?" Gasping, breathless, she asked. "Did she say...where she was goin'?" He kept his head turned away. "Tucker! What's wrong?"

He looked at the ground between them. "You don't got on much in the way of clothes there, boss."

Her stomach turned over and over. "Tucker," she said in a calmer voice. "I asked you a question."

He pulled his hat off and rubbed his arm across his forehead. "Sorry, no, I haven't seen her. I got here at seven thirty and her car wasn't here."

She stood silent a long moment, then mumbled, "thanks," as she turned and walked off, feeling deflated.

Tucker called after her, "Everything all right?" She only waved a hand over her head.

Trudging up the porch steps, she pushed into the house and went straight for the kitchen. She stopped at the island where it had all started less than twelve hours ago. She pounded her fists. "Damn!" She swung her arms wildly, knocking things over. Several crashed to the floor and something shattered against the back door.

"Damn it, Jo, you blew it!" She dropped onto one of the stools, beating herself up for going against her resolve to never open her heart only to have it crushed by another pretty face.

A minute later she got up and pulled the bottle from the cupboard and grabbed a glass. She refused to shed another tear over a woman. She looked a good long while at the bottle, then opened it and filled the glass half full. When she raised the glass, though, the smell made her want to gag. She returned it to the counter. She sat trance-like, recalling every word Maria had spoken last night.

Maria stopped abruptly in the kitchen door. Obviously Jo hadn't heard her come in. She surveyed the mess and watched for several minutes as Jo turned a glass around and around in her hand next to a whiskey bottle. She panicked. Was Jo regretting last night?

She approached with apprehension and put her hand on Jo's shoulder. "Is something wrong, Jo?"

Jo jerked around, spilling the whiskey. "Shit!" she yelped.

Maria grabbed her arm before she could move. "Jo honey, what's wrong?" She saw pain when Jo's eyes met hers. Her stomach flipped over when Jo only shrugged. Fighting the building anxiety, she leaned close and slipped her arm around Jo's shoulder. "It's kind of early for drinking, don't you think?" She kept her tone light and cheerful despite the growing turmoil she felt.

Jo looked away and rubbed at her forehead. "I got up and you were gone…all of you."

Maria heard the fear in Jo's voice. She ran her hands through Jo's unruly hair. "Oh, honey, you didn't think…" Jo dropped her head. Maria lifted her chin and looked into her eyes. "Sweetheart, I hope you didn't think for one second that I'm leaving here…or you."

When Jo's eyes filled with tears, she pulled Jo to her chest and hugged her tightly. "I'm not leaving, Jo." She placed a soft kiss on her head. "The baby woke me at five thirty and after I fed her I couldn't go back to sleep…thanks to you." She kissed into her hair again. "So around seven I rustled Matt out of bed and drove them to Kathleen's. I'm sorry, I thought I could get back and crawl back into bed before you woke up. We were up pretty late." She loosened her arms around Jo and leaned back. "I wanted some time with you to make up for falling asleep on you during the wee hours of this morning." She tipped Jo's chin up and touched her fingers to Jo's cheek. "I wanted some time with you alone, no distractions and no interruptions, time to make love to you." She tilted her head and gave Jo a smile she hoped looked sexy. "Would that be possible?"

Relief filled Jo as she stood and pulled Maria into her arms. "Not only possible, but likely."

When Jo leaned in and kissed her with urgency, Maria slipped her hand under the back of Jo's T-shirt. Slowly she moved her hand around to cup her breast and they moaned in unison. Maria's touch was hot as she stroked Jo's skin, igniting a spark low in her belly that spread like a white hot flame through her. Jo pulled back, breathless. Maria's swollen lips glistened and her eyes flashed with a desire that threatened to undo her. When Maria's thumb rubbed across one of her already hard nipples, Jo's eyes drifted closed. Maria's other hand wandered dangerously close to the waist of her boxers. The pulse between her legs throbbed. Her heart drummed so loud she was sure Maria could hear it too.

Maria's lips touched her ear. "I want to touch all of you, Jo Marchal." Maria pulled her hand from under her shirt and put it against Jo's heart. "Every part." She led Jo to the bedroom and backed her against the side of the bed. Slowly, deliberately she stripped off Jo's shirt. Her eyes were a soft caress on Jo's skin. When the back of Maria's hand brushed down her stomach, Jo shivered. Maria pulled the boxers down, drawing her fingers over Jo's thighs, her fingertips raising goose bumps in their wake. After guiding Jo down onto the bed, Maria removed her own clothes and snuggled against Jo's side.

"Tell me how to please you." Her fingers grazed over Jo's stomach.

Jo touched her fingers to Maria's cheek. "Touch me."

Maria moved her hand to cover Jo's breast. "Here?"

"That's a good start." A smile curved her lips.

Maria caught her nipple between her thumb and finger, gently pulling it fully erect. She leaned over and flicked her tongue across the hard peak. She sucked it between her lips and Jo moaned. Maria gave the other breast equal attention, soliciting another throaty moan. Jo closed her eyes, relishing the stimulation to the sensitive nerve endings. Sparks fired in every part of her body.

Maria's fingers returned to her nipple. "You like this…" She kissed the corner of Jo's mouth. "After last night and early this morning, I certainly do."

Jo opened her eyes. Maria touched her in ways no one ever had. It wasn't just sexual. It was gentle, curious and loving. Oh, it made her wet and she wanted Maria to take her to ecstasy with a need she'd never known. She wanted to feel Maria in every part of her.

When Maria's hand slid down her abdomen, into her damp patch of curls and finally reached her center, Jo couldn't breathe. She gasped when Maria's fingers moved through her slick wetness.

"God, you feel so good," Maria whispered into Jo's ear, her fingers sliding back and forth. "Does this feel good?"

Jo couldn't speak, her clenching thighs answered for her. She was drunk on passion and when Maria raised her head to look into her eyes, Jo saw the same passion burning in Maria's eyes. She slipped her hand into Maria's hair. "Please, Maria, kiss me while you touch me."

Maria covered Jo's lips as her fingers worked her swollen flesh. Jo's body thrust against her hand. She groaned Maria's name when the climax shook her, collapsing back into the bed while she continued to stroke her, Jo's thighs quivering in response.

Against Jo's lips, she murmured, "That went way too fast. I want much, much more of you."

"I think that's possible if you give me a couple minutes." A smile tugged at Jo's mouth.

Maria rested her head on Jo's chest, listening to the steady drum of her heart. She knew she'd never felt this kind of complete, fulfilling connection with anyone—ever. She removed her hand from between Jo's legs amidst moans of protest, then slid it around Jo's waist.

"Was that as good for you as it was for me?"

"Mmm…" was Jo's only reply.

Maria raised her head meeting Jo's sparkling bright eyes. "That's it, just mmm?" She circled her fingertip around Jo's navel.

Jo exhaled deeply. "You've rendered me speechless and boneless. I think I could die a very happy cowgirl." The corner of her mouth curled.

Maria narrowed her eyes. "There'll be no dying now that I've found my true happiness." She brushed her lips over Jo's. "I think I might be in love with you, Jo Marchal. I know that I want to spend my life feeling like this with you. Want to be with you like this—always." She watched as Jo's eyes drifted closed and held her breath.

Maria's words made Jo's heart feel so light she feared it might float out of her chest. *This* was all she had ever wanted, everything she'd ever dreamed of. A happy family and someone she could trust with her heart. And she knew in her heart she could trust Maria with it.

"Like this, huh?" Jo wrapped Maria in her arms.

"Just like that…"

Jo pressed her lips to Maria's temple. "I have a good feeling that's possible too."

Bella Books, Inc.

Women. Books. Even Better Together.

P.O. Box 10543
Tallahassee, FL 32302

Phone: 800-729-4992
www.bellabooks.com